Scarlett Shroud

Joshua Kendal

This book is a work of fiction. Names, characters, places, dialogue, and incidents are either the products of the authors imagination or are used fictitiously, and any resemblance to any person living or dead, events, or locals is entirely coincidental.

authorjoshuakendal@gmail.com

ISBN: 978-1-7381925-4-0 (E-book)
ISBN: 978-1-7381925-6-4 (PB)
ISBN: 978-1-7381925-5-7 (HC)

For Her

Chapter One

RECORD COLD SPOT. I couldn't have read that right. Could I? I back off the throttle and pull over. Mom prefers isolation, but really, a record cold spot? I climb off my bike and lift the visor on my helmet. Crisp morning air saturated with pine fills my lungs. Something I hadn't noticed on my drive from Great Falls, until now. I round the sign, and sure enough, I read it right.

RECORD COLD SPOT
THE COLDEST OFFICIAL TEMPERATURE
EVER RECORDED IN THE CONTINENTAL
UNITED STATES OCCOURED AT A MINING
CAMP NEAR HERE JANUARY 20, 1954
WHEN THE TEMPERATURE DROPPED TO
70 DEGREES BELOW ZERO.

Despite the July heat, a chill runs over me. "Home sweet home." I flip my visor down, jump on my bike, and crack the throttle. Zero to sixty in two-point-three seconds.

Adrenaline surges, warming me, and butterflies flutter to life in my stomach.

I love my bike. The high-pitched whine of the motor, the acceleration, it's everything a superbike should be, and the deep crimson paint job makes it super sexy. My matching lipstick doesn't hurt either. But the best part is the freedom it gives me, freedom like no other. Sure, it's older, a 2011, but that's what makes it—and me—inconspicuous. Well, as inconspicuous as a woman dressed in black on a crimson Ducati 848 can get. I could afford a brand new one every day for a hundred years and not put a dent in my family's fortune. I love it, but it's a constant reminder of how I have to keep a low profile, and not lounge around in extravagant mansions filled with expensive toys. I let my mind wonder, as I often do while speeding down a highway. This is the only place I can forget my burden. I may stand out a little on my bike, but a girl's gotta have some fun. No matter what Mom says.

A low profile. My parents should have thought of that before naming me. Scarlett. After an actress in some old movie. *Gone with the Wind*, I think. I look more like Scarlett Johansson with her crimson dye-job when she played the Black Widow, or so I've been told. Thinking of her always makes me smile. She can't get any more badass: Russian assassin, holds her own with the men, intelligent, not to mention quick with the comebacks. Boys idolize superheroes in the movies, and after watching her on the big screen, she became an inspiration of mine.

But I've got something the Black Widow could never have—the Thirst.

It hit me at 11:46 PM on my sixteenth birthday, right down to the exact second I was born.

An insatiable thirst for blood.

It felt like I was in one of the numerous movies I'd seen depicting someone stumbling through a desert with cracked lips and a hoarse throat. Didn't help that my room collapsed at the same time, choking me with dust.

They don't call it sweet sixteen because of some old TV show. It's because the Thirst kicks in at sixteen, and human blood tastes sweeter than chocolate frosting on a cupcake, with a hint of copper.

'Course I'm unique, so I often wonder if it tastes different to full-blooded vamps like Mom, who fell in love with my dad, a regular old human. Wish I could remember him. But for that to have happened, he would have had to stick around until I was born. He left Mom before he knew she was pregnant. He up and vanished without so much as a goodbye. I know its still pangs Mom as she doesn't speak much about him, but when she does, it's only of the love they had for each other, a love I never got to experience. It's an odd sensation missing something I never had, yet every now and then, especially on my birthday, I find myself yearning to have that father-daughter bond.

I have to give him thanks for one thing he left me, though. I look up at the clear sapphire sky littered with wispy white clouds streaking from the surrounding hill tops. To the best of my knowledge, I'm the only vamp who can set foot in the sun—without bursting into flames, that is. That's just about the only thing Hollywood got right about my kind.

The downfall of having Dad's blood coursing through my veins, is that I'm looked down upon by vamps and witches alike. Some even consider me lesser than a werewolf.

I sniff the air, habitually searching for their scent at the mere thought of them.

It's hard to imagine looking at someone as less than a stinking drooling mutt, but I have thick skin because of it.

Mom says the witches are jealous of me, or rather of the day I was born. A day prophesized back to when Atlantis still stood, or something like that. I never did pay much attention to my studies in Salem once the Thirst hit.

The one thing I do know—that I have to know—is my purpose. Most people search aimlessly their entire lives to find their purpose. Mine was ordained the moment of my birth.

Save the world. The whole frickin' world.

Nice bombshell to drop on top of the Thirst. Thanks, Mom. As if a girl didn't have enough to deal with at sixteen. Then to find out it was prophesized to go down nine years later on my twenty-fifth birthday. That was a little much to swallow at that age, more so due to the vagueness of the prophecy and what I'm supposed to save the world from, let alone how.

Fire from above. One of the few things in the prophecy that wasn't a jumbled riddle.

I swear, every fortune ever told in ancient times came from some drunk staring up at the night sky and waking up with a vision. Amulets of power, Atlanteans, heroes of legend, it all felt like embellished stories passed through the generations to make them more entertaining. But one piece of history survived the ravages of time. The fact my fate was scribed on parchment by the only sorcerer to have existed gave the prophecy merit to vamps and witches alike.

The one, the world's savior, bred from drinkers of blood and man—

A single sentence cut off due to the ravages of time, shackling me to a destiny not of my choosing.

The world's destruction shall come from above.

The only clue laid out as to how Armageddon will happen. I keep picturing an asteroid slamming into Earth like the one that took out the dinosaurs. How the hell am I supposed to stop an asteroid? NASA could. Send up a ton of nukes and blow it to bits. But what could I possibly do? I accelerate faster, frustrated at the very notion of me fighting a massive chunk of rock hurtling toward the planet. It's not like I could catch the damn thing, no matter how strong I am.

As a girl, all I wanted to do was run and hide. As a woman, I put on a brave face, but I still want to hide from the responsibility. That's another reason the freedom my bike gives me is so appealing. Perhaps it can help me outrun the end of the world.

My entire life I've wanted seclusion. My companionship consists of Mom along with characters in movies and books, and I'm fine with that. I like it that way. That's why being chosen to save the world pisses me off so much. There must be someone better. Someone who cares about the populace of the planet more than me. It's not as if I want to see the world obliterated—I mean, I live here—but I'd be content sitting in a cabin in the woods with a library full of books, and high-speed streaming.

My mind stops wondering, and I back off the throttle as Lincoln comes into view around the bend. Lincoln, Montana. Population zip. A thousand people doing whatever it is they do in a secluded valley surrounded by the foothills of the Rockies. And me, hiding out in a rental cabin for just under a week. Five days until the Fourth of July, five days until my twenty-fifth birthday. Five days until the day I'm prophesized to save the world, somehow.

Chapter Two

I pull up to the pumps at the Mountain View Co-op. I can see why Mom chose Lincoln: It's small. The Co-op is a gas station and convenience store all rolled into one. I'm guessing it's the place to go in town if you need anything—the *only* place in town. Filled with quaint little buildings mostly made to look like log cabins, the town has a romantic seclusion about it.

I can't help but feel at ease, especially after my therapeutic ride. My version of the self-help craze.

An elderly couple strolls down the sidewalk holding hands. A father and his little girl sit on a tailgate licking ice-cream from cones. Fewer than a dozen vehicles, mostly trucks, are parked along the main road for three or four blocks. Almost all of them have their windows rolled down despite the lack of a driver. It feels like a sleepy and relaxed town—very relaxed, maybe just a little too relaxed for my liking. But probably not a bad thing when I'm about to go through the most stressful ordeal of my life.

A petite woman with a shock of blonde hair emerges from a coffee shop and *she* comes to mind, adding to my stress. I crane my neck, shift my weight, and confirm it's not Kara. That's all I'd need right now is to have my lifelong tormentor soiling the sleepiness of Lincoln. I can almost smell my singed hair from when I was sixteen and she 'welcomed' me to Sanctum by burning off my split ends.

I take a breath of fresh air, focus on the moment, and where I am. Across the street, I see my next stop, On the Rocks, a liquor store.

A man steps out of a small building, the Wheel Inn. Its overhang for the wood sidewalk, the high front face that serves no purpose at all and the horizontal posts set up for horses to be hitched, make the place look as if it belongs in an old Western. The bang of pool balls slamming into each other reaches me from inside before the man shuts the door, and I contemplate my next meal.

Pool halls are my favorite hunting grounds.

I won't need to feed anytime soon, and I know I shouldn't hunt in such a small town, especially one I'm laying low in.

Draped over the seat of a Harley parked out front is a worn leather jacket. I crane my neck, focus. The crest on it isn't one I recognize. Still, I could go for a game or two, see if there's any chatter about the Black Serpents. I'd researched enough about that particular biker gang to warrant further investigation, firsthand. The gang numbers around fifty and has been tried but never convicted to a list of charges. I've been keeping my eye out for their crest of three black snakes coiling around each other. Feeding on the good and the innocent is something of a faux pas. If the Black Serpents turn out to be the degenerates I assume they are, I'd be happy to make them into my next meal. Their club house is supposed to be west of Lincoln, a ways from what I can remember, and in a small town like this it would be good to have options to hunt elsewhere.

A yellow 1970s pickup truck rumbles up to the pumps across from me as I climb off my bike. Out of the truck steps a man far too handsome to be stuck in this town.

If I'm the Black Widow, he would undoubtedly be Thor. Late twenties, standing six feet tall with broad shoulders and blond hair with a slight curl tapered to the back of his neck, he's the picturesque cowboy in tight jeans and a plaid shirt. Aside from missing the cowboy hat and short-cropped beard on his chiseled jaw, he's Thor.

Fine by me—I like my men clean-shaven. Even stubble irritates my skin. It's unfortunate, as that seems to have become the trend, the caveman look. I consider it dirty. If you can't shave for your woman, you probably can't open a door for her. Call me old fashioned, but that's just how I am. Just how Mom raised me to be.

Thor puts the gas nozzle into his truck and looks right at me. My cheeks warm. I *am* going to like it here. If I'm to pass the next five days in Lincoln, at least I'll have him as eye candy. I know it's impossible, but I swear his icy blue gaze catches me blushing despite my visor still being flipped down. It's hard not too. His sweet smile confirms it—he's Thor all right.

I'm like any other person in their twenties, full of needs and desires. 'Course mine are a little more heightened than those of humans, thanks to the vamp side of me. I swear every hook-up app was developed by vamps to satisfy their more primal urges and make a meal of the opposite sex when finished with them. Unlike other vamps, I'm no slut, and I don't see the point in getting attached when I'm going to watch someone grow old and die while I stay twenty-five for eternity. Though an actual relationship would be nice, it's just not realistic.

Flirting, on the other hand, I find to be a rush—and it's time to have some fun with Thor.

I drop my backpack on the seat and turn sideways to face the store, giving Thor a profile shot as I unzip my jacket then rub my lower back with both hands, feigning stiffness. To top off my pose I thrust out my chest and arch my back. Maybe it's a gift I haven't yet fully discovered, but I swear I feel his gaze on me. Tracing me from my cowboy boots up my jeans, pausing for a moment at my leather jacket, and then locking in on my green tank. At least that's what I hope he's doing. The finishing touch—I remove my helmet and shake my hair side to side, mimicking the entrance scene of a leading actress.

I turn my back to him, put my helmet on the motorcycle's tank.

Thor's reflection stares back at me in the gas pump's dollar gauge. It tells me all those hours watching romance movies didn't go to waste. I got his attention.

Don't make eye contact.

Leave him wanting.

I know the rules. I've played this game of cat and mouse before. I fill my tank, craning my head to the side, slowly massage my neck, rolling my shoulder.

With the click of the pump, I replace the nozzle, and take my phone out of my jacket. No text from Mom yet. I slip it in my back pocket and head inside the Co-op, dropping a fifty on the counter. I always keep a wad of them to save having to dig through my purse in my backpack. "Keep the change," I say to the clerk while watching Thor out of the corner of my eye.

Will he pass the test or not?

If I'm going to spend my time with someone, they better have something to offer. Looks he's got, but is he smart? Can he carry a conversation? Is he a gentleman, or does he think solely with what hangs between his legs?

I make for the door, and Thor opens it for me. He passed the test. Well, the first one anyway.

"Good morning," he says.

Oh my god he even sounds like Thor—somewhat—or maybe it's in my head. One thing for sure: His voice is deep and strong, yet kind.

"Morning," I say, returning his smile, letting him get his first real good look at me up close. I step past him toward my bike. I already got his attention and consider swaying my hips, but if he's interested then I don't have to.

"Excuse me," Thor calls after me.

Got him.

"Yeah?" I say, spinning around.

"I'm Lukas." He extends his hand.

"Scarlett." I take his hand in mine; his grip's strong. Farm boy strong, and he has the arms to back it up. A quick glance at his left hand reveals no wedding ring, nor the tan line or indentation of one ever being there. I can't help but wonder how this man has remained un-wed at his age, but after seeing the size of Lincoln I settle with the notion he hasn't found the right partner and hasn't settled. Another good quality: Never settle for less than you want, especially when it comes to swapping wedding vows with someone. I'm sure Lukas has had his share of women pursuing him, but unless there's something seriously wrong with him in the head, he's a catch.

"Would you like to join me for lunch?" he asks.

I am getting hungry, and I can still eat human food since the Thirst set in, unlike any other vamp I know. Being half human and half vamp has its advantages.

"That would be nice. But I've got to get settled in and unpack," I say, testing him again.

He isn't a poker player.

Disappointment is written all over his face, followed by a frown of confusion as he leans to the side and gazes at my bike with nothing but a helmet and a backpack on it. Check mark number two. He's smart—at the very least he's observant. Unpacking would take all of two minutes.

So, I throw him a bone. "How about dinner?"

He grins. Lukas is *definitely* not a poker player. "Can I pick you up at six?"

Pick *me* up, that's twice he's proved to be chivalrous.

"That depends how smooth you are," I say.

His grin grows.

Keep him waiting, just dangle the bait. It's all about anticipation and patience. I pull out my phone and show him a picture of the cabin I'd rented. "You know this house?"

"The old Miller place, just outside of town. You're staying there?"

"All summer," I say, planting the seed of two full months of my company. Who knows? I might actually stick around for a bit after my birthday and enjoy this sleepy little town along with its resident hottie, provided the world still exists. "Be there at eight. Bring some steaks." Hot woman on a Ducati who grills steaks in a cabin in the woods. Oh, I got him where I want him.

"I'll see you then."

I nod, pocket my phone, and turn for my bike.

The little girl who was eating ice cream with her father across the street on a tailgate is squatting beside my bike, inspecting her reflection in the chrome tailpipes. Long black hair obscures her face, but I recognize the yellow flower print summer dress and the ice cream in one hand that's melting, dripping down her knuckles.

I get close enough that she notices me, and she jumps up. Her ice cream falls from the cone to the pavement. A book in her other hand shoots up, and she presses it against her chest. A defense mechanism I recognize from my own youth. She looks to me, then to her fallen treat through Coke bottle glasses. Knobby knees stick out from beneath her dress, and her bright blue shoes do little to aid in her appearance, or even slightly match her outfit.

I bend to her height. "Didn't mean to scare you."

She locks eyes with me. Her gaze is steady, yet she holds her tongue and rolls her fingers tight around her book.

"You like my bike?"

She glances at it, then back to me, nods, letting her glasses slip down her nose. She's not talkative, and I guess she's a bit of a loner. It's not often you see a kid, let alone an eight-year-old, this shy. She reminds me of myself when I was younger.

"Here." I pull my wad out of my pocket, thumb out the smallest bill, and hand her a twenty. "Go get another ice cream."

She hesitates, staring at the bill.

"It was my fault you dropped yours in the first place." I slide the bill between the pages of her book.

"You leave that nice lady alone now. We gotta get going," her dad calls from across the street, turning from his conversation with another man. "Sorry," he says to me, raising a hand.

The little girl glances over her shoulder at her dad, then back at me, grins, and runs back to him. He opens the door to the truck for her, and she points back at me. Their voices are too muffled over the hum of the gas pumps to catch what they're saying, but when she pulls out the cash from between the pages of her book, I get the gist of the conversation. He's saying no, that's too much, go give it back. She lowers her head and turns to me.

I wave her back to her dad before she gets three feet from him, throw on my backpack and climb on my bike, wishing in some small way that the little girl's experience with a dad who cares for her was a memory of mine.

I brush the notion away as Lukas comes out of the Co-op.

I tuck my helmet between my legs, fire up my bike, and wink at him as I idle through the parking lot. Stopping ten yards away I switch off the engine walk to the doors of On the Rocks without looking back at him. Now I'm just outright teasing him, but I gotta have some fun on summer vacation.

After all, we might not live longer than five days.

That does it—the sobering thought of the prophecy pushes the thrill of flirting with Lukas to the back of my mind, along with the joy in the little girl's eyes at gaining another ice cream. Not so far that I don't forget to pick out a bottle of red wine to go with the steaks, along with my whiskey. Five days to fulfilling a prophecy calls for more than wine.

I put the bottles on the counter and gather some bills from the roll in my pocket. Between Lukas, the girl, her father, and the coming Armageddon, I'm moving around in a daze with my mind swimming in endless possibilities of a summer in Lincoln. What turning a quarter of a century means for me, is completely different than any human—or witch, for that matter.

A man opens the door, flashing sunlight throughout the store. A broadsword slicing through the air races through my mind, and I flinch.

I'm safe, but the hair on my neck is on end.

The middle-aged clerk says something that doesn't register. "Sorry, what'd you say?" I ask him. His gentle features combined with his salt-and-pepper hair ease my tension somewhat, but not enough.

"I need to see your ID, miss," the clerk repeats.

I can't be bothered to dig through my backpack to find my ID. I can't clear the image of a sharpened sword swinging at my head.

"You already have." I stop listening; it doesn't matter what he says. Another gift from being a half-breed is coercion—basically, mind control. It doesn't last, but it has its advantages. I push the bills toward him then shove the bottles in my pack.

The clerk takes my cash.

"Keep the change." Right now, I need to get back on my bike, need to run. Let the wind dry the sweat building on my palms.

No sooner have I left the pungent liquor store than I'm back on my bike. All that matters is the sign that says 70. The ten blocks or so it takes to cross Lincoln seem to last forever, but finally, there it is—my 70-mph sign, my taste of freedom. I slap my visor down and crack open the throttle, lifting my Ducati's front wheel from the pavement as I pull a deep breath into my lungs and hold on.

Oh, how I love my bike.

I let it pull me—and my thoughts—away from those who are hunting me.

Chapter Three

I find myself skipping smooth, flat stones from the shoreline of the Little Blackfoot River. The undulating water draws away my fear of being hunted by the Broadsword. Water always does ease my tension, especially rivers. As a little girl, rivers were my go-to if I was stressed. Then I got Old Red, and as good as she is some habits die hard.

Sitting on the cool rocks beneath a low concrete bridge, trying to escape from the world, it turns out escape from my anxiety was just a few miles west of Lincoln.

The drone of a vehicle on the overpass annoys me and flushes heat to my chest. A semi passing overhead intensifies the warmth and with it the embarrassment of imagining a sword slicing through the air back at the liquor store.

Mom's warning about the Broadsword creeps to mind. *Run, just run, if you ever find yourself against a member of the Broadsword—run.*

I sit up straighter, searching the banks of the river, confirm my bike is safely tucked away in the shrubs above. My heart pounds. No one's there. I draw air through my nose, sampling what the late afternoon breeze has to offer. No werewolf, no human, no scent but my perfume and the fresh water.

Still, Mom's lecture continues.

Merciless hunters on an endless pursuit to rid the world of magic, the Broadsword, every one of the Broadsword, is highly trained in how to kill vampires, witches, and werewolves. The wolf part I don't mind—one less mutt for me to put down. Though I've only taken down three, with more than a little help from Mom and other vamps or witches, each time was simultaneously satisfying and terrifying.

I sniff the air again. Even though I know I'm alone, I can't help but double-check my surroundings for the Broadsword. I've never even seen one, but I know what to look for. Every one of them has a pale gray undertone to their skin. Makes me think they'd have a hint of death and decay to their scent—as if they're all hollow husks with one foot in the grave. No one can say why, or even where they came from, or why they hunt us. Always searching. Searching with weapons that actually work on immortals. No stakes, no garlic. If they came at me with any of those, I'd happily take them on. I'm lying to myself, and I know it, but it gives me a sort of strength. Silver, though, they'd be armed with for sure. That one Hollywood got right, at least for the wolves and vamps. Good old-fashioned steel is just as effective on witches as silver is on vamps and wolves, and a bad enough wound will kill any immortal.

A bead of sweat rolls down my temple. The river hasn't washed away my fear. The more I remember Mom's teachings, the more heated I get. *You are unique, Scarlett. The only child of a vampire and a human that survived to birth. I wish the burden didn't fall on you, but it does. Since it does, you will be pursued, but you will be strong in mind, body, and spirit.* I need to cool down. The shade of the bridge isn't enough to beat the late afternoon sun.

I glance to my bike above me, tucked in the bushes just off the side of the road, and the memory of hundreds of windy cooling rides draws some heat from me. But fully clothed it won't be enough to satisfy me, especially when I have a secluded part of the river to myself thanks to the bridge above.

It was just your imagination. No one was there, no one knows you're here, they don't know you're here. Now breathe, relax, and cool off.

I push aside the shrubs, crouch down to the water, and submerge my hand. The July heat hasn't done much for warming the water gliding between my fingers.

I want to cool down, and a dip in this slow flowing water would do the trick, but a little too much for my liking. Any thought of a quick dip slips away with the heat from my hand.

The bank gives way under my boots. I slip, plunge into the river.

The water is freezing.

My ass is soaked, and the spray of my not so graceful landing splashed up my ribs. I gasp, push myself up, fighting to gain grip with my boots and my hands on the slimy jelly covering the riverbed. I grab at bushes and dry stones, and pull myself onto shore, content with my thoughts of abandoning a quick dip, but also pissed as water sloshes in my boots with every step.

All I want is the warmth of the sun on my skin. The water was far colder than I wanted it to be, but even such a brief plunge in the river cooled my mind. The sun's rays do little to ease my shaking limbs. Shivering, I wring out my tank on the sides and the bit around my stomach. My jeans are soaked, and cling to my ass. I try to wriggle them to my knees.

Through clenched teeth, I taste something in the air that wasn't there before. One whiff of sweat and I pause. I'm not alone. It's not a wolf's sweat—even in human form they have a slight dog smell to them. That leaves only two options: human or a member of the Broadsword.

I whip my head around. Two men wearing coveralls and no shirts are a few yards away.

Their skin is well tanned. They're human.

Both in their early twenties and drunk on moonshine from the looks of the pickle jar half-filled with a clear fluid. I turn up my nose as my enhanced senses confirm the jar's contents. The term *slack-jawed-yokels* never fit a pair better.

"Seen enough?" I ask shortly, not expecting a reply from the likes of these two.

"Water's cold today, huh?" says the one with shaggy dark hair holding the jar. He stares at my tank clinging to me as he elbows his snickering friend. "Saw your bike, thought you might need some…ah…assistance."

Guess I didn't conceal Old Red as well as I'd hoped.

The nerve—he's still staring. I've been here before, drunks out for a lay. Hoping to find some down-on-her-luck girl with car troubles. "Go home, boys. You're drunk, and I'm not interested."

"Come on now, what do you say to another dip in the river with old Zeke? Got the best 'shine in the county to keep you warm." He swirls the pickle jar's contents and steps closer.

Zeke, I laugh to myself. *The name fits.*

The bulbous noses, the squinty eyes, traits passed down by lineage, traits I recognize from my research. The Williams brothers. They fell off my list after delving deeper into the Black Serpents. I can't recall the brother's name, but Zeke stands out.

"Go home and sleep it off before you regret it." I turn my back to them, wrestle with pulling up my jeans so as not to roll my panties up to my waist. I have a temper—must be from Dad. It's short, very short, especially when dealing with characters like these.

A hand slaps my ass.

I straighten, jerk back, almost giving myself a wedgie as sopping wet denim makes it to my hips.

"Back off!" I shove my palm into Zeke's chest, impressed at my self restraint. I could have broken every rib he has. Instead, he stumbles to the ground.

"What cha wanna go doin' that for? Just havin' a bit of fun," says Zeke, clutching his chest.

"Yeah," Zeke's brother pipes up.

Both of them have a rap sheet, mischief, theft, possession of stollen property. All of it juvey stuff. But more recently they upped their game, out on bail from sexual contact, harassment, something like that. They hadn't made their way up to sexual assault, yet, from what I recall.

"It speaks," I say to the brother. "But does it sit? Or do you just follow your master around pissing off innocent girls? Getting them drunk on this moose piss." I slap the pickle jar from Zeke's hand, and it smashes against the rocks.

Zeke's brother is at a loss for words—no shock there.

Zeke, on the other hand, is fired up. "Bitch," he says, standing up and raising his fist as if he's about to hit me.

I almost laugh. Hit me? I could let him—any bruise he could make would heal in moments. I could step to the side, easily avoiding his blow and kick him in the ass, sending him into the river.

Or, I can surrender to the Thirst.

It's been two weeks since I fed. I only need one human a month to survive; unlike other vamps who can't eat human food and need to feed weekly. So, do I teach these boys a lesson on how to treat a woman? Or do I make sure they never lay a hand on one again? I've stocked and hunted criminals before and aside from the moonshine, they wreak of lawlessness. They have given me the opportunity to avoid tracking down a pool hall other than the one in Lincoln to hunt in, and they've soiled my calming river. I decide my hunt for the Black Serpents can be postponed.

All this goes through my mind in the time it takes Zeke to throw his fist at my face.

I catch it in my palm. The look of shock he gives me is priceless.

I tighten my grip, snapping the bones in his hand.

He opens his mouth to cry out. Before he can, my foot in his gut sends him flying through the air against the concrete support with a dull thud. The four yards of open air he'd passed through followed by the sudden stop blows all wind from his chest, forcing him to gasp with his eyes wide in disbelief.

I surge forward, closing the gap between myself and Zeke's brother.

"Wait, wait. We didn't mean…no—" He falls silent the moment my teeth penetrate his neck and elongate my fangs.

Ugh, gross—the taste of his sweat is worse than it smells. I prefer my prey to be bathed and well groomed, but I'm committed now. I shut my eyes and concentrate on the sweet, coppery, life-blood filling my mouth, and try to let its sugary content overpower the smell. Even filtered through his liver the mixture of shine in his blood doesn't make it any easier.

His corpse falls to the stones without enough blood left in it to twitch.

"I hope you taste better than him," I say to Zeke. The terror in his eyes, shifting from myself to his brother as he tries to scurry away on his backside, almost makes me feel compassion for him—almost.

The second I sink my teeth in him, I know I'm in for one hell of a night.

His blood alcohol level is through the roof.

If I don't pull back, mine will be too, and that's not how I had planned on my evening going. I want to get there the old-fashioned way with Lukas. Hopefully my vamp metabolism can burn through Zeke's alcohol saturated blood so I can still enjoy my night.

I let Zeke fall from my grasp to flop on the stones in his death throes like a fish plucked from the river. Mom's lectures about not wasting a drop are as clear as if she were beside me, but moonshine-laced food could make me unladylike, and I have a date.

I tug at my blood-stained shirt while I wait for Zeke to die. Looks like I'm going back into the river to clean my tank. Mom was right. *Always wear dark clothing*; blood doesn't stand out as much.

I pull my keys, cash, and phone from my jeans, thank God they're still dry, and drag the two corpses to the river's edge. I jump in, fully clothed, and have to fight the urge to get out again; it's not like I'm going to die of hypothermia or anything. Reaching below the surface, I take hold of a rock the size of my torso and heave it to the side.

Vamp strength—gotta love it when it comes time to dispose of evidence. My pride in doing what no human could fathom accomplishing is washed away with the river. I'm not the only one who's stronger than normal humans. Aside from their skill with weapons, the members of the Broadsword are strong—really strong. Not as strong as me, but they are a close second. They're human, after all, although somehow enhanced.

I shake my head and concentrate on the cold water whisking the heat from me, instead of dwelling on the thought of assassins scouring the globe in search of me.

I scan the river's banks and try to pick up a scent, or a footfall not drowned out by the churning water. Satisfied I'm alone, though I keep an eye on the banks, I return to my task. I relocate six more stones despite the slippery slime covering them, leaving a pit in the riverbed. In goes Zeke, held down by the first rock, followed by his brother. One by one I place the large rocks on their bodies, crushing the air from their chests in their final resting place.

Chapter Four

It's forty miles to Lincoln, and halfway there I'm forced to drive with one eye shut in order to focus. Zeke's moonshine is potent, and my metabolism hasn't burned through it as I'd hoped. I chalk it up as the reason I keep thinking about the Broadsword and their leader. Who the hell is he, and why does he want vamps, witches, and wolves wiped from the earth? If anyone knows, they haven't told me. I get why I'm a target but hunting me—supposedly the only person capable of stopping Armageddon—that's asinine. Who ever he is, he's a grade A asshole.

I check my mirrors for anyone in pursuit of me and decide Zeke's moonshine is making me paranoid. I spend the rest of my drive replaying movies and books in my head. The last few miles are eternal, but I make it to the driveway to the cabin Mom rented.

Fallen pine needles crunch under my tires as I pull up, and I give my head a shake, blinking the cabin into focus. It's not the nicest place I've stayed at, but it's not the worst either.

I remove my helmet and stagger as I get off my bike.

The pine scented air is fresher than it should be, and I control my urge to smile for no reason. Zeke had some top shelf 'shine.

I bang on the door. Lean against it, swaying back and forth. Of course no one's here, Mom isn't supposed to arrive until tomorrow night.

I pull out my phone, and again I have to focus through one eye to read the instructions Mom sent me to get in the cabin.

I type the four-digit code into the keypad, and on my second attempt, the little red light on the lock flashes green, followed by a click. Stepping into a small foyer, I fumble around, find a light switch, and drop my pack on a wood bench against the wall. The bottles inside clink off each other enough to remind me to be a bit gentler. *That's the problem with alcohol, blood-alcohol.*

Ha. I laugh aloud. Blood-alcohol. That's the first time I put that together.

Normally, I can take down a bottle of whiskey no problem. I heal quick so my liver processes it, sobering me faster than any human or witch, but I've never been this inebriated.

A split staircase presents itself before me. The left set lead down to a padlocked door in the basement. To the right, they lead up to the portion the Millers rented out to us. I sigh, wishing someone was here to help me make the climb.

Swaying, I look outside for any danger, then shut the door and lock the deadbolt.

I silently thank the sturdy railing for helping me get to the top, along with the kitchen counter that keeps me upright.

An open floor concept leading to the living room with a fireplace presents itself before me. Three doors running along the hallway to the right must lead to the bathroom and two bedrooms. It's the glass double doors to my left leading outside that I need in order to settle in.

We moved around a lot when I was a kid. Every place we lived in had a second-floor terrace or balcony of some sort. Handy to see if a threat is coming. Until I inspected it thoroughly there was no way I would sleep soundly. Old habits die hard, Mom knows that. Still coddling me at twenty-four, she made sure I would be comfortable when she booked this cabin.

Unlatching the glass doors, I step onto the elevated deck and run my hands over the lacquered log railing. Smooth, well kept, lined with four chairs and three end-tables. This deck is designed for lounging about and staring at the wilderness.

I plop into an Adirondack chair that leans back a little too far for my liking. But I'm becoming too drowsy to relocate. Well fed, with a head swimming in 'shine, I feel like I've just finished an entire thanksgiving turkey.

Rolling my head side to side, I finish my inspection. No stairs whatsoever. A thick solid rail surrounds me. Bears, that's why. Best not to give access to the cabin's glass doors in bear country. This is as good a place to let my liver filter out Zeke's 'shine before Lukas gets here. My eyelids grow heavy, and I gladly let them fall shut. With the sun warming my face, the brilliant array of yellow and orange trying to penetrate my eyelids, I listen for the rumble of Lukas' pick-up truck.

~ * ~

The incessant hooting of an owl disturbs me, waking me from my 'shine induced coma. I passed out. Must have been brief as my mind is still foggy thanks to Zeke, and Lukas hasn't arrived yet. The chill of the crisp night air on my face makes me pull the blanket to my chin. Its rough material in my hands makes me think of a multi-colored Mexican blanket that the country is so famous for. It has a nice smell; comforting, with a familiar masculine hint.

My eyes shoot open. I sit up.

There was no blanket on the deck when I passed out, let alone one wrapping me in it. It's black, white, and red striped, just large enough to cover me.

In the dark, my vamp eyes can see almost as good as if it were a sunny day. Makes for a more proficient hunter.

Beside me is a bouquet of red roses with a folded piece of paper tucked into their thorny grasp. Their enriching smell helps clear the fog from my mind even further, and the rough jagged writing on the note brings a school-girl smile to my face.

Scarlett,

You were sleeping so peacefully I didn't want to disturb you. If you want to join me, I always start my day with a hearty breakfast at Lambkin's.

Lukas

I flip the card over. His number's on the back.

"Nice young man."

"Jeez." I jerk in the chair. "Mom." Her voice is unmistakable. "How long have you been there?" Mom has a way of blending into the shadows that I just can't seem to master.

"Long enough to meet your gentleman caller waiting patiently for you to wake from your slumber." Mom sometimes speaks as if we're living in the 1800s; I think she figures it's romantic and charming. At least I know she approves of Lukas and didn't make a midnight snack of him. "I assume you fancied him, so I thanked him for keeping you in his charge until I arrived.

"I hope you didn't say it like that."

"I could have said more. For instance, how irresponsible you were to drink yourself into a stupor."

I frown and stared down at the deck. After twenty-four years, she still knows how to make me feel like a child yearning for her approval, hiding my mistakes to never disappoint her.

"But I love you. And don't want to embarrass you. Especially to a man perched on a tailgate shielded from the nights chill." Mom indicates the blanket covering me. "Periodically calling your name while waving a bouquet of flowers. Waiting patiently for you to come to your senses. Yes, I observed him for a time. Concluded his intentions pure, accepted his offerings on your behalf, and sent him on his way." She waves her hand above the bouquet, drawing the aroma upward. She has a way of scolding me, yet comforting me, so I might make a better decision the next time around. "Now get up, much has happened in my absence."

She steps inside the cabin like a phantasm, floating on a breeze. I'm always amazed how gracefully she moves, effortless, and without a sound, even in three-inch heels on a wood deck. She's the definition of class, making her simple black dress elegant. She can't help it, it's natural, and it's something I firmly believe skips a generation. Her light blonde hair, never with a curl out of place, makes her the spitting image of Marylin Monroe. Sometimes, when I was younger, I'd imagine she was *the* Marylin Monroe from the history books, rubbing elbows with the most influential people in America. Of course, that was absurd due to Mom's allergy to the sun. But it made sense why Dad fell for her. She's stunning, never aging a day past twenty-five. She would have told Lukas we were sisters, as was our usual cover story.

"How was Salem?" I ask, following her inside and sitting on a stool at the counter while she pours some coffee and hands it to me. I welcome the cup's warmth on my chilled fingers. The coffee has an earthy dark roast aroma blended with French vanilla and hazelnut. My favorite.

"It's gone."

"What's gone?"

"The Sanctum is gone. Burned to ash as if it had never existed."

"What?" I spill a quarter of my cup on the counter. "The Sanctum is guarded by the most powerful covens of vamps and witches. How could it be gone?"

Mom wipes the counter with a cloth. "It *was* guarded. No longer. The Broadsword saw to that. Every single one of them, if I had to presume."

My chest tightens. I have to force myself to sit straighter and cool my composure to not let on the feeling of the world closing in on me. The Broadsword has been on my mind far too much. It's hard for them not to be, though, as it won't be long until I save the world, or they succeed in destroying it by stopping me. God, I wish they never existed. That their relentless leader had never been born. The Sanctum seemed indestructible. It is…was…comprised of catacombs carved from the rock beneath Salem that ran for at least half a mile, at least that's how it felt when I was wandering around dank, torch lit tunnels. "I can't believe it could even burn."

"Everything inside it could burn and did."

"How can you be so calm about this?" We just lost the most powerful vamps and witches in existence. I try my best to not show it, but I'm freaking out.

"Because losing control of our emotions will not bring it back. Or help us now." In all my life I've never seen Mom lose her calculative demeanor. She's always living in the moment though remaining composed and trying to teach me how not to lose my temper and strike without thinking it through. I may look a lot like her, but she knows I'm more like Dad when it comes to wearing my heart on my sleeve. "I was fortunate. I was on my way out of town when I saw the flames."

"I just can't believe it." The Sanctum was the only place vamps and witches intermingled. It was also the place everyone—myself included—went to learn about their heritage upon turning sixteen. It would have been nice, if it weren't for the witches. Mean and jealous of us vamps. They got the reputation as wart covered green faced psychos with big noses who eat kids. While us vamps got typecast as romantics who lounge around sipping blood from crystal. Not to mention the whole immortality thing.

"Believe it. I got as close as I dared without risking detection. As far as I can tell, none made it out." Mom places her hand on top of mine. A stark reminder that even though we're immortal, and heal fast, we can die just like any other being. "Witches and vampires are going to have to work together despite our differences if you are to succeed. The Broadsword is more of a threat now than ever. All the assassinations they committed in the past were just training scenarios. Training for one massive strike to cripple our world."

"Succeed? You mean save the world from God knows what." If I ever had a chance of getting any help, it would have been from the elders at the Sanctum. They're the ones who knew the prophecy the best; they guarded the damned parchment that's been the bane of my existence. "We're totally alone." I stand from my stool. I'm heated and right in Mom's face. I've never acted out, spoke to her in such a rude manor, but there is a breaking point.

"Calm yourself, Scarlett."

Three words. Three words is all it takes, and I sit again, take hold of my cup, brooding. Within moments, my frustration has left me. I have no idea how she has that effect on me. In truth it might not even be her. Ever since I attended the Sanctum I've never given in to an emotional outburst. I always chalked it up to the Thirst, and Mom's understanding of it to calm me down, just as she remains collected herself.

"Sorry." I stare into my cup, regretting every time I gave Mom a hard time.

"Our isolation is and was key to your safety. And I have taught you well. You only forget my lessons every now and then…when it comes to courting a handsome young man." Mom grins, attempting to lift my spirits. I can't imagine what I would do without her. "But now, that isolation ends."

"What do you mean?"

"I told you, we will have to work together from now on, and you will never believe who I found on their way to the Sanctum when I was leaving." A shuffling behind me makes me turn my head. "You remember Kara."

If ever I knew of a person I hated more, an arch enemy, a nemesis, I don't recall. Kara and I have been at each other's throats since the day we met. She's the physical embodiment of everything I hate about this world. A damn good reason to let the world end. "How could I forget." I glare at the blonde bombshell across the cabin. She's so skinny I don't know how she has the strength to hold her head up.

"You think I like this? Protecting your fat a—"

"*Kara.*" She's silenced by her mother behind her. A little taller than Kara and twenty some years older, there is no doubt they are related; they're so similar in build and appearance.

"No." I turn back to Mom. "Not her. Anybody but her." I point at Kara. I hold my tongue at the look of disapproval on Mom's face. That was rude, though not completely uncalled for. "Sorry, Aunt Brenda. Its just that—"

"It's fine, dear," says Kara's mom, crossing the living room. "The two of you have butted heads since day one."

Kara's mom, whom I've come to know as Aunt Brenda due to her frequent visits after she and Mom met at the Sanctum, thankfully only resembles Kara in appearance. I never understood what a witch and a vamp had in common, but she visits us like clockwork on the first of every month, stays for a night, then leaves the next morning. At first, I thought it was to discuss my studies. Aunt Brenda became somewhat of a private tutor to me at the Sanctum. But after time, and listening in on their discussions, I learned better. They talk about the covens, and men.

Mom never had much to say about Dad, at least when I was in earshot, other than how she missed him and still had a place in her heart dedicated to him. Their courtship, as Mom called it, was short but filled with passion and a love like no other. Aunt Brenda had fewer loving words when it came to her husband. Married out of obligation due to an unplanned pregnancy, and no longer able to deal with the fact his wife was a witch, and his daughter would be on her sixteenth birthday, he turned to drugs when Kara was five. After numerous stints in and out of rehab, he abandoned them both when Kara was eight.

I hate Kara, but trashing each others' dads was one line neither of us crossed. 'Course she had it worse than me. Dad didn't know I existed; Kara's dad left her for a needle pumping crap into his veins.

That is the only thing about Kara that makes me feel something for her other than hatred.

To this day Aunt Brenda still comes for her monthly visits. Always polite, she greets me, asks me how my latest book is, then heads off to chat with Mom. The upside is she never brings Kara with her when she comes to visit. I learned enough about her life after Sanctum by listening in on Aunt Brenda and Mom. Kara's sole goal in life is to party, dance, drink, and bang as many men as she can. She's like a has-been celebrity with too much time and money.

"Scarlett, we are at war. I do not need to tell you how vital it is we succeed. Right now, they are our best chance."

Kara is our best chance, come on, Mom.

Mom speaks in such a calm voice my blood boils off any remnant of Zeke's moonshine. The little bit of composure I gained is gone as fast as it came.

"I'm not spending another second with"—I hold back for Aunt Brenda's sake—"her. I need some air." I stomp out the double glass doors, fully aware I'm acting like a child, but I don't care. It feels good to let out how pissed off I am. It's something I never do. I throw Lukas's blanket over my shoulder and spring over the rail. Aunt Brenda calls for me to wait. For a brief moment my outburst subsides, but then I'm on the ground, infuriated again.

With my helmet on, and Lukas's blanket around my waist, I fire up my Ducati. Rocks shoot from my back tire into the trees, and then the cabin as I spin around. I crack the throttle and don't look back.

Chapter Five

I'm on the road for about an hour when the sky changes from a starlit night to a brilliant collage of burgundy traced with streaks of auburn. Mom will be down for the day, sleeping, and there is no way I'm going back to the cabin. It doesn't matter if Aunt Brenda's there. So, I turn onto another highway, letting my bike try to do its job of whisking my hatred away, but it's a hard task when it comes to wiping out memories of Kara.

The names she called me hurt, despite the old saying of sticks and stone. *False savior, half-breed slut, abomination, freak of nature, unworthy harlot*...she had a long list. She burned my hair, turned it into snakes, well, the illusion of snakes anyway. The Medusa spell she called it. One of her favorites to cast.

Sweet sixteen. What a time to learn of my heritage, let alone having the innocence of childhood beliefs in normality ripped from me. Growing up basically on night shift due to mom's allergy to the sun was normal to me, especially because we lived a fairly isolated life. Then came my first summer in Salem where I learned how witches lived their lives immersed in the populace. Makes sense, they're born from humans, might as well live amongst them. It's they're ancestry that brings out the witch in them, they're blood, and what brings them to Salem. It's what brought her to Salem. Kara, lurking around every corner ready to cast some ridiculous spell or outright chase me down with a lynch mob bearing torches, actual torches. No wonder I dove into books and movies, they were an escape from reality, and there was no way in hell I was going to breathe a word of my torment to anyone, especially Mom. That would have made things worse. Sympathetic eyes trying to console, or worse yet a lecture as to how to deal with bullies. No, my burdens are unfortunately just that, mine.

I open up the throttle a little more, letting the wind try to take some rehashed rage from me. As if making friends wasn't hard enough when you were sixteen. I was almost happy to move around when my studies ended. I got all the companionship I needed, or wanted, thanks to Mom, movies, books, and social media. Which was strictly forbidden. *Don't even think about plastering your face on the internet. Never have lives less lived been more chronicled in history than on social media.* Mom's words. I open my throttle a little more.

I get it. Can't have anyone finding out immortals exist. But it's like saying you've got a third head when you say you're not on Instagram, Snapchat, Twitter, or whatever the newest fad is.

All my phone's been good for is texting, my playlist, movies, and of course the GPS tracking. Can't get too far without Mom knowing where I—

Sirens sound behind me. *Oh crap.* Red and blue lights flash in my mirror. The needle is hovering around 115. I slow the bike and pull to the side of the road. *What an annoyance.* Now I'll have to put Mom to work—her contacts at least—and after the way I stomped out, that'll be a fun conversation.

"Turn off the bike, miss. Remove your helmet," calls out a big bellied sheriff stepping out of his car.

Crap—another cop pulls in behind this guy. What, they have nothing better to do than to travel in packs today?

"Thanks for the warning officer," I say to him as he comes up beside me.

"Warning? I asked you to turn off the bike and remove your helmet."

Concentrate, you can only control one cop at a time, but if your focus is split between two cops you can't even do that. My pep-talk to myself better work—the other guy's getting out of his car.

I flip up my visor and stare at the sheriff. "Thanks for the warning," I repeat.

"Right. The warning, just keep it under sixty, okay, miss." He nods and turns toward his car.

The other officer meets him halfway. "What do you mean a warning?" he says as clear as if he was standing beside me after they exchange words. "You radioed over 110. What did she do, batt her eyes at you?"

I'm not sticking around to control him too; I'd be flip-flopping between the two of them so much I'd be here all day. I wave and pull onto the road, accelerating at a more leisurely pace than I'm used to, while keeping a close eye on them in my mirror. They're still standing there, arguing. *Good. Keep it up, boys. Just a little further.*

I round the next bend and bring my bike back up to 60. Doing 115 in a 60 zone, *not smart girl.* Now Mom's gotta get hold of her nerd-linger friends, again. She's gotta wipe my face from the state's data base as soon as the footage is uploaded from the cop car, again. I have to tell Mom I won't get caught, again.

I'm surprised she hasn't torched my bike yet.

It's things like this that explain the whole social media no-no-thing. I remember Mom complaining about one witch posting some video of herself night diving from a really high cliff, then slowing unnaturally before she hit the water. It went viral. The nerd-lingers had to build a worm to sniff out her digital footprint. A multi headed worm like a hydra. Mom said it took weeks for her friends to erase every like and share.

I get it. Why inform the Broadsword where you are and what you look like? They didn't find her—the girl—but they could have.

Crap. Did I just see…? Yep, flashing cherries through the trees behind me.

The cops figured out something wasn't right. My mind control only works on one person at a time and doesn't last long. But it's gotten me out of a few situations. Not this one though. That's okay, Old Red will. I pat my crimson gas tank, get a good grip on the throttle and whisper to my bike, "Let 'er buck." My Ducati can easily do 150 mph and still corner like it's on rails.

They don't have a hope in hell of catching me and Old Red.

~ * ~

I retrace my route from the cabin, and Lincoln, zipping down the back roads of the foothills.

Lincoln's pretty quiet in the morning. Old Red is sexy as hell, but right now, in this town, I wish I was driving a truck. And I know just where to find the one that comes to mind.

Parked outside the Lambkin's Restaurant Lounge and Casino, just like it should be, is Lukas's old yellow pickup. I pull around back and tuck my bike between a pair of trucks, unwrap Lukas's blanket from my waist, and toss it over Old Red. As hidden from sight as I can make her.

I check my phone. I've missed a few texts from Mom and Aunt Brenda telling me to come back to the cabin. A number not programmed in has a crying face emoji under it and two selfies.

One of Kara holding my backpack and pretending to drink my whiskey, another of her wearing thick, black-rimmed glasses, holding the book I've been reading, and her thumb pointing down like my choice in literature sucks. After all these years she still knows how to find a place inside of me that regulates my body heat and my temper. I delete her text harder than I should and crack my screen. I curse her, and myself, for doing such a stupid thing. Thumbing over the crack, my phone responds, giving me some peace. I figure she got my number from Aunt Brenda's phone. She can get under my skin like no other. Since the day we met, every encounter since then, and even the thought of her brings a tightening to my chest, a whitening to my knuckles from clenching my fists. I've learned, through Mom's guidance, how to remain in control of my emotions, but Kara pushes my limits.

I take a breath and round the little shop with the smell of its fresh brew escaping out an open window. It's not French vanilla, but it's a dark roast. I pause for a moment to let its scent fill my lungs, take my anger away—and then I catch a hint of bacon. Breakfast, especially bacon, would be nice after a night on the road.

I follow the aroma inside the log cabin façade. "Just take a seat anywhere, shoog. I'll be right with ya," a waitress in her forties with blonde hair done up in a bun at the top of her head says, passing by me with a tray full of orders. A quick whiff of the place makes me crave a plate of crispy bacon. Anything after that is just the side dish.

I nod with a smile. "Thank ya." Ya? What am I saying? It's *you*. Thank *you*. Lincoln is definitely rubbing off on me.

Scanning the restaurant, it makes me think of a place where everyone says hello to each other, even strangers. Kind of how I imagine Canada to be. Rough wood flooring, booths, and walls. I bet the only reason the chairs and bench seats are smooth is from years of denim sliding along them. Lukas is sitting at a booth in the corner reading a paper by himself. A newspaper. It strikes me as odd he doesn't have a phone in his hand like most people. The paper indicates he might not be a social media addict, making any conversation about it easier to explain why I'm not on any. *If* the topic even comes up. My cracked screen comes to mind, and I have to push down thoughts of Kara.

I walk toward his booth, and it hits me: I'm still wearing the same clothes from yesterday when we first met. I'm dry, but I haven't showered since the river, and, thanks to Kara, I left the cabin without having done my hair or makeup.

I duck into the restroom, take my jacket off, splash some water on my face and run handfuls through my hair. It's the wet look today. The good thing about riding a bike is that all the essentials a woman needs is kept in her pockets. My phone, keys, a wad of cash, and my crimson lipstick are all I have with me, but they're enough. I put on my jacket and zip it up to conceal the tank I wore yesterday, wishing I had brought my backpack and the spare tank I always keep in it. I put on my lipstick, purse my lips, head back into the restaurant, and walk up to Lukas's booth.

"I'll have the usual, Sue," says Lukas, running his finger down a page of the newspaper. "You hear the Williams brothers went missing yesterday outside of Avon. Cops think it might be foul play. All they can find is their…" He finally looks up to find me and not Sue hovering over his table. "…truck." His cheeks flush as he grins. "You're…not Sue."

No, I'm not, and the Williams brothers are buried at the bottom of a river. I'm certain their deaths can't be traced back to me, but it would be good to know what the locals do. "Thought I'd take you up on your invitation." I try to play it cool.

"Please. Take a seat." Lukas half rises from the bench and holds his palm out to the one across the table. His mom raised him right.

I slide into the booth. "Trouble?" I ask, indicating the paper. "Foul play isn't something I'd expect to hear making the news in a town like Lincoln."

"That's the word on the street."

On the street. He's so cute. There can't be more than a dozen streets in the whole town.

"Town gossip," he goes on. "They say their truck was found by a bridge and blood on the wall under it."

"Pretty specific for town gossip," I say. Now that I think about it, when I threw Zeke against the concrete, there may have been a trickle of blood that stained the wall from his head.

"The Sherriff tends to talk a lot, and so does his wife. Once she hears something the whole town knows it within hours."

"You concerned?"

"Nah, those Williams boys are full of vinegar. Hopped up on 'shine all the time, getting in fights, passing out in barns that aren't theirs, and…and that's just a tip of the iceberg that got them locked up for eight months. No, I'm not worried. Doubt anybody else in town would be either aside from their parole officer. They'll turn up."

Mom did teach me to be a good judge of character, and Lukas hesitantly omitting their sexual misconduct in the presence of a woman proves to me I was spot on having the Williams brothers on my list of potential snacks. Whether the cops think there's foul play or not, the towns folk don't seem to, or don't care. Well, at least Lukas doesn't, and if the other people of Lincoln are as level-headed as he is being, they'll chalk up the sheriff's wife's gossip as no more than just that. Gossip from the busybody that has her nose in everyone's business.

Sue drops another menu on the table. "Nice to see you not eating alone for once," she says to Lukas, whose cheeks flush deeper. "You two take your time deciding what you want."

It's like I'm in a romance, just like at the gas station. Sue is the hard-working waitress with an open ear to people's woes, who no doubt has sound advice or a short story to clarify someone's confusion, and she's attempting to fix Lukas up. It's sweet, this hometown feeling. I finally understand firsthand, the attraction all those starry-eyed girls in the films felt when they met a small-town country-boy. The creamy white cowboy hat hanging on the coatrack at the end of the booth cements my understanding. It's all about a fantasy. A romanticized version of reality that differs from that of city life.

"Coffee?"

"Yes please."

Sue fills my cup.

The bell hanging over the door rings, and Sue turns from the table to welcome another customer to the restaurant.

What levity I feel inside, or showed on my face, diminishes in a heartbeat. The customer Sue greets at the door…is Kara.

Chapter Six

I lock eyes with Kara. *What is she doing at the diner?* Stealing away my peace, that's what. I do my best not to scowl at her evil smile as she starts across the restaurant.

Lukas says something. "Sorry, what?" I ask him. Kara's presence has drowned out my surroundings in a veil of rage. I have to concentrate on softening my eyebrows from the scowl meant for her.

"I hoped you might show up," says Lukas to me.

"I…um."

Kara walks past our booth, eyeing Lukas seductively, and making sure I notice. She stops at a booth across from us, sits, and stares at us, drumming her ivory polished nails on the table top. "I wanted to apologize for last night," I say, turning back to Lukas. If he noticed Kara come in, he's good at hiding it. He holds his attention solely on me. Wish I could do the same for him.

"No need. I get it. A long day on the road, the fresh air, the peace of Lincoln at night. I've slept under many a starry night myself."

He's smooth. For all he knows I rode for an hour, but he doesn't strike me as the sort of man to point out a woman's flaws. I pull my zipper up a little higher, ensuring the tank I wore yesterday is covered up. "Thanks for understanding."

Sue leans closer as she passes by us. "Be right back to take your order, hon."

"Thank you." I wrap my fingers around the warm cup and lean over the wafting steam, draw in the dark roast's fresh aroma, shut my eyes, and force the rich scent to push Kara's presence to the back of my mind. I open my eyes to find my cup overflowing with cockroaches. "Ah"—I flinch—"hem." I pull back from the cup, feigning clearing my throat, hoping I don't look a fool startled by a fine cup of joe.

"The chicken fried steak and eggs is excellent," Lukas says, opening his menu without reaction to the infestation spreading from my cup across the table; the roaches are meant for my eyes alone. One of them scurries across the table and over Lukas's sleeve.

Kara likes her illusions, and *ohhh* how I've grown tired of them.

I shoot a look at Kara. *Keep it up and I'll bury you.*

Kara reproduces her evil smile, then stops mumbling, and the roaches vanish.

"Excellent?" I keep my voice upbeat, keep the conversation going with Lukas. "I'll be the judge of that," I say, forcing my mind to stay in a flirtatious state, and my ass in our booth; there is no chance of either happening until I deal with Kara. "Excuse me for a second. I'm just gonna go wash up. If Sue comes back, order mine with an extra side of bacon."

"Will do," replies Lukas.

I do my best to move both with intrigue for Lukas and domineering rage for Kara. I nod to the bathroom and step inside.

It's empty. Perfect.

The moment the door shuts behind Kara, I throw her back against the wall. Her throat is in my hand. "Can't cast a spell if you can't mumble," I say, my face inches from hers. I'm not the sixteen-year-old girl she'd tormented. I tighten my grip, lift her dangling toes a good foot clear off the floor. "You really wanna throw down with me, witch? I'm game, and you'll find I'm no longer the juvenile vamp you first met."

This feels good—too good.

Four years of regretting not standing up to my tormentor is coming out in a rush. The veins in Kara's neck throb, pulsing beneath my fingers; the one on her forehead bulges from the pressure. Her ivory nails dig into my wrists, tracing drops of crimson from them in a futile effort to free herself.

She tries to speak. I tighten my grip.

I could snap her neck like a toothpick. It'd be easy. My chest burns with the urge to drive her through the tiled wall. Kara's lips are turning blue. Her skin tone-colored lipstick can't cover the lack of oxygen anymore.

Violet flashes in the mirror beside Kara.

She can't have mumbled any magic.

My reflection staring back at me has violet eyes—not blue.

I'm not flushed, I'm beet red, snarling through gritted teeth, frowning so hard I wouldn't be surprised if the crow's feet around my eyes became permanent.

Kara's eyes roll up.

I squeeze mine shut, draw a deep breath, and drop her to the floor. I'm shaking, simultaneously proud at my restraint and pissed off. My reflection looks more like the woman I'm used to seeing stare back at me—blue eyes and all.

Why they appeared violet is a mystery, but I chalk it up to Kara somehow getting a partial mumble out to work some kind of spell on me.

I drop to one knee beside the coughing witch gasping for air, sprawled out on her side with her blonde locks half covering her face. "We done?"

Kara nods her agreement between coughs.

That was satisfying—my childhood bully submitting before me. I'm actually glad I didn't kill her. This is *sooo* much better. Humiliating her. Enforcing knowledge that she's helpless against me, magic or not. She knows I can end her life with a gesture.

I just wish I had done this a decade ago at Salem in front of all her followers.

A tear—I'm guessing involuntary—runs down Kara's temple, and I feel something unexpected. Remorse. I let her live and could have killed her. But that single tear reminds me of all the tears I shed thanks to her. Hers may be from actual physical pain, not emotional, but it's as real as mine were. A slew of movie scenes run through my head, none I can place specifically, but the gist of them. The meaning the heroine must take away from choosing not to do a deed that would come so easily to the villain.

If you act like her, then you're no better than her.

I stand, wet a paper towel and wipe the blood from my wrists. I stopped myself from going too far. I won't apologize for what I did, though there is a part of me that wants to. If anything, it's to show her that I'm the bigger person. But that in itself feels like I'd incur some bad karma.

I toss the towel and run my fingers through my hair. The reflection staring back at me is composed, with an air of confidence that wasn't there before. I grin at myself and leave Kara alone to put herself back together.

I'd been crushing the life out of Kara longer than I thought. Lukas is sitting at our booth waiting patiently, his breakfast untouched.

I sit, pick up a piece of bacon. It's still sizzling, as if Sue just dropped it off. It's cooked just right—not floppy, crispy but not burned. "Umm," I say as it hits my tongue. "You might have been right about the steak and eggs, but I'll bet they can't hold up to this." I wiggle a piece of bacon between us.

"If there's one thing I know, its breakfast. I'll take that bet." Lukas nods, picking up his fork and steak knife.

~ * ~

We finish our breakfast with the regular chit-chat of a first date sprinkled in with just the right amount of flirting. Where are you from, how many siblings, what are your plans for the future? All the usual stuff.

Sue clears the table and refills our coffees.

I dish out my rehearsed, scripted past and far-fetched future filled with mundane normality to Lukas. When he asks what brought me here? Today, that one stumped me. I'm so used to saying just passing through or visiting a relative. This time, the nuclear fall out scene from *Terminator* runs through my head.

I can't very well tell him I'm in Lincoln because this is ground zero of the battle for the planet. At least that's what has been deciphered from the prophecy. *In the midst of rolling hills under an endless sky foreshadowed by the sinking sun beyond the mountain, the savior shall rise to meet the onslaught of fire from above.* That particular pearl is why Mom and I traveled as much as we did. She was scouting. Lincoln, and the surrounding area, is a match to the prophecy's description. Along with some other tidbits sprinkled throughout. I always zoned out thinking about what *fire from above* could mean. I catch myself doing it again, and I settle with a girls-only summer vacation to answer Lukas.

"All girl's trip?" Lukas repeats with an inquiring tone. "I should count myself lucky you joined me."

He's fishing, so I throw him a line. "Well, I do owe you for the blanket. Which I intend on giving back, by the way." I raise my coffee cup. "We just needed some girl time, you know…Talk about our hair and clothes and stuff." I wink.

"You don't strike me as the type."

He may not have a poker face, but he's reading through the scripted version of me. He's smarter than most men I've met. 'Course it's not like any of them passed my tests. Lukas strikes me as different. As if he truly is the lead in a romance where a happily ever after is in sight for the woman tasked with a life-changing issue. Mine's a hell of a lot bigger than any on the silver screen, but the idea of living out a movie is tantalizing.

I stare out the window, holding my cup in both hands in front of my face. "Maybe I'm not, but there wasn't anyone keeping me back home." There's the subtle hint at a nugget he might have been digging for. I glance back at him—he gets it.

No…I don't have a man waiting for me somewhere.

You're welcome.

"The four of us decided to check out the mountains with no schedule." Figure I might as well include Kara and Aunt Brenda in my lie as they are living with Mom and me, for the moment. "Aside from going to the world-famous rodeo of Lincoln, that is." I've done my research on the place. On the Fourth of July weekend, a crazy number of fireworks are set to blanket the sky every night of the week-long rodeo that's kicked off with a parade and carnival. It's plastered all over the town's website.

Lukas sits up with pride. "Come to see me in action?"

So, the hat hanging on the coatrack isn't just for show. I have to admit, that intrigues me just a tad more than I already was.

"That depends. You any good?"

"It's been a while due to work, running the farm and all. But…I'm famous here."

"I bet you are." I finish my coffee.

What am I doing? I'm losing myself. Flirting with him is one thing, but I find I'm entertaining the long-lost delusions of a little girl who knew nothing of the Thirst. All those times as a child romanticizing about the perfect wedding race back to me. Wearing one of Mom's white shirts like a dress, my teddy bear draped in a black one as the groom. I can't help it that Lukas resembles, if not personifies, my childhood fantasy of the perfect someone to settle down with, raise kids with, and grow old with. But those delusions I had as a child I put aside a long time ago, thanks in part to Dad abandoning Mom and leaving her heartbroken. I've allowed myself to date but solely for entertainment purposes. Getting attached to a man would ultimately end in disaster. He's going to die, and I won't. Period.

I decided to harden my heart then, just as I decide to now. Re-erect barriers Lukas's chivalry has threatened to tear down, push childish dreams to the past where they belong. I'll still have fun with Lukas, and if he's as good of a man as I think he is, I might escalate us to a physical relationship, but one I can walk away from at a moment's notice.

The door to the bathroom opens. Kara's dolled herself up to her usual Barbie self, although she looks like a spooked deer on a dark highway. She ducks back into the restroom.

"Act natural." Kara's voice is as loud in my ears as if she was sitting beside me.

I sit up straight.

Telepathy, nice trick. Every witch has some unique gift. I've heard of others having it too. I never knew Kara had it. Always thought it would be cool. Now that she's in my head, I don't much like it.

"We're not alone."

I perk up. *What do you mean we're not alone?* I think to her, looking at the restroom door, trying to communicate back.

"Don't turn around, don't panic, just get out. Leave with the guy. Try to act like you live here. I'm slipping out the window. I'll meet you out back."

My urge to spin in the booth is hard to contain. If someone says heads up, most of the time a person looks up. I don't trust Kara, especially after I just kicked her ass. She's plotting something for sure. Though, I did show her I'm no longer one to be trifled with. But there's something in her voice. Like fear. I draw in a breath, and sure enough, despite the bacon, toast, and coffee, I pick out fear's faint scent. I've hunted for long enough to tell which direction it's coming from, and it's mixed with Kara's lilac perfume. *What's got you spooked?* I think to her.

"Are you out yet? Hurry up."

There's more panic to her voice. I'm guessing she can't read my mind—that's why she's not responding to my thoughts. That's a relief. But if I can only hear her, and she can't hear me, then that's a pretty crappy gift.

"This was fun. We should do it again some time," I say to Lukas.

My curiosity gets the better of me. I don't turn; instead, I pull out my phone and turn on the selfie option on the camera, run my fingers through my hair.

"I agree. How about tonight?" Lukas asks.

My phone shows two men sitting a few tables behind me—one older, one younger, and both with pale gray skin.

The Broadsword.

I'm far from tanned, but in my phone, I watch myself turn whiter. I didn't think that was possible.

"Walk me out," I say standing up, pocketing my phone, throwing a fifty on the table and drawing in a deep breath. I hold it in, force blood to return to my face, flushing my cheeks. Vamps aren't particularly tanned, and I don't want to give these two anything that might out me. I let my breath slip slowly between my lips then draw in another through my nose. Its an old meditation trick, but it works. Yes, I'm a vamp. But I'm out in daylight, roaming around. There's no way they could know of my unique condition, could they? Could they be part of the group that burned the Sanctum to the ground?

I need to get out, ride away, clear my head and think rationally. I need Mom.

I stretch my lower back as I stand at the end of the booth, waiting for Lukas to rise from his bench. "You didn't have to do that. I invited you out," he says, gesturing at the cash on the table.

"You can buy dinner." I let myself enjoy what could very well be the last time I set eyes on Lukas's handsome face. Armageddon doesn't scare me at all right now. If the Broadsword found out who—or what—I am, I'll be dead before my corpse can fall to the floor. "Not tonight. Girls' trip, remember."

He climbs out of the booth, puts his hat on. I put my hand on his cheek and press my lips against his. He's caught off guard, but settles into it with a hand on my hip. Sure, I wanted to kiss him, but I also know that public displays of affection are good deterrents to wandering eyes settling on you. His lips are soft, and he smells even better up close. I pull back, open my eyes to find a grin enhancing his already prominent cheekbones.

"Soon though." I turn him toward the door and keep his broad shoulders between the Broadsword and myself. "I'll give you a shout," I say to Lukas as we pass the table with my would-be killers. The kiss worked. The men at the table are concentrating a little too hard on their menus. They're related all right, no doubt of that. Same noses. Same strong chins. They even sit the same way. I've heard tales that Broadsword pairs are often comprised of father-son teams. An endless lineage of death dealers taught their trade from the time they can speak. Trained from birth to hunt anything non-human.

I try my meditation breathing again. It doesn't help.

Lukas opens the door for me. I step out to find two big black Harleys parked out front. "Goodbye, Lukas." I smile at him, then make for the back of the building.

"Bye, and thanks again," Lukas says to my back. Under any other circumstances I would have strutted away, letting my hips do more talking than my lips ever could. But today, it's all I can do to keep from sprinting to my bike and racing back to Mom.

Chapter Seven

My Ducati vibrating beneath me gives me hope. Hope that I can escape before the Broadsword figures out what—and who—I am. I coast up beside Lukas pulling out of his parking stall and toss his blanket through the window, shoot him a wink, and pull onto the road. I'm not sure why I paused to return the blanket—eating up valuable time like that isn't smart—but I had too; it felt right. And I could use a lot more of that feeling now.

"It's just me."

"Jeese." My bike wobbles. In my mirror is a rusted-out Trans Am. Its once-black paint has faded to a dulled dark gray, and there's a mass of blonde locks framing dark sunglasses behind the wheel. Someone needs to teach Kara about stealth. I may be on a crimson superbike, but that just passes for hot. A woman of her looks in a muscle car with a flaming bird on the hood, she's just looking for attention like she wants to be in a 70s rock video shining the hood with her ass. Sure, it's fast, but come on. She might as well be driving a beemer, at least that would blend in better than rare American muscle out here.

We make it out of town, and I push past the turn to our cabin.

"Where are you going? We need to warn them."

Use your phone, dummy. Now I wish she could hear my thoughts. I hold up my fist and stick out my thumb and pinky. Just to be sure she doesn't think I'm rocking out, I hold the universal sign of a phone to the side of my head. Kara fumbles around a bit, then I see her lips moving. I can't hear her, and my hair hasn't turned to snakes so I guess she figured out what I meant. She never struck me as overly bright, what with the Barbie doll look and all. Truth be told, I don't really know her, the real her. All I remember of her is a spoiled brat who was mean to anyone not in her clique, along with the stories Aunt Brenda told Mom on her visits.

"I told Mom about..."

I pull onto a gravel road a few miles past the cabin, and my back tire skids out a foot to the side. "Easy, Red. You take care of me, and I'll take care of you." I ease off the throttle; she's not a dirt bike.

Kara follows close behind me. Her Trans Am handles better on gravel than my Ducati.

"Where are you going?"

You're gonna learn not to jump into my head whenever you please. I give Old Red a jolt of gas, and an array of rocks fly from my back tire, peppering Kara's windshield. She backs off a few more yards with no reply.

I follow the winding road to a sign with a guy holding binoculars and pull over to the lookout. Kara rolls to a stop as I flip up my visor. She gets out, slamming the door. As I pull my helmet off, I catch her mumbling. The cracks and chips I put in her windshield shrink to leave a perfectly clean piece of glass.

I look out over the guardrail as Kara walks up beside me. She follows my gaze to our cabin below. "Nice view," she says, putting together what I was up to.

"Yep. There's no point in leading anyone to Mom during the daytime. We keep watch till she's up. She'll know what to do."

"Mom's got her covered till then, said to lay low." She huffs. "Run and hide, nothing new there."

Kara gave me a heads up in the diner. Probably saved my life. 'Course she could have just been looking out for herself. She needs me to save the world so she can go on whoring it up. As much as I hate to say it, I have to. "Truce?"

"Even though you just smashed my windshield…I get I was following close behind you but—"

"I did that because you were in my head." I guess she didn't get it.

"Fine. I won't do it again unless it's absolutely necessary. Okay?"

"See that you don't," I say, certain she'll do it again, spook me, and make me crash Old Red. I look back at my bike and have to admit that's why I got so mad at her. I could have wrecked Old Red and lost my freedom. The notion of caring more about my ride than the mental intrusion is absurd, but my bike is how I clear my mind and losing that freedom is not something I'm willing to entertain. I get off Old Red, set my helmet on her seat, step over the guardrail, and lean against it, arms crossed.

Kara follows my lead. We sit there for a minute, overlooking the valley and our cabin.

Kara breaks the silence. "Sorry, I got scared."

I never thought I'd hear her apologize to me. Being so near our would-be death-dealers brings out different sides of people. I know that. I have been the bringer of death to many people. It's different when you're on the other side.

"Me too," I tell her. "I've never seen one in person. Let alone two. You?"

Kara shakes her head. "All I could picture is them dancing around a fire with me staked in the middle of it." That must be a witch's greatest fear.

She mumbles and a cooling breeze flows over us, flipping our hair back.

"Nice trick," I say. She waves my words off as if she does that as easily as blinking. I mean it. I'm a little less heated. I take a breath. "What'd your mom say?"

"The usual. Be careful, make sure you're not followed. Run, don't fight, run."

"Sounds familiar. You ever hear of anyone beating them?"

"Nope." She sighs, grinding the toe of her boot into the ground.

"What do you know about the Broadsword?" I ask. "Not just that we're supposed to run from them. But what do you *actually* know?"

The girl I once knew to be so chatty is silent, reflective, almost a different person. She shrugs. "Been around as long as we have. Witches and vamps, I mean. They always work in pairs. Skilled with every weapon known to man. No witch has ever gone up against them and lived to tell the tale."

"I wonder where the tales come from then," I say, giving her a moment to ponder my words. She starts twirling her curls around two fingers. As a kid I was sure she did that to show off her perfect locks—not a split end to be found. Now, I'm starting to think she is actually considering what was said to her. "Sounds like you know about as much as I do."

"Warnings and ghost stories. If it wasn't for our education in the Sanctum, our kinds would never cross paths."

"I still can't believe it's gone. It always seemed impenetrable," I say.

"If the most powerful covens were guarding it, and they couldn't defend themselves against the Broadsword. What chance do *we* have? Really. The four of us against an army of them. It doesn't matter that they're human. Okay, really enhanced humans. But against numbers large enough to drop the Sanctum, we're screwed." Kara kicks a rock, sending it tumbling through bushes down the hill. "So much for the prophecy. There's no stopping them. Ah…sorry…I don't mean—"

"No. I get it. We can't win. We don't even know how I am supposed to do…whatever. I hate this. That blasted parchment has consumed my life since I turned," I say.

"It did bring us together. No matter how vague it is."

I study her, trying to decipher if she's joking. It's the prophecy that kept our two kinds from going to war for centuries. We all need a place to live. Unlike the wolves, mindless and built to do nothing but slaughter anyone—they're fair game for both witches and vamps to strike from the face of the earth. So, an understanding was met, not so much like a peace treaty being struck, but an understanding. We keep to our own kind. Something a little harder for me being half human, but apart from the hallways at the Sanctum, witches and vamps never intermingled. I figure she's being sincere. "And our moms seem to have hit it off. Despite the rules about separation."

"Yeah. I always found that weird. How they came to be friends I have no idea. It's not like you and I got along great. It was probably because you and I quarrelled that they were forced into a friendship," she says.

Didn't get along great. Quarrelled. I can think of much harsher words to describe our relationship. Kara was a bitch to me.

"And being high-ranking members of their covens, they must have had some interaction," Kara says. "Planning for your twenty-fifth birthday and all. I get why we built the Sanctum ages ago. We're not immortal like you vamps, so we needed a place to house centuries of knowledge."

I was going to say our moms' relationship grew due to their similarities in raising a child alone. But something creeps up from Kara's words. "Wait…you say built by witches?"

"Yeah."

"I heard we built it. The vamps. To house the knowledge of the elders and provide a safe haven for when we came of age. We just let the witches in to act as our daytime guardians."

"Guardians?" Kara raises her voice. "We're not lapdogs, we're just using you to finish the job. Save the world then kick you to the curb. Salem belongs to us witches. We've earned it."

"Calm down. There's obviously more to this than either one of us has been told. I mean, do you even know who wrote the oh-so-precious prophecy? Do you? 'Cause I don't. Think about all we've been taught. Tons about each other, and the wolves."

Kara spits on the ground at the mention of the beasts.

"The Broadsword might as well be the boogeyman, and we're all supposed to blindly follow some scribblings that were probably made by a drunkard with a wild imagination," I say. I'm still fired up from running into the Broadsword, and the more I question things, the more heated I'm getting.

Kara takes a couple of breaths; I'm guessing she's as riled up as I am.

"Ever wonder why we call it a coven?" Kara says more like she's repeating a question she's pondered for years rather than looking for an answer from me. "Witches coven. Vampire coven. Separate species. Separate councils. Two head covens ruling over all the other ones spread across the globe like parents ruling over their kids."

"No, but now they're gone, and right when I'm supposed to do…whatever."

"Right when we need them the most." Kara huffs. "Guess keeping you in hiding wasn't such a bad idea after all. The elders couldn't even save themselves."

The rumble of two Harleys rolling down the highway make us both look up.

The Broadsword.

I hold my breath as they approach the turn to our cabin, conflicted with thoughts of charging down through the trees as fast as my legs can take me, or running for the hills as I've been instructed to so many times over the years.

I sigh as the bikes pass by the turn. As does Kara.

We stare at each other, listening, waiting until we're sure the Harleys continue past the gravel road turn-off. It's as if we have a shared gut feeling.

"We're not getting anywhere with us speculating," I say once they're gone. "And now that we know we're not leading the Broadsword to Mom while she's sleeping, I think we should head back."

"I agree."

"Besides, I need a shower and some clean clothes."

Kara grins. "I agree."

"You're one to talk." What's happening? My childhood bully and I are joking. I'm tired. That's it. Even though it's not yet noon, I'm beat. "Let's go, we should get some rest until Mom wakes."

Chapter Eight

"Ahhh, I needed this," I say, leaning against the wall, letting the hot water rain down my back. I never do feel quite awake without a shower. I turn it off, pull back the curtain. The mirror is so fogged all I can make out is a fuzzy blur of tangled crimson hair. I guess I was in there longer than I realized. I'll give the Millers credit for one thing: They swiped some nice towels. They're white and fluffy and easily soak up every drop of water on my skin. They're just like the towels you find in a posh Caribbean hotel. What I wouldn't give to be on a private beach again, especially right now. Curled up under a palm tree with a good book in my hands, letting the drone of the waves pull my worries away. Instead, I'm in Lincoln.

I slip the bathrobe on, and I thumb the dolphin crest on the left chest. Yep, it's "borrowed". Wish I could say the same for the pillow I'd slept on waiting for Mom to wake. I swear I punched that fluffy marshmallow into submission twenty times as I slept. I crane my neck to the side, working out the last bit of a kink the shower didn't get rid of.

I wipe the steam from the mirror, look myself in the eyes, steadying myself in trusting that Mom and Aunt Brenda know what they're doing. Run and hide. That's what we've been taught. The plan to stay in this cabin after running into the Broadsword seems like going against every fiber in my being. But we couldn't run during the day, not with Mom, and there's the whole sticking around town to fulfill the prophecy thing. Aunt Brenda's reasoning that the Broadsword was scouting and had no knowledge of our presence, otherwise they'd have pursued us, was sound. Thankful for the shower, better than the relief the river gave to me, I fill my lungs with moist warm air and swing the door open.

My clothes are laid out on the bed and immediately give me a sense of home, whisking my mind from threats of the Broadsword. No matter where we were, Mom knew how to give me that. It's the little things she did for me when I was a kid that I find I don't mind as an adult. It's her way of showing affection. I toss the robe on the bed and get dressed; my tank is still warm from the dryer. *Thanks, Mom.* I run my hands through my hair, letting my curls slide through my fingers. It's the wet look today, again. *I want something to eat.*

I open the door from the master bedroom to the aroma of bacon and pancakes. Mom is good. Funny how even at dusk I can get a yearning for breakfast. Must be from years of Mom saying I need a healthy meal to start the night.

"Good morning." I greet Mom every night the same way. She greets me back from her seat at the table beside Aunt Brenda and across from Kara.

From her slouched posture, Kara looks to have had just as restless of a sleep as I did, though she somehow maintains her normal not-a-hair-out-of-place look. "I don't know how you vamps do it," Kara says, cutting into a pancake. "Sleeping like this."

"You don't really get used to it when you can be outside in the daytime," I say, sitting. I myself had spent most the day pulling the covers over my head to block out the sun from disturbing my sleep. "Black out curtains help, but this..." I scoop a pile of bacon on my plate. "This makes it easier. Thanks."

Mom winks, sitting as elegant as ever across the table with her hands in her lap. She's always joined me for mealtimes. Even though she can't eat human food, she always set out a place setting for herself in her special way of making me feel closer to her. Old habits die hard.

"I'm starting to like the way you think," Kara says, piling a heap of bacon on top of her pancakes. She's growing on me. Her sins of the past seem less traumatizing than they once did.

"Can you see it, Linda?" Aunt Brenda says to Mom as she butters some toast.

Mom nods.

"See what?" asks Kara.

"It's time." Aunt Brenda ignores her, continuing on with Mom. "Do you want to start or shall I?"

"Scarlett is older by a few months; she would have found out first anyway. So, I will start."

"Start what?" I put down my bacon, confused. Mom is never like this. Polite to witches, pampering her child who is far too old for it, there's nothing out of the ordinary there. But never starting the night with such a serious look on her face, not to mention her tone. It makes me think I'm about to be scolded and sent to my room for something I didn't know I did.

"The reason the two of you have become more...tolerant of each other in such a short time despite your past transgressions is your kinship. *Our* kinship." Mom holds her palm up, indicating Aunt Brenda. "Vampires and witches. We share an attraction. Like magnets. A bond that pairs us for life. It's unbreakable and untransferable. You two connected at the Sanctum, and it has been reaffirmed with your recent proximity to each other. All vampires and witches share this connection. That's the reason for us keeping separate from each other aside from at the Sanctum. Spells are put in place to help dampen the bond from setting in, but sometimes, if there is enough passion between a pair, they can overcome the spells."

Kara frowns and looks as confused as I feel.

"Your passion for each other was far from loving, but it was passion nevertheless," Mom continues. "Thus, your unspoken bond. Most of the time a connection occurs between a boy and a girl. Lust that leads to lifelong lovers, lovers that can never be."

"So what, she's supposed to be my girlfriend or something?' Kara points at me.

Aunt Brenda shakes her head. "You like men far too much for that to happen."

"No dear," Mom tells Kara. "The bond is tied to emotion, similar to how you control your powers. Emotion can be pleasurable or hurtful. The two of you were *so* hurtful to each other."

Hurtful? Mom has a way with words, but not this time. Saying Kara was *hurtful* to me as a kid is a huge understatement. I downright hated her.

"You were told vampires and witches had to be kept apart to prevent war," Mom says. "Which is true, in part. The truth is, if a bond forms between a witch and a vampire we would lose our wits upon separation, become overrun with emotion, and be fit to spend the rest of our lives in a psychiatric ward. A witch's lack of immortality ensures this will happen, pulling the pair apart. If, on the off chance, a witch outlives a vampire, the result would be unfavorable due to their powers coupled with a total lack of control of their emotions. There is something in our blood, common to both vampire and witch alike that compels us, bonds us, to whomever we become emotionally attached to. No one knows why our species react this way. Humans don't cause it, nor does the abnormality of the wolfs bring on this eventuality. The attachment in your case ladies, was your deep-rooted distaste for each other. A bond that would not have come to be if you had concentrated your emotions on the opposite sex, as most teenagers do, rather than each other. We all go through this conversation when we came of age. When we stay twenty-five for the foreseeable future."

Mom looks me in the eye. The way the covens run this is atrocious. Keeping what we are from us until we're sixteen? Not telling us about this bond until we're twenty-five? Kara basically gets a boost in her powers, from what I understand. I retain the appearance of a twenty-five-year-old for eternity, or until I get killed.

This is wearing thin. What other pearl of secrecy is Mom going to drop on me next? Is there something else when I hit another milestone like turning thirty?

"And when we realize our full potential," Aunt Brenda adds, nodding at Kara.

"Why wait till now?" I throw my hand in the air. "Why not tell us when the Thirst kicks in? Why—"

Mom cuts me off with one raised finger, and reluctantly, I shut my mouth.

"Due to our rules of separation, only intermingling at the Sanctuary, and the spells put in place there has been no need for concern. Centuries have passed without such a bond forming due to these processes, until the two of you overpowered them. But most of all. Because *you*, Scarlett," Mom says, "are unique. We were not certain how you would react."

"What about me?" Kara chucks a piece of bacon onto her plate. "It would have been nice not to have bonded with her." She points a thumb at me. "Least I know you'll be the one going bonkers."

That does it. "What? Would you have been nicer to me? Like you're any better now. Would you have not been such a stuck-up entitled little—"

"Scarlett. That is enough," Mom says, not yelling but stern enough that I hold my tongue.

Aunt Brenda mumbles something.

Kara jumps out of her chair, knocking it to the floor. "No. Stop it. I'm not going comatose."

Aunt Brenda stops mumbling. "Then calm yourself. Stop acting like a spoiled brat and sit down."

Kara wags her finger and eyes Aunt Brenda for a couple of seconds. Then she picks up her chair and sits with her arms crossed. The spoiled brat comment is spot on. I wish I had thought of that. I've never lashed out at Kara like I just did, aside from at the diner. Even when we were kids. No matter how frustrated I got with her, how much I want her hair to turn to snakes and have her be the one tormented and laughed at, I never lost my temper. Unlike Kara, who seemed to always have a chip on her shoulder. Her saying *comatose* gets me thinking. Cools my head. What does she mean by that? Witches each have a gift. Kara's is telepathy. I'm not sure what Aunt Brenda's is. Witches tend to keep their talents to themselves, especially from vamps. Could hers be a knockout gift, like putting someone into a deep sleep?

"I apologize, Scarlett. For my daughter's outburst, and for imprinting her brash behavior on you."

Mom puts her hand on mine. "The longer the two of you are together, the more you shall take on each other's traits."

"Great," says Kara. Mom's glare has some effect on silencing her, but it's nothing compared to Aunt Brenda's tsk. It must be a mother-daughter thing.

What's so awful about me that Kara wants nothing to do with the way I am? Aside from the whole prophecy thing, I'm awesome. It's not like I want to be anything like her. Or am I already starting to act like her? Lashing out at the diner is out of character for me. It felt great, sure, but her tears brought up some guilt. The memory of my reflection staring back at me with violet eyes creeps up and puts weight to the growing knot in my stomach. Is it possible I'm taking on more than her traits? Could I be developing some kind of transferred witch magic? I push the notion away. It's absurd. Even just learning about this now, no matter how much I try, I can't recall any vamp ever having witch powers.

"All this secrecy is wearing thin," Kara huffs, verbalizing my own frustration. "The covens are as crooked as the government." Am I channeling her emotions right now?

"Breathe, Scarlett," Mom says in her meditative voice.

I look between her and Kara. Mom's composed and regal, where Kara is acting exactly like what Aunt Brenda said she was—a spoiled brat, despite being twenty-four years old. I picture myself in her chair. My arms crossed. My nose wrinkled. That is not something I want to become. I haul in air through my nose, slide my chair further from Kara, and breathe out through my mouth. If proximity aids our bond, I do *not* want to strengthen it.

"As I was saying, we kept to our separate covens," Mom continues, as if Kara and I had not had our little outbursts. "The strongest of us remained in Salem at the Sanctum, preparing the youth of tomorrow. It was not until the past week that we believed we deciphered what the prophecy referred to. When science finally caught up with scripture."

Aunt Brenda slides her phone along the table to rest between Kara and myself. A video of the sun throwing tendrils of fire into space plays on her phone. "The prophecy speaks of fire from above."

The video reads:

HUBBLE DETECTS INCREASING SOLAR FLARE ACTIVITY

Am I supposed to stop the freakin' sun?

Chapter Nine

HUBBLE DETECTS INCREASING SOLAR FLARE ACTIVITY

"That's from two weeks ago." Kara whips out her phone, and her thumbs drum on the screen.

Aunt Brenda rolls her eyes as if this is something Kara does often during a conversation. I wouldn't dare try that with Mom.

"There is plenty of science behind the theory, as I am sure you will soon discover." Mom's tone is that of disapproval of Kara's actions. "Past flares have lit up the night sky enough to read without candlelight."

"1859," Kara says without looking up from her phone.

"Northern lights spread as far south as Cuba." Mom takes a deep breath. "Since the mass introduction of the electrical grid, blackouts have occurred due to flare ups."

"89, northern US and Quebec," says Kara. "2001, New Zealand."

"Are you done?" Mom raises her eyebrows. Kara puts her phone down. "Yes, the radiation reached as far south as New Zealand. Planes in the northern hemisphere get rerouted all the time due to this radiation when solar storms flare up. The passengers are at such a high altitude with little atmosphere to protect them that the radiation poses a threat. I know *they* say it cannot reach the earth's surface…" Mom spins the phone on the table. "But *they* say a lot. And *they* cannot yet account for our existence."

"So, you think the 'fire from above' in the prophecy is radiation? And that's what I'm supposed to stop?" I ask. Like we're all gonna be microwaved or something. It's hard to believe, but Mom hasn't steered me wrong yet. She's withheld things from me, sure. The bond between Kara and me is a huge one, but her wisdom has always been sound. A knot forms in my stomach. "How am I supposed to stop the sun?"

"That we do not know. But we must have faith," says Mom in her calm, comforting voice.

"This sucks. If it's true," says Kara. "Let's say you're right. Let's say she can pull this off and the planet isn't baked. She's just a vamp. Not a lick of magic in her. You'd think that's what we'd need right now." Kara snaps her fingers, mumbling, and a tiny flame shoots from her thumb. "You know, fight fire with fire."

I like that thought. Or maybe it's the thought of someone else handling this whole mess and letting the burden of saving the planet fall on someone else's shoulders. "Makes sense." I can't believe I agreed with Kara, but it just came out. "What could I possibly do?"

"You have more power than you know, Scarlett." Mom places her hand on mine, pats it, and sighs. She glances at Aunt Brenda, as if she's at a loss for words. Something I've not known Mom to be.

Aunt Brenda nods. They've discussed this before. Rehearsed their speech. Makes me wish I had eavesdropped on their conversations more often. "You will do what you have to when the time comes," Aunt Brenda says. "The immediate threat is the Broadsword."

"No kidding." Kara huffs. "Aside from this bond."

Aunt Brenda ignores her and continues. "We always told you to run when you see them. That's because they're just the first strike—the men, they're the brute force and they're not to be trifled with. But should the men not succeed, which has rarely ever happened, the women do not fail. Stealthy assassins that take you from behind while you're distracted. Together, they're a coven in their own rights, made of humans with enhanced strength, speed, and agility. Each one of them corrupted by…him."

"Him. Him who?" asks Kara.

"The only other man to ever bear our gifts," Aunt Brenda says. "A sorcerer. The leader of the Broadsword"

"What?" I understand Kara's shock. I've never heard of a man having the power of a witch since the sorcerer who wrote the prophecy ages ago. Magic and men don't mix. For some reason, even if a witch has a son, the gift of magic isn't passed down to them.

"He has the ability to turn the hearts of the weak into coal. Blacken them, making them cold, ruthless, and willing to do what it takes to see his vision come true."

"Which is what?" I ask. "You obviously know."

"As far as we can tell," Mom answers for Aunt Brenda, "his ambition is to let the earth burn and rule over the survivors with absolute power. A diminished population is far easier to reside over than one consisting of billions. With his ability to sap all control from one's soul, I fear that world domination is not beyond his reach."

"We don't know exactly how you're supposed to save the world," says Aunt Brenda. "But we know that *he* is afraid of you. He must be to have created the Broadsword and sent them scouring the globe to find you."

"Now they're here, in Lincoln," says Kara.

"We've been isolated in so many remote places I've lost track. Unless they followed you here from the Sanctum." I look over the three women at the table, and somehow think it is more Kara's fault than the others. Kara, who I'm bonded to. How could Mom keep that from me? How could Mom keep a sorcerer hidden from me? "Assuming they don't know we're here, hiding," I correct Kara. "How am I supposed to pull off this—whatever it is I'm supposed to do with *a sorcerer*?" I stand over the table; my hands shaking.

"Sit down," Mom says. "There's more you need to hear."

"More? What more could there be?" I throw my hands in the air. Mom's stare would have stabbed me had her eyes been knives. I know I'm being disrespectful but come on. How much more can she drop on me in one night?

"Sit," Mom repeats, nodding to my empty seat.

I haul in a breath and slump back in my chair. The only reason I'm not jumping on my bike is because, despite being pissed off, something inside me needs clarity. I want to know everything. "No more secrets."

"You are the key to saving us all, Scar." Scar—Mom only calls me that when I've been hurt. When I skinned my knee as a child, or some boy broke my heart before I hardened it. "*He* won't kill you—he can't. You mean too much to him."

"We hope," says Aunt Brenda.

"You see…" Mom drops her gaze to her lap. She's fidgeting as if she's picking at something lodged under her nails, her unwavering confidence nowhere in sight. "When I said a pairing is for life, and that it can cloud judgment, I was speaking from experience. I did my best to ensure neither vampire nor witch would keep a close eye on you. They knew how important you were, and I played my role as an overprotective mother, but they never knew how truly unique you are. Aside from Brenda, I told them you were the result of me falling in love with your father. A man. A regular human man, and that you were of no threat to our oldest laws. There has never been a child born between a vampire and a human. Never."

"And there still hasn't been to this day, not entirely human that is," Aunt Brenda adds.

Their words make it hard to swallow. My chest gets tight, and I'm sure my cheeks have turned crimson to match my hair. If I'm not half human, then what am I?

"Your father" —Mom finally looks up—"is the head of the Broadsword."

The leader of the Broadsword, a sorcerer, is my dad. *My dad* is the one who wants to kill me.

I need to run. I need to let something out of me, to burn off some adrenaline, to put my fist through the table—to do *something*. Tears roll down my cheeks without control and piss me off further.

"I..."

I don't have any words to say. I can't find them. I stand and my chair topples to the floor.

"I can't."

I shake my head. I need air, and I need it now. I grunt, stomping my way across the cabin. My fist obliterates the drywall at the top of the stairway. I jump down the entire flight of stairs, kick the door down to the outside.

"Scar, I'm sorry." I've never seen Mom cry, but her once-composed demeanor now sounds like that belonging to a weeping child.

I grab my jacket, throw it on, and jump on my bike. I always wondered what having a relationship with my dad would be like. Now I discover he's the one who's sent an army of assassins after us, after me. Looks like I got a relationship with him after all. I just never imagined it was a surrogate one through the Broadsword.

"Wait!" Kara shouts at my back.

There's nothing but concern on the face of my long-lost bully. I thought her family was messed up, her dad being a junkie and all. And she's staring at me with pity. Not since I met Kara was I jealous of her, but now I catch myself wishing my father was simply an addict like hers.

She's had almost as many bombs dropped on her as I have this night. Part of me wants solitude. But another part of me wants her by my side. She's in this with me, finding out we've been lied to by our moms. By everybody. "You coming?" I say.

Kara climbs on Old Red behind me. Her arms wrapping around my waist somehow let me take a breath that isn't fueled with rage. "Hit it." She doesn't have to ask twice.

Rocks pepper the cabin for the second time since I've been to Lincoln; I'm beginning to like that sound.

Chapter Ten

"Oh God." Kara's arms tighten around my waist.

A pine tree crashes to the driveway in front of us, blocking our path to the road.

I squeeze the brakes.

Old Red skids sideways toward the tree, but it still isn't enough to stop us.

Kara mumbles.

A gust of wind hits us so hard I nearly tip the bike. We stop with my back tire flicking a branch.

"Nice one," I say, tracing the fallen pine to the trees. Beside its splintered trunk is the older man in black from the diner. His pale gray flesh gives him an unnatural, almost spectral appearance in the moonlight.

The Broadsword has found us.

"Mom," I blurt out, glancing back toward the cabin. The hundred-yard driveway seems longer than it should.

Run. Just run. I know what I'm supposed to do. I should hit the gas and not look back. Old Red's not a dirt bike, but I'm sure I can maneuver her through the trees, around the fallen pine, and onto the road. But I can't abandon Mom and Aunt Brenda. Besides, we'll have a better chance of survival if we outnumber them.

We have to fight.

I pray the stories of the Broadsword are wrong. That they're not as strong as they say, or as fast. That they *can* be killed like anyone else, regardless of the tales.

I give Old Red some gas, skid to the side, spitting gravel into the downed tree, and turn back.

The younger Broadsword steps out of the trees onto the driveway between us and the cabin. His stone-cold face tightens my chest.

We're surrounded.

"Hang on," I say, cracking the throttle open, hoping to go around him.

He moves to intercept us. A weapon glints in the moonlight—a sword.

Kara's grip on my waist tightens.

The slash is so fast even my reflexes can't avoid the blow, and his blade lodges in the spokes of my front tire.

Old Red lurches forward, lifting her back end up. Kara and I launch through the air.

I reach back, twisting, and pull Kara to my chest as we hit the gravel. The wind is blown from my lungs and my head bounces off the driveway; stars fill my eyes.

"Get up," Kara says to me, looking back at the young Broadsword. "Get up!" I rise to my elbows, gasping, trying to ignore the panic and force air to return to my chest.

"Come on." Kara tugs at my jacket, pulling me to my feet.

I shake the stars from my vision. We're a dozen yards from the cabin. Aunt Brenda's on the deck, and Mom's jumping over the railing.

Both men are making their way toward us, moving with the confidence of an easy kill in their sights.

The ground rumbles.

Two slabs of stone shoot from the earth, one on either side of my would-be killers. Standing twice their height, the slabs press in on them to squish them flat. The older Broadsword drops his blade and drives his palms against each slab. His strength is phenomenal for a human, he doesn't flinch, doesn't say a word, doesn't even look to Aunt Brenda mumbling. He just glares at me, his prize.

The young Broadsword leaps through the air with his sword raised.

I panic, step back, and raise my arms in defense. Though I know my flesh won't do any good against his steel. I curse my stupidity, my instinctive reaction that'll be the end of me. This is it; I'm going to die. Limbless, or skewered so many times I won't be able to heal before I bleed out. His speed is so fast I doubt Kara even sees him move. He's barely more than a blur to my enhanced vision.

Thankfully, so is Mom, leaping over me from behind and colliding with him in midair.

I pull in my first full breath. Mom has saved me, again. Like no other person on earth can, she gives me hope.

Their feet barely hit the ground and the older Broadsword sprints from the stone slabs, letting them slam together. He hammers his fist into Mom's gut, sending her through the air, splintering the thick balcony railing to pieces as she crashes through it, right into Aunt Brenda.

Both our protectors are thrown back inside the cabin so fast, and with such ease that I can't help but believe the boogeyman tales of the Broadsword must be true.

"No," I say to myself. The momentary hope Mom gave me leaves with the word. I want to flee, but I know that's not an option. I'm not sure if it's fear, bravery, or sheer adrenaline that kicks in, but I shout at the pair meant to slaughter us, "No!"

I find myself charging forward, my feet carrying me faster than my mind can keep up. It's like watching myself from a distance. The shadows seem to have a slight violet hue to them, whisking their lack of importance away and aiding my focus on my target.

The pine trees, the cabin at my back, Kara, and even the gravel sliding beneath my feet fade away. Nothing matters but the sharpened steel flashing in the moonlight, arcing toward me.

The young Broadsword swings. I duck, letting the blade flash through the air above my head.

His throat is beneath my fingers in a heartbeat. I lift him from the earth and punch him with all my strength.

The satisfying crunch of his nose under my fist sends blood exploding to the sides of his face. I swing him down as hard as I can, driving his head into the gravel.

His neck snaps.

Holy shit, I killed a Broadsword. Courage rises in me. *I can do it again. I can win.*

I turn toward the older Broadsword. His fist slams into my cheek.

I'm flung back. Blood vessels burst, warming the back of my neck. I cringe, tighten my shoulders, and crash into the cabin wall.

I drop to the deck.

My jaw stings in pain, telling me it's broken. I slump to my side, groaning, fighting to stay conscious.

His feet land on the deck in front of me. He smiles, pulling out a dagger.

I try to rise, but slump back down holding my ribs; broken from hitting the wall. "Fuck you," I try to say, but my jaw won't even let me curse the man about to take my life, so I do all I can and spit a wad of blood at his chest.

All my training at the Sanctum, the sparring sessions, the weapons training, and here I am cornered.

He steps toward me. I kick at his knee. Try to snap it backward. But he side-steps the hit. I pull my leg back, ready to kick again.

Fire takes my night vision from me, and my target.

Rising behind the old Broadsword is the bird from the hood of Kara's car, the phoenix. Bathed in flames, it spreads its wings wide, silhouetting the Broadsword's figure. The phoenix's wings wrap around the gray-skinned man before me and set him ablaze. I raise my arms to shield my face from the heat.

The Broadsword is yanked from the deck, roaring in defiance.

I drag myself to the deck's edge.

The Broadsword's roar turns to a scream of anguish as the phoenix cries into the night, and flames soar high above the cabin, illuminating the forest around us. Kara's lips mumble out her spell as she braces herself against her car, holding out her palm to her creation.

The phoenix lets out a final burst of flame.

I have to pull back on the deck from the heat trying to blister my face, and then the phoenix dissipates into smoke rising to the night sky. I look over the edge again. Kara is down, breathing heavy, slumped beside her car with her chin in her chest, drained.

Burned flesh turns up my nose yet gives me a sense of security. She did it. We did it. We did the impossible. *We* took down the Broadsword. The boogeyman himself. The younger one lay where I killed him, and the older one's charred husk smokes on blackened gravel. I roll to my back, pull air into my lungs. There's hope yet.

Mom's kneeling beside Aunt Brenda, pulling her up to sitting. I crawl to them and into Mom's embrace. I let my eyes water.

Glass smashes to the floor behind us.

Something metallic—and heavy—rolls across the floor. A high-pitched whine fills the cabin, and my hands are on my ears as fast as they can move. They're wet to the touch and warm.

Mom's holding her ears as well. Her palms pool with blood to the point ~~that~~ it runs down her wrists and cheeks.

An iron grip on both of my shoulders launches me through the air and down the stairs. My back embeds in the drywall, sending dust into my eyes making them water further than just from the pain of going deaf.

Through tears welling I see my savior, Mom, her arms outstretched from throwing me clear of the weapon assaulting our senses.

Then I feel the heat.

The very air burns my lungs as the cabin shakes to its foundation, and a wall of flame surges behind Mom. I reach out in a futile effort to hold her, screaming not from the heat racing toward me, but from the sight of Mom recoiling at the flames overtaking her.

I can't hear my voice, but my throat vibrates in a hoarse call for Mom. The lower half of her body is encased in swirling flames—flames that recoil against a fine violet haze shielding the upper half of her body. The haze surrounds me too, filling the stairway, forming a flickering barrier against the raging torrent threatening to engulf us.

Kara or Aunt Brenda have thrown up a barrier, shielding me, but not fast enough to protect Mom.

The wall of flames extinguishes as fast as it appeared, leaving the cabin charred and burning.

I drop my hand, reaching out for Mom, and push myself out of the hole in the wall, landing on my knees. A surge of heat hits me like I stepped into a sunbaked car. The violet haze has vanished, letting superheated air race toward me.

Shaky, dizzy, and unable to keep my balance, I crawl up the stairs. Mom's at the top. The lower half of her body is black; her dress is melted to once soft skin now turned to cracked, charred legs. Given enough time, she might be able to heal—I hope.

The smell of burned flesh overtakes that of the smoking wood surrounding us, and tears streak down my cheeks. I take her hand in mine. It's still perfect, still smooth with every tiny hair unsinged. She's unscathed from her head to her waist thanks to the barrier. Her lips move, but no sound reaches my ears over the ringing.

A hand on my shoulder makes me turn from Mom. Kara—she somehow made it to me from outside. My tears run unchecked with the thought of her helping.

Kara helps me to my feet, pulling under my arms. The ringing in my ears increases as I rise. My balance is shot, and Kara has to steady me. She pulls Mom by the wrist, dragging her, and the three of us tumble down the stairs through the door.

The cool moist air replaces the dry choking ash in my throat. Kara's face is as tear streaked as mine feels. *Oh god, Aunt Brenda. We've gotta get her out too.* I point back inside the cabin and mouth the words to her despite the pain of my broken jaw, though I'm still unsure if any sound is passing my lips. She shakes her head and drags me to her car, dumps me in the back. I push myself up the best I can, fighting the vertigo as Kara pulls Mom toward me.

Tears flow freely from Mom's eyes, and terror streaks across her face, her eyes wide as can be.

The car shakes up and down. The roof dents in a few inches, and a woman in skintight black leather lands on Mom's back, swatting Kara toward me. Aunt Brenda's warnings of the Broadsword and the deadly female assassins that follow the men race to mind.

The woman squats, puts one hand on the top of Mom's head, the other under her chin.

I love you, Mom mouths.

The woman snaps Mom's head to the side, breaking her neck, killing her with a single motion.

Mom's eyes dim; all expression leaves her face. I can't hear it, but my vibrating throat confirms my scream. "No!"

Kara's car fires up, and I get sucked into the back of the bench seat. Kara's face remains composed, determined. She mumbles, and we ramp up, then down, with pine branches whipping at the car's sides and undercarriage. She mumbled us over the fallen pine that blocked our path to freedom. We turn hard, she accelerates harder onto the pavement, away from the female Broadsword.

Chapter Eleven

We spend most of the night on the road. Kara drives white-knuckled at times. Our destination…anywhere but the cabin.

I'm in and out, fighting the vertigo, the urge to lose my breakfast, and drifting from unconsciousness only to be startled awake screaming for Mom. Whatever weapon the Broadsword used rattled my senses, weakened me, drained me.

Kara's telepathy came in useful. *Get some rest while you can. Shhhh. It's okay.*

All I can hear is her voice in my head, consoling me as best she can. I try to do the same for her, but we've given up on me trying to talk even after she relocated me to the passenger seat. All I've accomplished was her either frowning at me from being too quiet or jerking her head back from me yelling.

She's asleep now, curled up behind the wheel with her knees pulled in tight. The sun warms me through the windshield. It's welcoming, along with the return of my hearing and balance. Kara looks like an angel, my guardian angel, gently twirling her hair in her fingers as she sleeps.

She just saved my life, but part of me, the younger me, wants to draw on her perfect features with my lipstick. *Bitch* across the forehead in crimson would suffice.

Now, all I see is a woman who lost her mother, a woman in pain. Though she conceals her distraught like none other. As far as I can tell, she hasn't shed any more tears for her mom since leaving the cabin.

I take a deep breath, adjust the rear-view mirror, and look myself over.

My jaw's healed, with not a bruise remaining, but I look expressionless with hollow eyes. If I'd put on any makeup last night it would have run down my face, tracking salt stains to my lips and chin. I clean myself up as best I can, run fingers through my hair, put on some lipstick, and flip the mirror back. Mundane routine is a survival adaptation developed since we were cavepeople. Right now, it's all that's keeping me sane.

We must have been parked here a while, because the car's getting stuffy from the two of us breathing. The windows have begun to fog, blurring the phoenix now back on Kara's hood, so I roll mine down. Kara stirs at the squeak of the old crank, and I stop. Two inches is all I need to clear the air and hear the sound of something I need: churning water.

I gaze at my childhood bully and brush a few strands of hair from her face. We are more alike than I thought. I've got witch blood in my veins. I wonder if that would have changed Kara's approach to me when we were younger. Would she have accepted me? Both of us were deceived, or had the truth omitted from us at least. In my book that's the same thing. Both of us are fatherless—well, in a physical presence sort of way. At least hers doesn't command an army of assassins sent after her.

I ease my way out of the car and let the door rest against the frame so I don't disturb Kara further. The dry gravel road scrapes the soles of my boots as I stretch out the kinks of my beating. My ribs don't complain anymore; I'm fully recovered.

Looking out over the vast sprawling farmland makes me wonder where we are, but it doesn't matter. The short green crops edged with newly churned-up dirt in the field across the road give an earthy aroma to the crisp morning air. It's nice. A sign. The hope for new life this summer. A fresh start. I can't help but hope the same will be true for the world in less than a week's time, and it won't look like fields covered in ash with dried-up riverbeds.

Turning from the road, I step through the tall grass of the bank and make my way down. The babbling brook Kara brought us to fills the air, my lungs, and my mind with a sense of peace. "Thank you, Kara," I say, glancing over my shoulder to the car. I scoop up some stones and plop down on the bank. One by one the stones sink beneath the brook's writhing surface.

Questions run through my head for the better part of the morning. What Mom had said about her past, my past, Dad, and the solar storm soon to cook us. Questions that will never be answered. After a while I just lay on the bank staring at the vast Montana skyline, listening to the brook, recalling memories of Mom being alive. Trying to put into practice Mom's lessons.

Live in the moment.

The past is gone, and I'm not in the future. I'm here, and only here. *So, enjoy here while you still draw breath. Smell the fragrance of the world around you. Feel the tall blades of grass gliding through your fingers. Soak up the beauty of the great blue sky traced with fluffy clouds. Listen to the brook, the odd call of a frog, and the car door slamming shut.*

"Scarlett." Kara is up. "Scarlett?"

"Over here," I call back.

"Where?" She's frantic; her footsteps shuffling on gravel are sporadic. Her voice is high-pitched, short, and full of panic. I raise my hand and the shuffling gravel stops. "Don't do that. You can't just leave like that." She climbs down the bank and sits beside me, sulking, her arms wrapped around her knees.

"I wouldn't leave you," I say, putting a hand on her shoulder, attempting to comfort her. I sense that's what she's worried about, being alone. The truth is I don't want to be alone either. Kara lies down beside me. A single tear rolls down her cheek.

"What are we going to do?" she asks, wiping the tear away.

"I don't know. Whatever it is, we'll do it together."

She nods.

Part of me wants to talk to her, but mostly I want nothing more than to lie here in silence. I don't have the energy for anything more than that.

My eyes start to water, and I clench them shut. Kara's not sobbing uncontrollably, and it gives me strength. I've shed enough tears this night. I have to be stronger than this. Mom lied to me, lied to us. I want to be pissed off about it, about Dad, about knowledge withheld until I was going to turn twenty-five, but it all seems moot in the wake of Mom…I can't even think the word. I have to stand tall and fight those bastards who—I will myself to think it—*murdered her*. All because of my father.

"I want revenge," I tell Kara eventually. Want to put a sense of balance to things, if such a thing can ever be done. Sheer brute force, which I have plenty of, is a good place to start. I can almost feel the young Broadsword's neck snapping in my hand as I slammed him headfirst into the driveway. I want to feel that again, over and over, until my heart cries out no more.

Kara stays silent. I understand the bond Mom spoke of. I can feel Kara. It's more than her fluttering heartbeat, her shallow breathing, and her heat I feel beside me. It's her emotions. The anxiety that tightens her chest from what I said. The confusion of hatred, sorrow, and fear bubbling up in her and me, each fighting to overtake the other. Like a wave of emotion hurled from her to me. I use it, the hatred.

"Soon enough I'll have to make my way back to Lincoln and try to fulfill the prophecy," I tell Kara. I have to try. *No, I have to succeed.* Not for the world, certainly not because it's an unwanted duty thrust upon me, or even to make Mom proud of me. "I have to go back and stop them…their plans. Dad's plans; solely to enrage them, let them realize their lives have been wasted in pursuit of a ludicrous ambition. Then I'll feed on every one of them until none are left."

Kara's heart thuds faster, enough that I can pick it out over the churning water. I pick up the scent of fear.

"They took out the Sanctum." I push Kara's transferred fear back, away from me, and keep my anger fueled. "Probably tortured the covens to find out where I am. I'm the bait. But I'm also the trap." I nod, reassuring myself I'm making the right choice, wanting to slay them all. No matter how many of them there are. Satisfied that for once in my life I have a true path set out for me, one not prophesized for me, but one I've chosen for me and me alone.

"*We*," Kara corrects me after a few moments. "We have to go back to Lincoln. Together."

"Together," I say, shutting my eyes. My anger washes away, replaced with hope. I won't have to face my enemies alone.

Kara sighs. She's broken, taxed, and so am I. So, we keep silent and let the day pass.

Time stands still. I don't know how long we lay there like that, but I don't care. I'm living in the moment. I finally get what Mom was talking about. *Love where you are and whoever you're with.* That's exactly what I'm doing—forgiving traumas of the past and opening my heart to Kara.

I never want to leave this spot on the bank, but the rumbling in our stomachs urges us to get up. We'll get weak if we don't replenish ourselves soon. "We should find somewhere to eat," I say, breaking the comfortable silence between us.

Kara sits up beside me, running her fingers through her hair. "You're right."

"I wouldn't mind some clean clothes either." I tug at my dirty sweat-stained tank top. "And a shower." I still smell of smoke, and with every whiff it brings Mom's half-burned body before my eyes like she's lying just yards away, dying all over again.

"That part's easy," Kara says, her voice still weighed down with thought.

A warm breeze laced with a lavender scent races over my body, ripples my shirt, and streaks through my hair. It's surprising, yet nice, like a gentle summer breeze from head to toe. Kara stops her mumbling, and the breeze fades away. No wonder she always smells like lilac; she willed it. Here I was rubbing all kinds of lotions and perfumes on myself all these years and she had her own personal spa at her beck and call. "Nice trick," I say, relieved to no longer have the charred scent surrounding me.

"Wind's an element, and it carries with it the fragrance of flowers." Kara shrugs, climbing up the bank. As if what she just did takes no effort at all.

I stare at her, confused.

She shakes her head. "Didn't you learn anything? Earth, air, wind, and fire, the four elements. The four things every witch can control."

"I know," I say, annoyed as if she thinks I'm ignorant. There are limitations, thankfully. Like they can't just pop up a Mount Everest in the middle of a wheat field, but they can do some pretty neat things with them. I'd have fun with that power.

"I never did thank you for…what you did for Mom…in the cabin. Throwing up that barrier like you did. Giving me a few more moments with her," I say, following her up the bank.

"That wasn't me."

Chapter Twelve

"What do you mean you didn't put up the barrier back at the cabin?" I'm confused.

Kara looks me in the eye. "I've been meaning to ask you about that." The look of confusion on my face tells her everything she needs to know. "You have no idea, do you? How hard it is to use air to stop fire. I mean, it consumes it after all, and you not only did it, but you *tainted* it. Made a kind of purple wall of writhing air. Mom told me of witches who could taint the elements—only the witches of legend could do that, as they were the first of us touched by the source our power stems from, the world's first sorceress. I could only hope to do what they did…what you did."

My mind races. Dad is a sorcerer, the only sorcerer since the one who scribed the prophecy, which means I have witch blood; meaning I have witch powers running through my veins. It's as if Kara got her wish—and so did I, wanting someone with magic in them to be the one to fulfill the prophecy. I never imagined for a second it could be me. "But I don't know any incantations like you mumble."

"That's the crazy part," says Kara. "I was taught what I know. Taught how to control the elements. The incantations I mumble"—she winks at me—"are a way of harnessing my natural gifts, focusing them if you will. Kinda like how folklore says every witch needs a wand." Kara waves her hand in the air like she's fencing with an invisible assailant. "My point is, you got the power, girl. Like, *the power*." She wiggles her fingers like quotation marks.

She's opening up to me, with more levity in her voice and actions. I get it. She's got something to talk about other than our moms. I find her ability to move on infectious.

"You think that's how I'm supposed to stop it." I gaze up, squinting at the sun. It seems like an impossible task. If that truly is what I'm supposed to prevent. I point at the sun and blink the spots from my eyes. Movies, books, documentaries, and even my lessons in Salem surge forward. A giant ball of gas burning so hot it could light the planet's atmosphere on fire—supernova temperature I think it's called—a hundred times bigger than earth, the giver of all life, of wind, and creator of the seasons. Such a task is impossible. "How am I supposed to tame a star?"

"Beats me, but that's what you gotta figure out." Kara opens the car door.

"Kara?" I can't believe I'm doing this. "Can you teach me…you know…how to mumble?"

"Teach you my tricks, show you *my* secrets? You're gonna need a ton more than what I know to—" She glances up at the sky, twirls her hair around a finger, then stares back at me. "You did make that barrier." She sighs. "Come on." She gets in, shuts the door, fires up the engine.

I shake my head. A witch…me. I can't make sense of this. It's like I'm sixteen all over again, finding out I'm half human and half vamp. Now, I know I'm half vamp and half witch with power. Actual power. Power that can stop the wrath of the sun itself. I climb in the passenger seat and shut the door as Kara hits the gas. She flicks on the radio and "*Highway to Hell*" by AC/DC blasts through the car's speakers. *Fitting.*

"We need some grub before we start your training." She leans over, opens the glove box, pulls out a sandwich, tosses it on my lap. Then pulls out another for herself. "Eat." I'd question how long they've been in there, but the sandwich is cold to the touch. She must have charmed the glove box to chill things like a cooler can. I open the hard-plastic triangle, give it a whiff. The meat hasn't turned, but the sticker with a bar code and the 7-Eleven symbol on it makes me want to toss it back into the glove box. Keeping a low profile and constantly being on the move doesn't always make for the best diet. This is surprising, though. I always figured Kara for the type who preferred a four-course meal served to her by waiters wearing white gloves. Not a patron of gas station food.

I force myself to eat it, fast, and choke down the last bite as we pull the car into a field off one of the numerous gravel roads we've traveled on. "Now this'll be perfect," Kara says, still chewing on her sandwich.

I bounce in my seat, have to hold myself in place with a hand on the roof. "What are you doing?"

Kara doesn't answer; she just smiles and hits the gas. The trimmed wheat sprouting from the earth rakes along the undercarriage of the car, makes my heart speed up. I've never driven off road before, but the continuous impact of rubber on pokey stocks is dreadful, like driving on hundreds of spikes. We'll blow out a tire at any second. She speeds down a hill into a low point in the field.

BANG, BANG.

I cover my ears. "Someone's shooting at us!" Kara cranks the wheel, and we skid to a stop, kicking dust up around the car. "What are you doing? Go! Before they reload!" I whip my head around in search of whoever's shooting at us. "Had to be a shotgun. It was so loud." A double barrel maybe. There were only the two shots, and they were close together.

Kara frowns at me. She looks pissed. Not a hint of fear shows on her stern composure. "I assume that was you?" she says, raising an eyebrow.

"What? Go! Don't stop!" I spin and kneel in my seat to check behind us. The Broadsword is nowhere in sight. No men. No women.

Stealthy assassins. The women of the Broadsword are even deadlier than the men. Mom's warning from back at the cabin forces me to recall how she died, and by whom. The woman's black skintight leather, boots, jacket, every stitch and seam are as clear as if she's standing outside the car. Her face though, is out of focus, blurred and unrecognizable. But her hands aren't. They're crisp and clear, from the pigment to the lines on her knuckles, right down to the cherry-red nail polish. I shake my head. Force myself not to imagine those same hands holding the shotgun that fired at us.

"Calm down," Kara says with a hand on my shoulder. "It's like you've never had a blow out before."

"A what?"

"We blew out a tire."

A plant puncturing hard rubber, it had happened—or had it? I had just been thinking about it. I couldn't have done it, could I? My heart slows its pounding, drawing away my imagination, my fear. "Sorry, I…"

"This is gonna be a long day." Kara gets out, slamming the door shut. I follow, somewhat in a state of disbelief. The front tire is flat with half its rim buried in the dirt. "We gotta get that under control." Kara kicks the front tire on her side. She rounds the car, and with one look at the front passenger tire she sits on the hood, folding her arms. "One spare, that's all we got. Couldn't have blown out just one. You had to blow two." She shakes her head, pauses, then takes a deep breath. "Let's get to work."

"I'm sorry, I didn't mean to...I've never done this..." I throw my palm out, indicating the field. "Off-roading on spikes got me worried, didn't think I could—"

"Well, you did. And if we want to get back on the road and not sit here waiting to be found by some farmer with a real gun, or the Broadsword, you're gonna fix this. I'm all for your idea of hunting those assholes down, especially *them*"—she means the ones from the cabin, but won't say it—"but I'd rather we track them down instead of us being stranded out in the open like this."

"I get it, but how am I supposed to fix that? I can't just conjure up new tires."

"Well you're gonna have to. 'Cause I can't." Kara takes a few steps from the car, turns around, and holds out her palms at her sides. "Welcome to Kara's school of kick-assery. Where prodigies come to learn how to control themselves and not get us killed by accident or get seen. Our class setting today is the middle of nowhere, with no bathrooms, but it gives us some space not to be seen practicing the art of witchcraft."

She smiles. It's more of a, *we're here, so buck up, and hurry up*, smile. She's trying to make me feel better in her unique way. I trust her—to a degree—to teach me something about witchcraft, but there's a side of me, the youth in me that remembers how mean she was, that can't help but consider if she's going to pull something. A trick, a curse, something to torment me. I clear the notion. She's an adult and so am I. What transpired in the past is just that. History.

I look around. She was right when she said perfect and pulled off the road into the field. We're in a gully; more of a dip in the land surrounded by gently rolling hills of wheat. There isn't a soul in sight, not a farmhouse, not even the road. "I'm gonna teach you in an afternoon everything I learned over four years. So pay attention. Because when the time comes, and we actually find them, you better be ready for a fight. There's no doubt they'll be on high alert."

"Especially since we killed two Broadswords."

"Exactly." Kara nods. "Good thing you don't have the same allergy to the sun as other vamps, or we'd be screwed."

We only have a few hours until sunset. Kara gives me hope. Hope that we might stand a chance. Hope that I won't screw things up. It isn't much, but it's there.

I hold out my hand to her. "Lead the way." We walk away from the car, and it's gnawing at me—why now? "Kara."

"Yeah."

"How come I haven't shown any sign of having powers before this? I mean...shouldn't they have kicked in when I turned sixteen, like your powers did, like the Thirst did for me?"

"Beats me. Should have."

"That's enlightening."

"You'd think in the decade since it kicked in that you'd have accidentally conjured up something. Must have been suppressing"—she pauses, thumbs her gold locks between her fingers—"your emotions. Mom."

"What?"

"You don't know what my mom's power is, do you?"

"I—"

"Suppression."

"I got telepathy," she adds in my head.

"She got emotional suppression. She did it on me when I lost my cool so I wouldn't manifest anything in a fit of rage."

"Shit."

"Yeah, you got it." Kara says what forms in my head. "Mom visited Linda and you for years. Not so she could hang out with your mom but so she could suppress your emotions. Your power. Every witch's power comes from her emotions, and if you have none, you have no power." Kara huffs. "No wonder you were such a stone-cold bitch in school. Mom sapped your emotions from you."

"Me? I was the bitch?" What's that saying about the pot and the kettle? Doesn't matter. Kara graduated from the Sanctum with an A-plus in bitchery.

"Okay, I wasn't much better."

No shit.

"But Mom worked me too. You know I never even went to see Deserae in the infirmary after she accidentally set herself on fire. Dummy." Kara pauses, shaking her head at Deserae's mumbling mishap. By Kara saying it, I not only remember the name of the witch from the Sanctum who set herself ablaze, but I recall just how vacant Kara was from not only me as per usual, but everyone else as well. She was a hollow shell of herself.

Then it hits me. "I had private lessons with Aunt Brenda nearly every day. She'd spend the beginning and the end of it mumbling at her schedule. I figured she was writing without a pen."

"Now you know better."

I pause, dredging up Aunt Brenda's monthly visits. "She did it when she came to see Mom, every time I bet. Giving me my booster dose."

"If you're betting she was just working on you I'd say you're mistaken, given what we've learned of this bond. Your mom didn't go bonkers when your dad split and…whatever, it's done. But if Mom could do that for her, there might be another witch who can do that for us. Course, continuing on as an emotionless wreck isn't appealing, but I won't have to worry about that." She flicks two fingers up at me. "Immortality and all."

"Never trust a witch," I say. Mulling over her words, simultaneously feeling hopeful but with yet another splash of betrayal fueled by secrecy.

Kara tilts her head, raises an eyebrow at me, but holds her tongue. We stare at each other for a moment, sizing each other up, searching for the long-lost rivals who are buried beneath our façades, waiting for one of them to jump up and lash out at the other.

"We were both duped."

Kara takes a second, then subsides. "Some of us more than others," she says with the corners of her mouth turning up.

"Can we move on, past the bullshit?"

"Fine, you never could take a joke."

How in the hell does she think any of this is funny? Maybe it's her way of coping. Her way of getting through life with such a carefree attitude, or maybe it's because Aunt Brenda mumbled her gift onto Kara for so long it changed her, robbed her of something, and that's why she responds to her most primal urges as if they control her. Fight, fuck, or flee. I've never known

Kara to run and hide; that was, and still is, my M.O. But fight? Hell yeah, she's a fighter. As for the other, well, she earned her reputation for being easy back at the Sanctum.

For the first time in my life, I pity Kara. I don't show it or say it. "Can we just do this already?"

Her smile grows. "First things first. Forget all you were taught about witches and spell casting. Afterall, you're unique, your dad's unique, and we have no idea what you can do. All you really need to know is that it's in you, similar to an emotion. A feeling you get knowing you can create whatever you can imagine."

"But you can't just do whatever you want. There has to be limits."

"Forget all you think you know," Kara repeats herself, gritting her teeth. "We don't know your limitations. You might not have any. So open your mind. Like when you were a kid, imagining you were riding unicorns, feeding your pet sharks, or whatever it is you vamps dream of. You blew our tires with a thought, threw up a barrier to…" Kara takes a breath. "I'm guessing it's like an instinct to you, tied to your emotions. You are a red head after all."

She snickers, another taunt from the past. No doubt on purpose to get me fired up. Before we bonded, it would have worked. She holds up her finger, silencing me as I open my mouth.

"Let's start with something simple. Fire. It holds a special place in our hearts since we lived in caves. It keeps us warm, cooks our food, protects us from danger, and it kills us. Make a fire. Think about it and make one. Over there, away from the car." She points at a low spot of dry, cracked earth a few yards away that must've been a small pond during planting season but has dried up.

Good idea, don't let the newb burn down the wheat field you're standing in. "Just like that? Make a fire."

"Yeah." She snaps her fingers, and a tiny flame shoots up from her thumb, then she blows it away, back into the nothingness it came from. "Now get on with it."

Kara's a horrible teacher; her patience is about as thin as mine. She shows it like I do too. Or maybe the bond between us lets us share our traits with the other more than I'd hoped.

I stare at the ground, squinting. Try to imagine a fire burning freely with flames dancing in the breeze. "Nothing's happening."

"Try this: Don't just think of a fire, think of a fire with context. Like the fire chicken on the hood of my car." Kara points a thumb over her shoulder. I chuckle at such an absurd name for a phoenix; she knows how to reach me. Whether that's in a good or bad way, she knows.

Okay, context, she says. I don't dare want to bring the phoenix to life. I might burn up the car. Something easy then, a campfire surrounded by stones, perfect for roasting marshmallows on. I stare at the ground again.

"Got something?"

I nod to her question, keeping my gaze on the ground. It worked at the cabin and in the car. Why not here?

"Now feel it, tie an emotion to it. Feel the heat, burn your hand if you have to. Just do it."

Burn my hand. Is she in my head? I'd once rested my palms on stones around a fire just like the one I'm thinking of. Young and stupid and wanting a closer look at the coals that would cook my hotdog. I blistered my palms that night.

"Yeah!" Kara shouts. "That's my girl!"

I was so busy thinking about my hands, the pain of the burns, and the anger at myself for being so dumb, that I don't notice what I manifested. In the field before me stands a campfire, the very one from my memory, rocks and all.

"Wow," I say in disbelief.

"Damn rights, wow." Kara slaps me on the shoulder. "You not only made fire but did more than push rocks right up out of the dirt, I think you *changed* the dirt into rocks. I can't do that; no one can do that. Didn't see any push up from underground." Kara's talking more to herself than to me as she rushes to the campfire. "Made wood too?" She holds her hands up to the flames. "They're real." She kicks dirt at the wood and stones. "Illusions." She sighs. "Okay, that's a relief. At least we don't have to worry about you manifesting something out of thin air." She turns back to me, pointing a thumb over her shoulder. "Put it out."

"How?"

"Any way you want. I'd snuff it out, take away the oxygen and smother it, or use the moisture in the air. But there are no rules for you, remember? Go ahead, oh mighty one, make it rain."

Rain. Okay, that should be easy enough if I can make fire. *Forget all I know. Just do it.* I stare up, hold my hand out toward a white cloud. Focus on a storm with black clouds streaked with lightning, a downpour. Use your emotions,...pain...like the hot stones on my hand...like watching Mom. I clamp my jaw shut and the hair on the back of my neck stands on end. So do the ones on my arms.

Kara mutters something about ionizing the air then tackles me to the ground.

A loud crack fills the air and a bolt of lightning chars the earth a few paces away from us, followed by a dump of water.

The once-fluffy white cloud has grown to twice its size in a heartbeat. "Shut it off!" Kara screams over the rumble of thunder booming.

My heart races.

I raise my hand at the cloud. It's not going away; the black cloud flashes another bolt across its surface.

"Move!" Kara tugs at my arm, dragging me toward the car. She slips in the mud, scrambles back to her feet. We're drenched from the downpour. My boots sink in the soft ground, threatening to get stuck as I chase after Kara diving into the driver seat. I open the passenger door and the rain stops pounding me.

I did it. I shut it down.

I glance up—nope, not me. The rain's hitting an invisible dome surrounding the car. I get in the car to the sound of Kara mumbling and looking through the windshield, concentrating.

Lightning strikes the car and I scream, jumping in my seat.

The bolt surges around Kara's dome, protecting us and the car, tracing itself along the saturated invisible surface.

Stop. Stop. "Stop!" I shout at the sky. The cloud flashes one last time and softens to gray, then back to white, and the rain drizzles out.

Kara stops her mumbling, rests her forehead on the steering wheel.

"Sorry."

"I think that's enough lessons for now," replies Kara, breathing heavily.

Chapter Thirteen

"No witch has ever made it rain like that." Kara leans back in her seat. "They've manipulated water that's already there, like a river or the moisture in the air, but never made a thunderstorm from a nearly clear sky."

"Why'd you tell me to do that then?" I point up.

"See if you could." She shrugs. "Potentially limitless, remember?" She sighs, scanning the mud surrounding us. "A year's worth of rain in a minute. I was right to train you in the middle of nowhere. Messing with the sky wasn't the best idea though. That freak storm was probably picked up by satellite, probably caught the Broadswords' eyes too. Though it's not like they don't know we're going back to Lincoln to stop them, and the sun. Damn prophecy. I just got excited. Wanted to see what you could do, and I wasn't disappointed at the show."

I feel my cheeks flush. "Wish I had more control."

"Well, it's a good thing your birthday's not for another three nights then, isn't it? Practice, practice, practice." She smirks, reminding me of another one of Mom's pearls she dropped enough for it to be engrained in me.

Repetitio est mater omnium doctrinarum.

Latin for *repetition is the mother of all learning.*

Kara steps out of the car. "Now, let's get outta here."

The driver's side of the car lifts as Kara mumbles, then drops back down. She keeps mumbling, gets out, then walks around the front of the car. I crank down my window and stick my head out. Every footstep she takes lands on hard-packed earth. Mud dries and any trace of water flees before the sole of her boot hits the ground. A boulder pushes through the dirt and lifts the front passenger side of the car up. The tire dangling on the rim contorts itself into place, filling with air. "Thought you couldn't fix it," I say.

"The teacher teaches when the student is ready to listen," Kara says, sticking her nose in the air. She mumbles once more and a flame shoots from her finger, melting the hole in the tire where air is hissing out of. The boulder sinks back beneath the dirt from where it came. She jumps in with dry clothes, flowing hair, and the fresh scent of lilac filling the car. "Would you like to do the honors this time?" she says, referring to me tending to my sopping wet clothes. "Just don't blow yourself out the window." She smiles, throwing on her sunglasses, and hits the gas.

I have to admit she has me a bit worried, but I give it a shot. I imagine a warm summer breeze, a calm and relaxing feeling lying on a riverbank; something I've done a million times. But nothing happens. I close my eyes and concentrate harder. We thump onto the gravel road, and I reach for the roof again.

"Having trouble?" I can hear levity in her voice. "You should be smelling of roses by now. It's pretty much the first thing we learn at the Sanctum, you know."

"Shut up…gimme a second," I say, keeping my eyes shut tight. Why is nothing happening? I can feel the warm sun basking me in its rays, but nothing's happening. "Seriously, what gives?" I blurt out.

"You tell me." Kara rolls down her window. "I can't read your mind. What're you doing different?"

"Nothing."

"There's gotta be something."

"I'm not doing anything different. Hot sun…lying by a bloody river…a warm frickin' breeze…nothing." I slap the dash of the car, and my clothes ripple on my body with such force I try to escape from it and crawl back through my seat.

"Whoa." Kara jerks the car and has to correct her steering so we don't hit the ditch. "Calm down."

"I'm trying!" I'm caught in a hot mini tornado throwing anything not glued down all over Kara's car. Chewing gum, dirt, pebbles. I'm being pelted with the uncleanliness of Kara's car. Kara has to grab her sunglasses before they're ripped from her face. She locks up her brakes, and I lunge forward, bracing myself on the dash. Kara throws the car in park and bails out her door.

I do the same, but the tornado follows me. My hair reaches straight up as high as it can go. My jacket's trying to pull over my head, and my feet lift from the ground. "Enough!"

I drop to my knees like the mini tornado never existed.

"What the hell!" Kara shouts.

"I hate this." I rake the road with my hand, sending gravel into the field. An instant regret at letting my temper get the better of me as a sharp pain in my palm lets me know I'm now bleeding. "Ah come on!" I slap the road again in defiance of it hurting me.

A flash of violet light blazes from beneath my hand. The road splits in two; a crack three inches wide spreads out from either side of my palm.

Neither Kara nor I move. We're both processing what happened. I think it, but she says it, throwing her hands in the air and turning away from me. "Red heads—can't tell me they don't have tempers." She spins around, pointing. "It's your anger that triggers your powers. It won't be the only emotion but for the moment it's the easiest to tap into." She snorts. "Red heads."

I try to remain calm, take a deep breath. "Guess that's why Mom taught me my breathing; she knew." I stare up at Kara. "All those lessons about mantras, keeping a cool head, yoga…She knew." I fight a tear that's threatening to escape. Be it from anger or sorrow, I'm not sure, but I hold it back. "Aunt Brenda's mumblings. I remember being young, before the Thirst. I lost my temper plenty of times. But since the Sanctum, since the night I turned sixteen…nothing."

It hits me, the clarity of the Thirst kicking in, and the collapse of my room in a violet haze is finally explained. I run my tongue over my teeth, almost tasting the dusty crumbled rock billowing in my room. Thought I was seeing things, having been abruptly woken up, but the violet did run witchcraft through my mind. Didn't think it was *my* witchcraft. Just like the crack in the road, I inadvertently tapped into the witch side of me. Witches and vamps gathered, came to see the cause of the ruckus. I swear Aunt Brenda was there, mumbling in the crowd. Later they chalked it up to old walls and water damage that brought down my room, but now I'm certain that story was a cover-up by Mom and Aunt Brenda to keep my true powers, my true origins, a secret.

Kara puts her hand on my shoulder. "Well at least you're dry." She gives me a second to nod a kind of acceptance at what's going on inside me. "Come on." She waits for me to stand before getting in the car.

I climb inside. "How am I gonna get a grip on this before…you know?"

Kara hits the gas. "For now, just stay calm. Wind in the car is one thing. The campfire, that was a nice move. That little burst of energy there is a new one for sure. Not to mention the storm." She shakes her head. "We need to know what pushes you. What made you so angry you actually controlled the weather?"

"Mom…I was thinking about Mom, I—"

"Don't. Don't do that to yourself."

I can tell she's holding back, but her lip doesn't even quiver. The loss of our mothers is so fresh it's like a wound with an exposed nerve, raw and easy to agitate. Yet she's composed.

"As much as I hate to say it. You have to push past that night. Never let yourself go there again." I'm certain she's speaking more to herself than to me. "It's too dangerous to go there. If it's anger that does it, use your temper to work your magic until you figure out how to use all your emotions. But never go that far again, at least when I'm that close." She smirks. "There's no telling what you could conjure up, like that little light show back there. Save that for when we find the Broadsword. Use your instincts when we do. Let your purple power kick some ass and see what happens."

God, she's so carefree it's getting annoying, mainly the thought of myself ending up like her, but I do have to give her credit for one thing: she can move past something tragic and keep her head held high, searching for the next adrenaline-fueled adventure in whatever comes next in her life. The thought of winging it against the Broadsword doesn't sit well, but if Kara's right and I have potentially limitless power, I can't lose. Can I?

I'm tired, and a realization hits me, terrifies me. "How can I ever close my eyes again? What if I work magic when I'm asleep? I could, I don't know, turn you into a cow or something, burn down a city, start a plague."

"Rookies," Kara says. Her mood has lifted considerably more than mine. "Actual transformation hasn't been accomplished in ages. Even if you can, which I hope you can't, witches can't cast when they're unconscious. Its like a survival thing. You vamps can see at night. We can't accidentally kill ourselves in our sleep."

"That's comforting."

"But you're unique, so that could be out the window." Kara glances at me. She's trying to lighten the mood, and it's working—partially. "Kinda concerning that the first thing you thought of is turning me into a cow, though. Nice to know that's how you really feel about me."

My cheeks warm with embarrassment. "I—"

"Ohhh, you're still way too easy to get riled up. You'll have to work on that too." Kara slaps me on the thigh. "So, where we headed?" She pulls onto the smooth pavement of the highway.

"We go back to the cabin," I say, feigning confidence. "Start tracking them from there."

"I was afraid you'd say that. Well, they know we're in the area, and what we're driving. I see no point in hiding anymore." Kara mumbles again and the dingy dashboard in front of me shimmers in the sunlight. The whole car's interior does, like a wave flowing over it, leaving shiny vinyl, polished leather, and spotless flooring surrounding us. "A simple concealment spell. Always thought it was a shame to hide how sexy the fire chicken really is."

I sit up in my seat. The same wave slides over the hood, leaving polished black paint with the phoenix as new as ever. Through the side mirror, the wave glides to the back of Kara's Trans Am, completing its transformation. "Sweet."

"Wanna try? Not with my girl here of course." Kara pats the dash then takes off her sunglasses and holds them up. "Something smaller perhaps."

"Why not?" I say, taking her sunglasses in my hand, looking over her car as we speed past a delivery van. "What should I do?"

"Surprise me. You're going to anyway."

What can I do to sunglasses, make them a gaudy neon? I'll start with that. Just the color. Once again nothing happens until I get a little steamed at my progress. Keeping my temper in check this time, I watch as Kara's sunglasses follow suit with the shimmering wave that passed over her car. Dark lenses line themselves with crimson frames instead of black. I put them on with pride.

"Matches your hair, nice."

My confidence is growing, so I cockily run my fingers through my hair. Kara snorts as she holds in a laugh.

"*Much* better."

I flip the visor down. Staring back at me in the mirror are crimson sunglasses framed by matching curls with streaks of blond. I meant to turn it all blond, not just where my fingers slipped through my hair. I glare at my reflection. My hair shimmers throughout until it matches Kara's locks, then returns to my natural color. "I got this," I say, casually hanging my arm out the window.

"Yeah, you're a natural all right."

I ignore the mockery in her voice and glance in the side mirror. "Kara. That delivery truck we passed. Is it following us?"

Kara checks her rear-view mirror. "They're definitely keeping pace now, and I passed them pretty easily."

Chapter Fourteen

"It would make sense to call in backup, especially since we took out two of them," I say, staring in the side mirror at the man and woman in the van keeping pace with us. Both of them gray-skinned. I can't recall the woman's face from the cabin, can't tell if this woman behind us is the one who crippled my heart. "Do you recognize her?"

Kara checks her rear-view mirror, squints, then shakes her head.

Part of me is relieved, yet part of me is disappointed. I want to kill the woman who hurt me, hurt Kara, but am I up to facing her? This woman in the van will be practice, I decide. Practice for when I track down the Broadsword who wronged us.

"You wanted to go after the Broadsword. Well, here they are. So now what? I pin it…we might as well roll down our windows and wave at them."

"They're keeping pace, so I'm guessing they already know who we are. Probably got a description of us from the one at the cabin. They aren't the boogeymen we've been led to believe they are. We beat them once. We can do it again," I tell Kara. We got lucky before. I didn't know how to use my powers. Of course, I still don't, but I'll have to trust my instincts. I find it hard to swallow. We've never fought one of the Broadsword's women. Hell, we just learned of them. I hope Mom's warning that they are more deadly than the men is no more than a trumped-up tale of speculation. I clear my throat. "Take the next turn-off."

The sign on the road reads AUGUSTA, another small town east of the Rockies. She pulls off the highway. Time slows. It takes forever to wait and see if they take the turn, see if they're following us, hunting us.

"We've been made," Kara says, checking her mirrors.

"We can use that to our advantage. Because for once we know where they are."

"We're going on the offensive?"

"Like it or not, this is war, and I don't see another choice." We're already in it, our moms are casualties from it, and we need to bring the fight to the Broadsword. We need to stop being the hunted and become the ones doing the hunting. Get our revenge. *My* revenge.

"There." I point to a service station with two pumps. "Pull over to the side of the building."

"I don't like this," says Kara as she pulls up to the cream-colored brick wall, scanning the street. "There're too many people around." More than half a dozen people are within sight. Two couples chatting in front of the gas station. A burly man at the pumps filling his pickup. A couple of kids across the street sitting at a picnic table texting.

The delivery truck pulls over in front of an inn a couple yards away. The driver lifts her phone, blocking part of her grayed skin from view. She raises it a little too high to be looking something up unless she's eighty and farsighted—which she isn't. Thirties maybe, but no more than that. The passenger is a man, and he just stares out the windshield.

"So much for the theory of how they travel in pairs of the same sex," I say. "Let's go in the store and head out the back. Work our way around to take them from behind."

"And just how are we supposed to take them?"

"With that concealment spell you can do, we can sneak up on them looking like a pair of old ladies."

"Old ladies with bodies like these." She gestures with her hand up and down. "I don't think so. I can only work with what's there, not shape shift a person into a hunched-over granny."

"Can you make their delivery van look like it does right now, no matter what happens inside the windows? Keep the town from seeing what we're doing?"

"Yeah, but the second I do they'll know we're up to something. Remember how the fire chicken changed from old to new? That shimmer is obvious."

"Yeah, but that won't matter if I can get to them before they react."

"You're fast, Scarlett, but you'd have to move like lightning. And what are you gonna do when you're in the van? There's not much room for an all-out fight."

"Buy me some time then. Suck the air from their lungs the second you're done with the concealment spell."

Her face has fear written all over it, as I'm sure mine does. I'm used to hunting for food, but my food can't fight back like a Broadsword can. I don't let Kara see my hand shake as I reach for the door handle. "We can do this," I say, reassuring her, and myself.

Kara takes a deep breath and gets out of the car. "Okay."

I follow Kara into the store. *Crap, there's no back door. Now what?* Kara opens the door to the bathroom in the back. Sticks her head in, peeks back at me and nods me inside. Two stalls, a sink, and a window. It's a good thing we're both in shape. Kara, being more petite than me, slips through the window with ease. Squeezing through the tiny opening, I wriggle my way through the pane. "Not a word," I say at the snicker on Kara's face.

"Didn't say a thing." Even on the verge of a fight to the death she's lighthearted, bubbly.

We make our way down the alley. My heart picks up pace. This kind of hunting is far from what I'm used to. I move faster than a casual walk, which I'm sure is the pace for this town. We stop with our backs pressed up against the wall and the van right around the corner. A few calming breaths and we lock eyes. There's nothing more to say. It's time for action.

I can do this. I chose to do this, to hunt them down. Well, here I am, and there they are. The first of many Broadswords to fall. I hope.

I step out onto the street, and Kara follows, mumbling. The van shimmers and I kick it into high gear, closing the ten paces between the delivery van and myself in a second. I rip the passenger door from its hinges, toss it to the sidewalk. The door clangs on impact and immediately I know it's a mistake, it can no longer be concealed within Kara's spell. I don't waste time to curse my stupidity.

The passenger gasps for air—Kara's doing her part. I drive my fist into his jaw, breaking it, knocking him out cold.

I rush as fast as I can, but it's like I'm moving in slow motion, gliding over my first victim, reaching for the steering wheel. The driver works her lips, like Kara's doing.

Crap.

This gray-skinned woman is no human. *The Broadsword has turned a witch.*

I reach for her hair to drive her head into the steering wheel, but a wall of flames bursts to life, separating us and singeing my hand. I scream and pull back, raising my arms to block the heat.

My jacket sleeves are melting into my skin.

Ice crystals encase my arms from nowhere and turn to steam, extinguishing the heat, and stopping the leather from further bonding with my flesh. It's not a relief from the pain, but it stops it from worsening.

I fall back over the man, clawing at the steam with charred wet fingers. Something shoots past me like spears into the van's cab. I reach back to break my fall but find only air, and my head bounces off the concrete. My mind wants to shut down. I use the burns on my arm—along with those now on half my face and neck—to keep me coherent, conscious, and in the fight.

The intense heat from within the cab stops as quickly as it began. Kara's standing over me, mumbling with her palms held out toward the cab.

"Oh God," says Kara. Not the words I want to hear come from her lips as she looks down at me.

Every movement makes me wish for a quick death. A soft layer of snow blankets my body, giving me a moment of relief that quickly leaves as it melts on my burns. The Broadsword whose jaw I broke now has an icicle turning red protruding from his throat. The witch is dead, skewered to her seat through the shoulder, chest, and gut, with icicles dripping at their ends.

Kara pulls me up against the wall of the inn. I can smell myself: my burned hair, my charred flesh, my crisped leather jacket embedded in my arms. The image of the Broadsword Kara roasted at the cabin springs to mind, and I puke up what's left of the gas station sandwich. I convulse, my muscles lock, and a putrid dark-green acidic bile comes up after the sandwich, finally letting my body do what it wants to.

"No." The despair in Kara's voice forces me to focus on the van. The wall separating the cab from the cargo hold of the van shreds like it's made of paper. A young man pushes through the steel as the metal lacerates his flesh, lacerations that heal before my eyes.

The Broadsword has not only turned a witch, but a vamp to their cause.

Kara grabs me under the arms, pulls me back.

The young man grabs my boot from across his dead companion and pulls it half off. I push myself back, and the man's hand leaves the shade of the van.

His arm bursts into flames.

The sun. The van needs to be exposed to the sun.

The flat roof of the van rolls up in a metal coil bathed in violet, exposing its interior to the sun's rays. I did that. On instinct.

The young man cries out in anguish, along with more voices from within the van's cargo hold. His scream stifles as he disintegrates into a pile of ash on the van's floor. So do the others. More ash billows through the bent steel separating the cab from the cargo hold where he pushed through.

Kara gets me to my feet, and we wait. Wait for a witch to pop out of the back through the ash and attack. But no one comes. We won, though it doesn't feel like it. Even the salt in my tears confirms that, stinging the burn on my face.

Hushed warnings to run or hide fill the air as the few people on the street flee in every direction, hiding behind cars, dodging around buildings. Kara's mumbles propel me forward with concentrated gusts of wind, and she shoves me in the car. She jumps in, fires it up, and peels away from the building.

What the hell was I thinking? Take on the Broadsword? We might have had a chance, no matter how many of them there are, but now that we know they're comprised of not only human men and women, but witches and vamps, we're screwed. My stubborn selfish desire for revenge showed me just how outmatched we are, let alone outnumbered. Taking on two at a time would have been tough enough, but a van full of vamps…Thank God we ran into them during daylight.

I'm not sure how far we drive before Kara stops the car down a gravel road, but I'm drenched. Sweat's pouring out of me, mixing with the snow Kara blanketed me in. I'm burning up and shivering at the same time.

"Have to get my jacket off," I tell Kara. "Won't heal with it stuck in me." The words make my stomach churn, threatening to upheave itself again, but it's empty.

Kara helps me out of the car, then holds up a stick. I don't want to hear her next words. I already know what they'll be.

"Bite down."

The stick's bark on my tongue barely registers compared to my other senses working overtime. The rancid smell of my own cooked flesh mixed with burned leather, my heart hammering so loud it fills my ears, and pain…God, the pain is like nothing I've felt before.

I curse myself for attempting such a fool's errand. Wish I had opted to just hide out and stop the sun, somehow, instead of seeking out revenge.

Kara mumbles and my jacket shreds to pieces.

I bite through the stick as blood spews from me where the leather had melted to become one with my flesh, flesh now removed along with my jacket.

I catch sight of an inch of bone, stripped clean of the skin from my forearm.

I shudder, and everything goes dark.

Chapter Fifteen

The rumble of road beneath Kara's car forces me back to consciousness. I'm reclined in the passenger seat. I open my eyes to a bright sunny day, gauze wrapped around my hands and arms, and an aloe-scented cream caked on my neck and face.

"Feeling better?" Kara asks from behind the wheel.

I unwrap the gauze, wincing in anticipation. It tingles but doesn't hurt anymore. "Yeah, I'll be all right. Thanks, but you didn't have to bandage me up." My burns are gone, my bone is back beneath newly grown flesh where it belongs, and even the tiny hairs on my forearms have grown back. I flip down the visor. My hair's a wreck, but my neck isn't even pink from the flames that licked it.

"I found a cozy little place to rest up for the night. Needed something to do. It's a good thing you heal fast, girl."

"I guess that wasn't the best plan ever concocted."

"Ya think? Look at my hair. I mean I know I can pull it off…kinda actually like it…but I'd rather have made the choice to style it this way myself. Least I got the smell out."

She turns toward me. Her long locks on the left side of her head are gone, shaved short above her ear a couple inches. What remains on the top of her head is combed neatly to the right side. I want to laugh, but I did that to her, and it could have been much worse. I don't dare say I can still detect a trace of burned hair in the car.

"It's been a long night fixing you up, contemplating how the Broadsword is made up of both our kinds, and not just humans. Which we're not going to talk about. Your dad's running the whole show, which we're also not going to talk about. The way I figure it, we're in the clear for a bit. The Broadsword won't outright attack us in public or in the daytime if they're lining their ranks with vamps, *and* if we don't provoke them." She raises an eyebrow at me. She's right, our entire world has been turned upside down, but that's kinda been the norm since we turned sixteen. "We need to have some fun with that time. Besides"—Kara flips what remains of her hair over her shoulder—"you owe me one, and I'm cashing in." She tosses her phone into my lap. "Isn't that strapping farm boy putting on a show for you? He might have a friend. God knows I could use a little distraction from Armageddon. Well, maybe a big one. Broad-shouldered with dark eyes and big…feet."

I look at her phone, and open to a website.

67th Annual Lincoln Parade & Rodeo

"Parade's at eleven. We might miss that, but the rodeo's at one," Kara says. "Always have wanted a cowboy to call my own, for at least a night anyway." She sighs. "Better find a good one. World ends the next night. Hope the fireworks are good. And the corn dogs."

"Corn dogs?"

"You eat people. I eat corn dogs."

I can't believe she's like this—so casual about everything, about her hair, what we just went through, about finding out there's no limit to the lengths the Broadsword will go to stop me. Dad turned witches and vamps, murdered our mothers, and she wants to go trolling for ass? Is she thinking I won't be enough to stop Armageddon? I certainly am. Is that why Kara gave me her phone? She figures we're done for and wants to go out with a bang?

Part of me agrees with her, and the more I think about it the more I want to indulge in Kara's world. Let the problem of saving the planet drift to the back of my mind. Maybe she *is* rubbing off on me, but I don't know how I'm going to stop the sun anyway. So, I humor her. After all, I do owe her for her new do, not to mention saving my ass.

We head for Lincoln.

~ * ~

"Come on, girl. Gimme a smile." Kara smirks, sliding her fingers along the brim of her new black cowboy hat. "After all, there's no tomorrow." She hands me a hat from a rack set up on Lincoln's main street.

I fake a smile and take it. We missed the parade. The fresh mountain air still has a hint of popcorn and butter wafting from the kernels beneath my boots.

I pull the hat on in front of a full-length mirror. My eyes look like crap. I never recover well from crying, vamp or not. But the hat looks good.

Kara takes in a deep whiff, closes her eyes and grins. "You smell that?"

I smile, a real one this time. She knows how to enjoy the little things life has to offer, all right. "No guess as to where you're taking me next." Kara has literally sniffed out her corn dog.

I give the kind old woman selling the hats two hundred dollars. Her face lights up as she tries to give me change and I turn her down. An eighty-dollar tip is pretty decent, and it makes me feel better. Besides, as of tomorrow night, cash will probably be more useful to start a fire than anything else.

I've accepted our fate. I've accepted the fact that I didn't know how I was supposed to save the world a week ago, and I still don't. I never thought I'd be doing any of this—entertaining thoughts of sluffing off my responsibility—but the more time I spend with Kara, the more I feel like none of it matters. I wonder if that's how she goes through life without a care in the world. If my attitude to my lifelong purpose has been altered due to her influence thanks to our bond.

Breathing the fragrance of treats spotted throughout the small carnival unfolding before me, and seeing Kara take a rather unladylike chomp out of her corn dog, pushes me to actually enjoy myself and let go of my prophesized responsibilities. There isn't a damn thing I can do.

"Everything you wanted?" I ask her as she wipes mustard from her chin.

"It will be once I get another one, and maybe one of those overgrown pretzels," Kara replies, scanning the lineup of food trucks.

Two corn dogs, a giant pretzel, and a bag of popcorn later, we're at the end of the food trucks. She never ceases to amaze me. She should have been in a contest for the most snacks gobbled down, and to the best of my knowledge she's not gained a pound since leaving the Sanctum. Must be a spell she hasn't divulged yet.

We spend the better part of the day letting the rides spin us around, eating as much junk food as we can, and watching a lumberjack competition before we sit down in the stands for the rodeo. We both laugh out loud at the little kids trying to hang on to the backs of sheep trotting across the arena.

It isn't until the tractor comes in to smooth the ground torn up by the horses and calves that we crack our first beers. My treat. Kara has her ways of seduction. But that doesn't get far with beer girls lugging ice-filled trays up and down the stadium stairs.

We're three beers in when Kara elbows me in the ribs. "Isn't that your hottie from the diner?" She points across the arena.

Sure enough, there's Lukas, looking as handsome as ever in his white cowboy hat, strutting across the back field to a white painted chute. I have to admit, with all that's been going on, I haven't given much thought to a little romance. Now, seeing him, I can taste his lips from when we kissed. I'm more than happy Kara pushed me to come here and enjoy myself—I'm elated. I haven't had this much fun in years, and I don't want it to stop. Maybe this is what I needed. A taste of a life comprised of more than books, movies, hunting degenerates, fearing the Broadsword, constantly searching the night for wolves, and contemplating the overwhelming responsibility of saving the world. Maybe this is what I need to instinctively awaken the spark in me that can figure out what to do when the time comes. Maybe I can live carefree as Kara does—and still stop the Broadsword. Not only use my powers but control them to stop Dad.

I know I should be practicing to learn how to use my—what did Kara call it?—purple power, but my lack of control is worrisome. If I could harness my purple power as Kara does, now that would be a game changer. So far, I haven't controlled that part of me. Sure, I rolled up the roof of the van, but all I did was think that's what we needed, and it happened as if by instinct, nothing like how I controlled changing my hair color.

Part of me knows what we're doing is reckless. We're being hunted. We're out in the open. Our mothers were brutally stripped away from us, and here we are at a rodeo. But on the other hand, we're living and in the moment as Mom taught me. Wouldn't she be proud of me for doing such a thing and not only listening to her teachings but putting them into practice?

I've decided it: No more guilt. I'm going to enjoy every minute I have left. If I save the world, great. If I fail, chances are I won't be around to worry about it.

"Let's give a big welcome to Lincoln's own Lukas Sutherland!" the commentator announces over the loudspeakers. The crowd cheers for their hometown boy, and so do Kara and I. Kara whistles so loud I jerk my head to the side. The girl has a set of lungs on her. We're like giddy schoolgirls set loose from our mothers with a wad of cash and nothing to do but flirt with the boys, of which Kara has done plenty already. Put a beer in that girl, and what little reserve she has goes out the window. She even pinched a guy's ass as he walked past us, then completely ignored him. If I didn't know better, I'd swear she was seventeen and not twenty-four.

The chute opens, and we scream louder, standing from the wood bench as Lukas crosses the arena riding bareback. The horse jumps and spins, threatening to toss Lukas off. The horn blows and beer sloshes over my hand from raising it to the sky as he leaps from his horse and scurries away. The anticipation is intense, waiting for his score. Bareback isn't as exciting as watching bull riding, but I've never known a rider personally before. "Eighty-three for Lincoln's very own Lukas Sutherland!" the commentator says. The crowd loses it. He took first place.

"I'm gonna get…us another round," I say to Kara as I step onto the stairs.

"You go get that *round*." Kara winks.

I make my way down the stairs to the steel bars of the arena, climb up to the second rung of the tube steel fence, and whistle to Lukas, waving my hat in the air. Lukas turns, along with almost every other cowboy in the arena. I feel myself blush. The beer has given me a boost of bravery, or perhaps Kara's rubbing off on me. Lukas waves back and points toward my right. I put on my hat and hop down from the fence.

I have no idea how he came up with a single red carnation from the short distance behind the chutes to me, but he did. There's no hiding the smile on my face as I wrap my arms around him. "Congratulations."

"Thank you." His cheeks redden, and his gaze shifts from me momentarily before locking eyes again. He's taken aback at how bold I am, but I don't care. If I don't make my intentions obvious, how will he be sure I like him? Sure, I kissed him once, but there literally is no tomorrow, and he's hot. "What do you think of our little rodeo?" He slips the carnation behind my ear.

"I like the view." I run my finger down his chest. His muscles beneath his flannel shirt make me bite my bottom lip. I catch myself doing it and slowly let it slip from my teeth. He catches it too. His poker face is *really* horrible. His head is swimming with possibilities—of that I'm sure—and there's no time to play hard to get. "Got somewhere you need to be right now?"

He drops his gaze. Clear disappointment shows as he says, "Unfortunately, I do. I have to get the horses back to the farm before the rodeo lets out."

"Eighty-six, we have a new leader on the board!" comes the announcement over the speakers.

"Sorry to hear that," I say.

"Ah, I just ride for the fun of it."

"I wasn't talking about the score." I'm not letting him go that easy.

He perks up as he catches what I'm getting at. "We have a kind of a tradition here in Lincoln."

"Yeah, what's that?" I run my hand along his bicep to his forearm.

"After the rodeo, there's a bonfire party just a couple miles outside of town in the forest, and I would be honored if you would accompany me to it." He takes my hand in his, kisses my knuckles.

"Sounds great. How do we get there?"

"Do you still have my number?"

Crap, I never put it in my phone. I pull my crimson lipstick from my pocket and roll up his sleeve. "Drop me the location," I say pressing my shoulder up against his chest, writing my number in large digits along the inside of his forearm, branding him as taken to all other women. Kind of childish, but sometimes the oldest tricks are the best. With his arm almost wrapped around me I slide his hand to my waist and gaze up into his dreamy blue eyes. I kiss him on the lips. Just enough to cement our relationship. Not too much to say I'm a slut. "I'll see you there." I pull away and head for the stands.

"I'll be there by eight," he calls out to my back.

I raise my hand into the air and call back without turning around, "Eight o'clock." I don't see a need to draw his attention from my skin-tight jeans as I put a little more sway in my hips than usual.

I grab two more beers and make my way to our seats only to find Kara making out with a broad-shouldered cowboy. She isn't wasting any time. They finally take a break and notice me. "Oh, Scar, this is…" She has to think about it for a second. "Ben. Ben here is a calf-roper, and he's invited us to a bonfire." Ben's the third man to have invited her to the bonfire tonight. Men flock to her like flies to a candy apple. It's funny. "I'll meet you there." She gives him a peck on the lips. "Now get a move on, we need some girl time."

Ben stands from the bench and holds out his hand. "Scar, is it?"

"Scarlett," I correct him, shaking his hand, trying not to giggle. Not only is Ben the third man to invite Kara to a party. But she also said she'd *be there* to all of them. Each time I did my best not to play the role of the bitchy overprotective girlfriend. "Sounds like fun, Ben." I let his hand go and shuffle to my seat.

As Ben turns away, Kara slaps him on his ass. I'm sure she winked at him. She grabs the beer I had for her, takes a swig, and gazes over the arena at the cowboys getting the bulls into the chute. "That was fast."

She meant my time with Lukas, not the rodeo progression. "We're meeting at a bonfire," I say, taking a sip of my own beer. "I'm guessing it's the same one you've been invited to, three times. Should make for quite the show."

"I like to keep my options open," she says, then slaps me on the knee. "But look at you. Not as tongue tied as you once were around the opposite sex."

"Things change in a decade, you know."

"They certainly do." Kara stares at me with a devilish grin. "You think Ben'll bring his lasso?"

I smile.

Chapter Sixteen

The bull riding wraps up, but we haven't finished our beers yet so I decide before Kara tackles another corn dog we should stay and watch the trophies being handed out. "Scope out a few more prospects," Kara calls it, agreeing with my decision.

Lukas was out of the running; I saw his yellow truck leave pulling a horse trailer. The thought had crossed my mind that the reason why was because he was racing home to finish his chores and get back to me quicker. Kara stuck my carnation behind her ear, emphasizing her partially shaved head, lounging back on the empty bench behind us. She gets a few looks from men passing by and another invite to the bonfire. I swear she lives for the chase more than the finish line. I do have to admit, though, her idea of actually living it up before the sun cooks us has become uplifting…until I look across the stadium.

"Kara?"

"Yeah, babe."

"Am I seeing things here?"

Kara sits forward, dropping her sunglasses to the tip of her nose. "You gotta be kidding me."

Three men led by a woman are crossing through the arena from the chutes, all dressed in black with a grayish tone to their skin. The two wearing trench coats might have fit in with the crowd if it weren't for the July heat.

"They don't care about staying hidden."

"Can we get security on the field," calls the announcer as the four members of the Broadsword climb onto the wood plank stage that's been dragged into the center of the arena by a huge green tractor. I wanted to track them down, each and every one of them. Take my revenge for what they did. After our last encounter with the Broadsword, I changed my mind. I'm immortal, after all. I can hunt them to the end of time if I stop the sun. I curse them for stripping me of this time where I was able to be free, if only for a little while, to enjoy what life had to offer with Kara by my side showing me how to do so.

Two of the cowboys reach for the Broadsword. A single punch and one of the cowboys flies through the air, slamming into the steel railing of the arena.

The second cowboy is crushed into a mangled corpse from a double-fisted blow of another member of the Broadsword, scattering the remaining cowboys, along with the award presenters, away from the stage.

The sight entices screams from those in the crowd who haven't yet left the stadium. Some people trample over others, some pull out their phones.

"Show yourself," a voice different than the announcer calls over the loudspeakers. "We know you're here. You can spare these people's lives if you but surrender yourself."

I swallow hard.

"We gotta go," Kara says, grabbing my wrist. "They're dead anyway. Especially if you die."

"Go where? They'll just find us."

"*Scar.*" Terror has filled Kara's eyes. They dart from me to the exit behind us. I can't blame her.

"No. We can't outrun them." I can, but Kara can't, and I'd have no chance at outrunning them if I have to carry her. "We have to fight. *I* have to fight. I've had enough of all this." I'm actually starting to believe I can do this. Rather, I'm lying to myself to boost my confidence, for Kara's sake. Or maybe I'm just tired—tired of hiding, tired of running. Either way, I have powers. So do they; especially if the woman is a witch, but she doesn't have vamp blood surging through her veins and neither do any of them. I have to try. At the very least, I have to be rid of our hunters. I owe Kara that much, one more night before the last sunset. I owe her one more bonfire.

I move with all the speed I can coax. I doubt Kara even sees me move down the stairs until I reach the arena rail and swing myself over it. I get a hand on the stage and the earth opens beneath my feet, forming a hollow. I drop and my legs freeze in place, encased in hard-packed dirt up to my waist.

The female is mumbling.

"Thank you," says the voice on the intercom. A male Broadsword bursts through the window of the elevated announcer's booth, clears half the stadium, and lands, taking the impact with ease. "I'll make this quick." His sword's sharpened edges flash in the sun as he approaches the stage, swinging it with every step.

Make this quick? Like he's being merciful, like I'm such easy prey. If my heart wasn't pounding to escape my ribs before, it is now. "I'm not prey," I murmur. I'm the hunter. Me, not them.

The man on stage tilts his head to the side and chuckles. He actually finds me laughable.

I put my strength to work against the stage. It groans and creaks, and its wheels pull free from the dirt.

I heave with all I have, tearing the stage free from the tractor that towed it into the arena, and topple it forward crushing the Broadswords.

I wrench myself free of the compacted earth. Was it *that* easy? Did I get *that* lucky? Five Broadswords squashed with one blow?

The stage explodes, forcing me to leap aside, and take cover. Evidently it isn't that easy. Splinters of wood and steel fill the air above my head, flying about the arena from a forceful gust of wind.

Kara's poking her head up from behind the bench where we sat. A man a few rows ahead of her lies still on his side, a steel tube lodged in his belly. Others in the stands suffer his fate, skewered by bits of the stage, while others cling to their injuries. Those who had taken cover as Kara did have snapped out of their need to record everything, and scramble to the stadium's exits.

Kara winces with her hand on her shoulder. Her palm comes away, thankfully with no blood on it.

I did that too her. *I* got her hurt. It may be just a bruise, but it's there by my doing. I scream. The hair on my arms and neck stands on end just as they did in the wheat field, and a torrent of water falls from the sky, blanketing the stadium, saturating its dry dirt in a heartbeat.

I'm greeted with shocked faces from the Broadsword, and I like it.

Yeah, that's right, I made it rain. I am *the storm.*

I jump clear of the rain-soaked earth, pointing at my target.

The Broadsword is met with a bolt of lightning, passing first through the man who meant to take my head off, then to the pooled stadium. He twitches, and his smoking carcass falls to the mud, sizzling in the cool water, along with one of his brethren.

A third Broadsword meets me in the air.

He may be strong and fast, but his body is just as frail as a regular human's. I crush his windpipe under my fingers, along with whatever other vital stuff resides in his throat and toss his limp corpse at the witch.

She sidesteps, dodging her dead brethren, and the Broadsword beside her hammers a fist into my side before my feet touch down. A *snap* rings in my ears, followed by stabbing pain—another rib cracked or broken. His hit slams me into the tractor tire. The wind leaves my lungs. I gasp, but no relief comes.

The last man runs toward me. The witch mumbles skyward.

A section of bench flies overhead from the stands, Kara has my back.

The ten-foot length of wood drives itself in one side of the witch and out the other. She shakes, and her body hits the mud in two separate splashes.

A boulder the size of a car falls from above, driving the last Broadsword into the earth, splattering my face with mud and stinging my eyes.

The witch must have meant to crush me with it. She probably would have succeeded had Kara not intervened and ended the witch's life, along with the spell she was mumbling.

I pull myself up against the tire, force air into my chest. I peek around the tire to find Kara floating ten feet above the stands. Behind her, high up in the bleachers, is a mumbling witch.

"Nooo!" I scream with the little air I have in me. I move without thought. I move with fear taking over me and grab hold of the tractor's tire. It's far too heavy for me to lift, but my newfound gift kicks in and helps me. The tractor takes on a violet hue covering its green paint. I hurl it at the witch, and it crashes through the stadium, taking the witch with it.

I jump for Kara and the hue surrounding me helps again, propelling me further than my legs ever could. I'm not going to reach her before she plummets to the bleachers below, but my violet energy swirls like smoke, reaches out from my hands, beats me to Kara's falling body, catches her before she can hit the tattered stadium beneath her, and brings her to my arms. "Kara?"

"Next time"—she wraps her arms around my neck—"we run."

The violet energy fades from wherever it came from, leaving Kara in my arms. "Come on, I'll get you a corn dog," I say as the rain slows, trying to lighten the fact we nearly died for the second time in as many days.

"That's if you didn't squish the truck." She puts her feet down and lurches forward. I catch her before she falls.

"You okay?"

"Fine." There's pain in her voice. "For nearly being torn in two."

I drape her arm over my shoulder. She's too stubborn to let me carry her, and I won't dare suggest it. I get her to the stadium's exit. The rodeo grounds are deserted.

"Nice aim," she says, shaking her head.

I had thrown the tractor through the stadium, through the witch, and right into Kara's coveted corn dog van.

Chapter Seventeen

"Can you believe that just happened?" I say to Kara as she shifts her weight in the passenger seat. "Broad daylight…no regard for secrecy. The Broadsword must think there's no point in hiding our existence from the world anymore."

"I'm more shocked at what you did." Kara pulls out her phone. "No one has ever gone up against the Broadsword and lived to my knowledge, and you did it three times. Then there's the whole flying thing. And shooting lightning where you wanted. Badass, girl. You might still be able to pull this thing off tomorrow night. I'm just letting you be my chauffeur until it all goes down." She pats her dashboard. "Not a scratch now, or I'll set the fire chicken after you."

I laugh. Her car is sweet; it now looks like an old Cadillac. It still rides the same as the Trans Am though, still has the get-up-and-go, and Kara's pet fire chicken under an ivory white concealment spell seems to want to shine through the paint job. Her love for her fire chicken makes me think of my bike. I miss it. I love having Kara by my side, but the freedom, the solitude of gunning my bike can't be matched. I give her Trans Am some gas; there's no comparison.

"Well, you were right."

"About what?"

"They don't care about being seen. There's footage from the rodeo all over the net. You're famous, like viral famous." Kara holds up her phone. The top video shows me soaring through the air, surrounded by lightning. There are more videos below it, all with me as the star. "Win or lose, the cat's out of the bag. Personally, I hope we win. No more living on the road, no more secrecy. I'm gonna spend my family's fortune well. Maybe buy a modest hut in Bora Bora."

Modest, ha. Kara's family line reaches back as far as mine. I can't imagine what she considers modest. A ten thousand square foot castle with servants at her beck and call? That I can picture.

"What would you do?" she asks, tucking her foot under her leg and turning toward me like a little kid with a stolen piggy bank. "With the family fortune, I mean."

"I don't know, I never thought of it as an option."

"Well start thinking, Scar. We got it, might as well enjoy it."

The possibilities are endless. So much so that I can't come up with a single thing, especially considering our remote location. We hit a pothole in the road, and something comes to mind.

"I'd get a new bike. Well, the same one, just rebuilt."

"Dull, Scar, dull." Kara spins around in her seat and crosses her arms, murmuring something, not a spell, but something I can't make out.

"We need a place to lay low. Somewhere secluded but open so we can see someone coming."

"Why don't you wish for room service while you're at it. It's not like we know anyone around here who'll put us up for the night, especially after this." Kara wobbles her phone back and forth.

"Could go to Lukas's farm."

"In search of an afternoon romp, are ya?"

I exhale heavy, shooting Kara a look that says she's being absurd.

"Hey, if you're not interested in him maybe I—"

"Don't even go there," I say, cutting her off. "I don't have his number. See if you can look him up."

"Fine," Kara huffs, tapping her phone. "But he better be hospitable, or he'll have a bitchy witch to deal with."

~ * ~

We keep on the road until sunset. Turns out tracking down a person in rural Montana is difficult. I've basically been circling Lincoln. My phone dings an incoming text. I reach for it in the cup holder, but Kara beats me to it. "What? What is it?"

"Party's still on. Your cowboy just pinned his location. Guess he doesn't care about the media after all."

"Or it's the Broadsword."

"Lighten up, not everything's a trap," she says, zooming in on the location. "He probably thinks you're kinky. Do things to him no other woman can."

"Kara." Damn right I can, but I've never been comfortable with "girl talk" when it comes to my sex life. My warming chest confirms it and I turn from her so as not to reveal any flushing of my cheeks that might be occurring. Must be due to Mom's regal influence. Oh, how I miss her, and her advice. What would she have to say to me now? *Live Scarlett, live.*

"I thought this bonfire party was in the forest," Kara says.

"That's what Lukas said."

"Well unless Google is lying, he just pin-dropped a field. Suth-er-land Ranch."

His home. He wants me at his home.

Kara looks how I feel, concerned. "You might not be so paranoid after all. We'll be seen coming for miles according to this." She surveys the land, zooming in and out, moving the map side to side. Why the hell am I driving? Giving her a break because she got tossed in the air and stretched out a bit. She's fine. I want to see my phone. "Unless…" she adds.

"Unless what?" I crane my neck to see the screen.

Kara pulls it back. "Unless we go here. High ground overlooking the valley. Give us a chance to check it out. I can work a spell to reveal any concealment at the ranch. It'll give our position away, but we'll be far enough out that we can make a break for it if it's crawling with the Broadsword, witch Broadswords anyway."

"We'll be dealing with vamps now too."

"That's why I've got you." Kara shuts my phone off and puts it back in the cup holder. "Take the next left."

"Aren't we going to reply?" Mom always said it's rude not to reply. If someone takes the time to text me, I should take the time to text them back because I might not be able to tomorrow, and today that statement is more accurate than ever. There might not be a tomorrow, at least in the way we know it now.

"Let him sweat," Kara says, reaching to flip through the radio stations again.

~ * ~

It's 10:30 by the time we pull up to Kara's lookout. Lukas had texted me at sunset, 9:30. He missed our date, and I'm certain it isn't due to farm chores. "You ready?" Kara asks.

"Don't we need to get out of the car?"

"You're so cute. Just use your vamp vision. You see anything red, pin it."

I nod, and Kara mumbles a blanket of yellow sparks that cover the gravel road in front of us, then moves down the hill in a shimmering wave. She wasn't kidding that her spell would give our position away. The wave shifts the dark valley below—Lukas's farm—and the surrounding hills from black to darkened yellow, and then back to black again. I scan the wave as it moves.

Kara stops mumbling. "Anything?"

"Nothing."

"Well, unless the Broadsword is hiding in plain sight. The coast is clear."

"That's not very comforting."

"Witches like concealment spells. Even the elders use them to cover up gray hairs. If they were out there, we'd know it."

~ * ~

It takes almost a half hour for us to make our way to the Sutherland Ranch bungalow, partially because we were atop the valley, but mostly because I creep Kara's car down the quarter mile long driveway. The Trans Am's ability to drive without headlights on is a blessing when one wants to travel unseen at night, especially with me driving. A gopher scurrying across the road is as clear to me at night as it would be to Kara during the day. It's extremely handy when it comes to keeping an eye out for wolves. "So far so good," I say, eyeing the house as I pull up to it.

"Well, what are you waiting for? Go knock."

"You're not coming?"

"I'm not leaving my fire chicken until you tell me the coast is clear," Kara says, rubbing the stick shift. "Just leave the keys."

"He invited us, and we need a place to hide out. I can always use my coercion to help with that if I need to." I'd rather not mess with Lukas's mind, but if I have to I will.

"Go on," Kara says, not making a move to get out of the car.

I get out and shut the door as quietly as possible, then realize it's a useless action as the valley is dead quiet aside from the rumble of the engine.

Then I hear a howl.

I freeze, shoulders tensed, fists clenched.

More howls sound, one after another, overlapping each other, announcing a fresh kill, or fighting over one. But I've heard these howls before, and I relax. They're not low enough to be made by werewolves. The howls are coming from coyotes. When I was a young girl and I first heard their cries at night it sent shivers up my spine, made the hair on the back of my neck stand on end, made me want to run, hide, and lock myself away with as many walls between myself and them. Now, their echoing call is welcoming, as if they're my personal guardians sent to dispatch any rodents in the area, and in doing so ensuring a true four-legged beast is not on the prowl. No coyote, not even a pack, would stand a chance against a single werewolf.

Kara's sitting up straight, pale, and on high alert. "We're good," I say. She nods, yet continues peering out every window, trying to pinpoint the pack of coyotes.

She slides over the stick shift to the driver's seat before I turn and walk up to the steps leading to the covered deck. The door opens. Lukas stands silently in the doorway as I climb the steps. "I didn't think I'd hear from you again," I say.

"Thought you'd need a place to stay, after…" He drops his gaze, searching for words. I'm guessing he saw what happened after he left the rodeo.

"Thank you." I put my hand on his arm. He stares me in the eye. The strong cowboy I met earlier is filled with a mix of emotions: fear, anticipation, and intrigue. I'm unsure of which one will win out. At least the Broadsword has not found him. He holds the door open for me. I nod at Kara to come over, and I step inside.

Chapter Eighteen

Lukas's home is everything I'd imagined a Montana farmhouse to be. A single level log cabin with a wrap-around covered deck. Exposed wood beams throughout the open area interior. Every piece of timber gives a warm feeling thanks to the dark stained walls and floors. Aerial pictures showing the progression of time on the ranch hang from the walls. A set of horseshoes with hooks for keys to dangle from is nailed beside the door. A lamp with a cowboy carved out of lacquered wood for its base is in the corner. Large antlers are mounted above a roaring fireplace. Cozy brown leather couches are worn down to the ultimate comfort level surrounding an ornately wood-carved coffee table.

"Thank you," I repeat myself as I make my way inside. Lukas holds the door open for Kara. Her single raised eyebrow says it all—nice, but it's not to her taste.

"I wasn't sure you'd come," Lukas says, shutting the door behind Kara.

"I wasn't sure you'd call"—I lean against the island countertop and eye the muted TV above the fireplace—"after what happened." A video of me chucking the tractor across the arena is playing. The caption reads:

LINCOLN CAUGHT IN THE CROSSFIRE: SUPERPOWERS REAL!

"I still can't believe you hit the corn dog truck," Kara says. "Look, there's me. Ugh, such a bad angle, can't even tell it is." She's taking coming out of the closet far too well. "So, Lukas. What's your take on all this?" Kara gestures toward the TV.

"I don't know what to think." He pauses, making his way to the other side of the island. "You're all over the news. The president is even supposed to speak soon. People are scared."

"What about you?" I ask him.

"I'm…waiting to hear your story, firsthand. Not the mainstream media speculation."

"I owe you that much for letting us stay," I tell him. Truth is, there's something about him I trust. Something that makes me want to let him into my life, and the only way that will ever happen is if I'm honest about who I am.

"Better grab a drink, big boy." Kara pulls out a chair at the dining table. "It's a long story, and you're gonna need one."

Lukas nods and pulls three beers from the fridge. He slides one across the island to me, goes over to the table, hands Kara one, and sits across from her. "I'm as ready as I'll ever be."

~ * ~

Lukas sat there as Kara and I laid it out in front of him: My origins, the Broadsword, the prophecy. It's not every day you learn the end of the world is right around the corner. Not to mention the woman you've made out with is a unique blend of the world's magics of legend. He took it pretty well, sipping his beer, listening to our every word. His stonelike posture relaxed, a bit, after I told him how I choose my food, and how rare I need to feed in comparison to other vamps. Kara replenished his empty drink, and hers, more than once. "And then we got your pin-drop, and here we are," I say, still leaning against the island, taking comfort in his calm demeanor.

"He hasn't run out the door screaming yet." Kara hoists her beer into the air at me. "Might be a keeper."

I give her a look to hold her tongue, though I know she never will.

"So, now what?" Lukas asks as his phone dings for the fifth or sixth time. He'd ignored it while he listened to the truth of the world and ignores it again. He's a gentleman—of that there's no doubt—and sharp as well. I had no idea how he would react; to my surprise his composure is far better than mine was when Mom spilled the beans. "We just wait and see if you can stop a solar eruption. While the entire planet searches for the two of you, the most famous people ever to set foot on earth?"

"Pretty much," Kara says. A door slamming shut outside makes her jump out of her chair. "You expecting anyone?"

Lukas shakes his head and leans in his chair to look out the window. "It's my cousin."

The front door swings open. "You gonna answer your phone or what?" Lukas's cousin says, bursting in. He stops in his tracks at the sight of me. We're famous all right; he's frozen stiff.

"Hear me out." Lukas stands from the table.

"What the hell?" his cousin shouts.

"Ben," Lukas says, stepping forward. I thought I recognized him. The cowboy in front of me is the very same one Kara was making out with at the rodeo. "Gimme a second to explain."

"Explain!" Ben's hysterical. "She trashed the town, they declared martial law, and you're hiding them!"

Martial law? Kara and I glance at each other. We were so busy laying it out for Lukas we forgot about the TV. We both turn toward it. The headline at the bottom of the screen reads:

LOCKDOWN: MARTIAL LAW DECLARED IN MONTANA

"They'll shoot us just for being in the same room as—"

"Careful, Ben." Kara cuts him off. "Calm him down, would ya?" she says to me.

I nod. "Ben, take a seat. You're safe. Everything's fine," I say to him. Ben stares at me, blinking, as if he's trying to resist me. He's ramped up. "Just sit down," I repeat myself, commanding his mind.

Lukas shifts his gaze between the two of us. I told him of my gift, and he sees it at work on his cousin. His brow raises ever so slightly, but he remains silent holding his beer.

Ben sits in the chair Kara was in as she walks over to the kitchen and pulls another beer from the fridge. "Relax, Benny boy. We'll take care of you." I'm not sure if she meant to scare him or comfort him. I don't think any of us in the room knows until she sets the beer in front of him. "We had a good time in the bleachers, let's not ruin it. The night's still young." I swear I catch her wink at him as she heads to the living room and picks up the TV remote.

"*—ose of you just joining us, martial law has been declared in Montana due to the world-wide panic ensuing over footage of an apparent battle between superpowered people at a rodeo in Lincoln. We'll be playing the footage in a moment. We have to warn you what you are about to see is graphic and violent, and viewer discretion is advised. The National Guard has been dispatched along with local law enforcement and will be going door-to-door in search of the suspect. A curfew of six PM has been set for all residents. Those from out of state are advised to take shelter in their arranged accommodations prior to six PM as well. The government is asking for your help in locating the young woman in the video we are about to show you. This is not a hoax. More than three dozen separate videos* *have been compiled to render the best likeness of the young woman in question. Once again, this footage is extremely violent and small children are advised to leave the room.*"

The four of us watch the compiled footage from the rodeo. I have to calm Ben once more during the seven-minute compilation. The fight felt like it took longer in real life than it showed on the TV. It must have been the adrenaline: slowing time, speeding my reflexes, slowing time again, all so I could react and survive. It was like watching a way cooler version of myself playing the part of the Russian assassin, but with powers.

"The young woman with blonde hair being carried away by the suspect is also wanted for questioning."

A close up of my face pops up in the bottom right-hand corner of the screen. There isn't a clear shot of Kara. That's one saving grace—at least I managed to protect her identity by keeping witness' camera phones on me.

"The suspects are to be considered armed and extremely dangerous. If identified, do not approach them. Contact your local—"

Kara mutes the TV. "Like your old man and the Broadsword weren't enough to worry about." She throws the remote on the couch and goes back to the fridge, holds up a beer. "Anyone else?" The guys nod, so do I. "Good thing you keep a stocked fridge, we'll be into that wine soon enough."

"Lukas, will anyone else be coming home?" I ask.

He shakes his head and pulls out his phone, then puts it on the table. "Ben's the only one who's been texting me."

"What about a wife, girlfriend, your folks?" Kara points a thumb to a photo on the wall as she hands him a beer. "You can't tell me you own this nice place, run this farm all by yourself, and you're all alone."

The jab about a wife or girlfriend doesn't go over my head. Kara's looking out for me. But I checked out Lukas's ring finger earlier, and Sue's comments about him finally not eating alone at the diner are proof enough for me. The photo Kara pointed at is at least two years old or more. Lukas is less filled out; his hair is cropped like Ben's short military style.

I know it before he says it. My heart stops for a second, as I'm sure Kara's does.

"They're gone…car crash. I was in college. Six years now since I inherited it. Felt wrong to abandon the place to be an engineer in the city. So, I stayed, kept the homestead going, and I'm single." Lukas glances at me, then down. I was right to think he's intelligent. An educated man, and one with pride in his family name. I want to comfort him, but he's a man and his composure is strong, sitting there telling it like it is.

Kara does her best to sound sincere and pull her foot out of her mouth. "Sorry," she says, cracking open the can for him. "I know what it's like, so does she."

"Can you guys tell me what's going on? Like who you are, and what the hell you did to me?" Ben asks once again, coming out of my influence.

"Relax, handsome, you're in good hands." Kara gives Ben his beer and slides her fingers along his cheek. He blushes. Someday she's gotta teach me how she holds a man in her pocket so easily. I'm good, but she's without a doubt better. If we hadn't been in hiding our whole lives, she'd probably be named a queen by now. She walks behind Ben, rubbing his shoulders. "We all have our talents; you've seen hers in action." She nods toward the TV. "Mine…" She leans down beside his ear and whispers just loud enough that I catch it. "Well, let's just say it's a little more intimate."

Ben raises his brow, and I almost giggle out loud.

"Believe me, buddy. We need these ladies more than they need us," Lukas says, leaning in his chair, looking out the kitchen window. "Trust me."

He sounds like he said that last part as more of a question than a statement, and Ben's response proves my assumption correct. "You know I do."

Lukas stands from his chair. "We have to hide you ladies. We got company."

Two sets of headlights are coming up the driveway, each topped with red and blue flashing lights.

Kara looks out the window. "We don't need to hide. I got this. Besides, can't hide the car with the out-of-state plates. These guys probably knew you since you were born. So just follow my lead." The guys look at her a little confused, but they don't question her.

The two cars park, blocking our Caddie and Ben's truck from backing away from the house. Both cars are painted the same as the sheriff's who had pulled me over a couple days back. "No mind games." Kara points at me. "They won't last long enough to do any good once they leave." She rounds the table, picks up the remote, and unmutes the TV as the sheriff knocks on the door.

Kara mumbles.

"Lukas. It's Caleb, son, open up."

Lukas's worry is all over his face. If this sheriff knows him—and it sounds like he does—the second that door opens, we're made.

Chapter Nineteen

Lukas opens the door. "Evening," the sheriff says. He's a big-bellied man in his fifties and fits the small-town movie depiction of his job to a T, right down to the bulbous nose and bushy gray eyebrows. "Mind if I come in?"

Crap, he's the same cop who pulled me over, and Lukas is hesitating. We're busted for sure if I don't do something.

"Don't be rude, Lukas. Invite that strapping man in. Want a beer, Officer?" Kara asks as Lukas backs away from the door.

"Okay, guys."

Kara's voice is loud and clear in my head, and from the look on Ben and Lukas's faces, she's in their heads as well.

"You can hear me; I can't hear you. So don't try and think your way into questions for me, just listen."

"No thank you, miss." The sheriff tips his hat.

"Lukas, say hi already."

"Uh, how's it going, Caleb?" asks Lukas finally.

"It's gonna be a long night. I see you've heard." Caleb indicates the TV.

Caleb's partner walks in through the door. He's well built in his late twenties or early thirties, and much thinner and taller than Caleb is with soft brown eyes. "Lukas. Ben."

"Hey Jake." Ben raises his beer.

"Jake." Lukas nods.

"So how bout that beer, Officer…Caleb, was it?" Kara says. I swear she has a bit of an accent to her voice. It's the first time I've looked at her since the cops knocked on the door, and it hits me as to what she was mumbling. Even disguised, she's just as stunning as ever: hair black as night, matching black tank and jeans, a barbed wire tattoo on her left arm, lips painted crimson like my bike, with eyelids shadowed in a smoky gray.

"Keep your cool, guys."

I look at my reflection in the window. My hair is black as well, and poker straight with a handful of strands dyed white and dropping down to frame the right side of my face. Not my face though—Mom's face.

She made me look like Mom.

I choke up. I even have Mom's dress on. Instantly I see a wave of bravery grow in the reflection of the woman in the window. My chin raises a bit. My shoulders pull back. I'm stunning.

It's a smart move on her part to disguise me as Mom. We're similar in height and build—and my face is plastered all over the news whereas Mom's isn't. Not to mention my face is the one that screwed with Officer Caleb's mind to let me out of a traffic ticket.

"Who might these ladies be?" Jake asks.

"You're up, Ben. Lukas met us online—sisters from Kansas. Down for summer break. Renting out his spare rooms."

"This is…" Ben holds his hand out to Kara.

"Kara and Scarlett—"

My breath catches. *Crap Kara, don't use our real names.* Now I wish I had telepathy to stop Ben's introduction.

"In case you forgot," Kara finishes, *"but for now we'll go as Lana and Chloe."*

"Lana, and this is Chloe. Come to visit from Kansas," says Ben.

"Wink at him and whisper sisters to him."

Ben hesitates, glances at her.

"Do it. Wink."

Ben winks at Jake and coughs the word "Sisters." Then takes a sip of beer to clear his throat. Jake grins and drops his hat to try to hide it. This is how she does it. She plays both sides. Man and woman alike. She anticipates a move like a chess game.

"Make a joke about Lukas not telling you about us."

"My cousin here wasn't even going to tell me he rented out the spare rooms. Lucky for these ladies I stopped by to keep him honest."

"Don't push it too far. Small lies, vague details. But not bad, just tone it down. Lukas. Beer them."

Lukas is staring at me. He's not involved with the cops at all. It's like he's in disbelief of Kara's concealment spell. I get it, but he's got to pick up his game. I nod toward the cops, urging Lukas to say something.

"Lukas. You're up."

Lukas clears his throat. "You have any leads?" he asks, shifting his eyes from me to the living room, and away from the cops.

"Ask them if they want a beer."

"Not yet, it's like they up and vanished," replies Caleb.

"They won't stay and be a third wheel. Just ask them."

"You sure you fine gentlemen don't want a beer?" Kara asks again since Lukas won't.

"No thank you, miss. Been sober seven years now." Caleb looks at the TV showing footage of me. "'Course I may start up again. What with all this."

That's why Lukas didn't offer him a beer. I walk around the island, rest my elbows on it and lean forward. I let Mom's dress hang low to show my cleavage…her cleavage. A trick she taught me. You want a guy to look at everything in a room but you? Show some cleavage. A lady must know when she needs to use her wares. "Have you heard anything more than what they're saying?" I tilt my beer in the direction of the TV.

"That's it," Jake answers me, avoiding eye contact and staring out the door at their cars. "We should get going though, Caleb. There are a lot more places to check tonight. Take 'er easy, fellas." He tips his hat. "Ladies."

"You're right. Oh, just one thing before we go. Can I see your IDs, ladies?"

Crap.

Caleb tries to look me in the eye but goes back to addressing Kara. "Protocol." I'll have to persuade him into thinking he has, just as soon as Jake is far enough away. Jake turns back around to wait for Caleb.

Crap.

"Right here." Kara pulls an ID out of her back pocket.

"Kitchen counter, by the sink."

On the right side of the sink is a wallet, leopard print design, and indented with my driver's license in a soft plastic cover on the top. I pick it up, and as soon as my fingers run along its surface, I know what she's done. I'm holding one of those green and yellow scrub sponges used to clean dishes. That's why she made it indented with a leopard print, for texture. Kara can without a doubt think on her feet. I walk around the counter, hold up the wallet for Caleb. "Here you go." Mom's picture and all. Kara's good.

"Can you take it out of the wallet please?" Caleb asks.

"Don't try to remove it. You can't."

I figured that much. "I don't think it would survive," I say. "Left it on the dash too long. Melted the plastic to it." The plastic yellows and spots with tiny bubbles.

Caleb takes my wallet. "Light," he says lifting it up and down an inch.

"Not much to fill it with," I say, taking another sip of beer, trying my best to act casual.

"There never is," says Caleb. "You look familiar. We met before?" He frowns now that I'm closer to him, and he looks over the license.

Crap.

At first, I thought it was a smooth idea, Kara mumbling me to look like Mom, but the cops would have looked into the cabin explosion. If they did, then they would have found the corpses, found Mom. That's why Lukas was giving me shifting glances to the living room. He wasn't shocked, he was trying to warn me that, like the pictures of me on the TV, the cops would have seen Mom's face, and Lukas met her when I was passed out. He is a smart one.

I take the wallet back and drop it on the middle of the island as I drain my beer, buying me precious moments to think. "Not till now." I put the empty can beside the fridge, pull another one out, crack it, and lean on the island again. *Come on cleavage, do your thing.*

Caleb turns red and drops his eyes immediately. "I suppose not. Good night, fellas." He tips his hat at Kara and shows the top of it to me, still not making eye contact. "Ladies," he says as he follows Jake down the steps.

"Let us know if you find 'em," Lukas calls out to their backs.

"Will do." Caleb salutes and gets in his car, followed by Jake getting into his.

Lukas shuts the door. We all breathe a sigh of relief, and each of us takes a large gulp of beer, Ben drains his. The ting of the empty can on the table combined with his head turned down shaking makes me regret coming to Lukas's home, but we had nowhere else to go. Ben has played along so far, and if he's to stay on our side, he needs to know what we're up against. I make my way to him and see my reflection in the window shift from that of my mom's appearance to my own. He looks me up and down, confused. I sit down.

"Thank you, Ben. If you're willing to hear me out"—I put my hand on top of his—"I'll tell you about a world beyond the one you know. My world."

He glances at Lukas, and then to Kara bringing him another beer. "Why not," he sighs. "If we're going to jail for harboring fugitives, I might as well know who we're harboring," he says, glaring at Lukas.

Chapter Twenty

Ben and Lukas are definitely related. Ben sat still, aside from pounding two beers, and listened to me just as Lukas had. He didn't interrupt. He just kept sipping his beer.

When I'm finished, Kara says to him, "How do you like me now, handsome?"

He gazes at her as she leans against the island on an elbow. I study his face. "Is it weird I'm more attracted to you now?" He huffs, as if to himself, and takes a long pull of his beer as he leans back staring toward the ceiling. Setting his can down, his eyes are pinched at the corners more than normal. A country boy's smile, without actually smiling.

"A little," says Kara. "But I get it." She runs her fingers through what's left of her hair, flipping it back over her shoulder. "It's hard to be around this and not be."

The corners of Ben's lips curl up. "There's one thing I don't get," he says. "Well, there's a lot I don't get. But if this Broadsword is coming for you like an army, why don't you call in your…um…good witches and vampires?" He swallows hard. He's trying to make sense of everything I told him and find a solution. I'm certain his mind is playing it all for him like he's at a theater. "Raise your own army. I mean…where are they all? You've been getting ready for this forever." He frowns. He's getting frustrated. "So where is everybody? Where's your backup?"

"Aside from the Sanctum, we live mostly in solitude. I don't even know how many of us there are," I tell him, answering for Kara.

"We were taught to keep our numbers low, not draw attention to ourselves," Kara adds.

"That's stupid," says Ben.

"*Ben*," Lukas says, trying to curb his cousin's insult.

"No. I'm sorry. It's stupid. We're about to turn into Chernobyl and the only people who have a chance of stopping these guys got their heads buried in the sand." He stands from his chair, then makes for the door.

"Where you going?" asks Lukas.

"Get my gun. Least I'll be ready when…" The door slams shut behind him. I can't make out the rest of what he's saying, but his rant continues all the way to his truck, through the slamming of its door, and all the way back up the stairs and into the house. "And that's another thing…werewolves. If they're as dumb as you claim them to be, then how'd they stay hidden for so long? Can't you magic their minds to your side like you did to me?"

"It doesn't last that long," I say. "Plus, that's kind of a unique trait of mine, and I can only influence one person at a time."

"That's convenient." Ben slides a pump-action shotgun on the island, followed by a box of shells. "This even gonna work on them?"

"Witches and the Broadsword, yes. Vamps, only if you put enough holes in us, and if you don't give us time to heal."

"This sucks." He turns his back to me, leans over the island, rocks back and forth on his elbows, straining his muscles.

"Calm him down a bit," Kara says in my head as she puts a hand on his shoulder.

I reach out to him. "Take a breath, relax." My gift forces his mind to relax his body and, in turn, allows the tension to shed from his body long enough for him to remain in this state of his own accord.

"At least you didn't find all this out when you were sixteen like we did. You're a grown man. You have a shot at being rational about it. I sure as hell wasn't at that age." Kara lets his shoulder go, leans with her back against the island beside him, pushing out her chest. "Hell, I stormed off in a fit, smashed age-old junk on display as I went." She glances at me and winks, allowing Ben a moment to give in and let his attention be drawn to her boobs before he quickly looks back at his beer. "You'd think they'd have had the sense to move that stuff to a place where they didn't tell us we were the monsters of the world." I'm not sure if it's her way of getting through to him, or if she's just venting. "'Course once my powers kicked in and I learned how to use them, it got better. I didn't mind so much that I was what kids dressed up for at Halloween. Actually, I think I even did once myself as a kid." She winks at me again. "Green paint and all. Ugly as hell."

"You're *not* ugly," Ben says

That's another way she does it, other than treating people like chess pieces. Draw out the gentleman in him. The side that tells him to comfort a woman, whether she's a witch or not.

She locks eyes with him and curls her lips up in the smallest grin. She's letting him see the humanity in her…I guess.

"You're sweet." Kara's voice softens from her usual playful demeanor. I swear she's even blushing, or at the least mumbling a rosy shade to her cheeks. "You're not so bad yourself." Flirt.

The room falls silent aside from the TV. Kara glances up at Ben and back to the floor. I do the same to Lukas. We're all thinking it: If this truly is our last night, then we should go out with a bang. Give in to our more primal animal instincts. We're all adults, after all. The tension in the room is thick, and the best way to cut through it is with sex. I still want to be pursued though, as I'm sure Kara does. After all, half the fun is in the anticipation, the chase, and the build-up to the main event.

"Fire's dying." Lukas breaks the silence and gets up from the table with the remote held to his lips. "YouTube." A slew of country music videos pops up under his recently viewed section. As the first song starts, he holds a hand out for me to take. "How about a glass of wine by the fire? And perhaps a dance. If you think you can keep up, that is."

"I've got a few moves you've probably never seen." I take his hand, and stand from the table.

"Ben, can you grab some glasses for the ladies?"

Ben, already on his way to the cupboard, doesn't say a word as he pulls out some glasses, and Kara produces the bottle of wine from the fridge she'd eyed up earlier.

I make my way into the living room as Lukas puts another log on the fire. I can't tell if it's the heat from the flames or my heart picking up pace that warms my chest. I only have one thing on my mind as Lukas bends over, stoking the fire in painted-on Wranglers.

Let the hunt begin.

Chapter Twenty-One

A rooster's call from outside the open window wakes me. The fresh air mixed with a hint of bacon cooking makes me pull in a deep blissful breath. Lukas isn't in bed. The side he fell asleep on has its sheets tossed over. I roll over and slide my hand along them. His body heat still lingers along with his musky scent. I shut my eyes, replaying the night's embrace. If that was my last night on earth, he made it a good one.

I reminisce until I can't take the smell of bacon wafting through the door anymore. Lukas's plaid shirt clings to me as I stand, crackling with enough static electricity I have to tug at it to let it fall to my thighs. The crisp morning air coming in from outside caresses my legs as I search for my jeans. I finally spot them on the dresser, folded with my tank and bra on top—what a gentleman. I pick up my tank and think about Kara's lilac trick, then recall the attached full bath, and the shower. Lukas's shirt hits the bed and I shut the semi-transparent shower door. Steam fills my lungs as I let the hot water roll down my back. Oh, how I love a nice hot shower. This is turning out to be the start of a great birthday, no matter what the night might bring.

"Ahem." Lukas's voice comes from the bedroom. "Breakfast is ready."

"Can you hand me a towel?" I slide the shower door open an inch and stare out. He's dressed like he's about to take me out to a county dance. He looks *way* too good for this early in the morning, a true farm boy. Up before dawn, he's ready for a full day. He steps closer, handing me the towel.

"Thanks." I slide the door open, take it, toss it to the side, then wrap my hand around the back of his neck and roll his collar under my fingers. He doesn't resist me from pulling him in, clothes and all. "There seems to be a spot I can't quite reach."

He presses his lips against mine, sliding his hands down my waist. I was right—my birthday is improving by the second.

~ * ~

I sit at the table, satisfied from my shower, to a quiet country breakfast with bacon, eggs, hash browns, and toast piled high on plates in the center of the table. "I could get used to this," I say, winking at Lukas as he sits at the table in his second set of dancing clothes.

Kara spreads some raspberry jam on her toast and agrees with me as she shovels back some bacon. Ben grunts. The wine didn't agree with him too well from the looks of his complexion. Green around the gills. I never understood where that saying came from, but it fits Ben to a T. He's a pale shade of green, gingerly sipping coffee with an empty plate in front of him. Kara and I exchange looks, like giddy schoolgirl's who have just been making out with a boy behind the bleachers, eager to tell someone, yet wanting to keep the memory just to ourselves. *A lady does not kiss and tell.* Mom used to say that every time I returned home from being out with a guy. That motto stuck with me to adulthood.

Ben puts his coffee cup down and the clink against the table makes him wince.

"Oh, come on. I thought you country boys could keep up," Kara says. From the way Ben jerks, I guess she kicked him under the table. He fakes a smile and scoops some eggs onto his plate. "Fine, since you asked so nicely." Kara mumbles, holding her hand out to the jug of water on the center of the table. The water inside floats out of it in a giant bubble, leaving condensation dripping down the glass. Ben and Lukas both perk up as the bubble hovers in front of Ben's face. "Now hush up. I need to concentrate." Kara closes her eyes and continues mumbling. The bubble separates into millions of smaller ones. Again and again, they separate until a fine mist swirls in front of Ben, spreading along his face, down his chest, and under his shirt. He shuts his eyes tight, and I'm pretty sure he locks his jaw as a fine sheen spreads over his skin. Slowly, the sheen vanishes from sight, drunk up by his pores. Kara stops mumbling. "You're welcome."

Ben's green complexion fades to its normal color, and he opens his eyes, no longer blood shot. "What was that?"

"Nice trick," I say to her.

Kara stuffs a forkful of eggs in her mouth, and between chomps says, "I just saturated every cell in his body. Hydrating him better than any sports drink could ever claim to do. No big deal." She smiles with a wad of egg bulging in her cheek. She's a stunning woman, but I'm starting to notice she has less than regal eating habits. She can get away with it, though—she's all dolled up and smelling of lilac again. Not a hair out of place where it hangs to the side, the side she didn't shave. I, on the other hand, am sporting the wet look. It actually makes my crimson lipstick pop a bit more, so I don't mind.

"I *like* you," says Ben, perking up and diving his fork into his eggs.

"I know," says Kara between bites.

Lukas isn't nearly as hurting as his cousin was. I figure he sweated out any alcohol in his system last night—and again this morning—thanks to me. "So, what's your plan, ladies? You're more than welcome to hide out here until…you know," he says.

"Right." Kara slaps me on the shoulder. "Happy birthday, Scar."

I have mixed feelings about this birthday. All my previous birthdays were fun, set as a night of celebration where Mom would take me out on the town. Sure, it was different than other kids' birthdays when I was young. It was just the two of us celebrating. It kind of turned me into a loner. I'd made the mistake of saying that once in front of Mom, and she corrected me by telling me I was a lone wolf. At the time that seemed cool—until I turned sixteen and learned the truth about werewolves. Even though I was a loner to the rest of the world, I always had Mom. Now, I find myself silently thanking Kara, and the guys, for coming into my life. Kara knew Mom, and Lukas even met her briefly. It's as if having them at the table with me gives me a gift of Mom's spiritual presence. My morning to this point hasn't been lonesome, dull, or disappointing, thanks to Lukas. I catch my cheeks warming and concentrate on Kara instead of recalling my time with him in the shower.

"What should we get you for your special day?" Kara claps her hands together. "I know. Something so special only the truest of friends could ever think to give you. Your deepest desire. Lucky for you, I *am* that friend. And I have the ability to grant you your wish."

"You can grant wishes too?" asks Ben with a mouthful of toast. He and Kara have similar eating habits.

"I'm not a genie, handsome. But I do have my tricks." She tugs me out of my chair. "Come on. It's outside." She drags me to the front door. "I didn't really forget it was your big day."

"Kara, what are y—"

She opens the door, and I'm speechless. On the porch, shining in the sun's early rays, is a Ducati—*my* crimson Ducati. Polished to a sheen. Its metallic paint flickers, just as sexy as ever. "Kara." I throw my arms around her and look over her shoulder at my bike.

"It's nothing you wouldn't do for me."

"But how? It was destroyed." I let her go, step onto the porch. "There's no way you could have found one." It dons on me as I run my fingers over the seat: This is not my Ducati. "What's the catch?"

"Well…" She crosses her arms and leans against the door as Lukas and Ben poke their heads around her slender frame to see my bike. "It's not really yours. Unless he gives it to you." She nods at Lukas.

"Me?"

"Let's just say it's really good on dirt. Looks good though, huh?" She's beaming with pride. She has without a doubt bonded to me. How else could she make me want to jump for joy and kick her in the ass at the same time?

"You saying that's mine? I wish. Only bike I got is that old…" Lukas pauses, stares at the barn. His eyes dart all around it and then back to the Ducati. "Don't think I'll ever get used to having you two do your thing."

"What? I don't get it," Ben says as Lukas turns to go back inside.

"It's my bike." Lukas pats Ben on the shoulder. "She magicked it into that." Lukas plucks a set of keys from the horseshoe hooks on the wall and tosses them to me. "Go ahead, give 'er a spin."

"*Your* dirt bike?" Ben says to Lukas, watching the keys fly through the air. "You can do *that*?" he asks Kara. "Can you make my truck a Bugatti?" He looks like a little kid at Christmas.

Kara chuckles. "It doesn't work that way. It's still his dirt bike underneath, it just looks like her old one. But I like the way you roll, handsome. Bugatti, you got good taste. I just might let you take me out for a date, if you can keep *it* up."

Ben grins. "Oh, I can."

I'm not sure exactly what she meant by keep *it* up. His childish enthusiasm toward her magic, or a poke from last night? Either way, they'd have their alone time to figure it out because I have my bike back. I swing my leg over the seat.

"Come on, Lukas. Let's see what she's got."

He grins and climbs on the back as I locate the disguised clutch with my foot. I can't see it, but it's there, and I fire it up. I launch us off the deck, and we catch some air as we clear the stairs, not as much as my Ducati would have caught, but some. A slight skid to the right, then to the left, and I have it under control.

"Woo!" I shout, pumping my fist in the air with Lukas clinging to my waist. His strong arms wrapped around me make me think that my days of riding solo are over, and for some reason, I'm fine with that.

Chapter Twenty-Two

I stand up in the middle of the field, pick up my tank, pull it over my head, slip it under my jeans, and secure my belt in place. Lukas tucks his shirt into his pants and zips them up. That man has stamina, I'll give him that. He might actually make a decent woman of me. Not that I'm not a decent woman already, but he, and his lifestyle, have a certain appeal.

Even after our tussle in the field, my cheeks warm from the thought of settling down. It must be my subconscious looking for a connection, a family, a yearning to fill the void since Mom died. Or maybe it's my time with Kara that's drawn out a more promiscuous side in me that wants the pleasure of Lukas's company to last. I give my head a shake. He's still mortal. One day, I'll have to watch him grow old and die, whereas I'll remain twenty-five forever. But there's nothing stopping me from enjoying the pleasure of his company, and all that it entails, right now.

I'm starting to sound like Kara. She *is* rubbing off on me, I decide. Thankfully her taste in men hasn't. Ben's good-looking, yeah, but he's a little forward for my liking, kind of how Kara is. Makes sense why they hit it off.

Then there's Lukas, smart and reserved, with a quiet confidence to him—and hot, so very hot, kind of like me. Funny how life brings people together. First Kara and me, and now Lukas. Just wish it wasn't under world-ending circumstances. On the other hand, Lukas has been extremely useful at distracting me from the coming night.

"We better get back." I stand the bike up and climb on. He's such a gentleman. Not once has he suggested he drive *his* bike. It *is* still his after all, yet he hasn't mentioned a word about Kara giving away his toy.

He hops on and wraps his arms around me. "Good idea, I'm getting hungry. I pulled out some steaks this morning. They should be thawed by the time we get home."

He knows how to eat and has to in order to keep up his cut physique.

Dirt sprays as we take off. The breeze from the bike doesn't quite cool me off from the heat of the midday sun, but it helps.

We pull up to the deck to find Kara sitting on a porch swing by herself, looking bored as she thumbs through her phone with one hand and twirls what's left of her hair with the other. A rifle on the swing beside her and the numerous casings on the deck tell me she's had some fun, but she's a city girl at heart. Room service and posh hotels are more her style. I hope there'll still be some luxury left for her to lounge around in after tonight.

"Good time?" Kara asks with a grin that doesn't show any sign of going away as she looks Lukas and me over. "Got some grass in your hair," she adds as I climb the stairs. "Lukas," Kara says, trying not to smile so much.

Lukas nods. The bit about my hair must have gone over his head, otherwise I'm certain his poker face would show it. "Where's Ben?" he asks.

"He found your steaks. Said something about his world-famous marinade."

"Ahhh." Lukas flings the screen door open. "He's gonna ruin them." He ducks inside, shutting the door behind him hard enough to rattle the screen.

"Wanna give it a shot?" Kara nudges the rifle beside her.

I pick up the rifle. There's an assortment of beer cans lined up on a picnic bench. The grass below it is littered with downed soldiers. "Loaded?" I ask. She shrugs.

I aim and squeeze the trigger. A can drops. I flip the lever action on the .22, reload, and fire off four more shots. Four cans drop to the grass and no more shells fly out from me cocking the rifle.

"Wow," says Kara, her voice droll and unimpressed as she continues to thumb through her phone.

"Mom taught me." She thought it might come in handy, or at the very least, give me the eye to identify different weapons and how many rounds could be left. I lean the .22 against the wall and sit beside Kara in the swing. "Whatcha googlin'?" God, I can't believe I just said that like I'm some sort of valley girl. Kara's humorous demeanor *is* rubbing off on me.

"Us. They haven't found us yet." She either didn't notice my valley girl slip, or she isn't going to address it.

"You don't say."

"How was your birthday ride?" She doesn't look up from her phone, and she doesn't have to. The smirk on her face is emphasized by her tone.

"I like it here."

"Yeah, you fit right in."

"No, really." I hold out my palm to the valley stretching before us. "Open fields, rolling hills all around us, mountains in the distance, clean air, no people. It's like it was made just for me to curl up with a book on this bench."

"You'd get bored without me, and him." She nods, indicating Lukas, then keeps thumbing through her phone.

"You can't tell me you don't like it here."

"It's okay. Nightlife is better than I thought it would be." I assume she's talking about Ben. "A five-star hotel overlooking a white sand beach with aqua-blue water surrounding me sounds better. With clubs that don't go down till the sun comes up, of course. That would suit me."

"I couldn't live like that. It'd be great for a bit. But this…this is living. Just look at it." I lean back, interlacing my fingers behind my head shaded from the hot July sun. The only sound for miles is that of nature, birds chirping, a horse snorting from beside the barn, and the slow drone of numerous cows mooing in the distance. "Like look at that. Now that's a screensaver if I ever saw one. A lone cowboy on his horse coming up for a coffee with his neighbor." I reach up and rap my knuckles on the wall. "Company," I call to the guys. "You might want to mumble us up some disguises," I tell Kara.

Kara glances up from her phone then takes a selfie. "There's a better one," she says, ignoring me. My phone dings in my pocket as soon as she starts thumbing through hers again. I like her, now. I just wish we could have been friends from day one. Maybe then she'd listen to me a little better.

"Pardon me?" Lukas pokes his head out the door.

"You got company," I repeat.

He looks down the driveway at the cowboy approaching. A puff of smoke wafts from beneath a worn brown leather hat. The brim droops slightly as opposed to being turned up in the normal fashion. A matching leather vest covers a red and black plaid shirt that stands out against the cowboy's white horse covered in brown spots. *Palomino* is the name that comes to mind, doubt that's right though.

"Huh." Lukas steps back inside. A few seconds later and he's back on the porch, looking through the scope mounted on a bolt action rifle—a thirty-aught-six, I guess. Makes sense he'd have a weapon like that on the farm aside from the .22; the thirty-aught-six would drop anything Montana had to offer with a single shot.

Ben steps outside with his shotgun in hand. "Who is it?"

"Don't know."

I stand from the swing.

Kara looks up from her phone. "No Broadsword would be dumb enough to come at us alone."

"Unless he's a scout, or a messenger." I start loading the .22 from the box of bullets on the deck.

"He's not armed that I can see," says Lukas, lowering his rifle to his hip, though he keeps the barrel pointed in the stranger's general direction.

"A Broadsword doesn't need to be," I say.

It seems to take forever for the cowboy to make his way down the long gravel driveway, leaving puffs of smoke trailing behind him as he gets closer. I pick up the sweet smell of his cigar.

"Can I help you?" Lukas's voice is sterner than I've heard before.

Another puff of smoke is the cowboy's only response.

"That's far enough." Lukas raises his rifle. "I don't wanna put you down, mister, but I will."

The stranger's no more than twenty paces away. Kara's standing by my side, glaring down the driveway. My finger's ready on the trigger of the .22. I jerk and nearly let a shot off as Lukas fires his rifle.

A puff of dirt kicks up beside the stranger.

"I didn't have to miss," says Lukas.

The stranger stops his horse and raises the brim of his hat.

Late twenties, a handsome, clean-shaven chiseled face, long, black curly hair down to his chin, and eyes so dark they seem to look into my soul.

"That's no way to treat your elder, son," the stranger says, climbing down from his horse.

Elder? He can't have more than a year or two on us. Something isn't right, and nowadays I'm not about to risk getting the drop on.

I fire my .22.

The air between the stranger and myself blurs—the bullet slows to a stop in midair.

I unload all thirteen rounds the lever action has to offer.

Lukas cracks off the remaining three rounds in his clip.

Ben unloads his shotgun.

Lead dots the blurred air before the stranger. He waves his hand, and every hunk of lead falls to the driveway. "Is that really the way to greet your father?" he says, staring straight at me.

Chapter Twenty-Three

None of us move. My father, the head of the Broadsword, is ten feet away from me—and he's untouchable. He has powers like that of a witch, though I didn't know a witch could stop a bullet by condensing the air. I'm shaking, quivering, pulling in shallow breaths. I have to do something, and my newfound gift knows it. I'm cocooned in my violet energy like a suit of armor trying to keep me safe, prepared to act on instinct to keep all of us protected.

"There's no need for that, daughter." A wave of crimson fog pulses from Dad.

The world slows down, and a warming sensation like being in a shower overtakes me. My violet cocoon dissipates, and I drift back to the porch swing, as does Kara. "Scar?" she murmurs, her voice shaky.

We're entombed in a crimson fog. Forced, albeit ever so gently, to do no more than observe.

Ben charges forward, swinging his shotgun like a baseball bat.

Dad catches it with ease. "Really?" he says. The shotgun barrel crushes to half its size under Dad's grip. "Sit down, boys." He shoves the shotgun into Ben's chest so hard Ben collides with Lukas. They both fall to the deck bathed in the crimson fog.

I can't breathe. My chest struggles to rise and draw air against the tightness of the fog. All I can do is watch, no matter how hard I struggle, no matter how much force I exert against Dad's crimson fog. Kara's eyes are wide; She's panicking, trying to breathe as well.

The crimson fog drops, and air rushes into my lungs. I grab my chest, lurching forward on the bench. I can move again. I can move my entire body aside from my feet still encased in the crimson fog billowing along the deck.

Kara mumbles.

Flames erupt beneath Dad's feet.

"Take it easy, young lady." Dad waves his hand, and the flames vanish faster than they'd appeared, making me wonder if Kara had even drawn them into existence or if I'd imagined them. "You're out of your league. And as the breeder here said"—Dad glances at Lukas then back to Kara—"I don't want to hurt you."

Kara's head jerks back. She's clawing at a tiny cloud of fog clamping her jaw shut.

"You killed my mother!" The words shoot out of me.

My jaw clamps tight. It's like my lips are taped shut. I claw at my mouth and my fingers meet no resistance, only my lips. No matter how hard I try, I can't remove the tiny cloud from my face.

"Let's start over, shall we?" Dad climbs the stairs. "It's a pleasure to meet you after so many years, Scarlett."

He pulls a chair from against the wall, sits, leans back, and puffs on his cigar—he hadn't even lost that in the scuffle. We're merely an annoyance to him, no more powerful than a mosquito.

"That was never supposed to happen." Dad flicks ashes from the tip of his cigar. "I never knew she was there, or that you were the One. I never even knew you existed. It wasn't until your mother had...passed..." He pauses.

Murdered. Go ahead, say it. Until she was murdered by your coven. Say it.

"It wasn't until my Broadsword said the One who eluded them resembled not only her but myself as well that I learned of your existence. And seeing you now, there's no doubt you're my kin. You do have her eyes, Scar, is it?" He tilts his head slightly, sighs, and locks his gaze on me. "Short for Scarlett O'Hara, no doubt. I preferred the movie, but your mother loved the novel."

Tears well, threatening to escape. No way am I going to let one fall. No way am I going to let him see me as weak. He took everything from me. My whole world.

"Stubborn like her too, from the looks of it."

I reach out to smash his face and my wrists are bound the same as my ankles before I can stand, holding me in place. I curse as loudly as I can through shut lips.

"That"—he points at me, taking another puff of his cigar—"you get from me." He studies my face for a couple seconds then cocks his head down and to the side. "Passed down through my blood from your grandmother."

It's as if he's deep in thought, recalling an old memory. Not a memory that could be of me; he left before I was born. He stares me in the eyes. I don't know him well enough to read his face, but I recognize regret when I see it, and I remember what Mom said. *He could twist a mind into following him.* I squint, do my best to sneer at him.

He looks over my companions. "Interesting company you keep. Shouldn't get too close to a witch though, or haven't you been taught the rules?" It's Kara's turn to glare. "At least half the rules, half the truths." He takes his hat off, resting it on his knee, then crushes out his cigar on the railing. "All I can offer you, my daughter, is the truth."

He unbuttons his worn leather vest and pulls out an oval-shaped leather pouch embroidered with so much silver thread it has more metal than leather on it. It looks old, very old. He opens a flap to the pouch and pulls out a single ruby, flat, no more than the thickness of a finger, yet the size of a baby's head, and sparkling from within as if a million suns are trapped beneath its polished surface.

"The truth starts with this. The source of it all. Everything touched by magic stems from this amulet. The last remaining relic from Atlantis."

Chapter Twenty-Four

Atlantis.

I should be more shocked at the mention of the fabled city, but lately my life has been filled with one surprise after another. Even after learning of my true nature, witches, wolves, and Atlantis, anything other than what was in front of me was nothing more than generational stories that could have been altered repeatedly, so I never took much stock in them. But my father sitting before me with a piece of Atlantis in his hand makes me wish I had paid more attention at the Sanctum.

"This is what brought down Atlantis and sealed our fates. You see, I was born in a time of peace. When the world was new. When men, women, vampires, witches, and even the werewolves you have come to despise so much got along in harmony. It was smaller then, far less populated."

Dad pauses, staring vacantly at the sky.

Born in the time when Atlantis still stood. How powerful could he have become with centuries of accumulated knowledge? And what the hell is with the space cadet look?

He chuckles. "Your grandmother brought order to the savages running wild in the new land."

He points a thumb at the guys then waves his hand like he's painting. A blue mist trails his fingers to form a canvas, and a woman with a shock of red hair appears within the painting. It's like looking in a mirror, if I was wearing battle armor.

A polished wrist guard gleams in the sunlight as my grandmother runs her fingers through her hair. Pulling back the tresses, she reveals the hardened face of a warrior and a smoldering seductress with eyes silhouetted in charcoal and lips painted red. Not even the Black Widow could pull off this woman's commanding presence. She remains poised with her fingers draped over her sword's handle as her crimson cloak flaps in the wind, revealing brushed steel shin guards covering her from her knee to flow over red leather boots. Triple-plated armor curves along her arm, and her brushed steel breastplate features a raised crest of a bird of prey.

"It's a Raven," Dad says, a glimmer in his eye as he watches me absorb the vision of my ancestor. He observes to the image, cocking his head. "She…*was*…The Raven."

Dad takes a long, deep breath, working his fingers in and out of a fist.

"My mother—your grandmother—the world's first sorceress. The one we owe our thanks to for our power took pity on the people already living in the new world when she arrived. She, and the others, taught them, unified them, showed them a better way to live other than fighting over the possession of fire and living in caves."

"*Dude, your bloodline is intense.*" I glance to Kara, shaking her head slowly.

No kidding. I'm the progeny of the world's first sorceress, only sorcerer, and an elder vampire. It's a little much to absorb.

He trembles for a second. His head vibrates and cocks to the side. He sits up perfectly straight, no longer shaking.

"Her?" His voice is hushed, and deep. "Not her. Me." It's as if he's speaking to himself. "My power. My amulet. It was mine to rule over, not hers."

Torment thickens his voice as part of himself that disagrees with…himself.

Dad closes his eyes so tight crow's feet form around them. He takes in a deep breath, exhales, then slouches in the chair. He tucks the amulet back in its leather home, leaving only a sliver of its edge open to the world.

"I'm not an evil man." He gazes off into the distance again. His voice deepens once more, his eyes squint, like there's a smile behind them—a maniacal one. "I'm doing what no one else can do. What no one else has the power to do. Return the world to its former glory."

He sits, staring at the hills for so long it becomes uncomfortable. It's not as if I have any ease in the situation, but this is making it worse. He's making it worse than I could have imagined.

Get it over with. The words can't pass through my clamped lips.

The inaudible sound brings Dad back from wherever his mind drifted to, alerting him of my presence that he sloughed off. "The sun will do the job for me. And you"—my hand moves toward him but is held rigid due to the crimson fog—"will not stop it." His voice is still deep, full of gravel, and nothing like the one that spoke of my grandmother.

"Just a taste now, child. I've set measures in place that ensure I alone may bear the amulet. You will not enjoy this." He sneers at me and holds up the pouch. My mouth goes dry. I want to slap the pouch away with my free hand, but it's held in place by the fog.

He presses the visible sliver of the amulet against my finger, burning it.

I shut my eyes. No, not me, the amulet makes me shut them. I shudder, my breath catches in my chest, and goosebumps pepper my skin more so than when I was submerged in the river outside Lincoln. My next heartbeat brings up anger with a rush of heat intensifying into a rage that would have made my blood boil if it could have. I want—no, I need—to kill…something. Destroy something. Anything. The amulet is alive, has a soul, and is relaying its essence onto me, an evil one. I'm shaking…shuddering…like Dad did.

"What power you have, child," says Dad, still in his deep, gravelly voice. "The possibilities are—"

The sun appears before me, and I'm blinded; even with my eyes shut this vision the amulet is showing me is far too real. Its churning surface speeds up, throwing streams of fire into the void around it. The bursts get larger. The fire reaches out further, licking at the earth's surface, overtaking the planet. Burned wood, searing flesh, and choking ash overwhelm me.

I vomit.

I'm back on the deck, dry heaving at the crimson fog billowing around my feet. All the rage that had risen in my heart is gone and has been replaced with panic. I struggle to control my body enough to draw air. Struggle to remain composed, even though I puked, in front of Kara, my rock, and Lukas.

Dad shudders again and sits upright. "It won't last long." His hand is on my shoulder, his voice is considerably different, like it was when he first arrived. I shrug at his touch, but he won't let go. My stomach's knotted, and I double over further, held in the swing only by the fog restraining me. "Now you know what will come to pass, a rebirth. A new beginning for the planet. The depopulation of the weak, the undesirable, the useless eaters of the world. It's out of my hands. You think the strength I've displayed, the power I've shown you thus far, are the only gifts bestowed upon *him* by the amulet? *He* can't be stopped."

Shut up. Just shut up. The unbridled rage from the amulet is gone, but I still want nothing more than to smash his face with my fist despite my charred finger. My knuckles sting—they're wet, and warm. Dad's hand is no longer on my shoulder, it's covering his nose. Blood gushes from beneath his palm.

I struck him without thought. God, I wish I could have reveled in it—the impact, the breaking of his bones—but my rage blinded me and threw me into an instinctive fight or flight action.

My dry heaving subsides, and I focus. The amulet is on the deck, freely exposed to the sun.

"Well." Dad stands from his chair, backing away from me. "That's enough family time for a bit." He pulls his hand from his face. His nose, bent to the side, stops bleeding and reforms itself back into its normal shape as he wipes the blood off with his sleeve.

I'm free of the fog. His injury must have distracted him, let his spell fall.

I charge, reaching out for his throat.

He sidesteps, shoves me down the stairs from behind. The gravel from the driveway bites into my palms. Ignoring it, I spin around, scramble up the steps.

He's fast, but he's still just a man. I can stop him. If I can hit him once I can do it again.

Kara's free of the fog too, and Dad doesn't see her.

She kicks the amulet from the deck through the air over my head. Dad backhands her across the face, sending Kara through the swing to the deck in a mass of splintered wood.

I reach for him.

"Enough!" Dad punches me in the chest. The air leaves my lungs before I hit the driveway. "Insolent whelp. How dare you strike me." He has perfect posture again, and his voice is full, more than deep—its ominous, soul-crushing, and outright terrifying.

The man before me is not my father—not at the moment, not in the head. *He can't be stopped.* That's what Dad said. *He*, not *I*, but *he*. Every movie I've seen about split personalities runs through my head, makes me want to kill this other personality, and makes me pity him.

I rise to my feet and get knocked on my ass before I can find my balance, let alone take a swing or a proper breath. Something hit me, hit all of us. Something too fast to see.

Whatever it is that laid us out didn't hit Dad—it came from him. He somehow cleared the air around him with so much force Kara and the guys were tossed to the far side of the deck, clear into the railing.

He raises his hand at the amulet. It floats into his palm, then flashes a crimson tendril out of it, pinning me down. "This cursed bloodline will not stop me from carving out my kingdom." He slips the amulet into its pouch, tucks it beneath his vest, and more crimson tendrils reach out to Kara, Lukas, and Ben.

He looks to the sky, closes his eyes, and breathes deep, letting his chest rise and fall.

"Calm down." Dad's voice is soft again, but he isn't speaking to me. He's speaking to himself.

Chapter Twenty-Five

"You're quite the little spitfire." Dad's crimson tendril lifts me, holds me tight, pinning my arms down. "I can't have you lashing out at me again, at least not until you've heard me through. Restraining *him* is becoming increasingly more difficult the closer we get to the event."

The earth before him splits, and five crystals push up from the dirt, each one growing into the shape of an easy chair.

"Have a seat."

Dad's tendrils plop me down, followed by Kara, Lukas, and Ben. The tendrils fade and I make to rise, to chastise him, to rip his head off, but like the others I'm engulfed in Dad's paralyzing crimson fog. It's not as tight as it was before, but it's damn hard to draw a breath, and I can't imagine how the others are doing without having my strength. I glance to them.

"They'll be fine. They're not as unique as you are, daughter." He's right. They'll be fine, at least for now. They're pinned by swirling clouds at their ankles, wrists, and mouths. Kara's looks a little thicker around the mouth than the guys' do.

A fire bursts to life in the middle of our little sit-in. Though my burned finger is almost healed after touching the amulet, it still aches from the heat from the fire, and I curl it into my palm to shield it.

"I swear, no harm will come to you from either me or *his* people," Dad says, lounging in his chair, sipping something from a gold cup. We all have gold cups in our hands. The sweet smell of wine catches me. Did he materialize it, and the cups, from thin air? If he can do that, what else can he do, and more to the point, what can I do to stop him?

I glare at him as best I can.

"You are of my blood. It's because of that reason alone that I would like to explain myself. After all, family is what really matters in this world."

Family? Is he kidding? There's no way I would ever consider him family. Being related by blood is one thing, but being a family is a whole different one. Split personality or not, he took mine from me.

"Are you willing to listen to what I have to say?"

The crimson fog drifts away from my mouth on the breeze. This kumbaya sit-in is nuts. *He's* nuts, but what else am I supposed to do against the sorcery he possesses, especially with the amulet's power at his beck and call? "It's not like I have a choice," I say as snidely as I can.

"Right you are, daughter. Trust…is the first step to communication." The fog holding us all in our chairs dissipates. "I trust that there will be no more foolishness." He looks over each one of us individually.

Kara glares back at him, and folds her arms across her chest, crossing her legs. Ben rubs his wrist as if he's been in handcuffs. Lukas holds his composure better than his cousin and Kara as he leans forward, elbows on his knees. I doubt he'll make a move to charge Dad as his poise is similar to when I told him of the real world, less the table to lean on.

No one speaks. Dad takes a deep breath, then sighs. "Smell that? It's putrid."

What the hell is he talking about? We're in the middle of the country. The air couldn't be fresher. "What?" I say sharply.

"The pollution, daughter. In my time the air was clear, the ocean was clean, and there was more than enough for everyone. I get why *he* wants to change it all." He's drifting into thought, staring up again. "That all ended with me. The only child of the world's first sorceress." He strikes me as someone who's spent a lot of time alone, talking to himself, drifting off following his thoughts, not maintaining eye contact. "Can you see it, little one?" he asks Kara as the fog encasing her lips dissipates.

"See what?" Kara snaps. She's obviously as pissed as I am about our inability to do a thing against Dad.

"You'll see it, if you're any good." Then to me, he continues. "And so should you, thanks to my blood. It wasn't until I saw your little stunt on TV that I realized just how unique you are, Scarlett. Other than your grandmother and myself, no witch has manifested thought into the physical realm, the visual realm. Conjuring spells, mumbling is it," he glances to Kara then back to me, "That's the norm, but solidified energy, that's a family trait." He raises his wine, toasting me. "When I took hold of the amulet—"

Dad whips his head down and to the side, fast. "My amulet." He growls.

His chest rises and falls rapidly, as if he's enraged and about to charge into a fight.

He squeezes his eyes shut, and with a long deep breath he turns back to me. His face simultaneously calm, and yet downtrodden, his gaze locked on my feet. "*He's*...difficult to suppress. Not surprising." Dad takes a slow breath. "He was powerful enough that in one single night he murdered every Atlantean, his brethren, claimed their sorcery for himself, and plunged the city into the crushing depths of the sea. Your grandmother and a handful of others managed to defeat him, trapping his essence within this amulet. I inadvertently freed the Last Atlantean from within it." Dad pats the amulet concealed beneath his vest "His control, his power, his rage, they're unmatched. Like nothing I'd felt before. He took control of my mind, and body, and using me to wield...it...he destroyed my peaceful world. A once serene utopia built on cooperation between vampire, wolf, and man, was thrust into chaos. He shattered it as fast as he brought down his own city. Split the covens, turned them against each other by cursing their bloodlines to be driven mad if separated. Thus, the decrees you abide by."

He's talking about the bond I have with Kara. If ever there was a way to break it, surely it would have been discovered since caveman times. The inevitability of going insane when Kara eventually grows old and dies fuels my anger. I won't have Aunt Brenda here to quell my madness as she did with Mom when Dad left her.

He raises his cup at the guys. "Be nice, gentlemen, she's your salvation. She won't be able to stop it, but she can aid in the rebuilding."

"What are you talking about?" I glare at him harder, resisting the urge to leap across the firepit and tear out his throat. "Salvation? *You're* the reason any of us are in this mess."

"Your powers...are like his," Kara murmurs to me.

I glance at the bulge in his vest where he keeps the amulet.

"Clever girl," Dad says to Kara. "The power of Atlantis. The source of all of us," he repeats. "Why do you think I only let you have a taste of its power, of his essence? Don't want you ending up like me, not alone for a moment. I didn't heed the warnings." He huffs, thumbs the bulge in his vest. "Seems like a lifetime ago. Thought I could handle it. It's been with me so long I'd wager it saturated my cells and I passed some of its essence onto you. How else could you wield its power, willing my fog away as you did?"

"I—"

"And then there's the rodeo." Dad forms a ball of crimson energy in his hand, writhing with layers of smoke that dive in and out of its surface. "What I mean is, you have no control to challenge it, or *him*." The ball elongates into a solid sword, the crimson blade even seems to reflect the sun.

Dad stands up, shuddering, and locks eyes with me. "And you never will." His voice has dropped again.

He raises his other hand, his fingers tense like claws. Our crystal chairs wrap around us, encasing us. I'm helpless to move anything other than my head.

Kara mumbles.

Dad snaps his fingers and swipes his hand down. A glowing amber ball shoots out of Kara's mouth and follows Dad's motion to roll beside him in the grass.

Kara mouths something, but no sound comes—she's mute.

Violet flashes all around me, illuminating my crystal prison, there's something different about it though. There's...more...violet. It's thicker, stronger, a far cry from my initial purple power as Kara called it.

Dad struts toward me, and he grips my face, squeezing my cheeks in one hand so hard I swear he's going to dislodge my teeth under his grasp. I try to break through the crystal, kick him off, but it doesn't budge.

Crimson energy flows from Dad's amulet beneath his vest, along his arm, and after a brief standoff pushes my newfound power back to the depths of my soul from where it came. Leaving me utterly defenseless.

"You come from this mortal shell, but your power is mine by right. As is yours, witch." Dad glances at Kara, then turns his attention back to me, and pushing my head to the side he releases me, stands up, and gazes out toward the foothills. "Same with the beasts. There will be no free radicals in my kingdom, I shan't allow any of my creations to breed unchecked again."

His creations? Again? Is he somehow responsible for vamps, witches, and wolves coming into being? If he did, maybe I can reason with him—Dad, not this other personality that I want to destroy.

"With that amulet you could stop the sun's flare. If you don't, there won't be anyone left to rule over in your *kingdom*," I tell him.

"Immortality, ensures I can wait for the land and water to replenish."

He grins at me, tracing his gaze over my body from head to toe, slowly. Gives me the creeps.

"The strongest humans should survive, along with a few fortunate ones, and those graced by my gifts as you two are." He waves his sword between Kara and me. "If they're talented. They'll be able to handle the annihilation of the old world."

"Why not rule over everyone as the world is, if you're so powerful?" I say, taunting him. Egging him on to show off his great power, save the planet from the sun, and take the burden from me. Maybe that's how I'm supposed to save the planet. By outwitting the one person with seemingly unlimited power, one who can wield all the magic of Atlantis.

"I could, child. And I will, but its populace is too great to be bothered with. Starting anew is much more appealing. Besides, the earth already has no more to give at such an exponential growth rate. It took a hundred thousand years to reach a population of a billion people." He's talking to himself again. "And only another two hundred years to reach eight billion people. Seven billion people popped up in such a short time. Give it forty more years and I'll be looking at thirty-two billion people on the planet that I'd have to control. There have been several major extinction events in the earth's history, and it is long overdue for another. The planet's population is spinning out of control. Mankind and my creations have become a cancer on it and it's about to be cut out." Dad slices through his crystal chair, cleaving it in two. "Dwindle it down to controllable masses." He nods to himself, then bends down, rakes the ground with his fingers and studies the dirt sifting between them. "The world will replenish itself with time, but under my rule. It came back from the devastation that wiped out the dinosaurs, and with a little sorcerous aid I'll not only survive but thrive, along with the subjects I deem worthy."

"So you're supposed to be the world's greatest activist on climate change and population control." I sneer. "And your way to spread the word is to cook the earth?"

The grin he gives me immediately makes me regret turning his attention back to me and my skin crawls. "As for you," he says. "You could have been useful, but your bloodline deserves retribution. Thus, you shall not live long enough to follow in the footsteps of your ancestor and drive another blade through my heart." He raises his crimson sword. "Now, I shall carve out my kingdom."

My chair disintegrates, crumbling to pieces, and drops me to the ground.

Dad thrusts at my heart. I'm not fast enough to bat his blade aside, but I don't need to be.

He stops his strike a few inches from my chest.

He's shaking, vibrating with gritted teeth, as if he's struggling within himself for control of his own body.

Dad drops, breathing heavy.

Him on his knees, me on my back, we stare at each other a moment.

"Sorry," he says between breaths. "I swore no harm would come to you by my hand. For your safety, daughter, it's best we part ways. I'll do my best to make *him* think he ran you through with his blade."

Dad stands up, brushing the dust from his vest. He waves his hand, snaps his fingers, then our crystal chairs return to their original state, releasing the others and again leaving each crystal armrest with a full glass of wine. "You'll be needing this back," Dad says to Kara, snapping his fingers, sending the amber ball back into her mouth.

Kara clears her throat, tests her voice.

Dad's hand pauses over the bulge of the amulet, and he mumbles something to himself, quiet enough even my ears can't catch it.

Between his palms a yellow energy sparks to life, forming an orb.

He sculpts the orb, and it elongates to a pointed staff spanning the width of his shoulders. Blowing across its length, streams of orange spring to life throughout the writhing yellow staff, and it floats toward his horse.

The energy is absorbed through its muscular chest.

The horse shudders, scrapes at the dirt under its hooves as the glow splits in two beneath its hide and slides to its ribs.

Wings grow on either side of his steed.

His pegasus acts as if the massive wings have been with it since birth as my dad climbs on its back. He kicks the pegasus's flanks, and it takes flight, beating its massive wings.

Chapter Twenty-Six

Dad circles overhead. The ground rumbles. The wine in my cup on the armrest of the crystal chair has ripples in it.

The earth splits at the end of the quarter mile long driveway, and stones shoot skyward, launching clumps of rock and dirt into the air.

The rock forms a wall surrounding the ranch, replacing the barbed wire fence, and stretching out so far even my eyes have trouble following it. The wall is made of white smoothed stone glistening in the waning light, capped with torches every few paces. It's at least twenty feet tall and stands twice the height of the double arched doors in its north face. I stare at it, amazed at how small it makes me feel, recognizing it as a wall that would surround a medieval castle, or city due to its circumference. Just one of those doors looks as if it would test the limits of even my strength to move.

He lands his pegasus in front of the massive entrance. "I can't leave you defenseless, daughter. I have no doubt you'll survive what's to come to pass. You won't be able to stop it, but I'll ensure you have what you need to prosper." Dad holds his palm up above his head. "Doors of oak, able to withstand a siege for a fortnight."

Protruding from the door frame are black grates of wrought iron as thick as my wrist and forged into hundreds of diamond-shaped holes.

"A gate just small enough to allow a spear to pass through for close quarter combat."

Spears? He's lost his mind. He may have lined dozens of them along the wall, but really, what does he think we're going to have to defend ourselves from?

"Handy for the wolves, daughter. Along with the survivors who are sure to try and take what you have."

He must have read something on my face that made him add that. He waits a moment, lets me look over his manifestation with visions of wolves attacking. It makes sense the more I think about it, but from a medieval point of view.

He points to either side of the entrance. "As are these." On the interior of the wall, just behind the piled spears now sits a row of six catapults on either side of the gate. "Boulders, clay pots full of oil, and baskets with silver shards as ammunition." He really thinks we're going into a medieval battle. "Netting tied to the boulders and soaked in oil, any foe cresting the wall will be pulled over to the forest of pikes lining the other side if launched at the opportune moment."

I'm speechless, as is Kara. It's hard to comprehend what he created.

He points at a row of giant crossbows stationed behind the catapults. "These beauties, mounted on a swivel, can fire twelve bolts in rapid succession, effectively turning one man into ten. A masterpiece of engineering the likes of which the world hasn't seen in centuries." He's speaking from experience, I guess. The crossbow's bolts are as long as I am tall, and each is tipped with blades extending an arm's length from the shaft in all four directions like an X. "Silver tipped for added efficiency." Silver? He's certain of hard times to come, certain of wolves to come. If we live, that is.

"What? He's never heard of a gun?" Kara mutters.

"Take in the honorable and the good-hearted, teach or turn away the wicked, just as your grandmother did. Forge an army, daughter. Train them to work the land and the defenses and prepare them. Raise a formidable force to not only protect yourself, but to challenge him. You can't stop what's going to happen, but perhaps if you keep your wits about you, you can end the rein of the Last Atlantean."

Did my dad just suggest I *kill* him? I agree the Atlantean needs to go, but at the cost of Dad's life? I don't know if I could do that, kill my father.

He bows, and my hip gets heavy. I grab at it and find a handle under my fingers. He's conjured up a sword in a sheath belted to my waist, Kara and I each have one.

"Happy Birthday, Scarlett."

Dad salutes us and kicks his pegasus into flight without another word. The four of us just stand there as he shrinks into the distance, a speck swallowed by the vast Montana sky.

"Holy shit," Kara says, breaking the silence.

"Yeah," I agree. Build an army out of what's left of the world to take on Dad's other self? Is he nuts? I couldn't do a thing against him a minute ago, and Dad thinks I can end this sorcerous plague he's telling me I have no chance of preventing. He could stop this. He could stop the sun. With his amulet, I'm sure of it. He could stop the Last Atlantean. I hate to think it, after all these years of wishing I'd meet my father, but the thought rings loud and clear. *Suicide.* Even if he can't stop the solar flare, and he truly wanted to protect me from his other self, he could put a bullet in his head.

I shake mine, dispelling the notion.

As much as I want him to pay for what he did to Mom, for creating the Broadsword, for what he's claiming he's going to do, I now know none of that was, or is, in his control. After meeting him and watching how tormented he is trying to wage an inner war against an Atlantean, I want him to live. I want him to be free of his curse. He is my dad after all, and the only family I have left.

"He's got issues. Like…can you say let's draw more attention to ourselves? The Army has satellites, you dolt!" Kara shouts to the horizon. "Like they're not gonna see this," she says, throwing her hands in the air. "Whole world's looking for us and he puts a *huge* frickin' target on our backs, literally." She points up. "I can't cover up something this damn big. Even if I could, a wall surrounding this much land blinking in and out of existence on Google Earth kinda tells everyone where the fuck we are." She kicks the ground, sending specks of dirt toward the wall.

"I hate to say it, but if he's right, we're gonna need all this."

"You're talking like it's all over."

"You heard him just as well as I did."

"Don't tell me he got to you, Scar. I mean…sure, he makes sense in a crazy kind of destroy-the-world way. But there's gotta be a better way to go about it than killing half the planet. And he's gonna decide who gets to live on what's left of the planet? Are you kidding me?"

Ben's phone rings, followed by Lukas's.

"I'm not giving up. If he can do all this, maybe I can too." Dad showed me one thing—anything is possible.

"You don't have his amulet. That's how he did this." She points at the wall. "You think he could with out it? I never heard of anything remotely close to this kind of power."

"You heard him—it's in my blood, the amulet's power. What if I'm all we need? What if I can stop the flare by myself? Somehow. No matter what he says."

"No, I'm fine, Mom," says Ben.

"Somehow? Notice he forgot to mention that. How you can even do it. Convenient. Hell, he probably wrote the damn prophecy," says Kara.

"God, I hope not," I tell her. "If he did, then why give us any warning about it if he just wanted to let it happen? His other half, I mean."

Kara shakes her head. "You mean the genocidal maniac half of himself. Magic I get. The things he can do, okay, I'll buy he's got power. It could even come from Atlantis like he says. But—"

"But we've been lied to our entire lives," I say.

"Exactly." Kara points a finger at me. "So what's to say he's not?"

"You saw him—he's a mess. But I believe he's telling the truth. Look around. He's got some heart in him. He has to. Otherwise, why give us these defenses?"

"It's a bloody target on our backs, is what it is."

I can't deny that.

"I know, I can see it too. Ben's with me, Uncle, we're fine," says Lukas on his phone.

"No, don't come over here, Mom," says Ben. "I'll explain everything. Just sit tight, I'll be right there." Ben hangs up his phone. "This thing's big enough Mom can see it from our ranch."

"Yes, he's on his way home, Uncle. I'm staying." I can hear Lukas's uncle through the phone, not his words but the tone. "Okay, okay, we'll come together." Lukas hangs up and looks at Ben. "How are we gonna explain this to your folks?"

"Tell them the truth," says Kara. "Wait and see if the world goes to shit tonight. If it doesn't, start an amusement park or something."

"Kara—"

"What?" She cuts me off. "We're all over the news. They've stopped giving updates about the sun's activities, or the world's for that matter. We're in the middle of a real-life witch hunt, a nationwide one."

Memories of her chasing me with a lit torch come to mind.

"What do you think will happen when they find us? Assuming we live through tonight. Assuming anything happens at all. You think the government is just going to sit us down and ask us questions politely? I doubt that."

"Experimentation," I say.

"Exactly. We'll be poked and prodded and God knows what else until they've had enough of us. Then they'll cut us open to see what makes us tick."

Kara's right riled up, and I get it—we're being hunted. The government is an issue, but there's also the Broadsword. I don't really trust Dad's promise that he won't send them after us anymore. Part of me wants to, but after years of hiding and watching my back, it's hard to just let all that instinct and training go.

I stare at the wall and recall Dad's words about the wolves. We're being hunted by them as well. Does Dad know something he didn't divulge? Are there strays in the hills?

But now we have the bloody National Guard after us. Kara is right to worry. I'm worried. A single person can rationalize a situation like Lukas and Ben did, accepting there are things about the world they didn't know. But people at large, they're a different story. The masses are dumb, panicky, stupid animals. Especially when they're led by media with overactive imaginations, and world leaders who are more geared to going to war over oil and making a profit than trying to understand something like the supernatural. Area 51 comes to mind. Just look how a rumor like that has brought up one conspiracy theory after another.

I envision myself beside Kara on an examination table surrounded by doctors in HAZMAT suits with scalpels in their hands. Kara dead with her organs exposed to the world. I'm still alive, pinned down, and just as exposed as Kara. My heart is held up before my eyes in the hands of a so-called doctor, pondering how long I can live with my innards lying on the table beside me.

I push away the image. There's no time for fantasizing, especially about something as gruesome as that. "Go to your parents', Ben. You too," I say, walking over to Lukas. I kiss him, let his warmth drive my imagination away and ground me where I am in time. "If you can…if you're willing to…can you be my eyes and ears out there? Text us if anyone's coming our way, what the buzz around town is." I do my best to put on a brave face.

Lukas looks at the massive wall surrounding his ranch. "Will do." He hugs me, whispers in my ear. "I'll be back tomorrow. You be here. We'll have our steaks yet."

"That would be nice," I tell him, hoping there *will* be a tomorrow. His optimism isn't as infectious as I would like it to be. This could be the last time I get to lose myself in his brilliant sapphire eyes, so I memorize them, try to focus on them instead of thoughts of vamp experimentation.

Lukas lets me go and makes his way to the truck. Ben jumps in, fires it up. Lukas steps inside and says to Kara through the window, "Take care of her, would you."

She nods. She's as good at goodbyes as I am.

As they drive through the open gate, I take a deep breath. Mom's meditation tricks aren't enough to calm my mind. I want a drink. I pick up the wine Dad conjured. It's sweeter than anything I'd ever had. Rich from grapes long extinct. It's so full of flavor.

"What are you thinking?" Kara asks.

"I honestly have no idea. This is the first time in my life I want this night to come. I want it to be over with. I always feared it, and now, I just wanna see what tomorrow brings."

Kara picks up her wine and sniffs it. "Not sure what I'd do without my playlist." She's trying to lighten the mood, which oddly enough I don't feel needs lightening.

I should be pissed, but I'm not. I'm…kinda…tired.

Crap…the wine.

My eyelids are heavy, hard to keep open. "Kar—" I try to speak but my words slur, and I fall to the ground.

Chapter Twenty-Seven

I make a fist. Dirt sifts between my fingers. The air has an earthy flavor to it. A flame floats above me as the only source of light. A layer of black dirt high above me leads to walls of grayish-brown clay. I'm underground. "What happened?"

"Never take wine from a stranger, especially *your* dad," Kara says.

It comes flooding back to me. I'm suddenly flushed and pissed off. "He drugged me."

"His way of keeping you from stopping Armageddon. Lucky for us he doesn't know my hangover trick. I've been siphoning water into you for an hour or more trying to flush the toxins from your body."

"And we're underground because?"

"I wasn't taking on the National Guard by myself, not without my secret weapon." Kara points her finger at me like a gun.

"National Guard?" Kara was right. Dad painted a target on our backs when he conjured up the wall around Lukas's ranch. How else would the National Guard have found us so soon? It's easy to spot from far away, and they were already on the lookout for us.

"Haven't heard them scurrying about up there for a while now." She looks up. "I hauled you into the basement and bored a hole through the wall. Tunneled about fifty feet or so before I had to take a break so I could hydrate you. Not the easiest thing to do, you know." She pokes her finger in the clay. "Pretty dry down here, and you're not exactly light to drag along."

"They didn't shoot at you, did they?"

"I didn't give them the chance. You hit the deck. Huh, guess that's where that expression comes from. Anyway, Ben texted me about the Army speeding toward us, gave me the time we needed. So here we are." Kara pulls out her phone and the dugout lights up with its blue light. "Twenty to eleven, almost time for you to do your thing I'd imagine."

Just over an hour, one single hour, that's all we have left. 11:47 PM, the time has been etched into my brain since I learned about the prophecy. 11:47 PM, the exact minute I was born, the exact minute the Thirst kicked in on my sixteenth birthday, the exact minute I expect I'll have to stop the sun. I've been waiting and preparing my entire adult life, and most of my teenage years, for a moment in time that's just over an hour away. My stomach's churning. I chalk it up to the fact Dad drugged me and not because my subconscious is counting down to Armageddon.

I stand up, my lungs fill with smoke, and I cough.

"Yeah, sorry about that," Kara says. Dirt falls beside me. Kara mumbles a hole the size of my hand into existence above us. Fresh cool air gusts throughout the dugout, replacing the smoke.

"How does fire that isn't burning anything make smoke?"

"I don't know, it's magic."

"Thanks, I couldn't have made it this far without you."

"I know." Kara smirks, raising her chin.

"Think we can take a look up top?"

"Sure, but you're the one who's sticking her head up there to be shot like a gopher popping up." She mumbles. Clay steps form to the top of the dugout. The fire dies to a small flame the size of my finger, and the ground above the steps opens enough for me to squeeze through.

I listen. Nothing catches my attention. It's dead calm, eerily quiet. Not even the calls of the coyotes sound out. My stomach tightens, and I have to push back the thought that they were taken down by a wolf and that one is lurking in the shadows. I can't pick up a scent of one, only the remnants of men.

I poke my head above ground. We're beside the barn. Kara's gone more like eighty to a hundred yards from the house. Hard to tell underground, I guess.

I drop back down. "No one's here."

"Weird. They gotta be hiding, waiting for us to show ourselves."

"I can't pick up a fresh scent, and the house looks empty."

"Probably bugged. Guaranteed they put a tracker on my car. There's no way they'd just leave this place abandoned."

"Yeah." She's right. They'll be watching or listening for us to pop up. "We need to get out of here, off the ranch." I could make a run for it, but Kara's not as fast as I am, and I don't want to leave her alone. "The horses."

"No."

"It's our only option." I climb out of the hole, scanning the ranch. My night vision tells me it's clear, and I'm guessing it's far better than anything the Army has.

Kara follows me up. "I don't know how to ride," she murmurs.

"How hard can it be?" We slip into the barn. Aside from the horses, it's empty.

"Where are we gonna go on horses?"

"Into the hills, away from here, wait till the time comes to…I don't know."

It makes sense; a horse can do better than a car in the hills. If we can just get to them unseen, we'll be in the clear, so to speak. At the very least, give me a place where I don't have to watch my back so I can do…whatever.

"Blanket first," I tell Kara, plucking one hanging on a railing, placing it on a horse's back. That much I know, blanket then saddle. The knob on the saddle goes to the front, and there's a buckle to hold the entire thing in place around the horse's belly. The weight of the saddle surprises me, It's heavier than I thought. Kara's eyes are wide, and her spine's arched back like she's afraid, or nervous. Her horse scrapes the dirt floor with its hooves as Kara mumbles the blanket and saddle in place. I guess the horse feels the same about her. Once her buckle is tight, she holds up her fists, shaking them up and down. She means the reins. I find some on the wall and examine them. "I have no idea how to attach this."

"Your idea sucks."

"We'll go without the reins. Just hang on and let the horse do the work."

"Isn't that like driving without a wheel?" She wants her car, and I get it. I want my bike, even if it's Lukas's camouflaged dirt bike.

A high-pitched buzz comes from above.

I press my finger to my lips and point to the roof. Kara looks up. Her ears eventually pick up what my vamp hearing already detected. "A drone," she whispers. I nod. Leave it up to the military. They probably had one circling high above or sitting on the house with its camera scanning the ranch. "*Now what?*" she says telepathically.

"We destroy it and they're on to us," I whisper back.

"If we try to ride these things, they'll see us for sure."

"Can you take us there underground?"

She shakes her head. "*Too far.*" The buzz moves to the main doors of the barn. Kara runs over and looks through the gap where the hinges are. She holds her arms wide to her sides. It's a big drone. Probably one with a long battery life in it and all kinds of gizmos. The operator can't be far away. I don't think the controls can be worked over a mile, but that's what I know from movies. Who knows what the Army really has? What we need is speed and stealth. Like the drone.

My horse neighs, and I get an idea.

Dad did it.

Can I?

So far, I've needed anger or fear to access my power, but Dad did it when he was calm. Kara can do it at will and Aunt Brenda worked her over. Perhaps all I need is any emotion, and not an outburst. Anger, fear, anxiety, joy, love, anything. They're all in me, all the time, I've just chosen not to run wild with them. Concentration is the key, and considering where we're at, what do I have to lose?

It's worth a shot.

I do my best to mimic his movements, and a golden staff forms in thin air before my eyes.

"No." I hear Kara hush from the door. I have to, there's no other choice. The staff splits in two, and each-piece floats toward a horse's chest. The horses throw back their heads as it approaches and sinks beneath their flesh. Sweat stings my eyes as I try to imagine the energy doing what it did for Dad. Thin hairs grow from the horses' sides, grow larger, fatter, then sprout feathers and form into wings.

I collapse to the floor.

Kara makes it to me and pulls me up against the wall. "I'd rather we stayed on the ground."

"Haven't you always wanted one since you were little?" I try to enjoy the fact that I just pulled off something I thought was impossible. I guess Kara's becoming more and more used to strange things happening. She doesn't even congratulate me; instead, her response is a face almost covered with terror—she's afraid of heights. "You won't fall," I tell her. She doesn't glance away from the pegasus. "Just mumble a carrot into existence in front of it or something and get it to go where you want it to." She scowls at me. "Just get on. I'll take care of the drone." I push myself up.

Slowly, Kara approaches her winged horse. I pet the neck of mine and she does the same, following my lead to the T. They're nice horses, or at least I think they are. Up until this moment, the most interaction I've had with a horse was watching them at the rodeo.

Kara climbs into the saddle and grips the knob on the front so hard I swear her knuckles pop. I make my way to the barn doors and pick up a pitchfork hanging on the wall. Fitting—torches and pitchforks, I *am* the angry mob now. The drone circles around the barn and makes its way back to the doors.

Kara wasn't kidding. The drone is huge. It's the size of her car, and it's hovering about ten yards in front of the door at eye level. Now's my chance.

I kick the barn door open, leap at the drone, pitchfork held high.

With both hands I bring the pitchfork down. The handle vibrates and snaps in two on the drone's wing. Apparently, the military stuff is tougher than the ones in the movies.

The drone lists back—the wing I hit is intact, but it's dented.

It moves toward me.

I panic with only a splintered piece of wood in my hand. Then I feel weight on my hip. The sword Dad gave me is so light I forgot I had it. I pull the blade free of its sheath, swing at the dent, hacking a wing off.

The drone flops to the ground, kicking up dirt from a propeller.

I stab the thing in what looks like the camera, a bowling ball with glass circles on the front shatters as my blade sinks to the pommel. I pull it out to the satisfying sound of metal scraping on metal. The propellers slow and stop spinning.

I look around. No vehicles, no other drones are in sight, and it's as quiet as a Montana night can be.

I run inside the barn, climb on my pegasus, wrap my fingers in its mane and kick with my heels. The horse neighs and charges forward past the drone's dismembered bits. I pull on its mane and wings beat at my sides, lifting us skyward. I figure I've only got a half hour left before I have to wage war against the sun.

Chapter Twenty-Eight

I can see why women are obsessed with horses. There's a rush, letting it speed you to your destination. Of course, my horse has the added benefit of flight. Flying was nerve-wracking at first, but now that I've settled in and let the horse take over, it's become peaceful. That is if it wasn't for Kara sucking air through gritted teeth every time her horse drops, which is in between every wingbeat. If enough time passes, I'm sure she'll learn how to whistle a tune through a clenched jaw.

"Kara." I point at a foothill littered with trees and the clearing at its top. She mumbles the wine bottle sized carrots hovering before our pegasus' faces to drift toward the hill, and the horses follow the lead.

My pegasus's hooves touch down softer than I expect. I pat its neck and wait for Kara. Her steed touches down, and she's on solid ground before it can stop beating its wings.

I climb down. "Did you see the soldiers?"

"We're never doing that again," Kara says, breathing heavy, doubled over with her hands on her knees. "And no, I didn't." She sits down, pulls her legs in, wraps her arms around them. "I was too busy trying not to let the carrots vanish while hanging on for my life."

"It wasn't *that* bad."

"Easy for you to say. Your bones don't take months to heal if you fall off that thing."

"Guess I'm just tougher than you." I sit beside her, and she grumbles. "The soldiers are a few hills away," I say, pointing between Lincoln and Lukas's farm. I'm pretty sure they didn't see us, and I haven't seen or heard another drone in the area."

"*Satellites*." Kara throws her hands in the air, annoyed. "Heat signature, infrared, night vision, zoom lenses, we're screwed."

I put my hand on her shoulder. "It's okay."

She sighs and lies back in the grass.

I follow her lead. There's nothing more we can do at the moment but wait. I hesitate to check my phone, to see the time, but I decide if something's going to happen it'll be obvious.

The constellations are out. I can always pick out Orion first; seeing it reminds me of nights spent playing outside with Mom. The stars are brilliant and abundant—and have a green taint to them. "Um…are you seeing this?"

Kara focuses on the stars above. "Oh, *come on*, can't a girl get a little peace?"

"What are you worried about? You don't have to do anything."

"Aside from keeping your ass alive like I've been doing since I first rolled into Lincoln." She takes my hand in hers. She's trying to play the role of the supportive tough girlfriend, but her palms are sweating, whether it be from the flight on her winged horse or the sky above it doesn't matter. She's scared, and so am I.

I let Kara's lilac perfume wash over me, and I shut my eyes.

My breath catches.

The sky's not black—it's brilliant. Emerald green, sapphire blue, and violet lines snake their way around the stars. A tear runs down my temple. "Shut your eyes," I say.

Her hand squeezes mine tighter. "It's so—"

"I know."

"This is what your dad meant. If I can see it. Funny how something so pretty can be so scary at the same time."

I open my eyes and the colors fade away with my eyelids, leaving only a black night sky dotted with green-tinted stars.

I hold my hand up; it's bathed in violet. "Something's happening."

"Scar?" Kara's normally optimistic eyes are watery.

She mumbles. No, she says something, but her words don't register. I'm standing above her. Oh God, no I'm not—I'm levitating above her, encased in my violet energy.

Her hand pulls free of mine despite our grip tightening. I rise higher in the air, surrounded by writhing tendrils of my violet power reaching out from my aura. But it's different than before I met Dad, before I touched *his* amulet. It's no longer a purple power, my violet energy has become…enhanced, like I felt at Dad's kumbaya. As if there's more to it than just me, like it's another part of me, attached yet separate; my…other self.

Salty tears reach my lips. This is it. The ancient blood awakening in my veins is guiding me, urging me instinctively skyward. I follow my gut and push myself higher. My hair flutters in the wind of the higher altitude. A rush of heat passes over me. I clench my fists, and I understand.

I can feel the sun's energy—not on my skin, but a tingling sensation within me. I'm connected to it as if I'm part of it, or rather my other self is. The awesome power of our life-giving star is reaching out to the planet, reaching out to *me*, and a thought grows inside. I can control it, deflect it. Finally, after a decade of uncertainty, I know what must be done.

I must become the earth's shield.

My aura hits an invisible roof and spreads out across the Montana skyline.

I can see way more than I should, as if I'm flying, speeding over the earth in all directions.

It's incredible: the dark green foothills below me, Lincoln, the lights of Great Falls, the snow-topped mountains, the fields littered with crops, the ocean, the dense forests, the lakes and islands, a rugged coastline, and then another ocean, the Atlantic.

My consciousness—my other self's consciousness—is surging across the earth, and I can see it as if I'm there myself.

I'm doing it. I'm going to succeed. My shield of violet energy is encasing the planet and using the sun's own destructive force to power it.

I feel a vibration, a dull hum or something that spikes every time I pass over a city. If I had a mirror, I'm sure I'd see my hair standing on end from the static electricity surging over my skin.

I'm flying over it all—all of North America and spreading my shield over the oceans.

My hand jerks like I've been stabbed. No, burned.

Physically my hand's fine, but it aches down to the bone. My other hand jerks, followed by both my feet. I try to cry out, but my throat is too dry to coax a sound from it. I'm not bleeding or charred, but I might as well be.

My entire leg jerks. This time sound leaves my lips, and I know what's happening to my limbs. The shield is an extension of me, of my power, and it's being attacked—retreating from the crimson aura destroying it.

Dad is fighting me.

He's using the sun's power as I am, but he's got the amulet. I can sense it, feel it like I'm back on Lukas's porch. The power of the amulet, willed by the Last Atlantean to assault my very essence, is trying to take over.

I've lost the Atlantic. It's gone. I can't see it. I've lost a lot: the Caribbean, the Gulf of Mexico, that strip of sea below California, they're all gone.

My heart pounds in my chest.

Vegas, there's Vegas. I recognize that famous fountain outside a hotel from the movie where Brad Pitt stood by it with a slew of actors after pulling off an impossible heist.

I have to win too…hold the line at Vegas.

My hands and feet burn more than fire could ever do to them. I hear myself scream.

He won't push me back further. I can't let Dad do this. I have to push him back. Make *his* limbs burn. I have to show him…exactly…who…I…am.

I draw a line. My other self draws it with me against the crimson wave. My head cranes skyward. My limbs reach out as far as they can. My nails dig into my palms and my chest rumbles with a roar I set free.

The crimson assault stops in its tracks. A primeval head-butting of source energy parts the very air in a shockwave where I'm pushing back, where I'm winning.

Instantly all tension leaves my hands and feet followed by my arms and legs. I'm limp. Have I won? Have I lost?

The horizon flashes with an amber glow. I'm in agony, being attacked more so than anything Dad has done. I curl into a ball in an attempt to stop my nerve endings from screaming.

It doesn't help. The amber surges toward me. It's the sun's flare.

Dad's using its awesome power better than I am. He's guiding it, stripping away my control of it. It's no longer aiding me; it too is attacking my shield.

I force my limbs to straighten, to take on a pose of power and confidence.

I push back with all I have, screaming with every bit of energy I possess to stand my ground, to hold onto Vegas. Amber flashes above me, surging over my violet shield, and is deflected into space.

I'm exhausted beyond what I thought was possible, and my shield falls, dissipating above me to leave the night sky filled with stars.

I collapse, powerless, and plummet toward the ground.

Chapter Twenty-Nine

"Shhh. It's okay," Kara's voice reassures me, her fingers tracing through my hair. Kara's fingers? She's alive? I'm alive? "You did it, Scar. Just relax, I've got you."

"Where?"

"We're safe."

I wipe the crust from my eyes and my vision clears. We're in a tiny wood cabin, an old one, from the looks of the rough-cut slats that form the walls. It's more like an upscale hunting shack or a hermit's home that has been long deserted. There's a dingy window with faint moonlight trying to shine through the grime on it, a small table with two stools, and a single cot so worn out its springs poke my ribs. It's warm thanks to the fire flickering in a rusty old wood stove. Something fragrant fills the air and makes my stomach growl. Kara has rescued me once again. "What happened?"

Kara tucks my hair behind my ear. "You did it. You lit up the night better than the Fourth of July and stopped Armageddon." She stands up from sitting on the edge of the cot and the bed frame creaks. "Of course, you needed me to save your hide. I had to catch you with the wind so you didn't break your neck. You're making a habit of needing me to save your ass, you know, and frankly, it's getting tiresome. I think next time I'll let you fend for yourself." She smirks. It's nice to see she's in good spirits; it's infectious and it raises mine.

"What do you mean I did it?" I sit up, pushing the tattered wool blanket off me. "The last thing I saw was Dad's crimson energy pushing against mine, followed by a flash of light from the sun."

"Yeah. It was cool." From the top of the wood stove Kara picks up a blue pot speckled with white. "I didn't see any crimson, only your purple cloud taking over the sky. When that wicked bright flash hit it and I was still alive to catch you, I knew you did an *okay job*." She winks, pours the pot's steaming contents into a matching cup.

Did I win? Did I actually save the planet? I fought Dad and the sun over Vegas, not the entire planet.

"Whatever you did, worked," Kara adds. "We're alive, birds are still singing, grass is still growing." She hands me the cup and sits on a stool at the table.

I draw in a long deep breath. Did I save the earth as I was prophesized to? I had the battle of my life, energy wise. I'm still spent, weak, and drained. My eyes feel as if they're sunk deep into my sockets from lack of sleep, but it's worth it if I used my newfound power, my other self, to shield the earth.

I let myself breathe out, and along with the air my decade long burden weighs less heavy in my chest.

"Mom was right about the blackout, though," Kara says, spinning her phone on the table. "It's been a might bit boring watching you sleep for two nights with no one but those horses of yours to keep me company. I swear, if I have to ride one of those again, I'll scream. Especially if I have to do it while lugging your dead weight around. You know how hard it is to *drive* those things dangling carrots in front of their noses with you in my arms?"

"I've been out for two nights?" The power I put out drained me that much? The fact that I'm this bagged worries me about ever having to use my power on that grand of a scale again.

"I swear you snore loud enough to scare away any bears in the area."

"But Kara. Your phone doesn't work. Not at all?"

She shakes her head.

Please tell me you just can't charge it out here in this cabin, and that you killed the battery googling the world's response to my battle with the sun and Dad. "Did it die?"

"Yeah."

"Thank God. For a second there I thought you were gonna say it died when I did…my thing." I sip the tea she gave me. It's more comforting than flavorful. No more than a mix of hot water, pine needles, and fresh-picked blackberries floating on the top.

"It did."

I freeze. What if I didn't stop Armageddon entirely? What if something *did* get through my shield? Not the full force of the sun's flare, but its electromagnetic pulse. "Then why'd your phone die?"

"I'm guessing it got fried from all the electricity you were putting out. You were like one of those sparkling globes from a science lab. Hell, I think even my hair was standing on end a bit."

That could be possible, I guess. I hope that's what did it. "Not an EMP like you read about." I pluck a plump blackberry from my tea and chew it down. The look on Kara's face puts a pit in my stomach. She hadn't thought about that. "Kara…how close are we to a city or something?"

"We're deep in the hills, far from any road. There's a town in the distance, though."

We both go for the door. The air's thick with the scent of pine trees surrounding the tiny cabin. I was right about the cabin being abandoned. The trees have grown so close to it that it's hard to see a constellation through their branches. "Where's the town?"

"This way." Kara sparks a flame in her hand, uses it like a torch, and leads us past the pair of pegasuses up the hill to a clearing. She points into the night. "It's right over there."

There's nothing but endless darkness aside from her makeshift torch. Kara wouldn't have been able to find it in the dark, but my vamp eyes make out the silhouette of a town that couldn't have more than a couple hundred people living in it. Not a single light shines from it. Maybe it was too late at night for anyone to be up. "What time would you say it is?"

"Sun should be up soon. It's probably five or six, but it's kinda hard to tell. You don't think?"

"Yeah, I do." I do think Kara isn't entirely correct when she said I did it. I may not have let the earth fry, but something got through. Something like the blackouts in the past, but the power was back on within a few hours of those solar storms, unlike now.

Far off in the northwest, a tiny ball of crimson light slowly streaks skyward like the space shuttle creeping toward the atmosphere. It's so small I'm certain Kara can't pick it out from the sea of stars. "I think Dad may have won after all."

The tiny ball of crimson tells me he's far from completing his plans, and he still has his sights set on world domination. If that's the case, then my work is far from finished. Prophesized to save the world. Fire from above. Dad's crimson energy mixed with the sun's flare looked a hell of a lot like a raging fire. I can't help but wonder if *Dad*, not the sun's flare, is the true enemy that I'm prophesied to stop.

Chapter Thirty

The sun rises into the morning sky. Kara and I haven't moved from the ridge or said much. We just sit there in the grass, watching the tiny town for signs of life in the valley below us. No light comes from it before sunrise. No vehicles move about its streets, or on the highway connecting it to Lincoln. There are people mulling about in the town, but there's nothing to indicate an EMP didn't take out the power grid, among other things. Lincoln is much larger than the town we're staring at, and I decide it should be our first stop. I need to know if it's as dead as this town is, electricity wise.

The knot in my stomach hasn't subsided; it's moved up into my throat. What kind of world are we living in now? One without power. Surely that can be switched on soon enough. But something in the back of my brain gnaws at me. How my shield retreated, and only covered a radius around me reaching as far as Vegas, not the entire planet. My imagination tries to take over, showing me fields of ashes, crumbling cities, and charred bodies. I have to fight to push down the thoughts and be rational. Use reasoning and the information at hand to make logical decisions, not react to fear.

Kara suggests that the reason no one is traveling on the highway is because martial law is in effect. I hope she's right, but I doubt a curfew would be set during the day. The government, military, and the Broadsword are still searching for us as far as I know. I decide to make use of our winged horses despite Kara's threat to scream, and lead the way, winding through the hills, keeping low so as not to be spotted, searching for a good vantage point to check out Lincoln.

Lincoln's eery. Void of any sign of technology.

No OPEN FOR BUSINESS signs are lit up and no vehicles move. The town would have looked deserted if it weren't for its residents making their way to the school on foot or by bicycle. Not a single person is on their phone.

A faint hum comes from the north, grows louder.

I point in the direction for Kara, as her hearing isn't as attuned as mine. It's the rumble of an engine pulling a rusty old farm truck along the highway. Kara's wrong about the curfew, or the fellow driving the truck has blown through a blockade. Either way, it's the first sign of any working technology—and it's a welcome sight—until I make out the soldiers dressed in camo riding in the back.

The truck pulls up to the school, and six soldiers jump out of the back of the pickup. The townspeople file onto the football field as if there's a game about to start. We get as close as we can on our pegasuses, then leave them among some trees and file into the crowd. I get Kara to mumble us some disguises.

We stand in the crowd trying to look nervous and confused, as she's made us out to be a pair of tourists who don't speak very good English. It's her idea—hide in plain sight with a guise that no one would question. Two college girls with thick Russian accents out to see the Wild West, stranded on the road when the light show hit, and unable to communicate without broken sentences. Kara's idea is the perfect disguise as to why we're new in town and puts the townsfolk who approach us at ease.

The soldiers are at center field speaking with a short dumpy man I guess to be the mayor, and by his side stands a long-necked woman with her hands on her hips, chirping continuously. I can't help but think of my conversation with Lukas at the diner, and that this woman is probably the sheriff's wife who gossips to no end.

It never ceases to amaze me at how people become accustomed to routine. Not another soul other than the players are allowed on the field during game time. And during a crisis, the same is true for those in charge having been surrounded by people with their toes as close to the out-of-bounds line as possible. They're remarkably calm considering their entire world has shifted overnight, over two nights, whether they know it or not. I guess knowing your neighbor along with all their secrets has its privileges. I've no doubt that if Lincoln were a larger city full of strangers, its stores and homes would be looted by the greedy with the scared following, having no mind of their own to tell them not to jump off the proverbial bridge.

About ten minutes pass with no one else strolling onto the sidelines. I guess the entire town has shown up. I recognize Sue, the kind woman who served Lukas and I breakfast, and the silver-haired man from the liquor store. The big-bellied sheriff who pulled me over walks onto the field along with the two cops, whose names I can't recall, who questioned us at Lukas's ranch. The dumpy mayor waves his hat in the air. The crowd continues gossiping until the long-necked woman whistles to silence the town's folk.

The mayor gives a brief speech broken apart by the busybody adding her two cents. "Let me remind you all of what we spoke about yesterday. Stay calm…don't overreact. Help your neighbour, conserve water, every thing will be business as usual. Credit card machines and ATM's are down so cash only. You don't have cash, barter or trade. There will be no looting or hoarding. Share with each other. We'll get through this together as a town.

I sway side to side, impatiently rubbing my hands together, waiting for the soldiers to speak. The crowd for the most part doesn't interrupt the mayor's speech. They speak between themselves, but no one shouts out like you see during a debate for the presidency.

Finally, the mayor introduces the head Army guy as First Lieutenant Niclas Huntly. He looks like a Niclas—English, Scottish, or Irish I suspect, due to his red hair. Despite being no more than forty, the lieutenant has a stern look about him that demands respect. His short-cropped hair and chiseled jaw along with his rigid composure make me think he keeps his unit under a hard-pressed thumb. He waits for everyone in the crowd to fall silent before he addresses the people of Lincoln in a deep booming voice that easily carries across the field.

"These are the facts, people. The power is out. Nothing electronic is operational. Neither is anything mechanical that operates on a digital system. What is still operational is anything analog, or non-digital. That's why that old truck is still running. It has no electronic fuel injection. No electronic brain. At the moment we do not know what caused this, and no one will start to panic."

Lieutenant Huntly's words say what I don't want to truly believe. But he's right—it's as if the entire valley, if not a wider area, has been hit with an EMP.

Kara said that I gave off a crazy amount of electricity that fried her phone. I hoped she was right and that's all it was, but I doubt *I* could put out enough of a surge to power down a town, especially since I was conjuring my shield…but the sun could have.

"With that being said, the first step in any military operation is to assess the situation and establish communication," the lieutenant continues. "That is exactly what we've been doing in the surrounding towns, and all the people of Lincoln are going to assist us with that objective here. Does anybody here have experience in repairing vehicles?"

Three men raise their hands.

"Take who you need to assist you and get as many vehicles as you can up and operational, and once you do, bring them here. The school is now our base of operations. You people know what you have in your homes. If it is any form of communication equipment, preferably something that runs on batteries, bring them here as well, and we will assess them."

Not a single person speaks to one another; it's clear the lieutenant is now their coach, and they are his players. He's a natural leader, and that puts a pang in my stomach. These people will follow him blindly. A mob armed with pitchforks and torches comes to mind. I'm starting to see why Dad turned Lukas's ranch into a stronghold; I might need one.

"Martial law is still in effect. As is the curfew until we hear otherwise. My men and I will be working alongside your mayor to both coordinate and safeguard Lincoln, along with any neighboring towns. We do not know when the power will come back on, so we will act as if it never will, rationing the supplies Lincoln has to offer." He's well-trained. "As for the events at the stadium two nights ago..."

Here it comes, instructions for the mob to bear their pitchforks.

"…specifically, the women who displayed abilities we cannot yet explain..."

Light your torches and hunt them down.

"I want them alive and unharmed."

I didn't see that coming.

"If they can shed some light on what's happened, I want to give them the opportunity to do so. No one, I repeat, no one is to engage them. Report their location back to me and my men and I will confront them. Are there any intelligent questions?"

A slew of hands shoots into the air, but only one voice calls out. A feminine one. "Do you have any leads on where these women are right now?" The question comes from a young woman across the field. Even at this distance I can make out her grayish undertone, and her glare.

She's staring directly at Kara and me as if we aren't disguised at all, and she's working her lips, but no words reach my ears.

She's mumbling.

Chapter Thirty-One

"Get ready to run." Kara's voice in my head is loud and clear, and a bit panicked. I take her hand in mine, squeezing it tight. Stay put. We need to hear what Lieutenant Huntly has to say, and an all-out brawl with this witch in front of his soldiers is the last thing I want even though the lieutenant told the crowd not to engage us. I scan the crowd for the witch's counterpart. I doubt she's alone; the members of Broadsword never are.

"Do not draw any attention to yourself," whispers a voice at our backs.

Kara's instinct to flee washes over me, adding to mine. I turn my head to find a spitting image of Lieutenant Huntly, but with black hair and gray skin. I have to fight the urge to spin around with my fists flying, but his eyes have no malice in them, no indication of intent to stab me in the back. It's as if I'm staring into a hollow void, emotionless, and missing something deep within. The fact he doesn't want the crowd knowing we're here—or perhaps that *he's* here—confuses me. The Broadsword had no issue coming out in the public eye at the rodeo, so what's changed? Is it Dad? His promise none of his followers would harm me?

"That's where you people come in," says Lieutenant Huntly. "You are to be my eyes and ears."

"He's lying," the man behind us whispers.

Kara squeezes my hand tighter.

"They know of the sanctuary your father built for you. These men cannot be trusted."

"And you can?" Kara says forcefully.

"Your father decreed it. We are at your command. Now calm your energies before you make a scene."

He isn't talking to Kara, he's talking to me, and my other self. Kara's mumbling. So is the witch across the field. I can feel my other self following my instinct to protect me, protect us. I must be shrouded in a violet field as the Broadsword's hand is hovering an inch off my shoulder, unable to make contact.

Kara's mumbling—at me. Same as the witch across the field. They must be working together to conceal my other self because no one has pointed and screamed at me, yet.

Kara's hot-tempered, but at this moment in time she's more level-headed than I am; working with the Broadsword to ensure we don't stand out in the crowd. I have to follow her lead and calm myself for Kara's sake.

I shut my eyes. The lieutenant's speech, still ongoing, drifts away from my attention. I draw in a slow breath and shudder on its release.

"I am called Markus. I am at your command. Right now, it's best we leave this place, my lady," he says, bowing.

~ * ~

It's easier than I expect to slip away from the crowd as the townspeople throw a barrage of questions at Lieutenant Huntly. The witch, a slender woman with her short blonde hair done up in a mom cut, joins up with us before we reach the edge of town. I don't know what to think, what to feel, or even what to do other than keep Kara by my side. The Broadsword has hunted us mercilessly, and here they are by my side to protect me thanks to a few words from Dad? Really?

I call them on it, my lack of believing they've got my best interests in mind, then Markus tells us how Dad sent out one final group text before the power went out.

Get to Lincoln, Montana. There you shall find my daughter, Scarlett. Protect her and her castle with your lives. I have created a safe haven for her. Fortify it and do as she asks. You, my Soulless, are hers until you draw your last breath, or until I command you otherwise. Any Broadsword not within fifty miles of Lincoln, continue with the original plan.

I make Markus repeat the text to me three times. Not a word changes, nor does it differ when I ask Laurel, the witch Broadsword, to do the same. I still have trouble believing it, or them. So does Kara. "We need proof more than your word that you're loyal to us," I tell them.

"We need a test," Kara suggests.

"Like what? Have them stand on their heads?"

"Have them cut off their own hands," Kara says, glaring at them.

She wants proof, and I get it, though I'm a bit taken aback by her proposed method. Still, I can't think of a better way for them to prove themselves. After all, there are plenty of the Broadsword left in the world—and they're all coming here, coming to me, at least those in a fifty-mile radius. I'm not sure what that part of Dad's message meant, *Continue with the original plan*, but I'll find that out soon enough. Right now, we need unrenouncing proof of loyalty. Part of me still wants to go on the hunt for them as I had originally planned, until I got our asses kicked. Recalling my burns makes my decision about Kara's suggestion easy. "You heard her," I say. "Cut a hand off."

Blades whip out of sheaths, high into the air, and come down fast toward their own outstretched arms.

"Stop!" I scream.

I'm not sure if it's to stop them from mutilating themselves or because they're so close to us, slashing swords about. Either way, I'm not fast enough.

"Markus!" cries Laurel. She's unscathed, but Markus was faster than she was.

Markus grits his teeth and drops his sword, stained with blood.

"Is that proof enough?" Laurel asks, tears welling in her eyes. "Let me see." She reaches for Markus's arm. Reluctantly, he lets go of his wrist. The thumb size slice of missing flesh from its top oozes blood. He was fast enough to turn his amputating stroke into a glancing nick—a wide one, but not deep. Amazingly he hasn't said a word, not to me, or Laurel. He curls his lips in, pressing them together, breathing slow and heavy through his nose. "Open your fist."

Markus complies and his fingers reach out.

Laurel sighs, "You chipped the bone, but didn't hit anything vital that I can see." She holds his forearm with one hand, reaches into Markus's jacket with the other, then pulls out a small first aid tin. "Keep pressure."

Markus wraps his good hand around his wound. His blade came down on the top of his wrist, not the meaty bottom with all the tendons and strings and things that work the fingers. The look in his eyes screams *bitch* at me, yet he holds his tongue. His silence, Laurel's rushed speech, her sporadic movements as she sterilizes him, and her watery eyes make me feel like crap. They're human, well…a witch and a human. But they aren't the merciless, unflinching, blood-thirsty, emotionless boogeymen they've been made out to be. At least this pair isn't. Kara stays silent, but I can see on her face she feels the same as I do.

"I'm sorry. I just—" I start.

"I understand, my lady," says Markus through gritted teeth. Laurel runs a curved needle through his skin, closing the gash. "I would have done the same thing if I were in your position. Thank you for stopping us when you did." His gaze moves from me to Laurel. "Are you okay?" His whispering makes me think they're more than just partnered assassins.

"Don't worry about me," says Laurel, shaking her head.

"That's what I do." He glances to me, then back to Laurel.

My past tells me to order them to kill each other, but the look of these two, their grayish flesh and tending to each other, tells me I'm the heartless one for giving them the order to dismember themselves. They've proven their loyalty. Who else in their right mind would try to cut off their own hand? I take his words as saying she is his number-one priority, and it pangs him that because of Dad's command he must put me ahead of her.

"I guess they can stay. Scar?" Kara says in less than her usual confident voice.

I nod. I don't trust them, not entirely, but orders are orders, and Dad gave me complete control over their lives. Keeping a close eye on them is a must. I can't just turn off a decade's worth of mistrust because of a single act of obedience, but an army of the Broadsword at my command could come in handy if the townsfolk form an angry mob despite Lieutenant Huntly's orders. I have to think logically, after all. Like I'm critiquing a movie looking for holes in the backstory of a new ally. But there's something that gnaws at me aside from my conflict about my would-be protectors. Dad's words to them in his text. He called them his Soulless. They're alive, but not really, not when I look into their eyes that seem to have something missing behind them. And their skin tone does resemble that of a fresh corpse. It creeps me out.

They creep me out.

So, I decide to distance myself from them to give me some much-needed time to wrap my head around this, with the only person who has a chance of understanding what I'm feeling. "When you're patched up, make your way to the Sutherland Ranch." I point in the direction of Lukas's farm. "Discreetly."

Markus nods.

"Come on, Kara," I say, climbing on the back of my pegasus. She doesn't complain this time, just follows my lead. I guess she needs some time to process this as well.

We fly in silence. It's needed. Kara's proximity is enough to calm me without a word. I figure I did the same for her as her cheeks lose the angered blood rush she had when the Broadsword escorted us out of town.

We crest the hill of the valley that holds Lukas's farm and my jaw drops, literally. Dad had returned to the farm since we left it.

Between Lukas's house and the out-of-place medieval wall, nestled in the field's center is a freakin' castle.

Chapter Thirty-Two

As I fly over the wall Dad built around Lukas's ranch, the tiny castle in the center of the field comes into focus. It looks as if it's been standing for centuries, grayed in the shadow, hints of moss here and there on the north side. It's nothing like the pristine stone wall surrounding Lukas's ranch. Standing about five stories high at its peak, with another wall surrounding it, the castle looks archaic. Its construction is simple: a wall with a single gate designed in the same fashion as the one surrounding the ranch, just smaller. One single building spread out over a city block with a main tower in the middle. No imagination has been put into it; Hollywood wouldn't have used it even in a B movie.

Kara's so shocked she stops mumbling. The carrots in front of our horses drop and they start to veer off in the directions they please until Kara materializes the carrots again. We fly over the cobblestone road leading from the outer wall to the castle's, past Lukas's house, and set down just outside in the field.

The courtyard inside is shockingly unexpected. Lush, full of berry bushes and fruit trees that I'm not entirely sure will be able to handle the inevitable harsh Montana winter.

"How could he do this?" I ask.

"There's no way there was this much rock in the ground. I suspected it when he made the wall, but I'm sure of it now."

"What?"

"Growing the crystal chairs from the elements is one thing I've heard of, but our swords, the walls, the weapons, the castle, now this…" Kara plucks a plump orange from a tree, inspecting it, sniffing it, and tossing it aside. "He's changing matter into whatever he wants."

I'm stunned. More than that, I'm speechless. If he can do that, what can't he do?

"I know," says Kara. I'm thinking it, but she verbalizes it. "I *really* hope he's not going to change his mind and come after us."

"There's no point in that. We already had our world-changing head-butting match."

"So, do we leave? Hit the road and don't look back?"

Kara knows magic, and just as much about my dad as I do, making her far more qualified than me to make the decision of staying here. Really, why would we? This is a gigantic target. But…"If there's no power, and the hills are swarming with people hunting us—not to mention Sergeant Strict over there—then having a fortified bunker to take refuge in isn't really a bad thing."

"We're staying, then?"

"I say we give it a night, sleep on it, decide in the morning."

"It's not as if we have any other place to go. If all else fails, we can take off on those scary-assed horses you made."

She's right, and I'm starting to see that she often is. And like she said, we have our pegasuses. "Okay, one night."

Kara leads the pegasuses inside the castle's walls with her carrots, and immediately upon the carrots vanishing they begin to graze on the lush grass of the courtyard, far greener than the field surrounding the castle. I can't help but feel a sense of familiarity from the castle. It's as if my other self knows this is a place of refuge.

We make our way across the courtyard and through a set of arched double doors leading into the grand hall. It's like I'm home, yet there's an odd sense that gives me goosebumps.

A dozen spheres almost as big as me hang perfectly spaced along the shiny black wall that rises at least two stories to the ceiling. The spheres cast a golden hue through out the hall that mixes with flickering light from a huge fire burning in an open pit at its center. At the far end of the hall is a large stone table, and behind it is a single chair, more like a throne, made of sparkly white specks with veins of gold swirling throughout it.

Silent and bewildered, we exchange looks as we make our way through the castle, poking our heads into rooms until we finally find a wide staircase leading to the top floor. Which is one single bedroom large enough to rival most houses. It isn't until we're on the wrap-around balcony overlooking Lukas's land that I speak from the heart. Something is gnawing at me, and I have to get it out. "There's something wrong with my dad."

"You think?"

"I know I shouldn't care, but—"

"But he tried to kill us and the entire planet. He's bat-shit crazy, Scar."

"I don't think it's his fault."

"Okay." Kara sighs. "I'll bite. Why do you think Daddy dearest is innocent of attempted genocide?"

Kara's harsh. I can't blame her. But I have to trust my gut. "When I touched his amulet, I felt…a presence. Something evil. Like give-you-nightmares-for-the-rest-of-your-life kind of evil." I run my thumb back and forth over my other hand as I lean on the balcony, searching for words.

Kara makes to speak but shuts her lips and waits.

"He swapped personalities before our eyes," I finally say, more to the railing than to Kara as I attempt to make sense of what my gut is telling me. "His posture, his demeanor, his voice, even his actions are sporadic."

"Like sicking the Broadsword on us and then turning them into your personal lap dogs. Or giving us this." Kara waves her palm over the courtyard. I nod. "He's bat-shit, Scar. If you can believe a word he said, he'd be thousands of years old. He's a witch, or a warlock, or whatever. We don't live that long." Frustration's setting into Kara's voice. I know immortality is always a sore subject between vamps and witches, but I can't recall a time she let it show. "I mean—"

"I get it."

We both stare out over Lukas's cattle milling about, neither of us wanting to admit she is going to die eventually, and our bond will be broken. And if what our moms told us was true, I *am* going to lose all control over my actions without Kara. I *am* going to snap. Maybe even follow in Dad's footsteps. That scares me, the thought of losing my mind. Ending up like Dad with a massive split personality disorder is not what I envisioned my life turning out to be. 'Course he's got the amulet, which doesn't seem to help him in staying sane, and I touched it as well. Part of me wants to be the first to go and let Kara outlive me, but then I'd be subjecting her to spending the remainder of her life in a straitjacket.

"So, what are you gonna do?"

"I don't know." The truth is, I do. I want neither of us to go nuts. I want to find a way to strip our bond away so we don't. I want to find Dad and free him of the damned Atlantean plaguing him. I want to know what he was up to when I saw that crimson ball of energy shooting into space the other night. I want to hide away from the world, now that my birthday has passed, and curl up with a good book.

But most of all, I find myself not wanting to be alone. Reading or not, I want companionship. And if I have to take on the government, the Army, and this Last Atlantean to find it, then I will. Even if it's for a short time, and it's with Kara, and I end up going mad in seventy years or so, I want it.

"Well, let's start with dinner. I'm hungry, and I don't know about you, but I could use a drink." That's the best idea I've heard all day, and I tell her so. "You think your old man stocked a wine cellar in this joint?"

"Even if he didn't, Lukas's fridge still had some beer in it."

"And some food if it hasn't spoiled yet."

I hadn't thought about that. The power's been out for two days, and I doubt anything in a fridge or freezer would have survived in the July heat. My stomach grumbles at the notion of not being filled. "Let's see what he's got."

We make our way down through the castle. The moment I set foot in the throne room I feel uneasy again. Thankfully that passes when we step outside. Kara plucks an apple from a tree and studies it. "Why do I feel like a princess who's about to fall asleep if I take a bite of this?" She chucks the apple aside. "If those two Broadswords follow your orders, get them to sample every fruit and berry in here. I'm not gonna kick because your dad...well, you know."

Went crazy. I know, Kara. I just hope the proverbial apple *did* fall far from the tree.

I can't convince Kara to get on her pegasus any time soon unless we absolutely needed to. Which is a shame. I'm growing fond of the magnificent-winged horses. So, to appease her we leave them in the courtyard to graze.

The walk is calming and quiet. We make it to Lukas's farmhouse an hour or two before sunset, and the second we open the door to Lukas's house the stench of rotting food makes me pull back. Kara mumbles some fresh air throughout the house, and that helps a bit, but if we are going to stay here for any length of time, the fridge has to go. There's no point in cleaning it out so I haul it outside and prop it up against the barn, pull out any beer and set them down to air out. Kara jests about me being the heavy lifter and her the brains in our relationship. Being out of the castle and back in civilization has lifted her spirits, and mine. I haul out the kitchen garbage to a burn barrel out back. She yearns for luxury at a five-star hotel, and it appears as if she'll do her best to get that out of Lukas's home when she mumbles the house full of her lilac scent and flashes every candle along with the fireplace to life. From the looks of the house, Lukas hasn't returned from his aunt and uncle's place since he left.

Kara eyes a bowl of fruit on the table and I guess the fresh memory of the apple in the courtyard tells her to leave it be as she turns up her nose at it. She finds some jerky, chews some down, and tucks a jar of peanuts under her arm. "The red should go nicely with this feast." She kicks a foot out at the wine rack built into the island as she grabs a pair of glasses, goes outside, and plops down on the deck. She's trying. But it must be gnawing at her like it is me. With no power we have no refrigeration, gas, heat, or running water. I know it's a trivial thought, especially with all that's going on, but I can't help it. I want a shower—a hot, steaming one. One that will wash away my worries if only for a short period. I grab the bottle of wine Kara kicked at, unscrew the top, join her on the porch, and pour us some very full glasses. At least I have my Ducati. Rather, Lukas's dirt bike that looks like my Ducati. I raise my glass. "Here's to life's luxuries."

"Yep, we're living the dream." Kara clinks my glass and downs half her wine. She's trying.

"Someone's coming."

"You got ears like a hound dog, you know that?" Kara polishes off her glass. "Army dudes?"

"Sounds like Ben's truck." Sure enough it is. He and Lukas drive through the gate of the outer wall with the setting sun at their backs. "Guess we should close that."

"We'll get them to do it."

I smile, mainly at how the second a man shows up, she's got a task for him to perform for her. I give Kara the bottle and go inside to find a couple beers for the guys that don't reek of rotten food and find a half full case in one of the cupboards. The beer is warm, but considering the circumstances, I don't think they'll mind.

The guys step out of Ben's old truck as I walk outside. "How are you holding up?" I say, tossing them each a beer.

"Better now." Ben cracks his beer and takes a big chug of it. He clears his throat and grimaces.

"Fridge is toast," says Kara, filling up her glass, then pointing with the bottle toward the fridge leaning against the barn. "But the wine's a perfect temperature."

"Wine hurts too much," replies Ben.

"*Ahhh muffin.*" Kara's such a tease—and a flirt, more so than I could ever be. "How's this?" She mumbles, and the beer can in Ben's hand frosts.

He looks at it, stunned, takes a sip, and says, "Don't know how I ever got along without you."

Kara winks at him and takes another slug of wine.

"You ladies all right?" Lukas asks.

I can't think of what to say, so I wrap my arms around him, kiss him. He's so warm and such a good kisser I could lose myself in his embrace, so I pull back before he can get excited, or I do. "We'll make it," I say.

"I like what you've done with the place," Lukas says, nodding at the castle. "Really upped the property value."

"That was Dad," I tell him. "You don't seem that shocked to find a castle where your field was."

"Oh, we were, the first time we saw it."

"Damn right," says Ben, hoisting up his beer.

"Work never stops on a ranch, but I guess I never have to check the fences again." Lukas points a thumb at the outer wall.

"So, what have you boys been up to while the women were busy saving the world?" Kara asks.

Before either of them can answer, a lone howl echoes throughout the valley, sending a chill up my spine despite the July heat. It's far too deep to be made by a coyote. I look at Kara. She knows it too.

"We should close that gate," she says.

Chapter Thirty-Three

The cry of a wolf—not a normal one made by nature—marks the signature of a long night to follow. Thankfully werewolves rarely travel in packs. If they ever do, they're hunted down and wiped out. That's the only thing useful about the Broadsword: They hunt the wolves as much as vamps and witches do—even more so—but it's hard to tell exactly as the Broadsword is very good at covering up the remnants of a battle, along with their existence. "You guys better load your guns."

"Why do you make me think that's not a normal wolf's howl?" asks Lukas.

"Because it isn't," Kara answers. "Scar, you see anything?" She stands from the deck, abandoning her wine, wrapping her fingers around the railing.

"Nothing between us and the wall but cows." It stands to reason this wolf is at our doorstep because of Lukas's cattle. Directionless, bloodthirsty beasts that think with nothing but their bellies, wolves wouldn't be able to resist a thousand-pound steak roaming about. A barbed wire fence wouldn't slow a wolf, but the high walls around Lukas's ranch should be able to. "Can you mumble that thing shut from here?" I ask Kara, indicating the gate.

"You're the one with all the power."

That's a no.

"I could blow the doors around maybe, but working whatever latch locks it will have to be done by hand," she offers.

"I'll go." Ben puffs out his chest, no doubt trying to further impress Kara by showing bravery.

"That's sweet, babe," says Kara. "But unless you got silver in those guns, you're just gonna piss off a wolf if one comes at you. No, we got this." Kara mumbles her Trans Am back to its refurbished condition as she walks down the steps. As particular as she is for luxury, I'm grateful she never chipped her car to give it more kick. Guess she's as particular about her ride as I am. "Oh fire chicken, oh fire chicken," she chants, running her hand over the phoenix emblem on the hood. "Protect us, oh fire chicken. Get us there and back safely, and if need be, hand out a lickin'." She loves that car like I loved my bike.

"I'll take the bike in case we need an extra set of wheels."

"If we're leaving anything behind it'll be that." Kara points at my bike.

"Load up whatever you think will be useful into your truck," I tell the guys. "We're staying in the castle tonight."

As much as I want to pretend we're still living in a modern world, I know the reality of it. The more walls between a wolf and yourself, the better. Especially if those walls are high, smooth, and made of stone. Part of me thanks Dad, silently.

~ * ~

My heart pounds as we speed toward the gate. I've killed three wolves in my lifetime, but I always had help—Mom was a formidable hunter. To say the wolves are strong and fast is an understatement. I just hope Kara and I are strong enough together. Again, I find myself thanking Dad for the silver sword hanging from my hip. Kara insisted we bring them just in case, and I agreed without hesitation. I never thought of her as the sword-wielding type, but we all have our little fantasies, I guess.

Violet flashes in my side mirror. My other self must sense my concern as I'm trailing wisps of it behind me. Maybe we will be enough. Kara turns on her brights, stopping a couple of yards from the gate. "Stay in the car," I say, pointing at her.

"Like hell." Her words are muffled from inside of the car, but I make them out. "You'll need all the eyes you can get, vamp vision or not." She's right.

I run to the open gate. The towering oak doors are simple enough. *Shut them and brace them.* A pack would make short work of it if left alone, but it would slow them down. Although a single wolf could work at it until sunup and possibly get through. What I really want is to close the iron gate that separates the doors from the outside. It's mocking me, sticking out of the wall by only two feet, making me wish we had inspected it earlier in the day and, more importantly, how to work it.

"Any thoughts?" I say.

"There's gotta be a crank or something. A mechanism that slides it in place. *There*." On the wall, just before the stairs leading up to the foot-walk, is a wheel the size of a trash-can lid. A long steel handle sticks out of it. Kara takes hold of the handle and grunts. The wheel spins around once and the gate creaks forward an inch. "Come on muscles, gimme a hand."

"Good girl." I run to her and put my strength to work. Kara backs off when I start to spin it faster then she can keep up with.

When the gate's three quarters closed, Kara starts to mumble. One of the giant oak doors is hit by a hard gust of wind that pushes it shut over the iron grate. We're doing it! Metal grinds on metal and the wheel comes to a dead stop, successfully closing the iron grate.

A snarl comes from the other side of the grate, followed by a thud.

"Jeez!" Kara shouts, dropping the wood post she's trying to wrestle against the door. She stumbles, falls back.

"Get back! Get to your car!" I shout at her. She's done her part and figured out how to operate the grate, and just in the nick of time. There's no need to keep her in harm's way. She stares at me with wide eyes. I'm not sure if she's ever seen a wolf in person before, but she has now, and it's throwing its shoulder at the iron grate just two steps away. "Go!"

The wolf's gray fur, crimson eyes, and long teeth come in and out of the light from Kara's high beams. The grate vibrates with every hit of the wolf's shoulder. Dad's words repeat in my ears: *Strong enough to withstand a siege for a fortnight.* However long a fortnight is, I'm sure he's right. The iron is so thick that it doesn't even bow from the assault.

Kara scrambles to her feet. I grab hold of the remaining open oak door. Its hinges creak. It's heavy, so heavy I have to kick off the wall to get it to start moving.

The door is sticking straight out from the wall, ready to finish the other half of its path to shutting, when the wolf yelps.

Kara stabbed it through the iron grate with one of the long spears Dad had provided us. I had forgotten about them, but she didn't.

"Die, you rabid dog!" Kara shouts. I guess she dislikes being startled just as much as I do. My response was always to take off in an all-out run. Hers, apparently, is to strike back in a fit of rage.

The wolf backs away, taking the spear with it through the tiny diamond cut-outs in the grate.

I push the door shut. Kara grabs another spear and runs up the stairs to the top of the wall. "What are you doing?" I call out to her.

"Just get that door braced," she says without looking back at me, reaching the foot-walk and looking over its edge. "It's too dark to see it."

Another thud sounds off the grate, followed by scratching. Scratching that's moving up. "It's climbing the grate. Get down here!"

Kara takes aim, throws her spear. If she can't see the wolf she's blindly hoping for a hit.

There's another yelp followed by a dull thud on the other side of the gate.

Kara sprints down the stairs. "Got him twice."

I prop a post against each door.

We look at each other. Kara had hit it, it's off the wall, and the scratching doesn't return.

"Do you believe that just happened?" Kara asks, breathing fast.

I doubt she's expecting an answer, and all I want to do is put as much distance between myself and the wall as possible. "Let's get to the castle."

"Don't gotta tell me twice." Kara barely spits the words out and she's in her car.

Chapter Thirty-Four

We park inside the courtyard and secure the castle's double gates. The guys had grabbed what they deemed necessary: water bottles, various cans of food, a few bottles of wine, two and a half cases of beer, guns, and ammunition—lots of ammunition. Lukas must have been an avid hunter, or his parents were, because his stockpile could arm over a dozen people with rifles.

All our provisions are set out neatly on a stone bench that circles the stairway of the large room in the tower. The guys go over the operation of the rifles with us, "Just in case," Lukas insists. He's a gentleman, doing what he can to make us feel protected and safe, even though the women in his presence are far more powerful than he could ever dream of becoming.

After a few swigs of wine to calm the nerves, mostly Kara's, we tell the guys what happened at the gate. They tell us Ben's dad has kept them busy hunting for coyotes that killed a cow. They thought it had to be a pack, but when I tell them a single wolf would make short work of a cow, they turn white. The realization they could have run into a werewolf brings up bravery in Ben, puffing his chest out, saying it would look good stuffed and hanging over his fireplace. He even says he wasn't disappointed in missing the game he bet money on due to the power outage, while trying to reinforce it was his choice to track down and kill a werewolf. Lukas takes a different approach, begins questioning me about what could take one down—and, more importantly, what can't. I hold up my sword, then tell them, just as Hollywood has portrayed, about how the wolves heal almost instantly and you could literally watch a slash from a sword grow shut in seconds—unless it's from silver, making it harder to heal but not impossible if given enough time. The silver affects them like poison, and it burns their flesh if contact with it isn't broken. Silver bullets would be better than a sword, like poisoned pellets imbedded deep in organs, but since we have none, and they could be used up, I once again find myself grateful for the medieval weapons Dad provided. The swords, the catapults, the crossbows, and the spears would have to be enough if needed.

We should sleep in shifts, I decide, and after my explanation to the guys, there's no objection. We spend the night sleeping two at a time in the single room in the main tower. Kara's dubbed it the queen's chambers; I like it.

The two of us who are awake circle the wrap-around balcony, scanning the fields for any disturbance. Lukas assures me his cows will raise quite the ruckus if a wolf comes bounding at them like guard dogs—big, slow guard dogs with no bite. But they can *beller*, which is what Ben calls their bark.

I make sure I'm the one to take the darkest hours so my night vision can be most effective. We decide Kara and I should never be on the same shift in the event something with a little more oomph than a rifle is needed. It's a sensible move, splitting us up, but since this whole thing began, I've had Kara by my side, and somehow having her slumber just yards away from me doesn't feel close enough.

When dawn finally breaks, I never thought I'd be so happy to see its array of colors. Wolves revert back to their human form during the daylight hours, and I'm tired. I'm sure the others are as well.

Sleeping in broken segments, even a few hours at a time, leaves me groggy. Ben has a stash of instant coffee under the seat of his truck in case of an emergency and this qualifies. I make a fire—with more control than I had under Kara's tutelage—to warm up some water in a cast-iron pot down in the kitchen. Its earthy aroma fills the stone kitchen and wafts up the stairs. Within minutes, all four of us are sipping Ben's emergency brew.

The lack of sugar brings up the unanimous decision to raid Lukas's house of everything it has. The guys even bring the barbecue, though I'm not sure why. It isn't like we have anything to eat that hasn't spoiled, and I doubt Lukas has any designs of slaughtering a cow unless he absolutely has to. Five full half-tons later and Lukas's house is strewn about the castle. We each pick a room of our own—although I doubt we'll be sleeping separate anytime soon, yet it does give me a hint of the old day-to-day life to which I was accustomed. We sit down with canned-ham sandwiches for lunch, and Ben chooses our spot to picnic at, directly above the castle gate. The top of the wall is made into a foot-walk four feet wide and lined with stone teeth to hide behind. The guys have set up four folding lawn chairs.

"So these wolves," Ben says between bites, "you expect we'll see more tonight?"

"Hard to say," I reply. "We could have scared it off, but there's a lot of beef down there. It might move on to easier hunting grounds, it might not."

"I gotta warn my folks, let them know it's a damned werewolf that's stalking their herd," says Ben.

"No," I tell him, surveying our surroundings. "You should bring them here, at least until we deal with it. But just in case, plan for a lengthy stay."

I'm happier than ever that we're surrounded by a double set of walls, especially without another experienced hunter by my side. The guys may be able to hunt, sure, but there's no comparison when it comes to hunting a werewolf.

"I'll come with you." Lukas steps forward. "Uncle Brian's tractor is sure to still be working. We can load up what they have in the trailer and bring back more supplies."

"And wine," says Kara.

"Do you think you can make your way into town and see what the soldiers are up to before you come back?" I ask. "They know we're here, or at least that we were. I'm surprised we haven't seen them yet."

"Can't see anything but hilltops past that wall." Kara nods. "I hate to side with your dad, but he was right. We need to raise an army, our army. That huge wall way over there is useless without people to man it. Let alone tell us if we're under attack."

The more I'm with her, the more I get the sense she's a born warrior, especially after she reacted so fast to the wolf last night. She has a survival instinct that comes naturally to her, one that most don't have. She may yearn for the butler beck and call treatment, but something tells me she'll have no problem surviving the world we live in now.

"Raise an army to fend off *the* Army? How's that gonna work, Kara? Why would anybody want to fight *the* Army, especially on our behalf?"

"'Cause they're wrong. The people think we're the bad guys in all this because the government plastered wanted posters of us all over the news. So, let's show them we're not by using the wolves.

We offer the safety of the castle to the people in exchange for their aid in defending it from them, and as a bonus to us we only allow in any military types who don't want to experiment on us for being special."

"I doubt anybody will buy that."

"Look around, Scar. World's changed. We got to adapt, and so does everyone outside these walls. Any of them wants in, then they'll just have to swear an oath to us."

I get what she's saying, and I'd rather not have the people knocking at our gates with torches and pitchforks. Fight *the* Army? I can't see that working out for anyone. But Kara does have a point. If we could turn the Army, persuade them to work with us in exchange for sanctuary from the wolves, promise they can live beside us in harmony…*that* would be beneficial for everyone. Might give Kara and I the voices we need to convince the powers-that-be to not slice us open to see what makes us tick.

Besides, I'd rather have a formidable force at my side, if I need one, as I try to free Dad from the Last Atlantean. He's sure to come our way, sweeping across the land like a plague if his ambition is to conquer the world.

"Not only protection from the wolves," I tell Kara, "But from Dad and his threat to rule over everyone with a crimson fist." Somehow, altering my perspective as to why we are going to open up the castle makes me feel as if the entire idea didn't stem from Dad. As if I'm in charge of my own destiny, and those around me are my council, advising me on what my options are. Ultimately, however, it's my decision.

"Damn rights, Scar." Kara nods. "Because one thing's for sure, the four of us can't patrol *this* place day in and day out. And after last night, I think I'm gonna need a little more beauty sleep than what I got."

"You're gorgeous to me, darlin'," Ben says, winking at Kara.

Kara blushes. "Clean out Lincoln's liquor store too when you're there." She's trying to flirt back, but I can tell she's still tired and off her game. "We'll stay here and wait for you. But don't keep us waiting too long. A girl has needs, you know." She isn't *that* tired.

"You're right," Lukas says to Kara.

Kara flips her hair over her shoulder. "Of course I am."

"I mean about the wall," Lukas goes on. "We need a way to signal you that we need the gate open, and that it's us. Otherwise, we might as well leave it wide open. For all we know there's a pack of werewolves out there right now—or vampires, or witches, or who knows what. I don't want to invite any of them in with open arms if we can help it."

Lukas brings up a good point, a few good points.

"Use flashlights," I say, waving my hand in front of my sandwich like it's a flashlight. "From the top of the hill outside the gate. That'll work both day or night." Lukas nods in agreement. "If you have any friends in Lincoln, ones who won't be scared to sleep under the same roof as a vamp—"

"And a witch," Kara adds.

"And a witch," I amend, "bring them back here. I promise I won't bite." I grin.

Lukas looks away from me, frowning. I don't get the feeling he's considering candidates who could hold their composure. It's more like he realizes that I kill people and drink blood. Sure, he knows it, but it appears to have sunk in. I haven't fed since I killed Zeke and his brother, and I won't need to for a while. It's not as if I feel guilty about it—I have to kill in order to live—but at the moment I wish I hadn't teased Lukas about it.

"Be careful on the road," I say, trying to shift his train of thought. "The soldiers might want to confiscate your truck."

"Well, lets get to it." Ben wipes his mouth, stands, and gives Kara a peck on the cheek. "We've got a lot to do, and *I want* to be back tonight."

Kara grins. "I'm gonna lie down." She stands up, running a finger across Ben's chest. "Rest up for the night shift." It's Ben's turn to blush. "You can see them out, right, Scar?" She kisses Ben and heads down from the foot-walk.

The guys follow her down and jump in their truck. I open the castle gate for them, follow them along the cobblestone road to the outer wall, and pry the gates open. I look for a wolf's carcass but find only disturbed grass on the side of the road. Confirming not a scent is left lingering, I work the iron grate. The guys leave for Ben's place, and Lincoln, without another word. I know it's childish, but I can't help but notice Kara got a kiss goodbye, and I didn't.

Chapter Thirty-Five

Working the crank on the iron grate is taxing. Why didn't Dad conjure up something with more gears in it?

"My lady."

"Jeez." I jump back from the crank. Markus is standing in the archway. "You need a bell around your neck."

"I'll find one at the earliest convenience, my lady."

Right…the whole take-orders-without-question thing. "Never mind."

"As you wish, my lady."

"Stop calling me that. My name is Scarlett."

Markus nods his obedience. I still find it hard to fathom that I can tell him what to do, and he'll do it without question. He's like a well-trained dog.

"Where's your friend?" I ask shortly. I remember his companion's name, Laurel, but something in me still doesn't want to acknowledge that my hunters have become, for lack of a better term, my slaves.

"She's dead, my…Scarlett." He reads my face but doesn't answer me.

"How?"

"There was a wolf. She went down fighting. They both did."

The look in his eyes reaffirms my suspicions that they were close, possibly lovers, and it gets to me. Here I am pissed that I have a member of the Broadsword in my presence and now I'm actually feeling sorry for this guy. Assassin or not, he's still human…I think. "Sorry, she seemed nice." I didn't know her from a hole in the ground, but her words and her voice were soft, kind. It doesn't help that Markus keeps shifting his weight and glancing from me to his feet. I find myself wanting to know more about her, especially how she died. It's a little bit morbid, but when it comes to the wolves, any knowledge is power. I decide to try to ease it out of him in the off chance his eyes start to water. "I hope she didn't suffer."

Markus's chest rises and falls with a breath, I take it as him fighting a memory. I haven't given him an order, and he doesn't strike me as the type who volunteers information often. But I need to know.

"Where—"

"Less than a mile from here, last night." It's his turn to be short with me.

Might have been the wolf that attacked Kara and me. But if it wasn't, oh God, all we need right now is a bloody pack at our door. "A stray?"

"It was alone."

That's his way of saying he doesn't know. Getting answers out of this guy will be like pulling teeth. Part of a pack or a stray, either way one wolf running around in these hills is more than enough for me. *Mangy beasts.* "What's your plan now?"

He looks shocked, like he's never been asked to speak of a course of action that is his own, only ordered. "I…I don't have one. I mean…I never thought of…what ever you wish of me."

Dad kept the Broadsword tight under his command, all right. Markus seems more afraid of being able to think for himself than anything else. And if I'm to trust him, actually trust him, I need to know how he thinks. I asked him a question, and he kinda answered it. So, I wait, staring at him until the silence becomes uncomfortable. But I won't be the one who breaks.

Markus scans the wall and the castle, and finally, he speaks his mind. "We make preparations." He looks like he's done with sharing, so I urge him on with a look. "We're heavily fortified against an attack, not from any modern weapons, but that can be rectified. We should outfit your force in case the wolves come back in numbers, or something else does."

Something else? What does he mean by that? And what force? He can't mean me and Kara and the guys?

"They, like myself, are yours to command."

Markus holds his palm out to his side. I step toward him. On the other side of the oak door stands nearly a dozen or more gray-skinned people dressed in black.

My throat goes dry. It's all I can do to swallow. I've been hunted by these people, taught to run from them without thought, and there are more of them standing before me than I have ever wished to see in person. I feel like I'm ten years old and I'm begging Mom to chase the monsters from my closet—but she's not here, and the monsters are.

"You okay?"

Kara's voice brings me back to reality, or whatever it is I'm in the midst of. Even from the distance of the castle her telepathy works. Thank God.

The pack of Broadswords is just staring at me. Staring at me and Markus, waiting to be invited in. Being a vamp, I get the pun from the movies. But I finally know how those unsuspecting blondes in all those shows felt once they realized who they let into their home, or rather *what* they let in. I give Kara a thumbs up, though I have to tense my forearm to restrain myself from shaking, even though they're sworn to me.

Markus cocks his head at me, then glances to the castle. "So that's her gift."

If I thought I was uncomfortable before, I was mistaken. Confront me, surprise me, kill me, but not her. No one gets near her. "Get out." I point through the arch. I'm shaking. No, I'm tense. I'm clenching my jaw so tight it hurts.

Thankfully, Markus nods and walks through the gate. I can't get it closed fast enough. The iron grate hits home and I'm working the door when the Trans Am pulls up. Markus may have proved his loyalty by almost slicing his hand off, but I don't trust him, or them. Trust has to be earned, and they frighten me more so than if I was facing a pack of wolves. Wolves are just beasts, but the Broadsword…they can think, deceive, lie.

No sooner do I get the beam secured in place than Kara catches me before I slump to the cobblestones, fighting tears.

"I got you."

More than you know, Kara. More than you know.

Chapter Thirty-Six

"I can't take this," I say, sitting on the ground with Kara beside me, her arm draped over my shoulders. "Mom…Dad…the Broadsword…the world."

"My phone." Kara squeezes me tighter.

She's without a doubt my rock, always making light of the situation, trying to make me feel better. "Your phone, my bike." I try to follow her lead. Maybe if I fake her levity long enough, it might just rub off on me.

"I got you your bike back. At least it looks like your bike." Kara stands and tugs at my arm. "Just look around, Scar. We got the world by the balls. Two hot women with their very own castle. A couple of gentlemen callers. A horde of men just itching to follow our every beck and call. Some of them might even be cute, if it wasn't for the try-to-wipe-us-off-the-face-of-the-earth deal they have going." She winks. "I do like pretty things, you know."

I chuckle. She knows how to get through to me.

"What do you say we check them out," she suggests. "From a safe rock-chucking distance, of course."

"A rock-chucking distance?"

Kara pulls a rifle out of her car. "Rock, lead, whatever." She climbs the stairs leading to the top of the wall. "Don't worry, Scar. I'm a crack shot, remember. I'll protect you."

"I'm finally starting to believe that."

"You better, I'm the one with the gun."

We make the top of the wall and peer around the stone teeth that line it. Seventeen Broadswords mingle before the gate. They seem almost human, almost normal. None are vamps, that's for sure, or they'd be crispy piles of ash. The women might be witches, but without Kara mumbling something to reveal them, there's no way of telling. Markus is in the midst of the group, and he's the only one not paired up. It's obvious who is. It's as if they're joined at the hip in their respective hunting parties.

"Think we should make them do the hokey pokey? Or send 'em packin'?" Kara holds the rifle up and loosely takes aim at them, waving the barrel back and forth. "I could wound a few, let you suck their blood, blah, blah, blah," she says mimicking every cartoon about Dracula I've ever seen.

She did it to me back at the Sanctum, too. It infuriated me then. Now it's kinda uplifting. Not the thought of feeding on Broadsword, I can't imagine how they'd taste, bland perhaps. But the notion that vamps skulk around dark corners saying blah, blah, blah, is absurd.

"That won't be necessary," Markus calls out from below.

"Shit. They made us." Kara ducks, as do I, but she's the only one of us grinning.

I shake my head. She's like a little kid playing cowgirl. Sometimes a bit of seriousness would be nice from her, but not right now. I figure she's proving an unspoken point. That we've already put the Broadsword to the test in Lincoln. If the rest of them down there are sworn to me as

Markus is, they're mine to command, no matter how I feel about them. If I'm afraid, cautious, or pissed off, it doesn't matter. "Markus?"

"Yes."

"Is everyone down there sworn to obey me?"

"Yes."

They'll do as I ask of them, and Kara's egging me on. "Should we let them in?"

"Wouldn't be very good hosts if we didn't."

I weigh my options. Do I let them stand there for all time or not? Do I accept and overcome the fact that the boogeymen—and women—I've feared for so long are now my own personal army? When the time comes to take on Dad's other self they could come in handy. Unless he turns them against me with no more than a word. I admit to myself that's concerning, but it would be something I'd have to deal with if and when it happens. Either way, I have to start somewhere, and Kara and I are seriously short handed. "Keep that loaded and ready."

"Don't you worry." Kara taps her rifle. "Old Betsie here is ready to rock."

We open the gates and let the Broadsword in.

I can't get the concept of letting a fox into the hen house out of my head. Markus leads them in like he's their leader. Whether that's because he was the first of them to make contact with us or if he's actually in command of them isn't obvious. He introduces each of the Broadsword to Kara and me, none of them are witches, they're all human, as human as they can get with their enhanced strength, speed, and grayish skin.

With my approval, Markus leaves a pair of Broadswords atop the closed gate to keep watch and to send word when Lukas and Ben get back. After all, the four of us decided to keep the gate shut and use flashlights for communication, and I don't want the guys to be totally shocked when they return.

I was right about Markus, though. He's hard to get to volunteer information, harder than some of the other Broadsword. One man in his twenties, Matt, is so open and straight forward it's comical.

Matt sprinted like a kid to the catapults and the huge crossbows once our introductions were through, and he got my permission to check them out. Within minutes every one of us knew how to operate the gigantic ancient weapons thanks to him. More so due to him climbing all over them and talking aloud to himself as he figured out which lever did what. His boyish excitement is refreshing, and infectious. It doesn't take long for the others to chime in their opinions about the machines and ammunition. Nor does it take long for Kara to be the first to test one of the crossbows' massive bolts. She fires one clear over the wall so fast it's hard to keep track of which is surprising due to the bolt's size. She shouts a "Wahoo" and shoots another one into the field, scaring more than one of Lukas's cows as the bolt sticks in the dirt. The crossbow's range is impressive, soaring a couple hundred yards before impaling itself in the earth.

After Kara finishes her play time, we make our way to the castle. Markus leaves Matt and his female companion—whose name I can't remember—behind to man the giant weapons if need be. He sets the rest of the Broadsword to patrol the castle wall at various points where they can all see each other and raise an alarm. Each one of them is heavily armed with assortments of knives, handguns, rifles, semi-automatic guns, and grenades. One even has a rocket launcher and his coat's lined with its ammunition. And of course, they each have a sword at their hip, a constant reminder of who they are.

Markus tries to convince me that I should have my sword at my side at all times. It's light, almost as if Dad had magicked it to weigh as much as a feather, but I still don't like the idea of accepting it. It feels like I'm giving in to line up and follow orders like the rest of the Broadsword. The castle I get—it's protection, and I would be a fool not to stay in it. It is nice, aside from that main hall that gives me the heebie-jeebies every time I pass through it. The castle does have one excellent perk, though, the view from the main tower. Kara heads off to find a bottle of wine, leaving Markus and me alone on the balcony overlooking what I can't help but think of calling *my* kingdom.

It bothers me how little I know about the man beside me, and his kind, let alone his profession. Curiosity gets the better of me, and I hope I'll fare better than the cat. "Markus."

"Yes."

"Why are you gray? The Broadsword, I mean. Why do all of you have a gray undertone like you're sick or something?"

Markus pauses and looks down over the courtyard like he's embarrassed. "We have no souls."

Chapter Thirty-Seven

"What?"

Markus repeats himself. "We have no souls."

"How?"

"Your father took them."

"How..." The words are hard to get out. I know way more than the average human does about what's real and what's myth, but I've never heard of someone *actually* stealing a soul. The notion I had earlier about not drinking the blood of a Broadsword cements itself within me as a personal law not to be broken. "How did he...take it?"

"A spell."

Markus is infuriating. No kidding it was a spell. *Just spit it out already, and don't make me beg for every answer.* That's it, he can, if I command him to. "Okay, from now on you're going to volunteer what you know without me having to pry at answers. Understood?"

"I understand." Markus drops his gaze even more.

"So, tell me, tell me how it is you came to be like this." I wave my palm up and down before him.

"As I said, Scarlett. Drago took my soul with a spell. It, along with those of my brethren, are trapped within an amulet he keeps on him at all times. He stole our souls." Markus peers up at the Broadswords standing guard on the castle wall. "And with them, our will. Once commanded, we follow without question until we fulfill his wishes. Once we have, we are free of his influence until he commands us again, which he never fails to do. So, we remain in a constant state of obedience."

He looks me in the eye. I'm certain he's going to shed a tear, but one never falls. His lip doesn't even quiver. If I were in his position—soulless—I'd be a blubbering idiot if I had to talk about it.

"Like we are at this very moment," he finishes. "Sworn to protect you."

"And if I die?"

"We are free until he commands us again. But we won't let you die. We can't. To disobey isn't a matter of choice, it is an impossibility."

I can't believe it. The more I uncover, the more I wonder what Mom ever saw in Dad. I'm grateful I'm here but it's as if I'm the spawn of the devil himself. At least I still have my soul. "I'm sorry."

"You didn't do anything. Aside from making me come out of my comfort zone and tell you something we don't even speak of with each other. And let us not forget that you almost made me cut off my hand. Over a lifetime of it being attached I have grown quite fond of it. I guess I should thank you for stopping me in mid-stroke." He has a sense of humor I didn't expect from his stern demeanor.

"How is it?" I feel like a total bitch knowing what I know now.

"Healing just fine, thank you."

"If you weren't so damn fast you wouldn't have needed to get it bandaged. How are you so fast anyway? Witches aren't, and you're definitely not a vamp."

"I don't know. Part of the soul-sucking spell, or another one. Doesn't matter."

"Doesn't matter? I have trouble keeping up with—" I want to say *the Broadswords I killed*, but now that seems rude. *The true definition of a lady, or a gentleman, is someone who puts everyone around them above themselves to ensure they are as comfortable and welcomed as possible.* Mom always had a phrase that stuck in my head and made me wonder just how wise she actually was. I have my foot in my mouth and all I can do is redirect myself and hope Markus doesn't take offense. "Wolves. Wolves are bloody fast, and from what I've seen you are too."

"A young wolf, yes. But not an old wolf, or an old vampire. They are more…" It's Markus's turn to take his foot out of his mouth. "*Challenging* to keep up with."

"I'm not old," Kara says from behind us. "And I can kick your gray ass any time. Doesn't even bother me that I'd bruise one as nice as yours to prove my point." Kara arches her back as she checks out Markus's bum and flings her hair over her shoulder. "Think I put a bit of color to those gray cheeks, wouldn't ya say, Scar?" Kara hadn't heard the part about Markus being soulless or she'd have never said any of that—I'm sure of it. She's too compassionate despite the façade she puts on. She is right, though: Markus is blushing.

"He's got a story for you," I say to Kara.

"Better be good." Kara takes a drink straight from the bottle.

"It's an eye opener. Tell her what you told me…please." I know the *please* isn't necessary, but it makes me feel better. Like Mom would be proud of me or something. "I'll be back in a second."

"Where are you going?" Kara and Markus ask at the same time.

"To powder my nose," I say, descending the stairs. I catch something of Kara saying how I need to practice my magic more if I still need a mirror to put my face on, or something like that. All I know is I need to stretch my legs and go for a ride. Reflect about what Markus said, about who Dad really is, and who he isn't. An idea forms as I think about freeing Dad from the grip of the Last Atlantean, and as I run, images of a time yet to come surface. A time when he sits at the table with me, eating dinner, free of his curse, free of the amulet thanks to me. At the table sits Markus, his skin pink, his soul returned. My imagination, my soul, drives me forward, and after finding out the Broadsword has been stripped of theirs, I pity them and want nothing more than to return their souls to them, give them freedom.

When I make it to the grand hall, the hair on the back of my neck stands on end, whisking away my daydream. I scurry to the doors to relieve the tension. My uneasiness doesn't leave me thanks to the sound of a loud bell ringing, coming from the outer wall.

Chapter Thirty-Eight

This isn't the joyous mind-clearing ride I had in mind, racing toward the main gate on my dirt bike Ducati thanks to this bell ringing. I never noticed it before, but as it's being struck by Matt, I can't fathom how I missed it. It's embedded in one of the wall's teeth facing the castle. I guess we were so busy looking over the wall at the wolf or the Broadsword that we failed to notice it.

Markus shouts orders behind me. The Broadsword relocates along the castle wall in my side mirror, and there's a pack of them piling into Kara's Trans Am. I'm sure she's not ecstatic about that.

Matt stops banging on the bell and descends the stairs as I pull up to the gate. "What's going on?" I ask.

"Some guy by the name of Ben wants in. He says he knows you," Matt replies.

"Help me with the gate." Cranking the grate and the huge oak doors open is a breeze now that I have help, especially since Matt has strength similar to mine, but I'm pretty sure I'd have him beat in an arm wrestle.

Ben wasn't kidding when he said he was going to load up. He's standing beside an old tractor that's twice as tall as he is, and he's towing a trailer that should be attached to a semi. Behind that, another pickup truck even older than Ben's is loaded with a pile of stuff in the back. At its wheel is a heavyset man with gray hair who's a spitting image of Ben, and beside him is an older woman with heavily dyed curly short blonde hair who looks a little concerned.

"They who I think they are?" Ben asks, looking up at the pair of Broadswords on top of the wall.

"Yep. Turns out they have unwavering loyalty to me."

"I guess they're better than me standing on the hill trying to wave you down with a flashlight."

"You think you brought enough stuff?"

"Dad was in the war. He likes to be prepared if he can." Ben's dad gets out of the truck, walks around it, opens the door for his wife. These men are raised right around here. "It took some doing to get them to leave home, but after we told them about the werewolf—which made me feel like a lying little brat by the way—and convinced them you're on our side, it got a bit easier. Especially after Lukas vouched for you."

"Where is he?" I don't want to seem like a concerned girlfriend—after all, we haven't known each other very long—but I'm worried for him.

"He'll be here in a day or three; it's a decent trek to Rawlings."

"Rawlings?" I rack my brain. Somewhere in Wyoming, I think.

"Yeah, Mom got all bent out of shape once we told her about…all this. Wanted to check on Aunt Lorie. Ah"—Ben waves off the idea—"she's as tough as they come. Lukas is gonna have a hard time convincing her to pack up and come out here." Now is not the best time to be wandering around the country, but I get it, she's family, and a man like Lukas strikes me as one who can take care of himself.

"Benjamin, where are your manners?" Ben's mom says.

Ben rolls his eyes. "Mom, Dad, this is Scarlett."

"Miss," says Ben's dad.

He's promptly elbowed in the ribs by Ben's mom. "These boys of mine, such bad manners. It's Bert and Brian, dear," Ben's mom says, holding out her hand. I shake it. She's putting on a brave face, but I can smell the fear on her. I get it. I'm the harbinger of death according to the news. "So, you're what all the fuss is about." Her eyes are kind, and her smile is present, but it's forced.

"I suppose so," I say.

"Well now that we've had proper introductions, no thanks to my son here…"

Ben rolls his eyes again. I wonder how often he still gets corrected by Bert despite him being in his mid-twenties. I guess a mother's work never stops when it comes to her kids.

"We should be heading in. It'll be dark soon and the boys need to unpack while you and I have a little chat." The ripe scent of fear coming from Bert shifts from that of prey to predator. I can't help but think of the phrase *momma bear*. "I hear you have somewhat of a kitchen that needs tending to." She's a brave woman, and from the look of her she spent a lot of time in the kitchen. She's one of those poor women who has zero body fat above the waist but has hips like someone who's given birth to a dozen kids. The kitchen must be her safe zone. The place where she's the boss.

Mom's words about comforting others run through my head again. I consider saying I'm getting hungry but decide against it after recalling Lukas's reaction. "Sounds good. After all, these boys"—I mimic Bert's name for the men, undermining them as she did, and hopefully gaining favor with her—"would probably get scurvy eating nothing but steak and beans without us women to take care of them."

Bert smiles—this one isn't forced. "You're right about that. Load the kitchen first, son."

"Yes, Mother," Ben says, drawing out his words. This might be entertaining, watching Bert throw her weight around with the men. If anything, it will be a welcome distraction.

The Broadsword lock up once we're through the gate. The men unpack, kitchen first, and leave me and Bert alone in the kitchen. She busies herself organizing what she's brought, everything but the sink. She not only brought food, but full place settings, utensils, pots, pans, and a water cooler. It won't cool the water anymore, but she has four full bottles for drinking.

Water?

I never thought about that. Bert's supply here won't go very far. I'm so used to turning on a tap and having it readily available. We used bottled water for Ben's instant coffee, but it never registered then just how stripped of life's basic necessities we've become without electricity. I instantly feel dirty, grimy, and in need of a shower. I make a mental note to talk to the men about it. Maybe they can rig the well at Lukas's to work without the power being on.

I let Bert run the show and the conversation. Evidently, the guys have revealed who was with whom, either that or Bert pulled it out of them because she keeps going on about how Lukas is such a good nephew without a mention of Ben. I get it. Lukas's parents are gone and she's looking out for him even though he's a grown man. The aggressive predator scent rises from Bert with her every word. I'm certain she's gearing up to give me the *you better not hurt that boy* speech. It's impresses how protective she is, and it reminds me of Mom. Bert doesn't even bring up the lack of power, the out-of-place castle, or my incident at the rodeo. She does thank me for opening up the place and says the boys will head back to their farm to gather their herd. They lost another cow between when Lukas and Ben left until now. It's funny how Bert just slipped that in like normal conversation as she busies herself, like the looming threat of a werewolf on her land hasn't bothered her. It's like me being a vamp has no bearing either, when it comes to being a surrogate momma bear. I wonder if she thinks I'll bite her if she pushes things, but figure Lukas had enough to say about me that wasn't terrifying. Besides, the Thirst isn't upon me yet. Soon enough, though, I'll have to satisfy it. I know she's got questions the guys couldn't have answered for her. Who wouldn't? But she presses on about Lukas, and I let her with the occasional agreement.

When the words "As for the two of you together" cross her lips, I catch a hint of fear waft back to me. Thankfully, before she can get another word out, Kara appears in the kitchen. Her disruption is timed perfectly.

"Scar, we gotta talk."

"You must be Kara," Bert says, eyeing Kara from head to toe. "It's impolite to interrupt someone in mid-conversation." That hint of fear coming from Bert vanishes. She's looking out for her son now.

"Sorry." Kara barely acknowledges Bert. "But I need your vamp vision. Like now."

"What is it?"

Kara doesn't get to answer me—the warning bell does.

Chapter Thirty-Nine

I run outside, through the courtyard, and to the foot-walk on the top of the castle wall. "What is it now?"

"There's been two explosions to the northwest." A dark-haired woman points to the sky. Two wispy black clouds are dissipating in the wind against their blue backdrop. Smaller plumes trail them to the source of the explosions. "Big enough we heard them before we saw the smoke."

They look pretty far away. "Do you know what's over there?" I swallow, hard, and try not to imagine Dad heading my way on his rampage to take over the world. Surrounded by members of the Broadswords who can shift allegiances with a word from him is not the position I want to be in.

"There's a small town roughly in that direction, from what I remember on the map."

"What do you see, Scar?" Kara says, catching up with me, making me focus, immerse myself in the moment at hand instead of playing out scenarios in my head of what could possibly be out there.

"Same as you. What ever blew is too far away for me to see," I tell her. Kara would know as much about the area as myself. I need a local.

. Bert scurries through the courtyard in more of a fast walk than a jog. She's sweating. Poor thing.

I call out to her before she can set a foot on the stairs. "Do you know what's over there that could have blown up?" I point in the direction the dark-haired Broadsword had.

Between breaths, Bert says, "Every farm runs red."

"Red?" I ask.

"Red gas. Kept in fuel tanks."

"Could that have been what you saw?" I ask the dark-haired Broadsword.

"Doubt it," her male companion answers. "These were huge, and far away."

Bert climbs the stairs, catches her breath and squints at the trails of smoke. "Had to come from Ovando's gas station. It's only eight miles away. That's the only thing I can think of that would have enough fuel to make that kind of explosion."

"I'll send someone to check it out." Markus made it to the foot-walk. "You two use the truck and take the last quarter mile or so on foot. Recon only." The way Markus orders the other Broadswords around makes me think of Lieutenant Niclas Huntly.

"We'll go," I say, indicating me and Kara. I need to go. See for myself that it's not Dad. Put some physical distance between myself and the Broadsword and voice my concerns to Kara about them switching sides.

"No, you won't. We can't protect you out there," says Markus.

"She can handle herself. Especially with me by her side." Kara wraps her arm around my neck. She found the wine she was looking for.

"Too risky." Markus shakes his head.

"I'm going," I say, pulling away from Kara. "They can follow me if they want. But we need to know what's going on outside of these walls. Recon." I tease Markus, confident I can command—and if necessary, kill—the two Broadswords he's ordering to send with me. "You know you can't stop me."

"I am sworn to protect you, Scarlett. Even if that means from yourself."

Markus's words set off alarms in my head. Protect me from myself. What would he do? Tie me up and gag me? Feed me intravenously for eternity while he keeps me held up in these stone walls? My imagination about government experiments rushes up. I don't think so. "I'm in charge here. Got it?" I wait for him to reply; he nods. I guess that'll do for now. "I don't need protecting from myself. Now, I'm leaving. These two can follow us." If anything, they can take the first hit from whatever is out there if it's not Dad, kinda like a human shield. I wrap my arm around Kara's waist. "And you can stay here. Is that clear?"

"Yes." The way Markus is so quick to respond and obey without pressing his point, makes me study him. I wish I could read minds. I'm growing uncomfortable ordering him and the Broadsword around like I'm a slave owner. But after what he just said, I'm thankful he and the other Broadswords listen to me. Having your once would-be killers under control isn't a bad thing, but his words make me want to keep an even closer eye on all of them. God, I wish Dad didn't have the ability to control the Broadsword on a whim. If they were free of his influence, they would be far more trustworthy, especially if they lost their speed and strength.

"Bert, can you hold down the fort till we get back?" She looks at me with a newfound respect I didn't catch during my time in the kitchen with her. "Take care of the boys?"

"I'll get them fed," Bert replies with a grin. I'm not certain if it's due to me referring to the men as boys, or because she considers herself an excellent cook. Either way, I believe I've won her over. "And these ones too." She indicates Markus specifically. "As long as they behave."

"They will. Right?" I glare at Markus. He nods his agreement.

"I'm driving." Kara pulls her keys out of her pocket and takes off down the stone steps.

We hop in her car. She hammers on the gas. In no time we're speeding down the highway with Kara swerving a little outside the lines on her turns. In hindsight I shouldn't have let her drive, but what the hell's the real harm? It's not like we have to worry about cops. They got bigger fish to fry. 'Course I am at the top of America's most wanted list. Whatever.

I consider taking Markus's advice to pull off the road to make our way to Ovando on foot, but as we approach the open field surrounding it, I think better of the idea. We'd be totally exposed even in the fading sunlight, and if we need a quick getaway, I want Kara's Trans Am close by.

We park behind the first building on the edge of town, a blue Quonset with matching farmhouse. No one's home—or if they are, they're hiding.

Ovando is small, very small. Before we left, Bert told us it housed no more than a hundred people. But the whole town's so spread out that walking would keep you thin if you lived here. The nearest building to the Quonset is a good football field away. She was right about the fire coming from here. A trail of billowing smoke still wafts from the town's center about a quarter mile away.

Kara complains about wearing the wrong shoes as we walk through the tall grass around the Quonset toward the scattered buildings. A delivery truck painted with a sign saying Trixi's Saloon comes into view, as does the saloon the truck is meant to advertise. Trixi's has at least twenty motorcycles parked outside of it. Makes me wish I had brought mine, even if it is a dirt bike disguised as a Ducati.

"Think they blew up the gas station?" Kara asks.

"Not all bikers are like the ones in movies, *Kara*."

"They might be when times are tough, *Scarlett*." She sticks her tongue out at me.

The dark-haired Broadsword shushes us from behind. "Stay here, we'll check it out."

"Have fun." Kara waves them on and leans against the Quonset, inspecting the sole of her shoe. Our Broadsword guardians don't make a sound as they move toward the tavern. It's creepy, like they're hunting, and for once they aren't hunting me. They make their way to the back and hover around a window for a bit, then come back to us, undetected, silent as if they aren't even bending the blades of grass beneath their boots.

"Bunch of degenerates?" Kara asks them.

"Kara."

"If I'd have to bet on it, I'd say they caused the explosions for fun," says the dark-haired woman. Took over the town, and scavenged what it has to offer."

"Why the hell would they do that? The National Guard is roaming about looking for us. That'd be suicide to draw attention to themselves."

"Power's out, communication's gone, the night sky looked like it lit on fire," says the dark-haired woman. "Mankind is back in the Stone Ages, and there are those who will be opportunists, but whether it be for good or for evil who can say."

"I could see after a month or so, when food becomes scarce and winter sets in, but not after just a few days. People wouldn't turn on each other in such a short time."

"Imaginations can run wild," she says. "We are in the beginning of what was written in the Bible: Armageddon, hysteria, mass rioting, looting, all are possible if the heart is clouded with fear. And the fearful will follow the strong if it means their survival, even if the strong are homicidal maniacs. To those without courage it's better to follow than to be under the boot."

She makes sense, and I get it. Just look at what happens after an earthquake, a tornado, or even when the wrong team loses the Superbowl. Hell, businesses have even had their storefronts destroyed in celebration of a winning team. A not-so-long-ago newscast title about soccer hooligans wrecking a stadium somewhere in Europe springs to mind. Fans trashed the stadium, surrounding businesses, fought each other; a few even died if I remember correctly. Riots have sprung up from far less than what the world has just been through, and that's when there was law and order, not to mention the ability to call for backup to disperse the crowds.

"They even have what looks like townspeople hanging from the rafters," says the woman.

"Sounds like quite the party." Kara swirls a finger in the air.

"Hanging from their necks," the male Broadsword adds.

Chapter Forty

Kara's quick-to-jump-into-action reflex must be just that—a reflex. It tells her when to fight, and when to run. Her shifting eyes tell me she wants nothing more than to hop in her car and floor it. "We should head back. We know what caused the explosions. Job's done."

"Those people didn't deserve this," I say under my breath.

"I can't believe people could sink so far so fast," says Kara. "To actually kill the townspeople. And over what?"

"They're not all dead," says the dark-haired Broadsword. "Not yet anyway. There's at least a half dozen of them huddled in the corner."

We could just leave them alone, but the bikers could come our way and try to take what we have. Let alone killing the innocent people inside. The real problem is that I don't like bullies. The solution? I'm getting hungry, and monsters only come out at night. "That settles it."

I start for the saloon. I can feel Kara's aura, through our bond, tugging at me, urging me to follow her instincts and hit the road. But I won't let it control me. I can't if I'm to retain the part of me that's strong on my own.

"Where are you going?" Kara says, grabbing my arm.

"I've had it. I'm not going to stand by while innocent people are murdered." Coming from a vamp I know that sounds weird, but Mom always taught me to feed on the lowest form of degenerates that mankind has to offer, and as far as I'm concerned, these people are in need of a savior, a protector. They're in my backyard, and I won't let them down. I've done that to far too many as of late, and I'll be damned if I'll do it again. "Especially when there's something I can do about it."

"Scar."

"No." I pull my arm free of Kara's grip. "They're doing this in what is now our backyard." I point at the saloon. I'm pissed off, now. "It's only a matter of time before they come knocking at our door."

"Let them. We've got the Broadsword to help us there. And it's a big-assed door."

"We've got the Broadsword to help *me* here." I have no intention of letting Kara walk in there with me. I can do this alone. I can heal. She can't.

"I have to agree with Kara," says the male Broadsword. "You are putting yourself in harm's way when you don't need to."

Markus's words about saving me from myself echo in my head. Would these two try to stop me as Markus insinuated? I'm getting more pissed off. I need to let something out. Let the vamp in me get out. "You two stay here and keep her safe. That's an order."

"What's gotten into you?" Kara's frowning at me. My rock, my go-to girl is shutting me down.

"This is *my* kingdom."

"Your what?"

“I’ll be damned if I’m gonna let it go to hell. Stay here.” I turn for the saloon. Kara tries to follow me, but the Broadsword holds her back, following my command.

I’m on my own, and with no one to look out for but myself, what I have before me is a rare opportunity to cut loose. I’ve always felt as if I’m walking around in a world made of cardboard and glass. I’ve always had to be careful with my strength, holding back so I don’t accidentally hurt an innocent person. And from what my faithful lapdogs have described, these men are far from innocent.

My heart is pounding with anticipation as I open the door to the saloon. I’m vibrating. It’s dimly lit inside thanks to the waning sun coming through the windows. The laughter and conversation slows to a stop at my presence. It’s like a scene from an old Western movie. I’m the sheriff who just walked into the midst of a band of rustlers that need to be driven out of town.

Five women and three men are curled up beside the jukebox, holding each other. Two bodies swing from the rafters. The ropes around their necks make their eyes bulge from their sockets. Below them, broken on the floor, are two wooden stools with their legs splintered to pieces. The holes in the floor are a dead giveaway; the chair legs were shot out as the townsfolk stood on them. One of the men hanging in the rafters looks familiar to me. I’ve seen him in Lincoln, but I can’t quite place him.

“What do we have here?” a fat biker with a long gray beard says, eyeing me up and down from the table nearest me. “A new recruit for our club.” He smiles. Not a nice smile, one that has a deviant thought behind it, I’m sure. He makes my skin crawl, they all do.

Not all bikers are bad. My words to Kara come to mind as I scan the room of both men and women freely helping themselves to Trixi’s booze. Not all of them could be bad, could they? Some could be followers. Too scared to do the right thing.

“You gonna say something or just stand there, princess?” The fat man stands from his table. A crest stitched into his tattered denim vest has three black snakes on it, each coiling around the other to form a kind of three-headed staff.

The Black Serpents have come to me.

I was right to have considered looking into them further. The carnage at Trixi’s is proof of that.

I smile back at him, just a bit more menacing than he had. Like a hunter ready for the kill.

I slap him, hard. My hand stings for an instant and recovers by the time he hits the floor, face down—dead. I made my point. Death has come knocking at their door this evening.

“Anyone who disagrees with this”—I point at the men strung up to the rafters—“leave now, or join him.” I put a boot into the fat man’s side. He slides across the floor into his table, tipping it over, sending the other three bikers sitting there onto their backs.

Then it hits me; I remember who the man hanging from the rafters is. He’s the man who tried to send the little knobby-kneed girl back to me to return the ice cream money I gave her at the Co-op gas station in Lincoln.

I look back to the jukebox, and sure enough, huddled behind one of the women is the little girl, her Coke-bottle glasses stained with tears.

Blood slicks my palms from my fingernails digging into them. How dare these people murder a kid’s parent in front of her, and in such a gruesome manner? She’ll be traumatized for life.

Someone yells, “Bitch.” A bullet whizzes past me.

My other self shows its face.

The room lights up with my violet energy, casting silhouetted black shadows of people rising to their feet. Whether it's to charge me or to flee, it doesn't matter—not anymore—after seeing the girl. Those who are innocent or too coward to fight had their chance to escape. Now, I'll slaughter them all like the swine they are. I give myself over to my emotions, let the writhing inside me out, let control over my actions to be dictated by primal urges rather than rational thought.

I move as fast as I can, breaking bones and spilling blood as I charge to the center of the saloon. Gunfire rings out all around me.

My violet other self shifts, cocooning me.

It's like a foggy dream, a good one. One not filled with rage but with pleasure from every face I smash, every limb I tear free from its owner.

I'm watching myself in a euphoric state, from outside my body. Watching my other self take control, submit to a deeper, more primal urge.

The crowd thins from wannabe tough guys to a mass of useless meat on the floor. A few manage to escape out the doors; others make it outside from me tossing them through the windows.

The gunfire dies and is replaced by moans.

I lift the last man alive by the throat, hoist him above my head. His dark eyes are wrought with fear. The stench of terror emanating from the corpses at my feet surrounds me, feeds me. I sink my teeth deep into his neck, tearing a sizable chunk of flesh free from his body. His jugular spurts as I spit the piece of his neck to the floor. His thrashing slows as his life blood sprays his fellow degenerates. I latch onto the wound, savoring the spurting pressure against the roof of my mouth as I drain him. I release him and he falls still with a final twitch.

I suck in the satisfying, almost overwhelming aroma of fresh spilled blood, and catch my reflection in the mirror behind the bar.

My hair, my clothes, and half my face are drenched in blood. The blood doesn't shock me or scare me; what scares me is the face in the mirror. Bathed in violet, scowling worse than when I slammed Kara against the wall in the bathroom of the diner. A face that screams I've lost control of myself. A face that likes the notion of going blood-drunk far too much.

Kara wouldn't like this face staring back at me in the mirror and neither would Mom. I think of the little girl and the horror I just subjected her to. Her presence pushed me over the edge, and it's quite possible I just inflicted more trauma on her than any child should ever endure.

My violet aura fades back into the nothingness from where it came. I've tamed the beast inside me that yearned to be released, fed it enough to sedate it. It's a beast I never knew I had, and never want to see again. Nothing like the rodeo where I had control over my actions. This night is all about bloodlust.

I drop the corpse to the floor and look to the townsfolk by the bullet-riddled juke box. They're alive, and from the smell, one of them has soiled themselves. The little girl is wide-eyed and can't stop staring at me, but I don't sense fear from her, only awe and amazement. Perhaps I didn't scar her emotionally. Perhaps I gave her a sense of justice, even though it was through a bloody path. No words I have can comfort them, or her. They're free now, terrified, aside from the girl, but free. I wipe my mouth on my sleeve, nod to the girl and walk to the door stepping between mangled limbs. I have to step over a biker to get outside. No, not a biker—a Broadsword, the man who had accompanied us here that I'd ordered to take care of Kara. He'd caught a stray bullet in the head.

I search frantically in the dark, but I can't see Kara anywhere.

Chapter Forty-One

Gunfire echoes. A single shot, immediately followed by four more in rapid succession, too close together to come from a rifle, and far too loud to come from a handgun. I round the Quonset in a heartbeat. Kara's on the ground, cradled by the dark-haired female Broadsword a few paces from the old farmhouse.

I'm frozen stiff. I can't lose her. Not now. Not ever. Not by my doing.

Three men in military uniforms are a few yards in front of them, weapons raised, wisps of smoke rising from their barrels, but they're aiming into the night, away from the dark-haired Broadsword, away from Kara.

"Where is she?" a familiar voice calls out from the dark. It's Markus. He's holding a biker by the head in both hands as the biker claws at Markus's iron grip to no avail.

"The bar!" shouts the dark-haired Broadsword.

Markus snaps the biker's neck and flings the corpse aside, then takes off running.

One of the military yells, "Freeze!"

Markus speeds past him, far enough away and in a direction that the military keep their guns trained on him but don't fire. He slows when he catches sight of me and calls out to me. At least I think he does. All that matters is Kara, and Markus's hands on my shoulders snap me out of my frozen state. I shove him back, run for Kara with tears obscuring my vision. "Is she…?"

"She's breathing," says the dark-haired Broadsword; her blood-soaked hand is held firm on Kara's shoulder. "But barely."

"You were supposed to protect her," I say, dropping to my knees, caressing Kara's cheek. I blink the tears from my eyes, clearing my vision, sending cool lines tracing down my cheeks.

"Move," Markus orders. The dark-haired Broadsword sets Kara down and shimmies aside. Markus rolls Kara enough to check her back. "Bullet went through." He sets her down and pulls out a small tin from within his coat. "She's got a chance if we can stop the bleeding. Watch our backs," he orders the dark-haired Broadsword and the military. They listen, look around for any more bikers between glances back at us, specifically me.

Markus pours a bottle of brown liquid on Kara's wounds. Iodine from the smell of it. She writhes and moans for a second, then falls silent, not breaking from her unconscious state. Markus rips open a package with his teeth and pours a white powder on Kara's wound.

"Clotting agent," he says moving fast, so fast it's painful to wait for gravity to catch up to him and pull the powder to Kara's wound. He slaps on a wad of gauze. "Pressure," he says pushing my palm on it. I hold it as firm as my shaking hand can. My fingers warm and become wet, but my palm remains dry, the clotting agent is working. "Lift her up." I do, and the moment my hand releases the gauze, Markus wraps a tensor bandage tight around Kara's shoulder, neck, and chest. "Let go."

"Thank you." My voice is squeaky and weak. I'm drained, exhausted, and it's not from what I did in the saloon. It's from guilt. I got Kara shot. If I had just listened to her. Why didn't I? What the hell was I thinking?

My eyes water again and I'm fighting thoughts of Kara dying. A world without her. No, that can't happen. All the times she was there for me replay in a second. The cabin, Lukas's house, the castle, the rodeo, even the field she teased me at while teaching me to tap into my power. I clamp my jaw shut to keep my bottom lip from quivering. What good is my power now if I lose her? I fight crying out. As if staying silent and keeping it in will keep Kara from leaving me.

Markus picks Kara up and slides her into the back seat of her car. I crawl in and hold Kara's head in my lap. The thigh of my jeans where her back rests becomes warm and wet. I drop my head and do my best not to let my tears fall on Kara's face.

~ * ~

The dark-haired Broadsword explains to me what happened as she drives us back to the castle. She cries as much as I do. Her companion was her lover, and he's dead because of me. More than once she wipes her eyes clear on the drive. I've been so preoccupied with my own agenda that I had forgotten Mom's lessons about comforting others, so much so that I haven't even bothered to learn their names. Hers is Toni, and she's alone now. Soulless, and alone. For some reason I thought the loss of a soul would make them, and therefore Toni, emotionless. But that's far from the case. She's as broken as any woman would be who lost someone she loved.

I can't imagine how she feels because...I can't...*won't* let that rush of emotion overtake me. I'm on the verge of being in her situation, of losing Kara, and I wouldn't wish that feeling on my greatest enemy.

I replay in my head over and over again what happened in Ovando and what Toni told me, combining our two versions together to make sense of the night. How I all but abandoned Kara to satisfy some primal urge that should have been sedated by a cool breeze on a fast bike. How Toni's companion, John, had followed me to protect me once he fulfilled the order I gave him to stay put. Turns out orders have to be specific, or they can be taken any way a member of the Broadsword perceives it. I told them to stay and protect Kara. Kara was out of harms way, and I didn't specify how long they had to stay by the Quonset. That explains how Markus showed up in Ovando. I hadn't told him how long to stay at the castle, just that he had to.

Toni held Kara back after John left them by the Quonset. That's when the military appeared. Apparently, they were holed up in a cold room with two elderly farmers in the old house. They kept hidden until I went berserk. The fleeing Black Serpents who escaped the saloon ran into them—and Kara and Toni. There was a standoff. The bikers with pistols, the military with rifles. The bikers lost, but not before shooting Kara. Thankfully Markus arrived with his tin of medical stuff and the knowledge of how to use it.

First aid isn't something I ever had to worry about, but I'm learning the hard way.

Back at the castle, Markus cleans Kara's wound and changes her bandages from a field dressing to a "proper one," as he put it. I spend most of the night lying beside Kara on the bed in the queen's chambers, dabbing a wet cloth on her forehead, constantly looking over her bandage for any sign of her bleeding through it. We change her clothes and bedding three times. Markus says she's sweating it out and it's a good sign as she isn't at a feverish temperature. My bully, my rock, is fighting for her life. Markus assures me she'll be fine, but my damned imagination runs wild.

Even if our bond hasn't solidified to the point of driving me insane, if I lose Kara, I'm certain I'll need to be fitted for a straitjacket. She has become the constant in my life, and the more I think about it, she always has been. Mom was present more than Kara was, but Kara was always in the back of my mind. First from me despising her. Then from me wanting to, in some absurd way, show her I was capable of so much more than she teased me to be lacking. Strength, speed, night vision, yeah, those were natural gifts. But my heart, my drive, my skill, those I earned, and fantasized that Aunt Brenda would brag about to Kara after every time she visited.

Since we lost our moms, she's been a friend—more so—and part of me wants to believe it's due to something other than our bond. It's a love-hate relationship that is exhausting, and slowly leaving only a mutual respect and a companionship that will not falter. With her, I'm never alone—and as I caress her cheek, wipe the sweat-saturated hair from her face, I find myself never wanting to be isolated from her.

I fall in and out of restless sleep by Kara's side throughout the night. Reliving Ovando every time my eyes shut is exhausting, but the nightmares are well deserved. The part that isn't, is the voice in my head that accompanies the nightmares. The gravelly voice of Dad, of the Last Atlantean who's consuming him.

Telling me my bloodline will end with me.

Chapter Forty-Two

It takes eight days for Kara to heal for me to be convinced she's well enough to leave the bed. She's grown tired of me fussing over her and is filled with curiosity to see all I've told her about. I let her wander around the castle, exploring its changes, with me keeping my distance behind her. In the event she collapses I can be there in a heartbeat.

I follow her as she makes introductions. Another two dozen Broadsword trickled in over the time she took to recover, as did the three military men from Ovando along with any of the townsfolk who survived the biker raid. They consider me a kind of dark guardian angel. The fact I have a castle to protect them has some bearing, of that I'm sure. As for the Black Serpents who fled, there's been no word of them. Yet what really troubles me is Dad. There's been no sighting, not a peep. I think of the crimson ball he sent skyward after we fought, wonder what he's up to, and find myself running through too many science-fiction scenarios. I have to force myself to wait until he rears his head so I can confront him.

I never admit I lost control of myself in Ovando, even to Kara. She suspects something happened to me, though. I can see it in her eyes, a burning question that will need to be answered sooner or later, but I won't speak a word of it yet. She insists I try to hone my natural skills. I consider it and try to practice what I've heard of witches doing—controlling the elements—but after I split the earth open and suck Brian's tractor into it, I decide it's best to wait until my teacher is mobile in the likely chance that I will need an assist in undoing whatever I inadvertently manifest. It takes all I have, along with aid from my violet-self, to wrench Brian's tractor out of the cavern I made.

So, I keep myself in check. I meditate, a lot. Partially due to my nightmares filled with Dad's gravelly voice, and partially to find peace in the castle. It has a constant hum to it from people we let in. Word spread about the bikers and me, and about the wolves. Thankfully we haven't seen another one of them, but that was enough to convince the people of Helmville, a town smaller than Ovando a dozen miles south of us, to move in.

The buzz is all around, but it always falls silent when I approach. Avoidance, that's what I get—glances from people trying to look like they suddenly have somewhere dire to be the moment I enter a room. The only real interaction I get is with the Broadsword and with children who stare at me in awe as their parents try to scurry them away. Except for one little girl who was orphaned thanks to the Black Serpents. Melanie, the ten-year-old girl with long brown hair, thick glasses, and knobby knees. The same one I bought ice cream for, the same one who watched me take revenge on those who murdered her father.

Melanie, or Mel as she prefers, has taken a liking to me. Enough that she doesn't run away from my presence. For some reason, me slaughtering the Black Serpents didn't make her afraid, it made her look up to me. I chalk it up to the desensitization of first-player video games. She probes me about my immortal nature and the truth compared to Hollywood. I fill her in but give crypted answers to some of her questions. I like to watch her wheels spin, and some answers I just don't have. Like how I deflected the solar flare.

After that conversation she presented me with a bouquet of dandelions saying I didn't have to fear the sun anymore. I'm not one for kids—I tolerate them more than anything, but Mel has grown on me. Her mom passed away giving birth to her. I still have a father who's living and breathing, but I don't know him. I hope I get a chance to. The real him. But for the moment, and since I met Mel, I try to think of myself as an orphan as she is. It makes it somehow easier than admitting, even though everyone knows my father is the harbinger of death.

So, I dig into Bert's private stash in the kitchen and sneak Mel a chocolate bar for us to share every day, with aid from Sue from the diner. It makes me feel good to give her something, and I figure it helps with regulating her diabetes, though I never questioned her about it. Who wants to discuss their weaknesses after all? Sue is always Bert's distraction for me, and I found it comical how she all but volunteered to help me once she discovered what I was up to. I haven't put my finger on it yet, but it's as if there's an old rivalry between Bert and Sue. It stands to reason, they're about the same age. Probably went to school together and chased after the same boy at one time.

Truth is, Mel and my daily heist with Sue is a welcome distraction. Waiting has been intolerable. Waiting for Dad, the Last Atlantean, to show up and try to take over the world. I still think I have the right idea—building an army—and so far, it's happening, with Markus acting like my first in command, taking charge of the civilians and training them, not to mention the Broadsword. Stealing candy for Mel is uplifting, but the Broadsword are always here, just around the corner, manning the wall, reminding me of how much I want to set them free of Dad's hold on them. Part of me hopes he can help me control my violet wild child, but that's if he is himself and free. But if he can't even control his other self, how can he aid me?

It's too much time to ponder everything, so I do what I can to pass the time. Reading my book isn't an option as it burned up in the cabin, but Kara does her best to entertain me by conjuring up a TV along with any recent movies she's seen. The picture's fuzzy at times, and the plot is mostly choppy as whatever movie she conjures from memory is far from intact. So, after a few days even that bit of normality leaves me, and she gives up on trying to reproduce Hollywood on a stone wall.

Kara has come to know Toni quite well as she became her non-official nurse. Mostly they swap stories, keep each other company. It kinda makes me jealous, but I shrug it off as to her needing some female companionship other than me constantly hovering over her. Neither one of us wants to go stark-raving mad in the chance we become separated thanks to the bond. So, we figure we'll slowly pull away from one another—no matter how much it tears at us to do it. She brought up the idea. Of course she did, my rock; she's looking out for me, protecting me, again. I'm immortal, and Kara isn't. Inevitably, one day, she'll…leave me.

I push those thoughts aside and follow Kara into the courtyard, my favorite place to meditate. Which is now occupied by the Broadsword and humans. It makes me curious, how long they'll work alongside each other. Some have even forged friendships, but not with me. I'm alone, aside from having Kara, Mel, and Markus. He's the one who's really running the show around here, not me. He even put down a drunken rant from a dirty man in coveralls with a bent nose, Ike, who unlike the other humans in the castle, gives me the creeps. There's a familiarity about him I just can't quite place until I nonchalantly ask Bert what his problem is. She tells me old man Williams is always full of vinegar, and immediately my conversation with Lukas at the diner comes back to me about the missing Williams boys. Zeke and his brother are the spitting image of their father—or would have been had I not fed off them and submerged them in the river. The thought of Ike makes me scan the people mulling about for him. I catch him every now and then, staring at me, and wonder if he suspects I had something to do with his sons' disappearance. Today, he's nowhere in sight.

I lean up against the water tower and hang back while Kara circles her Trans Am, the only vehicle aside from my dirt bike Ducati that remains in the courtyard. Any other working vehicles are parked outside the castle's walls. Markus says it's smart to remind everyone who saved them, and our rides are the perfect lawn ornaments to do so.

Then there's the winged pegasuses, safely protected inside the castle walls and grazing on the courtyard's lush grass. For some reason they haven't flown away yet. Must be due to all the carrots the children sneak them. The mythical horses have become somewhat of a novelty to them, especially Mel.

Kara climbs in her car and honks, startling the pegasuses. They snort and flap their wings, kicking up loose debris on the ground. She laughs. It's good to see her smile.

A drop of warm water hits my shoulder, reminding me of my shower. I sniff the air. I'm in need of one. Kara's fragrant flower trick only goes so far before it just becomes a potpourri mix of old pedals, sweat, and oil. After a few days of everyone being here the castle began to stink; a few more and it became down right rank. Deodorant only does so much, and not many people had thought to pack some when they came here. Medieval times must have been an era where people lived with livestock because they smelled like the animals they cared for, and I for one do not want to get used to that.

So, I enlisted Kara's mumbling skills that are far more controlled than my imagination. Truth be told I think that's what sped her recovery, her usefulness. I had her mumble the water tower full daily once it was constructed in the courtyard—which took far too long to build in the hot July sun. Kara did great. She filled the tower with ease from the well she sprang up from deep in the earth. All the people know who she is, or at least what she did for them. Fresh water to drink and to shower with every day. The fact she did it mumbling from her window while I was keeping her bedridden to heal herself didn't hurt her reputation. Even the shower stalls made of plywood and garden hoses were credited to her. We have four of them, and we use them well.

Kara hops out of her car with her sunglasses on, and after a few more introductions she makes her way to the main gate. She's infectious; everywhere she goes seems to have a more pleasant aura when she's around. Everyone she speaks to leaves their conversation happy, until I pass by and their grins fade.

I make my way to her side and look out past the dozen vehicles and the herd of cattle busying themselves on finding the greenest grass the sun has yet to dry out. "What do you think?"

"It would have looked better if you hadn't kept me lying in bed." Kara sighs. "But you did good, even with minimal supervision from me." Her sarcastic side returned even before her strength did. "Any word?" So did her serious side.

"I sent Markus out four days ago. He should be back by now."

"Bert's getting worried. Did you see the kitchen? She'll have us cooked out of food in no time. 'Course *you* didn't see." Kara pulls her sunglasses down to the brim of her nose. "Probably had your face buried in a book while I was laid up." She winks. Her way of comforting me works to a degree, but the feeling of loss is still there. She checks over her shoulder, leans closer to me and whispers, "Ben's all out of sorts. I guess they were close for cousins. Real close, like brothers. And between you and Toni taking care of me like you have, and me recovering. I haven't been able to…comfort him. Ease his mind if only for a night."

We all need a little easing. I wrap my arm around her and pull her close. I don't admit it to her, but I miss Lukas, he's been gone too long. His return from going to fetch his aunt is far overdue, and so is Markus's return from searching for him. "They'll be back soon," I say, more trying to convince myself than anything else.

"Wanna go for a ride?" Kara says after a moment. "I'll even let you drive."

We need the gas and probably shouldn't. "I'm good."

"Come on, Scar. It'll do you some good."

She's right, but Kara also needs a win, and I know exactly how to give it to her. "Nah. Take Ben. Go *check* on the herd."

Kara looks at me with pity in her eyes for just a second, then her demeanor shifts with anticipation. She knows how to cover up a look she doesn't mean to give. She pushes up her glasses and turns around, halfway to her car she stops and says, "He's probably just broke down with a truck full of beer, sitting in the sun, and having a blast."

I don't respond. I just keep staring out over the field. I've almost forgotten what Lukas's touch feels like. I'm not stupid. Something has happened to him. I refuse to let my imagination show any scenarios.

One thing is for sure—eight days is a long time to be buying beer and checking on family a day's ride away.

Chapter Forty-Three

After a hearty meal of potatoes and creamy pasta, I set out for my post on the wall. Kara's Trans Am is parked in the pasture with foggy windows until the sun sinks beneath the horizon. She waves at me from my position above the gate as she drives in, and Ben blushes. She and Ben got their win.

Laughter, singing, and the strumming of guitars echo from the main hall of the castle just as it has every night since our guests arrived. Montana has a hearty people with plenty of resolve, I'm finding. Kara and Ben hop out of the car, and she practically drags Ben into the hall. It makes me happy to see her happy. She's been cooped up in her room listening to a party I wouldn't let her attend. I stayed to partake after dinner, once, but it was just awkward. She needs to enjoy what we have while we have it, and she's accepted by the group far more than I am.

Bert's fresh-baked pies send their fragrance wafting through the open doors of the main hall; I left dinner a little too early. We're running low on the food we gathered. Anyone we let in the gates has their supplies put under the scrutinous eye of Bert. If she knows about my little deception with Sue, she hasn't voiced it to me. Though I doubt she ever will, if she knows the chocolate is for Mel. None of the other women seem to mind Bert being in charge. She has an air to her that commands respect. The fact her son is dating the only witch in the castle doesn't hurt, either. I overheard a couple kids talking about Kara. I don't want to tell her she has a nick name, Enchantress.

I get it—she's gorgeous, she can work magic, and she's enchanting. I haven't heard my nickname yet, and I don't think I want to. I even had to stop Mel from telling me once.

I'm falling into a slump again where I think of Mom, and even miss the days at the Sanctum. At least there I was with my own kind. Not one witch or vamp has come to our doors. Turns out they're few and far between in the Broadsword ranks, so I'm not holding my breath that any will show up. Instead, I busy myself with plans of the future. Mainly, what I'm going to do about Dad and freeing the Broadsword. Markus said Dad's amulet is what he used to strip them of their souls, and since it appears to contain the Last Atlantean, I figure if I can tear it away from Dad and smash it, they'll all return to normal. I hope. The problem is getting it away from him.

I look at Lukas's house and the deck where Dad kicked my ass. How I'll do this, I have no idea. Where Dad is? That's another issue. I consider sending out scouts, but since Markus hasn't returned, I hold the order. Not knowing what's beyond these walls is one thing, but depleting my meager force is plain stupid if Dad's alter-ego comes at me with full force.

The other thing weighing on my mind is food, and the lack of it.

It's mid-July. Not the best time to plant crops. There are enough people living in the castle that the preserves they brought won't hold out more than a month or two once all the fresh stuff is gone. We've basically become vegetarians for the past few days so what we do have that's fresh won't go to waste. We've got Lukas's cattle, enough to get through the winter. But then what? A cow moos in the dark as if disliking the notion of becoming a burger.

Then there's the real issue, and probably the reason I'm so feared, and Kara is not. I *will* need to feed eventually.

They think I'm scary? What if I was a full-blooded vamp? I'd need to feed a hell of a lot more often than once a month or so. That would thin the ranks of the castle pretty fast, and as far as I know, there aren't any disreputable types in their ranks, making choosing my next meal a quest outside the ranch. Picking off the people we've let in one by one won't bode well for morale. Ike does cross my mind, if he's anything like the sons he raised, but so far, he hasn't caused a disturbance or uttered a word to me.

"Want some company?"

"Jeez." I jump back. "Toni. You seriously have to teach me how you can do that." I have to calm my heart.

"Do what?" Toni leans on the wall's tooth. She knows exactly what. "I can't help it if I'm light on my feet." She flips her long dark hair over her shoulder. "But you name the time and place, and I'll give you a few pointers."

"It's just an expression."

"I know." Her mood shifts. Of course she knows. She's not an infant, and I just brought to light that she is entirely under my command.

"I didn't mean. I'm sorry, I—"

"Forget about it."

I'm starting to learn Toni's a tough woman, aside from being a member of the Broadsword. She's holding herself together better than I am, and she lost John whereas I still have Kara. I don't have Lukas, but I'm not convinced he's gone, not like John is. "Quiet night."—I look over my shoulder at the firelight dancing through the open door of the main hall—"All things considered. You're not going?"

"Nope. Thought I'd hang with you and brood for a while." Am I that obvious to the eye, or is she just that good at reading people? "You know. Take in the sights." She turns away from me and leans over the tooth. "Aaaamazing," she says, though I know she can't see much in the dark.

"It's peaceful."

"Uh-huh."

"It is."

"If you say so."

"I do."

"If *the One* says it's true, then I guess it must be." Reading my face, she catches my confusion. "You know a lot of us considered you the boogeyman."

"Really?"

"Oh yeah. The only one who could bring down Drago's idiotic plan, the One. You were made out to be a legend. Then we find out you're half vampire and half witch, making you virtually unstoppable. The boogeyman doesn't seem to quite cut it anymore. It's nice to see there's some humanity to you." She pauses. "Emotional humanity, I mean."

"Thanks, I guess." I lean on the tooth next to hers for a minute. It starts to drizzle, and I immediately want to go in search of an umbrella.

"Your old man gets loose lipped when he drinks, and two-faced." She squints at the clouds, clearly annoyed at the threat of rain, then studies my face, and does better than Markus has in the past—she volunteers what she knows despite the weather. "It wasn't until he started dabbling with the amulet centuries ago that he started to call himself Xanatos on occasion. Made us call him that too. It was weird, seeing him shift. One minute he was kind old Drago, then the next he's Xanatos barking orders, then he'd get confused as to why we were addressing him as Xanatos."

"So that's his name, Xanatos. Dad's tormentor."

"He was the Last Atlantean. What his name was before Atlantis took him and trained him, I don't know, but he came to be known by his Atlantean name. Xanatos made the amulet. He destroyed Atlantis, and he's *inside* the amulet. He's one with it, and it with him."

Somehow, hearing Toni tell me my suspicions are correct about everything being tied to the amulet reassures me I've got the right idea about smashing it. Dad didn't steal Toni's soul, Xanatos did. Then it hits me—if it's contact with the amulet that made Dad lose control of himself, become possessed, then what about me? "I touched the amulet." Is that why I lost control in Ovando—Xanatos's influence?

"Just be glad you didn't hold it too long. Look at your dad. He was sane once, before he took the amulet."

"How do you know all this?"

"I know someone who was there when it all went down. Atlantis and the amulet and all."

"He'd be centuries old."

"*She* is," Toni corrects me, wiping a drop of rain from her forehead. "I only met her once in my travels."

She could have said *hunting expeditions* but I wasn't going to shift her train of thought.

"She's part of the reason for the hatred of the wolves, pissed Xanatos off something fierce. You should be a little nicer to them. It's not like they asked to be cursed. None of us did." Toni's trailing off. She's talking about herself now and how Dad relieved her of her soul. "Having no control over what you do is downright terrifying. I believe you got a taste of it at the bar if I'm not mistaken."

I stare at her as blankly as I can.

"Thought so."

My poker face is useless with Toni. I'm like an open book to her, and it doesn't feel good. I lean over the tooth, and peer down the wall; she does the same. I want to believe her, believe that the reason for my selfish outburst at the bar is due to Xanatos, but something inside me tells me it's not. He may be the catalyst, but in the end I'm the one who acted without thought, giving into a part of me that has been buried for a decade with spells from Aunt Brenda. I have to learn to control that side of me and not feel like a spectator watching myself from afar. I'm in a different place than Toni. I have a choice. She doesn't. She can't control her actions...God...what if she's the Broadsword who killed Mom?

I turn my head from her, hiding my face so she can't read it. I try my damnedest to recall the face of the woman who murdered Mom, but all I can manage is her hands wrapped around Mom's head. Inspecting Toni's hands resting on the tooth does me no good. There's only one way to know for sure, and that's if I ask her, order her to tell me if she's the one who ended Mom's life and Aunt Brenda's. I want to know who did it so I can take my revenge, but that feels like losing control as I did in Ovando. Does it matter anyway if I know who did it now that I've discovered the unwavering obedience the Broadsword has?

Toni, though I haven't known her long, doesn't strike me as a heartless murderer. She has no say in what she does; none of them do. If I were in her shoes—soulless—would I be driven to obey a command to kill someone, even Kara? The thought frightens me and makes me pity Toni.

I decide, though I'm struggling with it, I don't want to know who killed Mom. The reality of it is that she's gone, taken by a slave of the Last Atlantean.

I want to bring him down more than ever now.

A car horn sounds out in the distance, pulling me from my realization, and is followed by Matt ringing the warning bell. A set of headlights is speeding toward the gate in the dark, and the gates are opening.

"Someone breaking in?"

"No." She can't see what I can. "They're being opened by our people."

"Then why sound the bell?"

"Because they need help."

They're too far away to positively identify in the dark, but just like I can recognize Matt's form at the bell, I can recognize the form of the man in the passenger seat of the truck.

Markus has returned.

There are people piled in the box of the pickup, but not one of them is Lukas.

Chapter Forty-Four

The pickup truck speeds toward the castle faster than necessary. Markus, or someone else, must be injured and in need of more medical attention than they can provide for themselves.

"Open the gates," I call down to the people inside the courtyard. "It's Markus."

"It's about time," says Toni, following me down the steps. "I can't imagine what could have kept him away for so long."

"He found Lukas," I say.

Toni doesn't have my vision. Binoculars would help even the odds. I can't see Lukas, but I told Markus not to return until he found him. Since I can't see Lukas, I assume Markus is returning with bad news. I try not to envision Lukas dead, but a vision of me standing over his grave pops up.

"Right on."

I don't respond to her. I clamp my jaw shut, focus on my surroundings rather than my imagination, and steady my nerves.

They aren't the only ones at our door. Vehicles and a crowd of people on foot are pouring through the main gates led by a slim-figured woman strutting with a confidence that no human should possess in times like these.

The pickup pulls up to the gate, and Matt jumps out of the box. "Get Abby!" he shouts, opening the door. Abby, our resident nurse and our only link to the medical world besides Markus, was highly welcomed when she found her way to the farm. People coming out of the main hall run in different directions calling for her.

"Who's that?" I point at the people filing in through the main gate.

"Townsfolk. From Lincoln I think," Matt says, opening the truck door, slinging Markus's arm over his shoulder and pulling him out of the truck. Markus's eye is red from burst blood vessels, he's got a fat lip, and walks with a limp.

"How bad is he?" I ask, doing what I figure to be a decent job at holding the composure of the leader I'm supposed to be.

"He'll be fine. It's Lukas that needs Abby's help right now," says Matt.

I hold myself together and walk faster than normal to the truck's bed, unsure if it's due to an urgency to see Lukas or because I can make out soldiers' uniforms among the approaching crowd. I look in the bed and all my composure goes out the window.

I gasp.

My hand covers my mouth.

Lukas is unconscious and has been beaten so badly he's barely recognizable. His curly gold locks are near black from blood that's caked it into a mat clinging to his face—or what's left of it. Both his eyes are swollen shut, his nose is bent to the side and broken for sure. His once soft lips are cracked and puffed up on one side, contorting his mouth out of shape. His shirt clings to his body in dried blood. A bulging wad of gauze, stained red, is sticking out of a torn piece of cloth tied around his thigh. The knuckles on both his hands are swollen and split open. He went down with a fight.

"Abby!" I scream back at the castle.

Abby jumps back at my scream, she's already at the bed of the truck with a first aid kit in hand. One glance at Lukas and she takes charge, jumping into the bed, pressing her hands against his torso, feeling the back of his neck with her fingers, prying his eyes open one at a time. "We need a gurney or a board, something to get him inside without jarring him around."

I rip the tailgate free. "This do?"

Abby pauses, staring at the tailgate. I moved too fast for her to catch what I did, and from the look on her face she has to process why the truck is bobbing, and how I got the tailgate. "Um…yeah. That'll work."

She guides those of us around the truck into action as if we're in her OR. We haul Lukas inside, set him on a table in the main hall, and strip off his clothing. His ribs and stomach are black and blue. His chest rises and falls in fast, short breaths, as if he's struggling to breathe. Abby speaks quickly, but in a calm medical voice like on the countless doctor shows on TV. She throws out medical terms as she examines him that I don't understand aside from one: internal bleeding.

"Gotta relieve the pressure. I need a scalpel, a small knife, something sharp."

Someone holds up a pocketknife.

"Good enough. Sterilize it in the fire and get me whiskey, a lot of whiskey." There's confidence in her voice, but also urgency. "We have to relieve the pressure or he's not going to make it through the night." She pours whiskey on Lukas's ribs and takes the sterilized pocketknife. "What I wouldn't give for a ten blade," Abby says, slicing into Lukas's side, making a long gash that spills more blood than I thought possible. If she weren't a nurse, I'd swear she was killing him. "Come on, breathe." As if Lukas were just another one of us under her command, he listens and takes a deep breath. "Good boy."

"Is he gonna make it?" I ask.

"I'll know more once I get a good look at this leg." Abby peels the bandage and gauze off Lukas's thigh. The gauze sticks to the wound, comes off slowly, trailing strands of sticky red blood. She sniffs Lukas's leg, nods to herself. She's smelling for rotting flesh, that much I know. Aside from sweat, grime, and fresh spilled blood, I can't pick up an odd scent either. That gives me a sense of being useful, somewhat.

"God, what happened?" says Kara.

"Christ." Ben's as pale as a Broadsword.

"Nothing good." Abby douses Lukas's thigh with whiskey and starts picking at it with the knife. "I need a needle and thread for this laceration, and some tweezers."

Matt helps Markus to a chair at the table next to us. "Did we get him here in time?"

"I wouldn't have wanted to wait any longer," says Abby as she's handed a pair of tweezers and pours whiskey on them. "Someone get him a seat." Abby indicates Ben. He's making slow zeroes with his head. "Before he faints and cracks his head. I don't need another injury." She goes to work cleaning Lukas's wound with the tweezers, pulling hard dark chunks of something out of his leg.

Lukas's leg spits a stream of blood to the table, and then another. "No, no, no. Not the femoral." Abby's hands dive into the wound with wads of gauze.

Lukas cries out, sits up. Hands shoot out, including mine, and we pin him back down.

"Tourniquet."

I let the others take his chest, grab the bandage Abby removed, and wrap it around Lukas's leg.

"Make it tight."

I do as much as I can without risking further damage. I could easily overtighten it and do God knows what to him. The spurting blood doesn't shoot out as far. Abby stuffs gauze in Lukas's leg. If he snapped out of his unconscious state, it was only momentary. His head cocks to the side, and he lays still again, passed out. I'm not sure he even came too, or if he just reacted.

"Thread that needle and bend it into a curve like a half-moon. I need suction." She's getting frustrated. I take Lukas's hand in mine. "Screw it. Roll him on his side. Now!" The others roll him. "Faster, faster. Come on." Abby squats down beside the table. "Light."

"Here." Ben pulls his keys out of his pocket and hands them to the woman closest to Abby. The woman clicks on a small two-inch penlight.

Abby grunts at our obvious lack of supplies. "Where's that needle?" The guy bending the needle nearly stabs Abby in the palm as he gives it to her. She throws the soaked gauze aside and digs into Lukas's thigh, pulling and tugging at the thread with the needle and tweezers while Lukas's blood covers the table. She's taking forever. I should have learned medicine. With my speed I could—

"Got it," Abby says, pulling away, ducking her head side to side, peering into Lukas's leg. "Roll him." She grabs the flashlight and double-checks her work then sets about stitching the leg shut.

"Thank you." My voice cracks.

"If we don't find any more surprises he should recover," Abby says, running her eyes over Lukas's body as her fingers skate along his wound with the thread. "Provided this holds."

I clear my throat and wipe my eyes. "What happened, Markus?"

"Wolves," Markus says, shaking his head. "A *lot* of wolves."

Chapter Forty-Five

"Wolves?" I question Markus. "How many? Where?"

"The most I've ever seen, all to the east. We're in for one hell of a fight. Got us some allies, though." Markus points at the soldier entering the main hall.

I recognize him from Lincoln, his short-cropped red hair, his rigid composure. Markus brought Lieutenant Niclas Huntly to the castle. Wolves outside the walls, military inside them, brought here by a member of the Broadsword. Not much of this is sitting well with me. The government wants me, and that means so does the lieutenant. I take some refuge that he said he wanted Kara and me alive, but not much. At least I can count on knowing the wolves' agenda being food. Their number will have to be thinned no doubt, but the soldier extending his hand to me could have numerous plans for me that would be kept shrouded in secrecy.

"I'm—"

"I know who you are," I say, glaring at the lieutenant. "You're the one who's in charge of hunting me down."

"Us," says Kara.

"Us," I correct myself.

"Not anymore," says the lieutenant. "Your man here, Markus, filled me in. I relayed the intel to my superiors. You have no need to fear the military, or at least what's left of it that I can get in contact with."

"Is that so?" asks Kara.

"We can trust him," says Markus, stretching out on a bench, letting Abby examine his leg. "He had my back, and I had his." Markus and the lieutenant nod between each other.

Markus might trust Lieutenant Huntly, but I for one don't. It doesn't look like Kara does either. I find it hard to believe the United States government would so easily roll over, forget the manhunt, accept who I am, *what* I am, and give up its worldwide scapegoat. It's just bad politics, and I've never trusted a politician to speak with anything other than a forked tongue.

"You certainly had Lukas's back," I say, running my fingers through Lukas's hair. The blood caked under my fingers infuriates me even more. "What'd you do? Beat him to a pulp until he told you about me? Look at him. If I hadn't sent Markus to—"

"Scarlett—"

"Do *not* interrupt me, Markus."

He falls silent and lays his head down on the bench.

"I've been hunted my entire life, and he just expects me to shake hands and say, oh, okay, I forgive you for turning the world against me. Least with you I know where I stand." This time I don't regret insinuating I have complete control of Markus and the Broadsword. "And now, with no electricity, he was somehow able to reach his superiors and convince them I'm the good guy. I don't think so."

"She's right." Kara steps forward, resting a hand on my shoulder. Her grip is to steady me, not support me. I'm shaking, vibrating, and my rock is here to cool my temper. "Our faces are most likely the last thing the civilized world saw, along with the caption of *martial law* and *witch hunt*. We're etched into the minds of every man, woman, and child out there. Every time they are cold, hungry, or lacking anything, they'll think of our faces."

"What's wrong with that? You're easy on the eyes, both of you," says a thin-framed woman in her thirties, her blonde hair done up in a mom cut, leaning against the door frame, relaxed, confident, and picking at her fingernails. Instantly I recognize her as the woman who led the latest herd of people through my gates. "All they're doing is picturing the faces of their saviors. They'll come to realize that with time, if they live long enough."

"Who the hell are you?" Kara's as fired up as I am, or she's feeding off me.

"Name's Nikki, and I'm your new best friend." She blows away the debris from her nails. Kara lets go of my shoulder and takes a step forward. Nikki looks between the two of us. "The bond has set in I see, not too strong yet though, it will get stronger if you keep holding hands. Good thing it's not ramped up by romance or you two would be screwed. It isn't, is it?" The look on both our faces makes Nikki brush aside the notion that Kara and I are lovers. "Good, you don't need that clouding your judgment further." She isn't just confident, she's cocky. "These boys are going to try to convince you about all kinds of things." That was a direct shot at Markus. "Who they are, what their agenda is, who they take orders from?"

"But who are you going to believe? Me, that's who. Because like you, they hunted me. I'm pretty good though." Nikki snaps her fingers and a flame sparks to life an inch above her thumb. "And I'm sure you'll take the word of your equal over a jarhead and an assassin." The flame flutters into nothing and she slaps Markus's injured leg as she passes him, making him wince. "Don't care what you did back there. I'm keeping an eye on you, turncoat." She holds out her hand to Kara. "Good to see another witch in the game."

Kara hesitates. I'm not certain why Kara's put off by Nikki. Is it because she's no longer the only witch in the castle? It can't be her attitude. She's not exactly humble, and as far as first impressions go, I can't see myself wanting to be in her presence for long.

Nikki drops her hand and jumps up to sit on the tabletop. "It's an outdated custom anyway, invented by untrustworthy men to prove they didn't have a knife up their sleeve."

"Just because you're a witch doesn't mean we should—"

"Trust me?" Nikki says, finishing Kara's sentence. "Yes, it does. Like it or not, we have to reclaim the world. What would you rather do, hand it back over to the men? Look what they did with it the first time."

Kara's shoulders drop at Nikki's words. I'm not sure she noticed it, but I did. She and Nikki are like two peas in a pod, both strong-willed women. I feel about Nikki the way I felt about Kara when I first met her, so I may have the wrong gut feeling about Nikki. Only time will tell. The real question is, can these two women coexist with such similar personalities and not kill each other? I've seen it before, in the Sanctum. Kara butted heads with a new girl so much the girl abandoned the Sanctum. I'll never forget it because that girl did exactly what I wanted to do and got away from her tormentor, Kara, who has now become the one person I feel I can't live without. She's quickly becoming the other half of my soul, and that could get dangerous.

I step back from Kara, trying futilely to lessen the bond.

"How did you get mixed up with…them?" I nod at the lieutenant.

A writhing ball of mist forms between the three of us. Nikki's mumbling.

I swear every drop of moisture in the hall gathers to form a giant globe. The air tastes like the desert—Nikki's good. I'm certain Kara could perform this trick as well, but probably not with as much ease as Nikki. "Lincoln. Great Falls." Nikki stops mumbling just long enough to speak actual words.

The globe zooms in to Montana. The two cities highlight with condensed water. The water droplets zoom in again, concentrating on a small town west of Great Falls surrounded by open fields, their crops burned to ash. It's a moving painting. A picture *is* worth a thousand words.

"Did the entire town burn?" Kara asks.

"You would have seen the smoke from here if it had been during the day," says Markus.

Nikki clears her throat as if to silence Markus from interrupting her tale. The droplets morph into a half dozen people lying motionless on the street, then whisks west to another town surrounded by foothills. Its people are the same as the first town, lying motionless, strewn about the streets, though there are less, only four, in this town.

"Devastation."

The picture zooms in on one surrounding town after another, still heading west toward us. A pack of wolves move like a blanket covering the land, growing larger in number with every town they pass, leaving them deserted.

"What about Lukas? Lincoln?" I ask.

"Patience," Nikki replies then continues mumbling. "Lincoln."

The town sign appears. The lieutenant is commanding his troops and the townspeople from behind a barricade of vehicles. Gunfire erupts; stones are thrown at the pack along with Molotov cocktails; the barricade falls.

"Swarming."

Lukas is enlarged on the moving canvas, his rifle on the ground beside him, his fists swinging. He falls and is overtaken. Markus charges into the pack and bodies fly through the air. Lukas is pulled back behind the dwindling line of soldiers and townsfolk.

"Salvation."

Stone spears shoot up from the earth, impaling the wolves closest to the people. Nikki's standing on a rooftop mumbling with her arms spread wide, and the earth splits between the combatants, separating the townsfolk from the wolves with a great chasm too large to leap across.

"Thank you," I say to Markus. He nods, not to me, but to the watery movie.

"Are they…taking them?" says Kara.

In the brief moment I gave thanks to Markus, I missed what Kara saw. I lean closer. Nikki enlarges the picture. The townsfolk and soldiers who had fallen to the wolves on the other side of the chasm weren't being slaughtered, they were being bitten, left moaning and wounded on the ground—they were being turned into wolves.

My chest tightens.

Wolves are mangy beasts that think only of their next kill. How the hell are they working together in such numbers?

Chapter Forty-Six

"This can't be," says Kara. "They're organized."

"I was there," Nikki says. "As hard as it is to believe, they were organized, methodical, and driven. They moved with purpose, unlike what we were taught."

Nikki mumbles the water back to moisten the air it had come from. The dry desert flavor is replaced with the fresh Montana air, ionized from the rain outside, mixing with what remains of Bert's feast.

"They had more on their minds than blood lust and carnage; their hearts weren't corrupted like others." She glances at Markus sitting on the bench, massaging his leg around the wrapping Abby has done.

"There're so many. How can this be? Their numbers have always been kept low like ours, but more so," I say. I can't believe Nikki, I just can't. Markus not challenging her story irks me even more.

"Scar's right." Kara gets in Nikki's face. "What you're saying is that the dogs have created—"

"A coven, like in the days of legend, when the world was young and full of magic more powerful than either of us could hope to wield." Nikki looks me up and down. "Well, maybe not you."

"Fuck," I murmur. I can't hear another word. This revelation coupled with the uneasy feeling of the grand hall is too much to bear. A *coven* of wolves. One is terrifying enough to disturb sleep for a month. A pack is bone-chilling. I look to the lieutenant, hoping he brought more than just people with him, hoping the Broadsword brought more than just what armaments they had on their person, hoping that stashed in an undiscovered room in the castle Dad left us enough high yield explosives to level a city. But I know that is all wishful, desperate thinking and nothing more.

"I need some air."

I storm out the doors to the courtyard. The lieutenant says something as I pass him, but it doesn't register. I need out. I need to think, to ride. Kara's hot on my heels, but I don't even want her by my side at the moment. I need freedom, and I know exactly where I can get it.

I hurry through the courtyard and jump on the back of my pegasus. "Carrot," I say, trying to force an illusion into existence. Kara made it look easy, but with a little aid from my other self a violet carrot appears before the pegasus. I wrap my fingers in its mane and kick my heels into its sides. In a bound we're airborne, clearing the lush orchard, kicking up the fresh citrus scent from the trees. Over the wall and into the sky we climb, higher and higher until I take a breath and my carrot vanishes.

My winged horse pulls back and hovers for a moment before it continues forward, craning its head side to side in search of its vanished treat. I don't care where it takes me, just as long as it's in control and I'm free.

The wind blows my hair back. Aside from the bounding up and down, the ride on the pegasus is almost as therapeutic as on my bike.

"Nice view," says Nikki, bounding up and down on the other pegasus a few yards away.

"Go away." Every bit of her presence pisses me off. Her likeness to Kara, her brash approach, invading my solitude…and the smug look on her face makes me want to smack it off her.

"I could, but then I would miss out on all this." Nikki pats Kara's pegasus. "A woman should never ride alone, especially during these times."

"I can't—"

"Handle it? Yes, you can. You're stronger than you think."

"You don't know me." No one does, not really. Kara's got a good handle on me, but even she can get it wrong. Though at the moment I can't recall when.

"I know because I can see it. Your power emanates right through your aura. Against this night sky you're lit up like a purple Christmas light." Her gift from witch blood flowing through her veins, I assume. "It's pretty. And it's strong, so you'll live through this and for many years after that…as long as you stay your course. When you're ready to talk, and ready to dry off, I'll be in the penthouse suite." She tugs at her horse's mane, and they turn back toward the castle.

I'd flown further than I thought. The castle and the land's outer wall are miniscule. A flickering light catches my eye not too far away in the distance.

Lincoln, I can see Lincoln.

The town isn't burning, it's burned. Embers glow in defiance of the rain, and sparks skirt away from skeletal frames of buildings. I was just beginning to like that town, before the whole end of the world thing anyway. I focus, try to peer through the dark. Nothing. I can't make out a single wolf. Is that a good sign? Would they move on to easier prey rather than ones held up behind towering walls? They should, unless they're commanded otherwise. Dad must be behind them, ordering them to do his bidding as he did to the Broadsword. What did he say? *The wolves are at your door.* Something like that. But why control them? What would be the point in having them multiply? Unless he means to use them as his own personal army to obliterate the few survivors humanity has to offer. But it's not like his plan worked; we're just without power. The earth didn't cook. I can't help but think of the line I held at Vegas, fighting Dad, fighting the sun, and the gut feeling I didn't stop all of it. Did the earth cook beyond my shield? I can't worry about that right now. I've got bigger problems. Like what about the Broadsword? Have they outlived their usefulness in his eyes? I doubt that. If he controls the wolves, will he turn the Broadsword against me?

"I said it's not safe. Come on. Your girl's going to worry." I stare at Lincoln, ignoring Nikki, and still nothing moving reveals itself. "I don't think she likes me very much. The last thing I want to do is trade blows with a witch when the real enemy is lurking in the hills. Especially over a petty thing like swiping the only other flying horse in the world."

"She hates that thing." I can't help myself. Nikki does remind me of Kara and how she can lighten my mood. I draw in the crisp night air and turn my pegasus. "So, Nikki, you can see my…power." I guess that's one way to put it. Since Ovando, mine's grown, like a tempest waiting to be unleashed, one I'm not fully in control of—yet. Burying Brian's tractor with no more than a thought is testament to that, not to mention I can feel it growing in me, as if I'm full of energy that's waiting, needing, to be released.

"I see a lot." Nikki urges her pegasus to keep pace with mine.

"Like what?"

"Death." Her voice loses all levity. "I see death, when someone will die thanks to their fading aura. It's like everyone is walking around with a rainbow of colors surrounding them. If it's strong, they'll live for many years, but the more it fades, the closer to death they are."

"That's creepy. I don't think I'd want to know when I'm going to die. I'm finally used to the whole immortal thing if I don't step in front of a bus."

"Fat chance of that happening anytime soon."

"How do you live with that kind of knowledge?"

"How'd you deal with being the prophesized savior? You found a way, so did I. I'm choosey as to who I tell. Most people can't handle it. But death is something you're going to have to deal with, and soon."

We fly the rest of the way to the castle in silence. Nikki's similar to Kara all right, giving me time to think. If I have to deal with a death that isn't my own, then whose is she speaking of? Abby said Lukas would recover, but I can't help but ask. "Lukas?" Butterflies form in my stomach the moment his name passes my lips.

Nikki chuckles. "He's that good, is he?" She pauses. I don't respond to her, just keep my gaze forward. Anticipating, dreading her answer is tearing me up inside, weighing down my chest. "Don't worry, just let him heal up before you take him for a ride." Nikki smiles, a twinkle in her eye.

In a heartbeat the butterflies in my stomach surge upward. I give a nod, though I don't look at her, and breathe a sigh of relief. Part of me still wants to know who is going to die, but after experiencing Nikki's foretelling, more specifically the agonizing moments between the question and the answer, there's a huge part of me that doesn't want to know. But if I can prevent any further bloodshed of those I've chosen to protect, then I have to know. I can think of a few others who should know as well, and the notion of sharing the burden of knowledge eases the pressure.

Touching down in the courtyard, I invite Nikki, Kara, Toni, Markus, and Lieutenant Huntly to the queen's chambers. "Will you tell them what you told me, about your gift?" I ask Nikki.

She's taken aback. She said she was choosey whom she told about her gift, but I didn't think she'd be awkward about it. She hesitates and barely raises her head when she begins to speak. Her cool, cocky attitude is replaced with…sorrow.

That's when it hits me. The reason she's being so stand-offish compared to when it was just the two of us is that someone in this room will soon be dead.

Chapter Forty-Seven

"You don't seem very sure of yourself," Markus says to Nikki, leaning against a wall in the queen's chambers, arms crossed.

"Markus," I interject, trying to defend Nikki. I've seen her demeanor when she's truthful, at least when I think she is. Now, as she tells my council of her gift she's hunched forward, head lowered, and not as cocky as she was when she first arrived. I hope I'm wrong about my assumption that someone on my council will soon die, due to how Nikki is acting.

"He's right," says Lieutenant Huntly. "I have seen things that will make you wish you were never born…granted most of those were within the past few days. But truthfully, you can tell when someone is going to die?"

"No," says Nikki. "I can only guess how long they will live…from experience."

"Think she's telling the truth?"

I nod at Kara.

"So, who drops first then?" asks Markus.

"You need to relax."

"No, Toni, I don't. If she's got information I can use to do our job until we're free, I'll exploit it." Markus's jab at my death setting him free of his command doesn't pass over my head, nor does Toni's glare at him. "Sorry, it's just that—"

"I know," says Toni, lighting up. "It's been a long time for me too, but just because we have a duty doesn't mean we have to be rude going about it."

"What job?" asks the lieutenant.

"To protect me at all costs," I tell him.

"That's interesting, and it explains why all these…people have left the service of, well…"

"My dad."

"Enough of this," says Kara, hitting her fist against the balcony rail. "Spill it, or I'll show you you're not the most powerful witch in this castle. Just remember who taught Scar all she knows about magic."

I get the feeling Nikki could wipe the floor with Kara in a battle of mumbling. She taught me most of what I know about controlling my power, but perhaps it's time I pick up another trick or two aside from going on gut instinct. Not wanting to offend either witch, I ask Nikki, "Can't hurt, can it?"

Immediately I second-guess myself. An hour ago, I didn't want to know about my own death, and I hesitated getting Nikki to confirm Abby's diagnosis of Lukas. Now I'm asking Nikki to point out those of us who are soon to perish. What if it's Kara? I don't think I can handle that. I had a hard enough time watching her recover from a gunshot wound I caused. Hell, even her new do that she's sporting so well is a constant reminder that I failed to protect her, just like Mom.

No, not Mom—I can't let her memory cloud my judgement. Or can I? Should I? What would she do?

"Nikki, I know you're not comfortable with discussing this, but it would put everyone at ease. If it wouldn't trouble you too much"—Mom's diplomacy lessons rehearse in my mind—"could you enlighten us as to what you think is to come to pass?" Mom might as well have said it herself. "Are the people we're to protect in any imminent danger?" I wave my hand over the balcony indicating those below, hoping she'll pick up that I do not want to know who on my council is doomed; if I read her right.

Nikki takes a moment to collect herself and picks up a bottle of wine from the table. "I'm not just going to point at people and tell them their time is up. There are better ways to go about it," she says, sitting down in a chair, rubbing the bridge of her nose. "Like hinting to a loved one now is the time to spend as many moments with them as possible." Nikki raises an eyebrow at me. "Take that heftier woman piling food around your beau—perhaps she should spend this night in the arms of those she loves, eating, drinking, and reminiscing of the good times they've had."

"Bert?" I wrap my fingers on the stone rail and lean over it, searching frantically for Ben's mother.

"I don't know her name, but it is a suggestion that should be taken."

Kara and I lock eyes. She hasn't been with Ben long, but I guess he's her thread to a reality that no longer exists, just as Lukas is to me.

Kara points at Nikki. "Liar." Her voice cracks. My strong Kara who seems indestructible is resuming her role as an insecure sixteen-year-old girl. "You don't know her…him. You…you better pray you're wrong." Kara rips the bottle of wine from Nikki's hand. "What would a skinny bitch with bee-sting tits know about anything."

I half expect Kara to hit her; instead, she storms across the queen's chambers and stomps off down the staircase, cursing Nikki's virtue.

"That"—Nikki points at the stairs—"is exactly why I said I'm choosey as to who I tell." She makes her way to the pile of booze in the corner and starts rummaging through the bottles of wine.

The rest of us trade glances. Toni sets four paper cups on the table, and we follow her commanding nod to sit and wait. Even Lieutenant Huntly follows her silent instruction, albeit ever so grudgingly.

The more time I spend with the man the more he strikes me as impatient, impetuous, and a bit of a control freak. Butting heads with him seems inevitable.

Nikki selects her bottle of wine, tosses her thigh-length leather coat over her chair, and rolls up the sleeves of her pearl white blouse. She means business. She undoes another button exposing more of her chest as she stares at Lieutenant Huntly like he's a piece of meat. She's forward, there's no denying that. She stares until he shifts his weight in his chair, then strikes a flame with her thumb as she'd done in the main hall. "Warm for red, cold for white. Remember that, dear," she says, winking at me and pressing her lit finger to the neck of the bottle just below the cork. "So, you kids think you can handle the truth?" She eyes all of us but the lieutenant. "You can't handle the truth!" she yells, laughing and shaking her head. I know she's quoting some famous law movie, but at the moment I can't recall which one.

The cork pops out of the bottle.

"Neat trick," I say, trying to lighten the mood.

"Ah-huh," Nikki hums more than says. "I haven't met a bottle I can't open. Drink up." Nikki fills our cups one by one and puts the bottle to her lips. After a long pull, she sets the bottle on the table. "You want the snowflake version or the cold hard facts?" She's an odd woman. Funny, energetic, and a jokester like Kara can be, yet she has a tormented sense of humor.

"Just tell it to us straight," says the lieutenant.

"First things first." Nikki locks eyes with me as she wipes a drop of wine rolling down her chin. "Are you a positive woman, or do you revel in the dark side?"

I never considered myself positive. How could I be with the end of the world hanging on my shoulders for a decade? But the way she poses her question, I can't dare say otherwise. "Positive…I guess."

"Me too." Nikki turns from me and addresses Lieutenant Huntly. "You need to make preparations."

"For what?" he asks.

"Unless I miss my guess, the wolves will be here within a day or two."

"How do you figure that?" asks Markus.

"Almost half of the people in this palace of stone will be alive to hoist a glass for longer than a day or two." Nikki tilts the bottle toward me then takes another swill of wine. "Positive, don't you think?"

In other words, half the people in the castle will be dead in two days.

I wish I hadn't pressed her.

Chapter Forty-Eight

Bert passes away before dawn breaks the next day, just as Nikki predicted. A heart attack is Abby's diagnosis. Markus tells me of the stubborn old aunt Lukas went to bring back with him. He couldn't convince her, and as a result she missed out on the last few hours Bert had left in this world.

Those I consider my council have kept their lips tight about Nikki's other prediction. I can tell it weighs heavy on them, as it does on me. Half the population of the castle is going to live longer than another day or two, according to Nikki—but that also means the other half will be dead.

Markus and Lieutenant Huntly have become believers in Nikki's gift, though Markus wasn't as disbelieving as the lieutenant had been. They're spending their time ensuring every weapon available is lining the castle wall after Nikki's prediction about Bert's passing came true. I fear Nikki's gift is accurate, which drives me to cherish the time I have left with those of my council, particularly Kara. Nikki's uneasy demeanor when she told us of Bert and the rest got me worried that one of them would also perish. It's selfish, but I picture myself locked in a room with padded walls from Kara's early demise. Then it hits me. Its not bad enough I'll go insane due to our bond when Kara dies, but I have power beyond that of a normal witch. The vision of my padded cell explodes with violet, setting me lose to lay waste to the land, tearing down the castle, smearing its cobbles with the guts of the people within it. Lukas, Ben, my council, Sue, and even sweet little Mel stare up at me with lifeless eyes bathed in my violet aura.

I squeeze my eyes shut. I can't let myself go there, imagining what is to come. Witches are powerful; they can conjure things up, and I don't want to inadvertently conjure up this image.

I take a slow breath and focus on the situation at hand.

I busy myself with preparing a plot for Bert in the orchard where the sweet smells from the kitchen waft from the window. Ben had no objection to my suggestion of a burial plot. I ask Kara if she can rim the plot with flowers. She tells me its beyond her scope. She'd need the seeds. She could water them, plant them, but mumbling seeds from nothing is impossible for her. She urges me to try to conjure up some just like Dad conjured up the castle, but I'd rather not disrupt Bert's resting place. I didn't know her long, but I liked her, even her momma bear, protective nature over Lukas. So I pick some wild flowers growing outside the castle. Brian calls them alfalfa. He smiles and holds his composure as I place them on the mound covering Bert.

It seems right to give Bert a proper burial, despite the knowledge of what is to come. It gives the people overcrowding the castle a sense of normality; it's a distraction from Markus and Lieutenant Huntly's preparations, and the devastation that brought down Lincoln and the towns west of it. It turns out not everyone from Lincoln made it here. After Nikki did her water globe trick, I'm guessing that those people still in Lincoln, along with those from the other towns, are now wolves. I don't have the heart to tell the group that theirs will soon be ripped from their chests by those very same loved ones.

Kara's taking Bert's passing a little rougher than I thought she would—sympathy pangs for Ben, I suspect. Kara's the driving force that's keeping Ben from thrashing yet another room full of furniture and keeping Brian from smoking his entire box of cigars at Bert's grave.

Kara's also the one who insisted we *live the most we can out of the time we have left*. Knowledge of one's own demise affects each of us differently. Kara and I have basically lived with it hanging over us since we were taught about the prophecy. She became the party girl with ambitions for room service, while I retreated to the freedom of my Ducati, books, and seclusion. Markus and Toni, being void of their souls, almost welcome death as a release from their slavery. Especially Toni, who longs to be back at the side of her lost lover, John. Lieutenant Huntly focuses on the upcoming battle and nothing else, as if he can change Nikki's prediction. Lukas, though still unconscious, is still with us. He's broken, but at least he's bandaged and resting in a bed unlike Bert in her final place.

The whole situation sucks. After seeing how Kara reacted to Nikki's prediction about Bert, we hem and haw about telling the people. After the funeral, my council decides it's best that we tell the people. They have a right to know, a right to prepare for their time to end in any way they see fit. Unfortunately, it's decided that I should be the bearer of bad news. Kara has earned the nickname Enchantress. I'm positive my nickname will be Harbinger of Death.

When the time comes for me to dash all hope, I find myself atop the outer wall, far from the castle, staring in the direction of Lincoln as the lieutenant takes charge and informs everyone gathered in the courtyard. The buzz of the castle rises and reaches me even at this distance, followed by the rumble of a Trans Am.

"It's done," Kara says, jumping out of her car and climbing the stairs to the top of the wall, followed by Nikki.

"I know, I just couldn't—"

"You have to," says Nikki. "They're looking to you for hope, and we certainly can't let the men take charge. They don't have any power—well, Markus does, and Huntly's got nice arms, but that's not enough. Those people need to see Nova again."

I frown at Nikki.

"She doesn't know," says Kara. "That's what they're calling you, Scar. Nova, short for supernova, ever since you lit up the rodeo and handed your dad an ass kicking."

"Beats Harbinger of Death," I say.

"Scar—"

"Oh boo-hoo, so the world's about to go to shit and you're feeling responsible. Get over it," Nikki says, cutting Kara off.

"Back off." Kara stands toe to toe with Nikki in my defense.

"No, she needs to be reminded of who she is, and so do those people." Nikki points at the castle. "If they want to call her Nova, she needs to step up and give them a show. Give them hope that they can survive with her help. I can see auras. I have also seen strong vibrant auras vanish in a second with a shit decision. Right now, those people are losing hope, and I'll be damned if I'm going to die because she doesn't have a spine."

Kara slaps Nikki across the face. "How dare you—"

Nikki lunges at Kara's throat.

"Enough!" I shout, my other self throwing up a barrier between the two of them.

"'Bout time," Nikki says after a moment. "If it's the protection of her—or your bond—that pushes you to act, then we should put her on the front line alone, *Nova*."

The barrier flashes from violet to crimson and hurls Nikki off the wall. I can't control my other self at the threat to Kara. Thankfully, Nikki mumbles up a dust devil to keep her from slamming into the ground too hard.

I shut my eyes and grit my teeth. Haul in air through my nose and let it slip between my lips. The fire in my chest subsides, as does my other self.

"You okay?" Kara puts her hands on my shoulders.

"I'm fine. It's just…ever since I touched that damned amulet it's like my power surges out of me on instinct."

"That's more like it!" Nikki shouts at me, even though I laid her out. "But if you throw my ass off a wall again you better know how to use that gift of yours."

"She's right," I say begrudgingly. "You need to teach me."

Kara releases my shoulders. "I can't teach you. You've got more power in your little pinky than I do in my whole body. Your issue is control, not your power. 'Course if you hadn't given up after one tiny crack in the ground and practiced more like I told you to while I was resting, you'd be more confident. Like me." Kara has her ways, and her words prompt a huff of a laugh from me. The crack I made swallowed Brian's tractor. "Come on, there's an entire field out there ready to be lit on fire or flooded. You need practice, and I need to watch from a safe distance." Kara heads down the wall's steps.

"That's it? You're just going to let me…play?"

"I could turn your hair to snakes and really get you going, but for now let's take baby steps with your emotions," she says without turning back to me.

"Snakes?' Nikki frowns at Kara as she passes by her.

Kara digs for something through the open window then jumps up and sits on the hood of her Trans Am. "Just a fond memory we share with each other. Don't concern yourself."

After a moment of her studying Kara, Nikki sits beside her on the hood and says, "Okay. Let's do it your way, since you know her so well."

"I do," Kara smirks, putting on her sunglasses. "Go on, Scar. Let loose."

The two women so similar to each other yet so different just stare at me, waiting patiently…patiently for them. My chest tightens and my cheeks warm. I feel like I'm about to give a report in front of my entire class back at the Sanctum on something I haven't studied. I swallow hard, walk past the pair of witches doing their best not to show hatred for each other—or a genuine fear for their safety. There's a hint of concern in Nikki's eyes. That's why Kara grabbed her sunglasses, to hide what her eyes would say. She's a clever witch.

I half smile and turn my back to them, using my evasion to hide my thoughts.

For years I thought the prophecy was a heavy weight on my shoulders. Now that it's over with and I won, or so I hope, I feel more optimistic. Though, I still have thoughts of Vegas and how I lost sight of the rest of the globe my shield was encompassing. I don't want that to show in my face—my concern about being unsure of the world, not to mention how the hell I'm going to fight Xanatos and free Dad from the amulet.

Then there's the Broadsword. Their souls are caught up in the midst of this. It all seems too much to bear for just one woman. So I concentrate on the immediate—on protecting Kara and the people within the castle from the wolves. I don't know, maybe we can hunt them down in the daytime and as cruel as it sounds, chain them up outside the walls to be unleashed against Xanatos. There's been no word from the lieutenant's radio chatter about Dad, nor any more sightings of crimson beams shooting to the sky. I haven't pressed him further about the rest of the world, it's too big to worry over, especially with an organized pack of wolves stalking the night. Besides, he wouldn't have much to report as his intel is from a ham radio. Their range is awesome, apparently, but few people still have them anymore. One thing's for certain, though: I'm growing tired of waiting for Dad to return.

It's gnawing at me. We've grown an army—not sizable, but it's better than just Kara and me. But waiting for Dad to come to me is getting irritating. He knows where I am. So why hasn't he shown up? Why hasn't Xanatos? Deep down inside I want to leave. Not like before, not to clear my mind on my bike, but to set out to track down Dad, take the fight to Xanatos while he thinks I'm sitting safe behind high walls. Catch him off guard.

I'll give it enough time to deal with the wolves, then decide if I go hunting. I need to ensure I don't fail these people, again. Losing electricity is one thing, but losing their lives is something else entirely. Maybe I can change Nikki's prediction. She said she's seen auras vanish due to shit decisions. Well then can't the same be said for good decisions? Can I fight hard enough to bring half the castle's auras back from Nikki's premonition of death?

I have to try.

There's nothing before me except an open field with grass the animals have grazed short. I take a deep breath and gaze up at the sky. *Mom, give me strength.*

Chapter Forty-Nine

"Show me what you got, Nova," says Nikki, sitting atop the hood of Kara's car. She mumbles, and a dozen mounds of soil push up through the short grass to reach my height. "And remember, you've got to inspire the masses."

No pressure whatsoever, thanks a lot. I'm not sure I like my nickname, but it's far better than Harbinger of Death.

I look at the castle and the fanned-out guards lining the wall. Okay, I got this, something simple like Kara taught me. *Fire, I'll set the soil on fire.* I concentrate, clench my fists and stare at the mounds.

Nothing, not a thing's happening.

I hold out my hand toward the mounds. *Focus, fire like in the main hall.* Just the thought of the hall makes the hairs on the back of my neck stand up. I shake my head and shudder to rid the feeling. *A different fire, warm and nurturing like the one Lukas made for me in his house.*

Thin trails of smoke waft from half the mounds. *Dirt doesn't burn, dummy.* I need something combustible, paper or wood, or even better, a pine tree, like the ones littering the foothills. I don't want to set them ablaze, just little ones that I have to grow in the mounds.

Something tingles in my palm, and I can almost feel seeds moving through the dirt into the mounds. Saplings sprout from their tops and grow fine needles on them, burst into flames in an instant, and extinguish themselves just as fast.

"Relax, Scar, you can do this," says Kara. "Use your emotions."

Do this? I just made a freakin' tree grow. Must have been pinecones in the ground spread by the birds or the wind and I felt them, actually made them grow, and set them on fire. But she's right. Its impressive, but not enough. Magic is tied to passion. Controlled passion, not a rage pounding in my chest like at Ovando. But flying down a highway on my bike kind of passion. I fill my lungs with the burned pine scent and imagine cruising along beside a blazing forest.

Flames shoot up on either side of me, soaring to at least fifty feet, threatening to burn me.

I try to block the heat with my arms, and the vision of Mom engulfed in flames rises from memory. "Oh crap, oh crap. Go away. Burn out."

The flames rage on despite no tinder whatsoever.

"Kara! Help!"

I drop into a ball, close my eyes, cover my head. I need my thunderstorm now. I try to feel the rain instead of the searing heat, try to smell the ionized air instead of superheated air. It's no use—the flames close in, surrounding me. Smoke chokes my lungs. I cough, try to scream, but my dry throat only lets out a rough gasp.

The earth shakes and the heat vanishes as quickly as it had come. Cool damp dirt pelts my flesh, cocooning me. I spit soil from my mouth, squinting. The fire is gone. The grass surrounding me for a good twenty paces is turned up, its black surface still smoking.

"Scar!" Kara shouts.

I push myself up to my knees, and she cradles me in her arms.

"I got you." Her fingers run through my hair, dislodging clumps of dirt as they go. Tears streak down my face and salt replaces the earthen flavor on my lips.

"She alive?" Nikki calls out from a distance.

Kara's cheek moves up and down against the side of my head. "Just breathe. It's okay. I'm here." Kara continues stroking my hair, pulls me tighter into her chest.

Thank God she was there to save my ass, again. I was a goner for sure, and I brought it on myself. How the hell am I going to pull off defeating Xanatos and saving Dad, the Broadswords' souls, these people, and Kara if I can't control my so-called gift raging inside of me? "I thought—"

"Don't."

"I'm sorry."

"Long as you're okay, that's what matters." She kisses the top of my head, rocking me gently.

Nikki's standing above us with her hands on her hips. "That went well if you were trying a sort of kamikaze move. Too bad it would only work once. You would have incinerated a pack of wolves, along with yourself. Nice move with growing trees—that's a new one—but it's not enough. Now get up and show some strength. Act like you meant to do that. There are eyes on you. And for God's sake, try to control yourself. Bond or not, you two are way too emotional."

Nikki's right. I feel it. My insecurities, my fear, heightened by Kara's. Why else would I need her to be by my side, reassuring me? The knowledge of this brought to words by Nikki does not diminish the feeling, though it does shift it. It also makes me take more notice of our connection and how it's not so much my blood that's boiling but Kara's.

"Piss off. She almost died," Kara snaps.

"But she didn't die, and she needs to dust herself off and do better, much better." Nikki wags a finger at me.

"Forget her." Kara's sweet voice sounds in my head. "Not now, Nikki."

"We don't have time for this. She has to—"

"What, save the world and learn all our ways in a single week? Took us years to learn to control our powers," Kara barks. "Can you grow a tree from nothing?" Kara doesn't wait for an answer. "Didn't think so. Now piss off."

"No, she—"

"*Piss off!*"

Nikki glares down at us, nostrils flaring. "We're screwed," she says, throwing her hands in the air, kicking a clump of dirt and storming off toward the castle.

"Just breathe, Scar, breathe," says Kara.

"I can't do this. I can't control it." It's my own fault. I could blame Mom and Aunt Brenda for concealing this side of me, but I'm the one who failed to act, which pisses me off further. I tried, but I let a little mishap like sinking a tractor in the dirt sway me from honing my skills without my mentor by my side. What if I do more harm than good without that guidance and end up killing someone I care for, or even myself. That blasted amulet supercharged me, and I saw what it's done to Dad. I don't want to lose control over my actions, let alone my mind.

"Yes, you can, and you *will* with time."

"Wish I had more time or used it better." I pull away from Kara to find her eyes a bit glossy.

"You know what you need?"

"What?"

"You need to let it out."

"I just tried, and I don't dare let out my…other self with you so close by."

"I can handle myself, and that's not what I mean. Not the witch in you, or whatever your light show is. The vamp in you." Kara stands and holds her hand out to me. I let her pull me up. "You need to smash them." She nods toward the smoking mounds of earth. "Make them pay for daring to defy you."

I look at the mounds, then at Kara. She's right, again. "I like that idea."

"Go get 'em, girl," she says, slapping my ass.

She has a way of encouraging me with just her eyes, let alone her words. The coach's slap on the ass, coupled with *our* growing anger at what Nikki pointed out, gets me moving. Imagining the piles are wolves helps let out some frustration I've been holding back.

I run at the piles and turn it into a sprint while I play out a scene yet to come from a battle we're soon to fight. One where I am the most powerful weapon my army can muster.

My fist destroys the top half of the first pile, and then the second. Kara shouts a "Yeah!" at my back, though I'm certain I'm a blur to her. I kick clear through another pile and really start to enjoy Kara's idea. My pounding heart, letting out my anger, the rush of putting my fist through something, successfully accomplishing something I know I can do—it all gives me confidence. Confidence that I can obliterate a pack of wolves, even though I know I'm pummeling dirt.

Boulders varying from half my height to taller than me push up through the grass, along with more piles of dirt. Kara's showing me the way to let loose, and I intend on taking full advantage of it. I pick up a smaller boulder and spin around, launching it through a pile, and crush another one with an overhead blow from a larger boulder. If anyone from the castle is watching—and I'm sure they are—they're in for a show.

Pile after pile appears and I obliterate them all, until I get to the last boulder Kara has popped up for me. It's pink, streaked with white lines, sparkling in the sun, and almost the same size as the last boulder I tossed. It's heavy, way too heavy to pick up. My muscles strain and my joints pop at the exertion. Quartz, that's what it is. A dense boulder made of quartz, far heavier than one twice its size if it was made of sandstone. My adrenaline surge fades with the embarrassment of not being able to lift this smaller boulder, and that pisses me off. I heave at it with all I have, and the boulder is suddenly weightless in my hands.

My other self has come to my aid, encasing the sparkly pink boulder in violet tendrils. No, not tendrils—more like writhing jagged arms. Mom's phone flashes through my mind with the video of the sun tossing out its solar flares. That could be why I got the name Nova. My other-half projects flares. Flares that can do my bidding, I hope.

I glance over my shoulder. Kara's a good dozen yards away. I have to control myself, my ability so I don't get her hurt. I have to stay in command of my emotions and not let myself slip like I did in Ovando. I was fired up then, enraged by what the Black Serpents had done. It's no wonder I marked them as food, and what they did in Ovando proved it. Just the thought of them raises my temperature, brightens my other self.

I focus on the piles, imagining they're wolves again, and not the threat I faced that drove me to give in to my primal urges at Trixi's saloon.

I raise my hand high above my head. The boulder follows, leaves my palm and hangs in the air a good fifteen feet above me, suspended by a flare. I grunt, though I'm not sure I need to, and bring it down swinging my arm like I'm brandishing a giant mace. The boulder slams through a mound and craters itself in the earth. More piles pop up. *Thank you, Kara.* I swing the quartz up and spin it in a great circle, take aim, and arc it through seven or eight piles, reducing them to specks of dirt with one blow.

"Atta girl," Kara whispers, but I catch it.

Now *this* I like. I know how to smash things, hit things. It's natural, and very therapeutic.

I continue for another five minutes or so before I launch the boulder through the air, letting it skip along the ground kicking clumps of dirt every couple of paces until it comes to a stop.

Kara high fives me and tosses me her keys to the Trans Am. "I think you earned a spin." Kara mumbles and the turned-up soil I had burned softens and turns to mud. "I expect my fire chicken not to have a speck on her when we're done."

"I'll give her a good wash."

"Don't forget the wax." Kara climbs in the passenger seat giggling. "Now let's do some mud bogging, girl."

I don't know what I'd do without her. As I step into her car, I try to push down the question gnawing at me. Was I right in assuming one of the council members was going to die? After seeing Nikki's demeanour alter like it did when she revealed her gift to the others, along with her prediction of half the people in the castle perishing, and just how polar opposite her attitude was compared to today, I can't push the notion aside. Is Kara going to die?

Chapter Fifty

My exploits in the field did not go unnoticed. As we pull Kara's thunderstorm-washed Trans Am—her doing, not mine—into the courtyard, we're met with grins and nods of approval. Nikki even gives me a "Good job" when I get out of the car. It's a welcome change to the usual buzz of the castle that falls silent when I come around a corner.

We had been practicing, and mud bogging, for so long that we missed dinner. I don't mind, but Kara grumbles about it when she has to settle for cold potatoes and extra dry jerky.

Markus and the lieutenant kept themselves busy while we were away. They cut down a number of trees in the courtyard, a task that picked up pace thanks to Nikki's aid. They had the outer wall's defenses moved to the courtyard. I agree with their decision as we don't have the manpower to guard the entire outer wall. The stables within the castle have been filled with all the best cattle and horses. The animals that couldn't fit have been left to roam about the ranch leaving the stables just outside the castle empty, hedging our bets that some will survive the pending battle.

I question Lieutenant Huntly how a functioning military can even be possible without power, and he tells me, "The United Sates is not to be trifled with, and like the Boy Scouts, we are prepared."

It turns out that some senator back in the day had the bright idea to construct most of the States' critical defenses with a button. One that if pressed will switch controls from digital to analog and make stuff work without the electronics of today. I'm sure there's more to it than pushing a button on an aircraft carrier and the entire thing operates like it's back in World War II, but I don't question him further. He seems to know what he's talking about.

Aircraft carriers, submarines, and vital bases of operations have the button. The button was dreamed up so that in the event of a nuclear attack, the U.S. would not be left defenseless. I bet they never thought the button would be needed due to the sun, and my dad.

Dad, it turns out according to Lieutenant Huntly's ham radio connections, has been busy. When I saw the crimson streak shooting toward the heavens and thought Dad had more on his agenda, I was right. A witness reported not only a crater was left in Washington where a nuclear power plant once stood, but that a man and gray skinned women were responsible for it. Four hundred miles from where we stand, they launched an entire nuclear power plant into space.

If Dad is hunting down every nuclear reactor with the aid of witches and launching the radioactive material into outer space at least we won't die from nuclear fallout. The lieutenant tells me there's nearly a hundred reactors in the US alone, and it gives me the creeps. I hear nuclear reactor and I think of the meltdown at Chernobyl. It's scary to think about nuclear power plants with fried computer chips due to the solar flare's EMP. I consider asking the lieutenant about nuclear submarines, but then think better of it as all we can do is deal with the immediate threat surrounding us, the threat bearing long pointy fangs.

Nikki reassures everyone they'll live through the night once word of her unique ability gets out, though she won't reveal who's going to die no matter how much people plead her to. We number over a hundred within the castle's walls, and every man, woman, and child agree on one thing: If this is to be their last night on earth, they would make the most of it.

I've heard about it, read about it, even seen it in movies, but never thought I'd witness it. People about to go to war, and possibly die, choose to live every last breath with passion and pleasure rather than wallow in sorrow and despair.

Families that are still whole hold each other, play games, tell stories. The kitchen is raided due to Kara's rumbling gut suggesting so, and a feast is set out. Musicians play to their heart's content. Wine and hard alcohol flow freely. The strong skunk smell of marijuana wafts from the corners of the castle. Couples make love. Those who are single soon find themselves divulging in their own pleasures of the flesh with either a comely stranger or a crush they'd not had the courage to confront until now.

Guards rotate shifts with friends or loved ones by their side. Even Lieutenant Huntly softens his composure, after reappearing from a locked room with Nikki. The entire castle has a feel of joy, passion, and intensity I've never experienced before. It's like the saying "spring is in the air" has taken on a new meaning and been amplified tenfold. Maybe knowing when you are going to die isn't such a bad thing. It seems to bring out the best in people…well, at least these people. Aside from a squabble over a rousing game of cribbage, not a single fight has broken out. The castle has become peaceful, and yet at the same time euphoric.

The main hall and courtyard are full of people laughing, dancing, and indulging. They disappear to private chambers for a stint and return to carry on with the celebration of life. The same goes for Kara and Ben.

I abandon the festivities to check in on Lukas in what Abby has dubbed the medical wing. He's on the mend, but not enough for me to partake in some closely pressed together one-on-one activities, thanks to Abby warning me, wagging her finger in my face, and not leaving the corridor leading to his room.

He's asleep, and I sit beside him in a chair looking over his wounded face. He's getting better. His swelling has gone down. His prominent cheekbones have returned, and although one eye still has the remnants of a shiner he's just as handsome as ever. I take his hand in mine, dragging the white cotton blanket across his hospital gown. Where Abby got it from, I have no idea.

He stirs, and I pull back not wanting to disturb him, cursing Abby for being so resourceful.

I don't want him to wake up yet. I haven't given myself the time to think as to what to say to him—maybe that's why I want to lie with him, hold him, embrace him in a night of passion. It's easier than confronting him about how we parted ways. About how I said I wouldn't bite anybody he brought back to the castle. About how I never got a kiss goodbye. It's damned childish for a woman of twenty-five not to want to hash it out, but if we just *do it*, then all is well, isn't it?

He goes still, falling deeper into his slumber. I won't get the answer I'm looking for tonight. I stand, turn from his bed, and feel his hand take mine.

"Not going to say hi?" Lukas's voice is hoarse and dry.

I place his hand on the bed beside him, then give him the glass of water from the end table and sit down. "I didn't want to disturb you," I tell him. "You need your rest."

God, I don't want to do this, have this conversation. I draw in air, sample it. Abby is right outside the bedroom door. Her unique scent mixed with that of the latex gloves stuffed in her pockets is too strong for her not to be. Why won't she just run off to the party?

"I can make time for you." He smiles, turning up his cheeks, squinting his brilliant sapphire eyes. The faint kerosine lamp light coming from the corner of the room is enough to let them shine, lock in on me. I wish I hadn't let go of his hand. All I want is to feel his warmth again. His kindness, his gentleman-like ways, his words right now—all make me want to think I imagined the rift between us. "After all, you left what sounds like a pretty good party to hang out with me in the dark."

"I can see perfectly." Crap, that just shot out. *Good going, remind him you're a vamp.* It's not as if he doesn't know, but the last thing I want is for him to recall our last words together.

"I'll have to remember that," he says. He knows I have good night vision, though, from our shift work on watch when it was just the four of us. Did he hit his head so hard he's forgotten that? He hasn't forgotten me.

Before my mind can race in any direction he rolls to his side, sits up, takes my hand in both of his. "Just promise that if you're going to hunt me down, that when you catch me, we begin our evening with a dance." He bends, kisses my knuckles.

What did he say? Is he insinuating a replay of our first night together? Now I know I've let my imagination run wild. "I—"

"Hear music," Lukas says. "As do I. And…I think I'm up for a dance. Only with the right partner, that is." He stands, pulls me with him, trying unsuccessfully to hide a wince at the pain in his leg. "What do you say? Care to join me?"

"I don't think so," says Abby, storming across the room.

"Abby, it's okay, I'm fine. We were just—"

"No. You get that butt back in bed before I have to stitch up that leg again." Abby all but pushes between us, breaking our hold, and lowers Lukas to his bed. "As for *you*," she scolds me over her shoulder. "I warned you he needs his rest."

I pull away, grinning at Lukas smiling back at me over Abby's fussing, tucking him tight under a blanket around his torso.

"I'll come back later," I tell Abby, and wink at Lukas.

"I'll be waiting," he says.

"You'll be sleeping." Abby fluffs his pillow, sighs, and turns to me.

I don't give her the chance to chastise me. I duck out of the room and head down the corridor, satisfied that all is well with Lukas, and had Abby not interjected I might have gotten the unspoken answer I sought. I'll be back, and I'll be sure to distract Abby with an errand of some importance that requires her presence at the far end of the castle, perhaps the ranch.

The elated buzz of the castle doesn't slow or begin to die down until late into the night when I'm alone on the balcony of the queen's chambers, waiting for sunrise.

"Can't sleep?" Kara asks.

I shake my head.

"Me neither." She joins me against the railing. "I didn't want to miss the sunrise."

"It's not going to be your last one, Kara." *Oh God, please don't let it be her last one.*

"I'll outlive you, vamp or not, I'm a survivor." Wine sloshes from her plastic cup to the rooftop below.

"Don't I know it." I never thought of me dying before Kara. I had always figured I'd outlive her—after all, I'm the immortal one. But if I die before her and our bond drives her insane, I can't imagine what she'd do. I don't want to think about it. Of course, I don't want to think about me losing *my* mind either. So, I push it aside and focus on her. "Ben asleep?"

"I played him out," she says, winking. "Wasn't easy." Kara toasts the night. "That cowboy has stamina." She gulps down what she has in her cup and tosses it over the rail. "What's really on your mind?"

"What isn't?" I sigh.

"Yeah, it's gotta suck being you." Kara stretches and pushes out her chest. I'm not sure if that's a shot at my boobs being bigger than hers. In her drunken state she might not even know she's taking jabs or being sarcastic.

She does get me thinking, though. It's not all bad being me. Having the weight of the world lifted from my shoulders has been kinda nice, even though I'm far from completing what I've decided to do. "You think we can win against so many wolves?"

"Half of us can." Kara drops her head, and spits over the rail. "Which half depends on who we put out front."

"Markus wants us to hold up here in the queen's chambers. The lieutenant agrees with him. You, Nikki, and I are to use our power from here where we can oversee everything." I agreed with his idea. It's sensible, yet the vamp part in me—especially the one that put on the show in the field—wants to be down in the trenches so to speak, no matter how terrifying the wolves are up close.

"Blah, blah, blah. All this planning won't mean shit when they arrive. One of them was enough for me."

Kara must still be shaken from her first encounter with a werewolf. It takes time to get over seeing such raw, feral power. I had nightmares for at least two months after my first encounter with a wolf. I put my hand on her shoulder for support. "Dawn's approaching."

Kara glances up and then stares back at the roof below us. She takes a deep breath, stands, and turns around. "I'm going to bed."

"Don't you want to see it?"

"There'll be more." Kara waves away my question and crawls into my bed.

"Goodnight, Kara."

She grumbles something I don't catch. The dark begins to fade away and I hope, for her sake more than mine, that she's right. That we will see another one, together.

Chapter Fifty-One

Arguing voices disturb me, waking me from my dream.

It's daytime and has been for a while from the looks of the sunlight illuminating my room. I close my eyes and try to go back to my dream about racing against Kara in a yellow convertible, but it's faded away to no more than a fleeting memory. This is the first dream I've had in a long time without the gravelly voice of my father, rather Xanatos, threatening me.

The voices are coming from Markus and Lieutenant Huntly on the stairwell, arguing about waking me.

Kara groans beside me. "Shut up," she grumbles and tosses a pillow in their direction. Another pillow covers her head before the first hits the floor.

I sit up and crane my head to the side, cracking my neck in two spots. I slept in my clothes on top of the covers beside Kara cocooned under them. "What is it?"

Lieutenant Huntly crests the stairwell first with Markus hot on his heels. "It is well into the afternoon, and vampire or not, fourteen hundred hours is pushing it." It figures the lieutenant would be the only one with a working watch.

The fact that I slept most of the day away pisses me off. What if I was sleeping away my last moments with Kara? With Lukas? "Why'd you let me sleep so late?" I slide off the bed, scowling at the lieutenant.

"Blame him." Lieutenant Huntly points a thumb over his shoulder at Markus.

"You need your rest for the coming battle, my…Scarlett." He catches himself from addressing me cordially again. "So does she." He nods at Kara squirming beneath her pillow.

"Thick headed…" Kara smothers herself so much I can't catch her insult.

"Just gimme a minute will ya?" I grab a cup on the end table. Wine sloshes over its brim. I put it back down and squint at the rest of the room. Markus follows my eyes. He grabs a half-drunk water bottle in the corner and brings it to me. I spin the cap off and drain it to help alleviate the kitty-litter taste in my mouth. I need to brush my teeth, badly, and I desperately need to pee. There's no ensuite attached to the queen's chambers. I curse Dad silently for such an asinine design. "What do you want?" I say gruffly.

"You need to be filled in on the preparations we have made, and we need to update you on the battle plan we have laid out," says Lieutenant Huntly.

I want to tell him to stick it where the sun doesn't shine but opt for a more diplomatic approach, Mom would have wanted that. "After I freshen up."

"We are running out of time to—"

A pillow hits the lieutenant in the head. "Get out. Get out. Get out!" shouts Kara. Then she pulls the covers over her head.

The men are stunned, as am I. They look at each other, then to me. "We'll be in the main hall once you've...freshened up," says Markus. They leave the queen's chambers without another word.

When they're well out of earshot Kara throws off the covers and jumps out of bed. "Christ, my teeth are floating. I thought they'd never leave." She whips her head around. I get what she means, and what she's looking for. I'm not sure I can make it down to the bottom floor where the crappy castle outhouses are without dancing my way there.

Kara mumbles and hurls the bedsheet at the wall. The smooth stone before her contorts and shifts into two stalls, and the bedsheet floats down in front of them like makeshift doors. God, I love her. Kara disappears behind the sheet in one stall, and I half-dance to the other. Kara has mumbled a stone toilet, a seat, a lid, and strips of the bed sheet into a tiny roll of toilet paper. Where the toilet drains to, I don't know, and I don't care. After relieving myself, I step out of the stall in search of more water. I find two more bottles and toss one to Kara when she emerges from her stall.

"Don't waste that by drinking it," she says. I remember her hydrating trick as she mumbles the entire bottle into her pores. She does the same to me, and I feel better instantly. Kara reaches for another bottle—she doesn't recuperate as fast as I do, and she drank a lot more than me, seeping from the scent of booze pouring out of her bones. She fragrances us up with a breeze. "That'll do till we hit the showers," she says.

"Thanks...for everything." I nod at the stalls. What I mean to say is thanks for saving me, befriending me, having my back, and in general just treating me like a person and not an all-powerful savior of the world who failed. All that we've accomplished in the castle, that Dad made for me, still isn't enough to wrench the feeling from the back of my head that beyond what I shielded is no more than a scorched ruin.

"Men just don't get what a woman needs, or wants, or *doesn't* want first thing in the morning."

I laugh. "Come on, Enchantress. Let's get ready for the day," I say, as I head for the stairs.

We make our way through the castle, and I decide the first thing on my agenda is a long warm shower; breakfast can wait. But not for Kara; she opts to rummage through the kitchen first. I leave her to it and continue on for my little slice of bliss. It amazes me how when the entire world falls apart that it's the little things that keep me sane: a hot shower, Kara's lilac perfume trick—which I've gotten pretty good at—and a ride on my Ducati; dirt bike or authentic doesn't matter anymore. I contemplate taking it for a rip once I freshen up, put on my face, and do my hair. I get to the showers and they're full. Children giggling and splashing about indicate that my shower won't be available for a while, so I listen to my stomach rumbling and steer back to the kitchen, but not before I squeeze some of the communal toothpaste on my finger and give my teeth a good scrubbing.

Approaching the kitchen, I smell bacon. One of my most cherished luxuries in life that I thought we ran out of days ago. Turns out Bert had a stash of bacon she was saving for a special occasion, and Brian has been waiting all day to fry it up for us. Kara, looking as elegant as ever, is working on her second helping along with some eggs when I make it to the kitchen. I join her, and Brian keeps shoveling food in front of us until we can't eat another bite. I think it's his way of coping with losing Bert; she would have ensured we were well-fed and ready for a bout with an army of wolves. Just the thought of an army of them tightens my chest again. So, I thank Brian for the wonderful meal and plan on searching for the guys who had so rudely interrupted our rest, another of life's underrated pleasures. But somehow, I end up in one of the rooms Abby deemed part of her clinic, staring at Lukas.

"How you doing, darlin'?" says Lukas, closing his book the moment he notices me standing in his doorway. He's looking stronger, though Abby still won't let him out of bed yet. Her strict advice about bed rest along with her repeatedly using the phrase "no sexual activity" since she interrupted us reminds me of Lukas's cabin…and his shower…and the field of tall grass. The thought rushes blood to my cheeks, warming them for the second time this morning, and embarrassing me. Lukas catches it. "Are you okay?"

I check the corridor; Abby's nowhere in sight and her lingering sent is too faint for her to be close by. "I'm fine," I say, shutting the door behind me, and sliding its wooden lock into place. "You're looking better."

He chuckles. "I can see well enough to read." He thumbs the pages of his book and puts it on his nightstand. Turns out he has an extensive library in his house, and he decided he was going to reread every novel he owned. Though I doubt he can see that great. His eyes are still surrounded by puffy cheeks and eyelids, but the swelling has gone down even since the other night. His lips are no longer split thanks to Kara's hydration trick. "And I can also make out the most beautiful thing I've seen all day," he says, winking, though it's hard to tell for sure.

I shoot him a smile, cross the room, give him a soft kiss on the lips, not too long of one, and sit in the chair beside him. His once chiseled features are now covered in a short poky beard I hadn't noticed before, attempting to conceal his handsome face, but in a way adding to his sex appeal. He can pull off the dirty bearded look I thought I despised, but I still prefer a clean-shaven face. "You need a shave," I say.

"Oh, I know." Lukas rubs the scruff on his jaw. "I don't think Abby trusts me with a razor yet, and it's driving me nuts."

"It's not a bad look, though it's a shame to cover that face of yours." I lean closer to him. "After all, that's the only reason I let you pursue me."

"The only reason?"

"Well, there might have been another quality or two you possess, but none come to mind."

"Is that so?"

I glance at the latch locking the door. Lukas follows my eyes, and he blushes. He truly wears his emotions on his face.

"It is," I say, moving from the chair to sit beside him on the bed. "So, I might just need a reminder." I slip my hand beneath the sheet, run my fingers down his chest and circle his abs, being careful to not press too hard on the bandages wrapped around them. "I think one of those qualities has something to do with work ethic. You know, get the job done, no matter what."

"I think I can refresh your memory."

I pull the sheet back and climb on top of him. He winces and tries to hide it.

"Don't worry, handsome," I say, leaning in and pressing my lips to his. "I'll be gentle."

Chapter Fifty-Two

The handle on the door to Lukas's room jiggles, disturbing our peace. I spent a little more time with Lukas than I had intended to, curled up against him, drawing in his warmth. "Time for you to rest," I say, kissing him.

"Wanna come back later once I'm…rested?" he says, pausing as he checks me out pulling my clothes on, running my fingers through my hair and putting it back in place.

"I'll tuck you in." I gently trace my fingers down his chest.

Lukas grins.

I open the door to find Abby standing in front of me, arms crossed, scowling. "How's my patient?" Her long brown hair is tied back in a ponytail. For a slim woman in her late twenties, she makes me feel as if I have to listen to her even though she's only got a year or two on me. The white doctor's coat she's wearing doesn't lessen the feeling. But it suits her, emphasizing the knowledge she has over the rest of us.

"I'm fine, Abby," Lukas calls out behind me.

"You hush up and get some rest," she says to Lukas. "And as for *you*,"—I'm certain she's about to give me the speech about his injuries and the importance of rest so Lukas can recover—"thank you for checking in on him. You're a good friend."

I'm a little confused, then I catch a glimpse of Mel's thick glasses peering around Abby's waist. She glances in Lukas's room, then to me. She's fidgeting, thumbing the corner of a book with a child dressed up as a witch on the cover. "Just making sure he doesn't get lonely," I say. "And what about you, sweetie? Did you come to read Lukas a story before his afternoon nap?"

She nods, scurries past me and into the chair beside Lukas.

"She's a good kid," I say.

"We need to talk," Abby says, turning from Lukas's room.

I blow Lukas a kiss, shoot Mel a thumbs up, and follow Abby down the hall. When someone says they want to talk it's never a good thing that they have to say. But I'm ready for the speech. I'll nod, agree with her, assure her I was gentle with Lukas. Then I'll wait till she's asleep before I sneak into his room tonight. "Abby, I—"

"I don't know what to do with her. There's only so much I can do."

"Who, Mel?"

"She's taken a liking to you, and I assume you have to her."

"What's not to like?"

Abby glances back over her shoulder down the empty hallway. "The fact she's going to die a slow and painful death if we don't get our hands on some insulin, and soon."

I stop in my tracks, stare at her. I don't know much about diabetes—anything, really, except that it has something to do with blood sugar.

"She has type one diabetes, and I'm running out."

I never considered Mel needed shots to stay alive. "I thought all she needed was to drink some orange juice or eat a chocolate bar."

"Not with type one."

"Can't we just send someone out to get more? There's gotta be a stash of the stuff in one of the hospitals or clinics or something."

"We could, but it won't matter. I've got enough to last her for about three months, but it's not refrigerated so it won't last one."

"Kara could mumble up a freezer for it," I say, recalling the chilled glovebox keeping her 7-Eleven sandwiches fresh in her car. I would try, but I'm not controlled enough for such a delicate thing. The last thing I want to do is destroy Mel's insulin by freezing it solid. "That could buy us some time to find more."

"Yes, that could work, but it would only give us back the two months. Even if we have all the insulin in the state, she's still going to die. It has an expiration date, and I seriously doubt they're manufacturing any more without any electricity."

My heart sinks. Sweet little knobby-kneed Mel is going to die by my inability to do what I was supposed to do. "She's just a kid. There's gotta be something we can do."

"There is, and unfortunately it's all we can do until things change." Abby raises her hand, indicating the unlit torch beside the open window. "Until the power's back on."

"What? Name it." My heart's racing, there isn't anything I wouldn't do for that kid.

"She's going to need a friend, a hand to hold other than mine, when the time comes. All we can do is make her as comfortable as possible. It'll be tough, what with her fevers and inability to control her bladder, not to mention the other symptoms she'll develop. But you *will* have to be there for her. Lukas too, I think she has a crush on him."

I don't want to think about two months from now when her insulin runs out. Hell, I don't want to think about the imminent demise Nikki predicted. Part of me wants Mel to be one of the ones who falls so she doesn't suffer through a long slow death, but being torn apart by a wolf is no way to go. 'Course, seeing half the people being torn to pieces around you, and you living through it, that's a completely different level of torture. The nightly celebration of life in the castle seems even more important than before. We need to do more. I need to do more.

"There's gotta be—"

"If there was, we'd be doing it. Trust me."

Abby's somber tone cements that she has exhausted her possibilities. I don't want to say it, as if doing so will make it somewhat of a last request, but if Mel is going to pass, painfully, then she should enjoy every moment she has left. "She's fascinated by my pegasus," I say more to myself than to Abby. "Think I'll take her for a ride when she's done with Lukas."

"She'd like that."

"Can you make sure she finds me when she's out?"

Abby nods. "Unfortunately, Mel won't be the only one we're going to lose."

What now? I don't say a word. I just feel the weight on my shoulders grow, even before Abby continues dropping another bomb.

"Anyone on medication is going to have a rough time, and if they can't live without it, they'll die too."

"And there's nothing we can do?"

Abby shakes her head. I can tell it's weighing on her mind heavily and has been for some time now. When she first came to us, she was eager to check out those who needed checking, and the castle was eager to accept her. She gathered all the medical supplies she could, cataloging everything. Now she looks as if she's past the point of giving up, slightly hunched over with her head down—not a normal posture for someone so young. The stress is aging her. "I'll do what I can, but in the end"—she takes a deep breath—"it won't be enough."

She feels like I do. She's trained, studied, and prepared for years to save lives. And here she is, like me, helpless to alter the outcome. Though it must be a little worse for her. She wanted to work in medicine. Whereas I had saving the world thrust on me. "Just when you think things can't get worse, the world winds up and punches you in the gut. When's it gonna end?"

"Thanks to you, it didn't." She shakes her head. "All I can think is how I spent my life paying off student loans, searching for a decent paycheck while actually getting to do what I love and staying near home. I even got a mortgage on a cozy little place a couple of miles from town, but none of that matters now."

I never considered that, the economics. Everybody's life was turned upside down: school, jobs, mortgages, car payments, and loans, all of it vanished in a heartbeat. There aren't any more dates to restaurants or movies; there's nothing. I had always known and been prepared, kinda, for what was going to happen. The interruption of life's day-to-day idiosyncrasies that seemed so important at the time have faded into a past that's long gone, but not forgotten.

"We just have to roll with the punches," Abby says. I finally get where that saying comes from. I wish I didn't. "Keep moving forward, keep living, for all those we've lost, and for the one's we're going to lose. It's all we can do."

She definitely works in the field, and it shows. She's been trained for loss, trained to expect and deal with the inevitable, and trained to comfort others. This sucks, and here the day started off so much better. All I want to do is crawl back in bed with Lukas. But I know I can't. I have responsibilities that need tending to. Aside from reviewing the castle's preparations, and practicing with my power, I have to try to comfort Mel.

"We'll do it together," I say, forcing a grin.

Chapter Fifty-Three

I leave Abby to wait for Mel to finish her story, and no doubt check on Lukas's condition after my visitation. Even though I slept till the afternoon, this day has been eternal, and I finally catch sight of my twin soldiers discussing something. Markus and Lieutenant Huntly, two peas in a pod. Both men have a commanding presence, similar build, height, and facial features. If it wasn't for the lieutenant's shock of red hair and camo differentiating him from Markus's black head-to-toe ensemble, I'd swear they were related. That and the fact that under Markus's black mat of short-cropped hair sits a face of gray.

Toni chiming in from her post atop the wall gives me hope that there'll be some sense brought to it from a woman's point of view.

I cross the courtyard that now houses the outer wall's defenses, manned thanks to Matt's directions, and for the second time since the castle has filled up, I feel welcomed. Children are not being scurried away at my presence, adults don't turn their heads and cease conversation, though I do catch the name *Nova* being tossed around more than once in hushed voices. Nikki was right, I needed to show them that I am capable—and though I don't feel it, I catch myself walking with a bit of a strut. I curb it immediately. My little display of power in the field that offered me cheers upon my return to the castle is also the reason the world fell apart: I didn't know what I was doing. I still don't. I don't know how I'm going to pull off anything I've decided to do. Now to top off everything, Mel is going to die. Nikki's prediction is one thing, especially after Bert's passing, but somehow hearing Abby's medically trained voice tell me of Mel makes it worse. I stop, pet my pegasus, and for a single moment, I'm alone.

"You know your bike won't throw you off like that thing will if a mouse runs in front of it, don't you?" says Kara.

I was so preoccupied with my own thoughts that I failed to notice her. "It is a magnificent animal."

"You should know, you made them." Kara has obviously not gotten over her fear of heights, or maybe it's the lack of control her pegasus offers. Either way, it's entertaining to see her around them, or rather, keep her distance from them.

"I got lucky repeating Dad's spell. You talk to them yet?" I ask, nodding at the rest of my council.

"Nah, that's your deal. I've got better things to do."

"Really?"

"Yeah, I have to fill the water tower for your oh-so-precious showers."

"And our drinking water."

"Bah, we've got wine for drinking." Kara spins on her heels and makes her way toward the water tower, followed by two children tugging at her, pleading for her to work her magic. Out of nowhere, a series of stones shoot from the ground forming two semi-circles a few feet apart.

Cheers sound from the children, along with praise for the Enchantress. "Don't waste all the fruit," I hear her say to the kids. "Sure, I can help it grow more in time, but it's *sooo* tiresome." The kids laugh, pluck oranges from the surrounding trees and immediately begin to hurl them at each other from the safety of their makeshift two-foot-high forts. I consider telling them to not waste the food, but the children's parents will stop them soon enough. Besides, Kara is giving them the gift of play and levity from life's harsh reality, and why shouldn't they have that?

Kara knows how to intoxicate others with her words, actions, and her presence. Unfortunately, her antics have not gone unnoticed by everyone else. Markus and the lieutenant are staring at me with looks I take as less than pleased. Reality sets in, and the peaceful bliss of escape, be it by Ducati or pegasus, leaves me.

I climb the stairs, and thankfully, it's Toni who greets me. "She's got a way about her," she says, indicating Kara.

"Like no other," I say.

"How you holding up?"

Toni's question catches me off guard. Do I tell her what Abby said about Mel, about the others? I want to talk to somebody, but something inside of me wants to stay quiet, push my fears and anxieties down deep. Mom speaks for me. "I'm good if you are," I tell her.

She gives me a look of disbelief but doesn't press me. Instead, she turns her attention to the fruit battle playing out between the children and laughs, simply saying, "I'm entertained."

"Nice of you to join us," says Markus. I shoot him a look telling him I'm not in the mood, and he gets the hint.

Lieutenant Huntly doesn't. "We have a lot to cover, and if you're not too busy." His tone makes me want to pull back and leave, or outright smash his nose in. "We need to go over the preparations we have made to deal with the wolves."

"Scarlett," Mel shouts leaving the main hall of the castle. She's done reading to Lukas, and I'm guessing by the way she's waving and running toward my pegasus that Abby told her of my idea.

Her interruption of my "urgent" meeting lights a spark in me. A spark of normality, if there is such a thing in these times. "Whatever it is, I'm sure you can handle it," I say, patting the lieutenant on the cheek with my palm. "As long as she's got an eye on you." I look at Toni, winking. It's a play from Kara's book, but it works.

The "twins" are at a loss for words long enough for Toni to catch on to what's going on, prompting her to say, "I gave them my two cents. If you're going up"—Toni points at the pegasus—"can I come?"

I look at Huntly, then Markus, and say to all of them while looking at my pegasus, "Girls just wanna have fun, right Toni?"

"Oh yeah."

Chapter Fifty-Four

I strut down the steps with Toni hot on my heels. I'm not sure why I disrespected Markus and the lieutenant like that—after all, they're here to protect me. But it just came out. Mom would have been disappointed. I stop halfway across the courtyard, look back at my protectors scowling at me, and consider at least mouthing an apology. "They'll be fine," says Toni, patting me on the shoulder. "You need this. *We* need this."

Toni almost skips to a pegasus, taking Mel by the hand. She's right, I do need this. But shirking my responsibilities to go for a ride is irresponsible and too carefree. Sure, it's something I did in the past, go for a ride to clear my head, but I never wanted to run from my responsibilities entirely. Standing beside Kara's makeshift forts she made for the children's fruit battle makes me consider how she brushed off any involvement with the castle's defenses, and I realize why I want to get away from Lieutenant Huntly and Markus. My bond with Kara has strengthened, allowing me to tap into her jovial approach to life.

"You two give them some carrots or apples or something before we take off," I tell Toni, taking a deep sigh, thinking this could be one thing I could easily do. That relieves a bit of my tension of failure along with my burden of command which I'm still uncertain I'm worthy of. But at least it is something I can do in defiance of my bond with Kara. Her outlook on life is intoxicating, but I have to maintain a calculative mind. "I'll appease the boys for a minute, so they don't sulk the entire time we're gone."

"Fine, but I'd let them suffer," Toni says, leading Mel to the winged horses.

I race up the stairs to Markus and the lieutenant. "Five minutes," I say as rudely as possible, irritated more by my own initial reaction to run off and play than anything else.

I consider apologizing for my behavior, but my abrupt composure serves me. They use the five minutes well and make me regret treating them the way I did even more, but I get what I need from them in as short a time as possible. Learning what they've planned, I know I was right about them running the show. Boosting my confidence that I just might be worthy of command after all. It may be my castle, and I it's queen, but a queen must know when to delegate matters to those more educated about that matter, just like how I got Kara to work the water tower. Markus and the lieutenant scramble to voice all their preparations, interrupting each other to add vital pieces of information regarding either a defensive or offensive strategy. Toni calls out for me to hurry up, and I hold up my finger indicating one more minute. I let them finish what they have to say, make a few suggestions, and agree with my decision to let them take charge of the castle's armaments. I give them a nod of approval, a "Good job," and head down the stairs with a feeling that I've taken one step toward bettering myself, protecting the castle, and the people housed within it.

I climb on my pegasus, and Toni lifts Mel into my lap. "Ready, sweetie," I say to Mel. She bobs her head up and down so fast I'd swear she's having a seizure if it weren't for the giant smile on her face.

"How do we get them up?" Toni asks, climbing onto Kara's pegasus.

"Kara had a trick with a carrot, but I discovered something last time I was on her." I pat my pegasus's neck, hoping I'm right.

"What's her name?" asks Mel, following my lead and patting its neck.

"I'm not sure," I say. Then it hits me. I'm not even certain she is a she, but it feels right to call her something other than *horse* or *pegasus*. "Why don't you name her?"

Mel almost jumps up an inch, twisting around. Her eyes are lit up. "Really?"

"Really."

Mel hugs my pegasus's neck. "How about Spirit?"

As if in response my pegasus neighs and scratches the grass with its hoof.

"Spirit, I think she likes it. Spirit it is. And what about yours, Toni?"

"Oh, I don't think I should be naming Kara's."

"Trust me, she won't mind."

Toni thinks for a second, then grins. "Swiftwind.

"Goooood name," says Mel, her words drawn out and excited.

"Shall we, ladies?" I ask. They both nod, ready to take flight. "Run your fingers through Swiftwind's mane," I tell Toni as I run mine through Spirit's. "Now, gently pull back, and give her a little nudge with your heels."

Wings spread wide on either side of us. Three or four trots forward and the wings flap, lifting us from the ground. Mel squeals, wiggling in my lap. Spirit and Swiftwind take over the controls and, staying together, we fly out of the courtyard. "This is awesome," Toni calls out.

It is awesome. I realize just how much I like the feeling of wind rushing through my hair without a helmet. The best part is the reaction from my companions. Toni waving her arms out to her sides, following the rhythm of Swiftwind's beating wings. Mel's shifting her head to either side of Spirit's to look down, calling out everything she sees.

"Look how small the cows are. There's Nikki. Hiiiii, Nikki!" Mel yells, waving her arm in a broad stroke from side to side. "Hi, Matt!"

Nikki is on her evening walk, making her way to the outer wall. She and Matt both wave back.

It's refreshing, like a reward for not brushing off Markus and the lieutenant. What I originally said, how I acted back on the wall, it wasn't me. I chalked it up to Kara's influence, but part of me wonders if me lashing out at them, and at the Black Serpents, is due to my contact with Dad's amulet. Look what it did to him. I rub my thumb against my fingers and can almost feel its polished surface between them.

"It wasn't your fault," says Toni. "It was his. He's like a black hole, drawing you in, and the only escape is to relish in moments like this."

Mel glances at her, then to me, confused. Thankfully she dismisses it and continues searching below. It's eerie how Toni can read me. With no more than a look, she saw I had shifted, drifted away in unpleasant, scary thoughts. Perhaps it's just her observation to how I treated Markus and the lieutenant, then rushed to rectify the situation. She knows my father better than I do, and she knows the influence he can have all too well. I try to shake it off and nod.

"Look, look, you can see town," says Mel.

She's right—we've climbed high enough that Lincoln's remains are poking through the foothills. She can't make it out as clearly as I can, and I don't want her to. There's so little left of Lincoln that it would be a stern reminder of what's going on around us other than the magic of flying. "Let's follow the river," I say to Mel. "Gently to the left," I call out a little louder to Toni.

I tug on Spirit's mane, and she follows my instruction. Whether Swiftwind follows Toni's guidance or keeps pace with Spirit I'm not sure, but they keep up with us.

"Where do you think all of those people are going?" Mel says, pointing.

A caravan's approaching, a big one comprised of about thirty older cars and trucks; anything still able to run.

My hint of peace leaves in an instant. So does Toni's from the look on her face. "The castle," I say.

"I hope there's more kids to play with," says Mel.

The numerous rifles held by soldiers in the back of old pickup trucks make me doubt there are any children among the line of vehicles speeding down the road. "Maybe," I tell Mel, stroking the top of her head. "Let's get back so we can greet them properly. I'll take you for another ride tomorrow, okay?"

Mel sighs, "Okay."

I squint, hard. Every single person I can see—man, woman, civilian, and military—has a gray undertone to them. I look at Toni, point at the caravan, then to her. She gets that I don't want to say it aloud with Mel in my lap: *They're all Broadsword, and there definitely won't be any children.*

Toni whistles at Matt and Nikki atop the outer wall as we pass them by. She points in the direction of the caravan, and the warning bell sounds. It's more of a notification to the people of the castle than a warning of danger. Despite the lack of government aid, we are getting an army. One, combined with those in the castle, that could ensure we can overcome a coven of wolves. Maybe Dad thought we would need more under my command. The thought of him sending more people to my aid is conflicting—more help against the wolves is great, but that also means more mouths to feed, and doesn't he need help with the nuclear reactors? But what if it isn't Dad sending them, what if it's Xanatos? It's been a while since the power went out, since Dad sent his text ordering the Broadsword to obey me, and these guys have vehicles. Could they have just taken that long to get to me? Logic tells me otherwise. Am I staring down at the other half of Xanatos's army come to sweep across the land and carve out his kingdom as he said? Wolves from the east, the Broadsword from the south. He has to be controlling the wolves, they're too wild to move the way they did in Nikki's watery globe show. And this caravan is out of place, and too late to arrive from within the fifty-mile radius Dad texted about for me not to be suspicious.

"I'll need you to go get Abby," I say to Mel, as we touch down in the courtyard and the caravan pulls up to the outer wall.

Gunfire erupts, echoing off the castle walls.

I pull Mel in close, cradling her.

The shots come from outside the castle, not within. "Take her," I tell Toni, handing Mel over. "Get her back."

She takes Mel. I jump down off Spirit, sprint across the courtyard, up the stairs, and to the top of the castle wall.

The outer gates are open.

A lower portion of the wall is covered in ice. Three figures of men are frozen solid against it. Half a dozen people on the driveway are engulfed in fire, their rifles shooting sporadically as they collapse between the massive gates. Flames lick the lead vehicle of the caravan as if fueled by a torrent of wind that exists only in that area.

Matt is on the ground, lying motionless.

Nikki's beside him, on her back with a hand clutching her shoulder—she took a hit, but she's still mumbling.

A broadsword charges past the lead vehicle and over his fallen brethren, his rifle trained at Nikki's head.

Another shot rings out—and Nikki collapses beside Matt, dead.

Chapter Fifty-Five

"No!" I scream. All those at the outer wall are dead thanks to this convoy of the Broadsword.

Anger at the wolves, at the Broadsword, at Dad surges through me. Nikki is dead. The cockiest, most powerful weapon we have is dead. I'm more aware of who specifically is around me, and where they came from. Men and women from Lincoln and the surrounding towns. Lieutenant Huntly. Markus.

I grab Markus by the cuff of his jacket, slam him against the stone tooth of the castle wall. "Why? Why is Broadsword attacking us after being sworn to obey me?"

"I don't—"

"Why?" I shout again, bending Markus backward over the tooth.

"Scarlett, wait!" shouts Toni, climbing the stairs.

Is she in on it too? Is she going to turn on me? Will Markus? *Have* I let the fox into the hen house?

I put my forearm into Markus's throat, restricting his air as his hands latch onto my arm. "Stop right there, Toni!"

She listens and doesn't move a step closer. She's still under my command, so Markus should be as well.

"Don't move," I say to Markus through gritted teeth. I let him go, slowly, and he remains in the awkward position I bent him into. I lean out over the wall and shout at the top of my lungs, "Stop! Cease fire!"

They don't stop. The caravan keeps funneling through the open gate, over the burning bodies, past Matt and Nikki's corpses.

"Why aren't they listening?" I ask Markus, pointing at the caravan.

"They have been commanded differently than us." His voice is rough from the exertion of keeping himself motionless and bent over backward, or from me crushing his windpipe.

"Are you still sworn to me?"

"Answer her!" Lieutenant Huntly holds his rifle at Markus, frantically looking between him and the approaching army.

"Yes," Markus replies.

"We are," says Toni. "And we have to act fast if we're going to stand a chance against them."

I take a breath, try to calm myself, try to remain rational. "Get up," I say to Markus. "You can move now, Toni."

Markus stands up, and Toni rests her hands on a tooth. "Thoughts?" she asks.

Markus answers her with a single word. "Xanatos."

Xanatos—not Dad. "Why?" I know the answer. I've been waiting, *wishing* for him to come to me so I can free Dad and the Broadsword from his grip, save these people. Xanatos has come to carve out his kingdom, as he put it. But I can't spot him among the convoy. I search the sky. He's not here. There's no trace of his pegasus, of him overseeing these Broadswords.

Lieutenant Huntly trains his scope on the caravan. "We'll find out soon enough."

The caravan is inside the outer wall, nearly halfway to us spreading out in three groups, and climbing out of their vehicles. They stop their advance, waiting in their respective groupings. I was right—they're a mixture of humans and military. They're all Broadsword gray, and they're all armed.

One man in the middle group steps forward, waving a white flag. "All we want is the One. Hand her over to us and the rest of you shall live. Harbor her from us, and you will all die. You have five minutes to comply." He drops his flag and walks backward to his group, resting his rifle on his shoulder.

"I guess that's the end of the negotiations," the lieutenant says.

"Xanatos," Markus repeats, nodding, agreeing with himself.

"They have their mission," says Toni. "And there's no room for negotiation."

The One, he called me the One. That was what Toni said Xanatos called me in front of the Broadsword. Xanatos must have changed his mind about his followers not causing any harm to me. God only knows what he has in mind. I know he wants to rule the world, but why does he want me?

All eyes are on me except for those manning the wall, shifting between me and the caravan. I'm certain they're deciding whether or not to throw me out, save their own skins. I get it—I'm just one person, and the sacrifice of one to save many is an easy decision, though I wish I wasn't the one to be sacrificed.

I wrap one hand around the other and try not to shake. I try not to let it show that I'm terrified. I brought this life onto these people, this life of hardship and loss.

How can I do anything other than try to save them, those who made me feel as if I belong, as if I'm accepted?

Abby confided in me, if only because Mel had taken a liking to me, but she trusted me with knowledge she hadn't shared with anybody else.

Mel, sweet little knobby-kneed Mel who wants nothing more than to learn about magic.

Nikki, stern and confident, pushed me harder than I thought possible, never once holding back her opinion—it was a nice change from avoidance. Now she's dead, lying beside Matt, who made us all laugh with his childish antics, especially when he thoroughly inspected the medieval weaponry left by Dad.

Lieutenant Huntly has been straightforward with me as much as Nikki and has taken charge of protecting me and those I love.

Toni, who actually befriended me…under different circumstances I'm sure we'd hang out all the time, despite the fact that she lost her lover, John, thanks to my inability to control my other self in Ovando. She's never once blamed me for that.

How Markus holds back his thoughts until I pry them out of him infuriates me, but he always calls it like it is with no sugar-coating, and I value that.

Lukas, the handsome gentleman who has warmed my heart and given me hope that there might actually be a future for us together, even if I will outlive him.

His cousin Ben and his comical addiction to beer and Kara.

Then there's Kara, my rock, the one person in the world whom I hated and now can't live without. She's been with me through it all, right from the beginning. How can I possibly let her down?

I can't.

Mom's teachings about considering others run through my head, along with how she deceived me. In the light of things, and how I lost control of myself against the Black Serpents, I find myself forgiving her. She, like so many others, was duped by Xanatos. Dad may have loved her, and she him, but neither of them has borne any actual ill will against me. Xanatos, sure, but not Dad. Mom died to save me, so I could save the world. She was, despite her few shortcomings, the strongest, most regal woman I've known. I hold my head high, trying to emulate Mom, and turn for the stairs, ready to be the lamb sent out to slaughter.

Kara's halfway up the stairs, glaring at me. "Don't even think about it."

"I have to," I tell her, steadying my voice. I'm a threat to Xanatos, plain and simple, and he sent his assassins to take me out. "I failed once…and…I can't…"

"Enough of this," says Lieutenant Huntly, bracing his rifle in his shoulder. He takes aim, fires, and hits the Broadsword that gave the ultimatum in the head, killing him instantly. "You want her, come and get her!" He fires a round at each division of the convoy, prompting the Broadswords to take cover.

"Lieutenant?" I say in disbelief. He stripped me of my choice to end this fight peacefully, to save these people. If the Broadsword planned *not* to kill me until they brought me before Xanatos, which is doubtful, the people I've taken under my charge to protect would have still been safe and I'd be alive to continue my fight. I might have found a way to save Dad if the Broadsword brought me to him. Now that possible timeline speeds from reality as fast as the bullets that sped from the lieutenant's rifle.

He crouches behind the safety of the wall, his focus intense and unflinching on me. "This is our ship, and you are our captain. Sink or swim, we sail together. We owe you that much. And call me Huntly."

Chapter Fifty-Six

"That settles that." Kara grabs me by the shoulders, stopping me from descending the stairs to meet the caravan of Broadsword sent for me. She doesn't need to. Huntly killing their negotiator saw to me standing my ground. "You're *not* leaving me."

The words barely pass her lips and a barrage of gunfire rattles off the wall's stone teeth.

"Down!" Huntly shouts. That's one order he doesn't have to give. Every warm body on the wall is crouching, aside from the three dead who weren't quick enough. "Hold your fire! Save the ammunition!"

There are so many bullets flying that I doubt anyone will poke their head up to take a shot. I'm crouching beside Kara on the stairs, my ears covered, and eyes locked on hers. She shakes her head.

"Don't go all violet on me. Control yourself. Use your wits and we will get through this."

Someone presses against my back, wraps their arms around me, covering my head. I jerk and toss my aggressor off.

"It's Markus, he's shielding you. Let him."

"We have to get her out of here!" I hear Toni shout from behind Markus, then feel the impact of her and Markus shoving me forward, trying to push me down the stairs. My muscles lock, and I'm able to stop the two Broadsword at my back from plowing me into Kara.

"She's right—we have a plan, now follow it."

"That was for wolves!" I shout over the gunfire.

"Just move!"

I didn't think Kara could yell telepathically, but she can, and she gets me to follow her lead down the stairs. Huntly barks orders from the top of the wall, but I can't make them out over the gunfire. It doesn't matter, he's doing what we planned for him to do, hold the wall. I have my own place in this battle. I look up at the queen's chambers. A strategic one where Kara and I will be of most use.

A catapult lets loose, hurling its payload of stones over the wall.

"Stick to the plan." Kara's got a half-dozen paces on me, racing for the open doors of the grand hall.

There's movement surrounding me. The courtyard is alive with people running one way or another. The castle has become a living organism, with supplies tracing in and out of its entrances, being tossed to those stationed on the wall, or back down to them. Children are being ushered into the castle. The catapults and giant crossbows are being adjusted in accordance to orders from those above, redirecting payloads at the caravan. Markus and Huntly run a tight ship, well organized and trained, and as much as it annoyed me to hear them out, I'm relieved I didn't wave aside the knowledge they gave me earlier.

Kara makes it inside the main hall, and over the hum of gunfire, orders, and medieval weaponry being let loose, I hear three letters screamed out with the utmost terror behind them.

"RPG!"

An explosion rocks the wall behind me, throwing body parts and stone debris into the air. The castle's movements pause, but only for a second as those within muster the courage to move past the shock of such a weapon and carry on with their pre-determined task.

There's a sizeable chunk of the wall missing from the gate, and thankfully, I catch the shock of short-cropped red-hair of Huntly crawling over to it to inspect the wall's structural integrity. If the caravan has more rocket propelled grenades, they'll be inside the courtyard in no time.

"Move!" Markus ushers me inside, still making himself as large as he can to be a human shield as I run crouching down. More explosions sound outside as I climb the stairs. I lose sight of Kara and start to panic. I'm fast, but for some stupid reason I'm stumbling, having trouble working my feet. It's not because of Markus prodding me forward, I'm faster than him. But I lost Kara, and I'm not paying attention to what I'm doing. I'm frantically looking for her down every corridor, in every room we pass. Even though I know where she's headed, my subconscious is freaking out, and pulls my other self to the forefront.

The stairway to the queen's chambers light up with violet.

I stop in my tracks, brace for Markus to crash into me. Instead, he levitates over me with aid from my other self. I can't lose control, can't let the part of me that Dad influenced get out, can't let my primal emotions take over like I did in Ovando. That's how I almost lost Kara once, and I'll be damned if I'm going to let that happen again.

The stairs and walls are basking in violet. *Breathe Scar, just breathe, like Mom taught you. You can't help Kara if you're not coherent and if you're not by her side. You know where she is. She's safe.*

Time stands still, and the castle falls silent as I push the outside world away. There's no more attack, no more gunfire or shouting, only me digging my fingers into stone, crumbling the very steps I'm meant to ascend. Grinding tiny pieces of rock together beneath my fingers, I focus. The battle echoing throughout the castle returns, and the weight in my chest lightens. I open my eyes and the stairs are back to normal, no longer tainted by my other self's aura. I let out that breath and continue climbing up the stairs, pulling Markus to his feet as I pass him by.

I make the queen's chambers and find Kara, half hiding behind the wall, half overseeing the battle below, and mumbling.

I follow Kara's lead, move to the other side of the doorway leading to the balcony, and partially expose myself to look out. She's conjured up a windstorm, pelting the caravan with debris. Humans on the wall have to duck and brace themselves while my Broadsword followers are strong enough to push against it and periodically return fire on the caravan. Had the caravan been comprised of mere mortals, Kara's storm would have put them on their asses, but all it's doing is partially blinding them from dust particles and forcing them to use their energy to stay upright.

"Keep it up. I'll light the trench," I tell Kara. "There"—I point—"a dozen paces in front of them." I'm not sure if Kara knows of all the castle's preparations. But I went over the defenses set out by Markus and Huntly, and I'll exhaust every one of them to send these bastards to their graves.

Kara takes my advice; her wind redirects to where I pointed.

I focus, and a flame bursts to life in a trench I know is there but can just make out.

Fire rockets from either side of my flame, speeding along a trench that can't be deeper than half a foot, and spreads to circle the castle's wall.

"Oil worked," says Markus, overlooking our attack. "Now—"

"Hit 'em hard, Kara," I say, beating Markus to what I'm sure he was going to suggest as our next move.

Kara's gusting wind picks up. Flame leaps into the air, licking at the Broadsword caravan. Hair and clothing catch fire along with one ill-placed Volkswagen hippie bus. The fire won't take out many of the caravan, but the shots fired at them as they relocate for better cover can. More than a few of them drop to the grass dead.

"Can you see the markers?" Markus asks.

I nod, already searching for them. I paid attention to what he and Huntly had said, and it's making us an effective unit. Fighting like this—like a well-trained team—is exhilarating, putting speed to the blood in my veins, and my course of action. I catch sight of what I'm looking for. Tiny flags laid out in the field, color coded and matching lines and numbers painted on the crossbows, distance and directional measurements from practice shots. "West arrows red four!" I shout.

My command repeats from voice to voice until it reaches those operating the crossbows. They tilt one back and let loose a giant arrow, sending it into the caravan group on the left, and shredding through the roof of a truck along with a pair of Broadsword on the flatbed.

"East arrows!" Markus shouts, squinting, then looks to me.

"Yellow two!" I complete the command. His vision is no comparison to mine.

Our orders are followed in the same manner, and an arrow skewers a car on my right.

Something flies through Kara's wall of fire—another RPG.

The wooden main gate blows back into the courtyard in pieces. Not even the iron grating survives the hit. Bent and mangled, it hangs precariously from one side of the wall.

Nikki's prediction is coming true. Our defenses won't be enough to stop this army of Broadsword from charging into the castle.

I have to do more, and despite my newfound pleasure in fighting alongside my own army, I have to do it alone. They'll have my back, at a safe distance—from me.

"Stay here," I say to Kara as I step onto the balcony, preparing to put the convoy to the test against vamp speed and strength, coupled with my other self's power. I scan the field searching for the quartz boulder I wielded like a mace. No need to mess with what worked. Markus and Toni grab me, try to hold me back. Kara shouts something, but it doesn't register.

I'm levitating, taking Markus and Toni with me. My senses heighten, like in Ovando, and everything slows down. People scurrying for cover, flames licking the air, gunfire erupting—everything moves at half speed, and my mind begins to fog over like a dream, I'm losing control of myself, but I'm about to turn the tide, *take* control of this battle. I can feel it in my racing heart, the rage of a woman on the brink of giving over to emotions without a thought of anything but satisfying that urge to revel in the most basic of instincts.

My other self surges, energy flashes all around me, and turns me, pulling me back inside the queen's chambers. I haven't learned to listen to it, yet, only give into my other self's guidance. My heart's pounding, fuming to lash out at my enemies, and I'm being pulled away from them, but why?

A man and a woman bearing rectangular SWAT shields step out of a corridor from behind a mirror on the far wall of the queen's chambers.

My other self smelled them before I could and acted on my behalf. The reek of wolf's blood flows through their veins.

Chapter Fifty-Seven

I can't give over control to my other self completely, not with Kara so close by, wolves or not. *Focus on their shields.* I push through the fog in my mind, will myself to be more than an observer and subdue any hint of violet trying to illuminate the room.

Strip away their defenses, then take them out yourself.

I surge forward, half running, half levitating with every step, and slam my fist into the man's shield.

He takes it with ease. Even with the added strength from my other self he barely moves back an inch. The woman shouts something, but I'm too concerned with how a mere wolf in human form can withstand me *and* my other self. I rip the man's shield away from him, toss it aside, and kick at the woman's shield. God, she's nearly as strong as he is. I dented her shield, but she's still standing.

Shots fire, ring off the woman's shield, and chip the stone walls around her as she crouches. With her pinned down, thanks to Markus's controlled shots, I reach out for the man with violet tendrils leading my fingers. He ducks, and faster than I can keep up he crosses the room, bats Markus's gun from his hands, and grabs Kara by the shoulders, holding her out to me like a human shield.

"No!" I scream, charging for them.

I get within arm's reach and Kara pulls free of his grasp. No...she didn't wriggle free—he let her go...*to bow down on his knees.*

"We surrender," he says.

My fist catches him in the side of the head, knocking him to the floor. I wind up for another blow and the woman slips between us, using her SWAT shield to push me back.

"Scarlett, stop!" shouts Toni, getting between the wolves and my fist. "She's the one I told you about."

Vaguely, I recall Toni telling me about a wolf, a woman, who was there when Dad changed thanks to the amulet. That was the night Lukas came back to us injured. Seeing him so beaten made me forget about Toni's supposedly age-old wolf.

Markus leaps for the woman, and she moves her shield, blocking him. She's only got one arm. The other is missing just below the elbow. She's completely playing defense, and she shows no sign of struggling to hold her own against Markus.

The man rises, but only back to his kneeling position with his head down.

For a moment, no one moves, and I have a second to register everyone bathed in my violet hue mixing with the rays of the setting sun. Kara's across the room, holding up her hand as if she's about to mumble something at the wolves. Markus is pissed off, scowling, and rising to his feet. Toni's wide-eyed, almost scared...of me, yet she's between me and the wolves. The woman peering out from behind the shield just stares at me, composed and calm, like how I imagine a seasoned Russian assassin would. She's waiting to react, to move and countermove, without emotion despite my glowing appearance.

"You better douse that light before they pinpoint your location," she says.

I catch a glimpse of myself in the mirror. My face is beet red, crinkled, and I'm lit up like the Fourth of July. My reflection is more menacing than it was when I crushed Kara's windpipe in the bathroom at the diner, but not like it was in Ovando, thankfully.

I take a slow breath, try to purge the aura of my other self and suppress it down, deep within my chest.

I drop my fist to my side but keep it clenched and ready to strike.

First, he surrenders, then she gives me advice that sounds more like an order from her tone. An explosion outside echoes in the courtyard, and my moment is gone.

"What's your deal?" I ask, sharply.

"No time for pleasantries," she says. "I'm Lexa, this is Eric. You all right, babe?"

Eric stands behind her, rubbing his jaw. He's taller than most men, with short-cropped hair as black as night, and a face that could grace any magazine. Lean and muscular, he looks like a man who's spent countless hours in the gym. "She packs a punch."

"You want to make it through the night, you're going to need our help. Can you accept it, or shall we continue our dance?" Lexa says to me, not moving from behind her shield.

Toni's nodding fast, telling me to let these wolves help us, telling me to listen to Lexa. Markus picks up his gun, trains it on them. "Don't shoot them," I say to him, "unless they turn on us." Markus looks even more enraged than when Lexa tossed him against the wall, but he stays his hand.

"Now that we're all friends, and you're not going to shoot us anymore," says Eric, "it's time to get to work. If they can hold these guys off, the others will be ready shortly."

"You're not going down there," Lexa says, lowering her shield. "Not without backup."

Three bullets chip the outer wall of the queen's chambers. All of us but the wolves react, jerking back from the open doors or looking toward the danger. *These two wolves are fearless, or too stupid to know when to duck and cover.* Something in my gut tells me the latter is unlikely.

"We're close enough." Eric nods at the setting sun, then smirks. "'Course, after all these years it's nice to see you're still concerned about me. I think you've forgotten just how good I am."

"You think too much of yourself."

"What's not to love?" Eric lifts his chin, smiling.

"Fine," Lexa sighs. "But I'm coming with you. Someone's gotta watch your ass."

"It *is* a nice ass."

"Get on with it." Lexa shoves Eric. "You coming with us?" she asks me, dropping her shield. She's fit, like Eric, with eyes so blue they nearly resemble those of a wolf. Her ivory face framed by long black hair makes her gaze even more intense, as if she's looking into my soul.

"I—"

"Your grandmother wouldn't have hesitated to be the first to ride into battle," Lexa cuts me off.

"Or be the first to lash out with that sharp tongue of hers," Eric says to Lexa. "Glad she didn't inherit that—got her temper, though."

"Just change already, and don't forget to call them."

"Fine," Eric says, rubbing his hands together. "Ladies…and guy…you're in for a show."

Eric drops to the floor, sprawling out on his hands and knees, grunting at the stones beneath him. I know what's happening, even though I've never seen it take place firsthand. As impossible as it is, being that the sun is still up, he's transforming into a wolf.

Eric arches his back and cranes his head to the ceiling, his muscles swell and tear through his clothes, forming broad shoulders supported by layer upon layer of corded muscle. A fine sheen of gray fur tipped with silver grows through his skin. Fingernails grow into long thick claws. Teeth elongate, coming to points half the length of my finger, and his face contorts to that of a wolf vaguely resembling his human features. He's panting as his hair thickens and grows into a long shaggy mane of deep crimson down his back. His coloring, massive size, and longer-than-normal claws are unlike any other wolf I've seen or even heard of.

He's astounding, yet terrifying. Like a marvel of nature and magic.

I step back, clenching my fists, trying not to show terror on my face. The wolf that once was Eric breathes deeply; his shoulders rise as his barrelled chest expands, and claws trace gouges in the stone beneath him. The only other oddity this great wolf possesses—if there is such a thing aside from his existence—is a thin band of cotton wrapped around his waist, stretching to near its breaking point.

I look to the others, all but Lexa are slack-jawed and wide eyed. She catches what I'm guessing is the same expression on my face and says, "Yeah, I know. He's showing off. He's only unique 'cause he's the first of us, the source all wolves stem from."

Chapter Fifty-Eight

I can't believe what I'm seeing. Eric, *the* first wolf.

It makes sense now why he's so strong, so fast. I step back. If he was that powerful as a man, I can't imagine how he is in his wolf form. I pray he's truly on our side, as I'm sure everyone else in the room is. I don't even think silver could kill him. My sword, the one from Dad, all I want is to wrap my fingers around its handle, put it between me and Eric to have some feeling of strength and protection. My eyes find it, leaning against the wall beside Kara's, along with all the other rifles Lukas and Ben stashed in the queen's chambers.

"Don't worry," says Lexa, following my gaze. "We're far too old to lose control like the pups do. The other added bonus…" Lexa drops her SWAT shield. "Controlling the change."

Her too? Can she change into a wolf in the daylight? If so, this is a game changer when it comes to dispatching wolves. I'm almost embarrassed at the thought of killing a wolf with no regard for their humanity, especially after these two have offered to come to our aid, not to mention Toni's guilt trip of how it wasn't their choosing to become animals. "Can you…"

"Change like him. No, I have to wait for dark like the others, but unlike them, I can turn it off at night." Lexa reaches out, shoulder height, and runs her fingers through Eric's mane. "Slow through the courtyard, babe. We don't want any friendly fire."

Eric nuzzles his head into her side, then springs onto the balcony rail.

"Can we trust them?"

I shrug at Kara. I hope so.

Markus has kept his barrel trained on Eric while he transformed and looks as concerned as Kara sounds in my head. Toni's composed, even though she's transfixed on Eric. So far, Lexa's been right. Eric seems to be in control of his wolf-self.

I step forward, finding courage. "If you're going to help us, then we better not hurt you two by accident." I step onto the balcony and stand beside Eric. He stares down at me from his perch on the rail and cranes his head the way a dog does when pondering something.

I have to get the word out to Huntly and those still alive in the castle. No one will hear me shouting over the fight consisting of explosions and gunfire. What I need is something visual, like what Kara did on the wall. Something that will catch the eye's attention, warn my people not to shoot a new ally. Something simple, and direct.

I can do this…I have to do this, have to control my magic. Fire…small flames…just words…that's all I want. Wolves are friends. Thin lines of fire trace through the sky, following my finger's direction:

W O L

I'm doing it.

Lexa slaps my hand. It stings something fierce, and she's shaking her head at me. "Don't give away our advantage. If you're going to do that, do it inside the courtyard, low enough that they can't see."

She's right—I was spelling in midair above the wall where everyone can see it, including the Broadsword caravan. There's no need to let them know we have a pair of wolves on our side. For a moment the exchange of gunfire stops as all eyes concentrate on the flaming letters dissipating between the two armies.

Something registers; Lexa said for Eric not to forget to call the others. Does she mean the pack that decimated Lincoln and the towns east of it that Nikki showed us? Is Eric the reason the wolves are working as one, as a controlled unit instead of a horde of wild dogs? That would explain Nikki's lack of showing us casualties. That also means that Xanatos doesn't control the pack, and Eric does. The caravan doesn't seem as menacing, if my assumptions are correct. They're still a threat, no doubt, but if Eric can summon a pack of wolves large enough to rival the caravan, we should be able to prevail. If I'm right.

I want to ask Lexa, but another explosion rocks the castle wall. There's no time.

I trace a single line back inside the courtyard, and all heads follow. Sporadic gunfire resumes from the caravan as my people read what I'm burning in the grass:

WOLVES ARE FRIENDS

Questioning faces turn upward, and more than a few of them jerk back at the sight of Eric, hunched over, yet towering above me. A rifle or three instinctively raise toward the tower, but I get them lowered by shaking my head and putting a hand on Eric's broad shoulder, running my fingers through his fur, petting him. He's warm, hot, and his fur is soft.

Bullets pepper the tower, and I dive for cover. Apparently my location has not gone unnoticed thanks to my other self. Eric's on top of me, pulling me into the queen's chambers and shoving me against the wall. "Scar!" yells Kara, coming to my side.

"I'm okay."

Bullets sound off the tower's walls, trailing away from the doors, and Markus, leaning against the other wall, says, "Either those soldiers are the worst shot in the world or they're trying to miss."

"Trying to miss? They just blanketed us in bullets," says Kara.

"No, he's right," says Toni. "They're not hitting anywhere near the doors; since we've been up here the only ones that have rocked the tower seemed more like strays to me."

"They're keeping us suppressed, not trying to kill us." Markus frowns. "They want you busy ducking and taking cover instead of using your powers."

A bullet in the head would definitely stop me from using my powers. Why would they intentionally miss? Then it hits me. The ultimatum was that I get sent out to the caravan. "They want me alive." With the caravan no longer life-threatening, and wolves now on my side, my other self decides I'm safe enough and crawls back within me, giving me a clearer and more focused head.

"We can use that to our advantage. You might not want to stop the light show just yet if they won't take a shot at you," says Lexa, loosening her black leather boots and setting them against the wall, followed by her jeans and shirt, leaving her standing in nothing but her lace bra and panties.

Evidently Eric put on a show for us, bursting through his clothing like he did. Lexa, it seems, is more practical, saving her clothes for later by piling them in the corner. I don't blame her; those boots are wicked. One thing is certain: She's not modest.

Markus blushes, turning his gaze from her, and I get why. Lexa's in such good shape she has a defined six-pack—and this, coupled with long wavy black hair to the middle of her back, an ivory face, high cheekbones, and lips red as an apple, means she's a knockout. "You can run point. It'll be hard for them to shoot us if they have to dodge you leading the way, and last I checked bullets don't curve around things."

"No way." Markus shakes his head. "Not going to happen."

"She's right," I tell him, though I can't believe I'm saying it. "I have to try."

"What if she's wrong?" Kara grabs my shoulder. "We don't know she's right. We don't even know if we can trust her."

"You don't have a choice." Lexa walks through the open doorway, basking in the sun's final rays. Eric nudges my arm with his nose as if to say it's time. "They're getting bolder."

An old pickup truck crashes through the disintegrated gate, clearing the entrance for the others as the driver is gunned down.

"I can't do what I need to if I'm worrying about you, Kara. I need you to be safe, to stay here mumbling far from the fight. They can stay here to protect you." I indicate the others.

"No," says Kara.

"Like hell." Markus cocks his rifle, expending an unused bullet to the floor as if to make a point. "I'm coming with you."

"Fine, but Toni stays." I look Toni in the eye. "Please, stay with Kara, protect her…to protect me." I could have ordered her, but if this is one of the last acts I'm to perform on this earth, then I don't want it to be that of a slavedriver.

Toni nods.

Lexa shakes her head. "Ohhh, they're making this easy, funneling toward the gate. Come on, while they're dumb enough to do that."

Lexa drops to the balcony and follows Eric's lead, transforming into her wolf form.

Chapter Fifty-Nine

"Be here when I get back," I tell Kara, hugging her, trying to be strong, trying not to show any insecurity. If I become lost in the pleasurable blood-drunk rage I went through before, there's no telling how far I might go. I might be the one the world needs saving from. If Kara dies from my actions, I know that would push me over the edge, but part of me has hope. Hope that through our bond, and our kinship, that if I do snap, she'll be able to draw me back to reality. But she can only do that if she's alive, and the best way I can ensure that in a battle is to keep her holed up in the tower, away from the enemy.

"Make sure you come back," she tells me. I feel it in her heart, the worry of things to come. She keeps a brave face though, in turn giving me strength.

I fake a smile and follow Markus down the stairs with Eric and Lexa behind me. We enter the main hall, full of the wounded sprawled out on the tables and floor, and Abby barking out commands to her appointed helpers. The whole room reeks of blood, loose bowels, and death. One by one, every head turns our way, terror written on their faces. They must not have seen my writing in the grass as they're all staring behind me. Lexa, covered in gray fur tipped with a hint of silver like any other wolf, shudders and stands up looking at Eric. He rubs his paw against his muzzle and stands on his hind legs. I guess the stench is overwhelming to their wolf senses.

Seeing them side by side, I realize just how much Eric differs from Lexa, and any other wolf. Males are normally larger than females, sure, but his size is immense compared to hers. He's got a good foot or two on her, standing about seven feet tall or more, and his girth has to have packed on an extra fifty pounds of sheer muscle. Combine that with his crimson mane and matching eyes, he'll leave every one of these people with PTSD, as if they don't have enough trauma already.

"They're friends," I tell the room, and somewhat reassure myself they're on my side. I get now why Hollywood has made a trove of movies with werewolves; if anyone ever laid eyes on one, especially Eric, they'd be both terror-stricken and awestruck at the sight of a massive wolf that moves like a man.

We press through to the doors without a response from a single soul, and one face stands out from the crowd of wounded. Sue, my assistant thief, is staring blankly at the ceiling with a hole in her chest. Her blood is not yet dry from spilling her life from the wound. I grit my teeth. This must end, they must end. Sue's lifeless body stirs up thoughts of Mom's murder by the Broadsword. I can pretend that everyone in the caravan was Mom's murderer.

I train my sights outside the great hall, its uneasy feeling no longer a hindrance but fuel to what must come next.

We make the courtyard and Markus rushes toward Kara's Trans Am—bullet-ridden, windows shot out, and two flat tires make me think it'll never drive again. I follow his lead, sloshing through puddles, the water tower is toppled and split open, and the water has a crimson tint to it from mixing with blood of the innocents I've vowed to protect. I duck beside Markus behind the car, followed by Lexa and Eric.

The courtyard is in shambles.

There are just as many bodies out here as there are in the main hall, some spread out in the grass, one in a tree, and a few lying motionless on the wall's catwalk. One catapult is destroyed and burning. The huge crossbows are lacking most of their oversized arrows, hopefully they're stuck in some of the Broadsword outside the walls. The explosions I heard from the tower must have come from a few grenades and RPGs. One must have made it clear through the main gate as a portion of the castle has collapsed, Abby's medical wing. That's why she's in the main hall; she had to improvise.

My heart picks up pace—if it's even possible—because an image of Lukas flashes in my imagination, buried under a heap of rubble. I try to recall if I saw him in the main hall, but there were so many people in there only Abby's face stands out aside from Sue's. I want to run back in, but I can't. I have a job to do, just like Abby has hers, and so does Kara.

The phoenix rises from her Trans Am and surges through the gate, wrapping its flaming wings around an old car leading the procession into the castle. It explodes, blocking the path for vehicles to get inside. So much for the bottleneck attack Lexa had hoped for. I guess Kara didn't catch that part.

"We're going," Markus says, no longer having to shout over the battle. Both sides must be conserving ammunition. "Turn up the lights." He means my other self, so we can put our theory to the test that I won't be shot. There's no need to recall an emotion to get ramp up, there's plenty to go around. I don't want to, but if letting out a tiny bit of my other self will enable us to come out on top, then I have to. My reflection in the Trans Am's paint job brightens, and we make for the main gate with wisps of tendrils trailing me.

Bullets zing through the air around us for a moment, then stops or is redirected to the people on the wall. I guess they see my tendrils, and so far, our theory of them wanting me alive is proving to be true.

As I reach the wall and glance around the frame, I get a sense of our enemies' condition: They've fared far better than we have. A couple vehicles are destroyed, a rusty blue pickup is still on fire, two cars have boulders on them, and one is skewered with a massive arrow sticking from the trunk, though only a few bodies are lying in the grass. Their automatic weapons and explosives have had a more devastating effect on us than our rifles and medieval weapons have had on them.

We're losing, and badly.

A metal cylinder like a pop can is tossed over the wall; everyone who sees it ducks for cover as it clangs off the stables then explodes.

Dirt, wood, and stone flies in the air, horses complain from inside, and I get an idea. I need to make a distraction, a big one, and what's bigger than a half vamp half-witch shooting out tendrils of violet energy while riding a pegasus? "I'll draw their attention."

"How?" asks Markus.

"I'll fly over them. When I do, make your move, charge them. Spread the word."

Markus makes to interject, but I can see it in his eyes, he knows it can work, and he has no choice but to obey me if I order him to. I didn't say that was an order, but it looks like he took it as one. He takes off up the stairs to tell Huntly and the others.

Eric and Lexa stare at me, heads cocked slightly. Maybe they don't know about my pegasus, or they think I can fly by myself or something. Either way, they bow their massive heads then follow Markus.

I run for the stables. One horse is dead, all the other animals are agitated, scraping the ground with their hooves and mooing or neighing, along with my pegasus. "Whoa, Spirit," I say, reaching for her, patting her neck and putting a hand on her head. Spirit's wings spread and bang against the stall she's in, but she calms enough for me to open the gate, climb on, and lead her out.

We take flight, faster than Spirit has done in the past, and clear the wall. Barrels train on me but don't fire. Nearly every eye of the caravan is on me, their sought-after prize.

A *pop* different than a gunshot sounds from the grouping of vehicles on my right.

I turn to find a member of the Broadsword holding a gun with four balls attached to the end of the oversized barrel. He fires, and another *pop* sounds.

A net spreads in front of us, led by four shimmering black balls expanding into the night, just missing their target.

Spirit rears up.

The second net snags her wing, ties her up, and we fall.

Chapter Sixty

Spirit tries to free her wing, keep us airborne, but it's an impossible task. The net around her holds tight, and we plummet awkwardly on our sides to the earth. I tighten my grip on her mane with one hand, try to free her wing of the net with the other, but it won't budge. We hit the ground so hard I'm more bounced off Spirit than thrown from her. Jarring my back as my spine contorts and compresses, I land beside her, writhing in pain.

We crash land between the middle and right divisions of the convoy. I'm surrounded.

My other self ramps up, drinking in my surroundings and relaying them to me faster than my normal senses ever could: the Broadsword running toward me, a wolf howling from the castle, shots raining down from the wall, my people rushing from the gate. Everything hits me at once, along with Markus tugging at my arm, dragging me back. Somehow, he made it to me, left the other Broadswords behind in the castle and charged to my aid like a true guardian.

My back spasms as he pulls me, and air won't fill my lungs as easily as it should.

I want to pull away from Markus, take a second to recover, but there's no time. The first Broadsword from the caravan reaches us and dives at Markus with a knife. Markus fires his rifle awkwardly with one hand; it recoils, jerking upward, but he hits his mark.

The Broadsword drops with a hole in his chest.

Gunfire erupts all around us; it's deafening. No bullets zing close, but Markus drags me beside Spirit and covers me with his body. "Stay down!" he shouts. It's not like I have a choice—I heal fast—but whatever's going on in my back brings up visions of me bound to a wheelchair for life.

Spirit makes a torturous sound and thrashes for a moment, kicking, flailing her unbound wing, then falls still.

Markus stays atop of me, uses Spirit as a shield, rests his rifle on her side, and fires sporadically, emptying his weapon.

He falls off me clutching his throat.

Mounds of dirt shoot up, surrounding us—Kara has bought me a second.

"Markus, no," I say, dragging myself to him.

Lying on my side, I dig beneath his jacket for his first aid kit. He tries to speak but only dark red bubbles come from his mouth. His hand against his throat can't keep the blood from spurting beneath it. I stop searching for the first aid kit, put my hand to his cheek and do the only thing I can. I say, "Thank you."

His eyes glaze over, and he falls limp in my arms.

Spirit is dead. Markus is gone. My protector since this madness began gave his life for me. I want to grieve for him, shed a tear for them both, but I can't. My back is broken, or damn close, and it pisses me off further. My other self is doing something to my spine—lining, supporting, or healing it. Whatever is happening, I can't say, but I've stopped spasming and my back only burns just below my ribs like a hot coal has replaced one of my vertebrae.

A member of the Broadsword climbs over the dirt mound, reaching for me. The brief seconds of safety Kara gave me are over.

I rise, fighting the burning ember in my back, and the dirt circle becomes lit with my other self's violet light.

He lunges at me, weaponless with both fists balled, ready to knock me out.

I catch one fist, twist his arm to the side, bend it against its will, and snap his wrist bones.

He cries out in pain.

I scream in fury.

My fist drives his head into the dirt, crushing temple bones beneath my knuckles, killing him with a single blow. I pull back my fist covered in blood, and my back hurts less, healed or fuelled by my other self reveling at the life-taking blow I landed.

I climb over Kara's temporary Sanctum with my violet tendrils blazing brighter than ever before. "You want me! Come and get me?" I shout as loud as I can, both being the distraction my people need, and burning off any grief or fear, changing it to rage.

Grenades go off in the crowd of my ground troops, killing a dozen or more. Automatic weapons mow down the rest in groups at a time. The caravan is unleashing everything they have now that I'm within their grasp, and they're making short work of the people I'm supposed to protect, for the second time.

I leap into the air, high enough and bright enough to turn heads, and come down behind the lineup of vehicles on the right that the Broadsword is using as cover. They don't shoot. They charge me head on.

"Die!" I scream, charging back.

My chest becomes superheated, enraged. My back no longer bothers me.

I'm watching myself again. I'm controlling myself, yet not.

Bones crush beneath my fists, legs break under my kicks, and bodies are tossed skyward by violet flares. I use a car door like a giant scythe, swinging it through the air, slicing it through my opponents.

It feels like I'm back in Ovando, fighting the Black Serpents, but this time I'm surrounded only by my enemy with no one to care for aside from myself.

A violet fog billows from my hand and paralyzes half the men.

My other hand elongates the flare, dropping the car door to hoist a truck in the air. Mercilessly I slam it on top of still-mobile faceless enemies. I crush bodies to lumps of smeared flesh and broken bones. If it moves, I squash it with sheer joy thundering my heart against my ribs, until I alone am standing amid paralytic statues.

The battle between my people and the other two groupings of the convoy rages on. Gunfire, explosions, and a giant flaming phoenix fill the night sky. My people are leaving me alone, as is the rest of the caravan, and I welcome the opportunity as I turn to those I paralyzed in my fog. "You came to get me, well here I am," I say calmly, strutting slowly toward them and letting the fog drop just enough that they can wriggle about but not move. "You said we'd all die, that they'd all die…that *she'd* die."

I curl my fingers into a point and slam my fist into the chest of the nearest Broadsword. His ribs separate and give way for my hand to pass between them, pushing aside soft mushy organs as he screams. Something thumps wildly in my grasp. I get a good grip and yank his heart from his chest. Before the light fades from his eyes, I let him see my fangs sink into the strong meaty organ. I drain the heart of its nourishing blood and toss it aside.

"Next," I say, moving toward a woman still clutching a military-style automatic rifle. Unable to drop it, unable to aim it and shoot, the woman shudders and the scent of fear fills the air. I haul its intoxicating fragrance in and shut my eyes. "That's the stuff."

I feel my other self flourish, relish in carnal delight, and I tear through the rest by feel alone. Using the fog as a sensor leading me to the rushing pulsating hearts, I tear into each chest to either toss aside a heart or drain it of its blood depending upon the scent—the greater the fear, the sweeter the aroma, and the better the taste.

Letting the last one fall, I drop the fog and savor the moment: the chaos of the battle, the screams, the crisp night air drying blood to my skin, the fear wafting on the wind. This must be how a blind person feels with all other senses heightened.

Wolf replaces the scent of fear on the wind, and I turn up my nose, open my eyes. Their scent is repulsive, and it draws out a hatred from a memory I can't recall.

I leap on top of a truck's roof and check out what I've missed.

In the distance, coming from an arch in the outer wall I'm certain never existed before, surges a pack of wolves a hundred strong or more.

The caravan has finally taken a hit, thanks to me. The two remaining defensive groups look to have suffered some more losses, but not enough to stop them from pushing forward and taking us out entirely.

There can't be more than twenty heads atop the castle wall, and bodies are strewn out between the caravan and the destroyed gates.

Nikki was right. Between those I'd seen inside, and the dead out here; we're taking heavy losses.

Small groups trying to reach the caravan rush forward and are gunned down. One is actually pushing through, but not toward the living caravan—toward me, and its being led by a rolling mound of dirt taking the bullets raining down on them. Every one of them has gray skin. My obedient Broadswords coming to my aid no doubt.

No…not every one of them, one of them has normal skin and only half a head of golden locks bouncing with every step.

Kara is on the field.

Chapter Sixty-One

Sweat pours from my palms, slicking them further as it mixes with the blood staining them. The sight of Kara out in the open dries my mouth despite the blood filling it. *Why the hell is she out here?*

One of her Broadsword guards falls, then another. They're doing their job of protecting her, putting themselves between the caravan and Kara where the rolling mound of dirt lets a bullet sneak past. "Kara!" I scream, finding my voice.

My other self encases the vehicles around me, lifting them into the air, moving them around me, around Kara. We're encircled by steel tinted violet, and safe for the moment. "What are you doing?" I grab her by the arms. "And you"—I toss Kara aside and face Toni—"*you* were supposed to protect her, even from herself."

Markus's words spew from my lips at Toni, and she takes a step back. Her lips move but her words don't register; I'm too pissed. She put Kara's life in jeopardy.

Kara steps between myself and Toni as I reach for her throat. I have to stop myself from smacking Kara across her face: it's wrought with concern and her eyes have a slight redness. She's been crying or trying not to.

"Scar, stop!" Kara shouts, holding me back. Her hands on my shoulders piss me off further. I don't want to be touched. Kara's face is bathed violet from my other self feeding off of my rage for Toni's insubordination. "Look at yourself!"

Look at myself? "I know what I look like. I'm the most powerful sorceress the world has ever seen."

My breath is shallow in a heartbeat.

I'm scared. Scared of my own thoughts. Of what I want to do. I'm infuriated, and fearful of what I'm becoming. *Breathe, Scar...think of Mom, and her kindness.* I take another step back and turn around.

"I'm...sorry," I say, though I'm not sure it's loud enough for Kara to hear me.

A hand rests on my shoulder. "It's okay," Kara says. She wraps her hand around my waist, pulls me back against her chest, and rests her head on my shoulder, hugging me. "I got you."

"I know," I tell her, holding her hand on my stomach, feeling the coolness of her skin, and letting myself calm down. "Thank you. I needed you," I whisper. She pulled me back from a precipice. I can't imagine what she would think of me if she knew what I did to these people. Sure I killed them, and she'd have no problem with that, but it's the *way* I killed them. I was merciless and overly cruel.

"I thought you were done for, and I couldn't help you if I couldn't see you."

The deep violet hue illuminating everything lightens. I'm still acting like my father would have, like Xanatos. I can almost hear his deep gravelly voice rumbling in the back of my mind.

The ground vibrates.

The pack of wolves is charging toward us.

My other self flashes, lighting up the makeshift wall of vehicles surrounding us. A howl comes from the castle, and I see Eric at the gates, howling at the sky behind his SWAT shield with Lexa at his side.

The pack of wolves splits in two, kicking up dirt as they pass us by on either side.

That's what happened in Lincoln, that's what Lexa meant about control—Eric can control the wolves. He can guide them from their endless blood-drunk urges. He and Lexa make use of their shields and speed toward the center caravan grouping, roaring, and growling as they run.

The oddity of a wolf with a shield, combined with their snarls, must shock the Broadsword. For a moment all they do is stare at the pair advancing on them. Their attention is so focused on Eric and Lexa they fail to notice the pack of wolves emerging from the darkness at their side. This must have been Lexa's plan all along: distract the caravan and let the wolves take them out.

The wolves hit the middle grouping of the caravan and all hell breaks loose. Sporadic gunfire, howls, snarls, screams, and yelps echo in the night. Bodies are tossed around, some with their limbs attached and some without.

An explosion goes off in the midst of them, followed by another, then another. I can make out objects flying through the air into the middle group, followed by explosions. They're coming from grenades tossed by the caravan group on the far side of them. They don't care if they take out their own people just as long as they stop the immediate threat. With the amount of ammunition being unloaded and bombs being tossed, there is no way any of them are going to survive.

Bullets ring off the car I'm standing behind.

Kara and Toni duck, taking cover.

"No, no, no," I find myself repeating as I stare down at Kara. She was safe in the castle, safer than she is here, and it's because of me she's dodging bullets. "I failed…failed you…failed Mom…failed everybody." I turn away from them as another explosion rocks the center group, and my despair, fear, and anxiety morph. "Never again," I say, digging my nails into my palms. "I'll keep you safe, like you did me."

"Scar, I'm fine, really."

"Not until they're wiped from the face of the earth you're not."

My other self flares up all around me more so than ever before, and time stops. I plunge my flares into the dirt, carving out a massive heap of earth the size of a truck. Lifting it in the air I say, "Get in."

"What?" says Kara.

"It's not a request." Violet flares wrap around Kara and Toni, drag them into the crater, cover it with the vehicles for a makeshift roof, and I release the mound of earth, entombing them within. "You'll be safe in there," I say, turning my attention to the battle at my back, giving in to my other self with every breath.

I'm more than warm, I'm emanating heat fueled by unbridled rage.

I leap into the air, throwing tendrils in every direction, searching for something to take hold. I overshoot my mark and pass over the center group of Broadsword's engaged with the full force of Eric's wolf army. I come down hard, the middle group at my back, the remaining stronghold of the caravan at my front.

Energy surges from within me, rising from my skin and forming a violet dome around me. A bullet hits it and slows to a stop, caught in the flickering violet.

The foggy dream-like state I'm in feeds me with a rush of pleasure, and I shudder, drawing in a choppy breath.

"You wanted me," I hear myself say. My voice is deeper, darker, and full of confidence. "You have no idea who you're dealing with." One pissed off bitch, that's who.

No, I'm not watching myself from a distance. I'm in control, free of all inhibitions and restraints. I'm speaking from urges buried deep down within me. "I am power," I tell myself. "I am eternal." My flickering violet dome shimmers, veins of energy writhing on its surface, surging out and mimicking the release of my emotions. Mimicking the freedom of accepting who my bloodline is, who I am. "I am the Raven." My ancestor's chosen name and earned name as the world's first sorceress, a blood memory that writhes in my veins. A name from the distant past bearing strength, giving substance and a name to my other self, uniting us as one. I'm no witch. I *am* a sorceress. More powerful than any witch could hope to be.

"I…am…the Raven!" I tell the world.

The dome pulses and expands in fast-forward like a blur, lighting up the night, engulfing the caravan at either side of me—incinerating all it touches. Vehicle, weapon, Broadsword, wolf, nothing above the earth's surface is safe.

The dome vanishes as fast as it moved, and I drop to my hands and knees on scorched earth. I'm breathing heavy, tired, and spent from such an outburst of energy.

I slump to my side with my violet energy fading.

Nothing is left of my enemy. Nothing remains aside from blackened steel, burning tires, and skeletons stripped clear of their flesh, leaving no more than charred bones where bodies once stood.

I did it. I won. I saved them. I saved her.

All I want to do is close my eyes, let my lids shut. The Raven in me won't let that happen, not entirely. Together we fought, and as drained as we are from stripping the land of our enemies, we're still fighting as a symbiotic unit.

Reality blurs. Everything becomes fuzzy as figures move about in the distance.

The fuzz clears, and the world is crisp, full of clear images. The figures are closing in on me now, having moved faster than the speed of light. I'm confused how they could move like that, then I realize it's due to a time lapse from me passing out and fighting to stay conscious.

I shake my head, trying to clear the fuzzy vision overtaking my eyes.

The figures surround me, but I can't make them out.

Another time lapse.

All that's clear is a hand reaching down to me.

Chapter Sixty-Two

Something's burning. Something toxic like gasoline mixed with burned grass and charred meat fills my lungs. The air's so thick with it I can taste it, and I rub my tongue against the roof of my mouth to wipe it clean.

A hand rests on my chest, another lifts my head. Kara's blurred face appears before me.

"You did it, Scar. You stopped them all. You can rest now." Kara's voice is soft and nurturing. I know I took out the caravan, but her saying it cements it.

I want to take her advice and rest, recover, regain some energy, but I want to ensure she's right. Ensure I stopped the threat, stopped Xanatos's first wave of attack. I try to stay conscious, but everything fades away.

~ * ~

A chill runs up my spine, making the hair on my arms and the back of my neck stand on end. My head flops to the side, cradled in someone's arm. Someone's carrying me. Bodies lie before me, surround me, bandaged and bleeding in a huge stone room with firelight dancing across faces and stone walls. It feels like home, but also creepy. I'm in the grand hall.

I hear my name, and then nothing.

~ * ~

Lavender with a faint hint of lilac mixed with jasmine caresses me from my rest. Silk slides across my hands as I pull the covers up to my chin. The sun warms my face and brightens my eyelids as I roll, makes me think it's going to be a great day filled with blue skies. A birdsong floats in from outside the window, welcoming me to the coming day. There are soft feminine voices in the room as well—kind, sweet, and familiar.

I open my eyes to the dandelion bouquet Mel made me on the end table beside the bed. Stretching, I let out a sigh. "Morning," I say to Kara and Lexa.

"How are you feeling?" Kara rises from her chair, bringing me a glass of water.

I sit up, letting the covers fall from my chest. I'm wearing a clean white tank, though I can't recall finding one to go to bed, or even going to bed for that matter. Images of the Raven return to me, like waking up from a hangover and the final scene of a movie I passed out to replays for an instant, stealing my blissful awakening. I gasp. "Did I really—"

"Just relax." Kara hands me the glass. I take it and sip slowly, waiting for her to speak to comfort me as only she can. But something tells me nothing she says or does can pull the pit from my stomach. She holds my other hand in hers, pressing my palm into the silk sheet as she strokes my knuckles. "You had a big night. Do you know what happened?"

I hoped she wouldn't ask me that. All I want is to crawl back under the covers and forget the night before, like pushing a drunken embarrassment far into the past and praying nobody brings up what I did. I finish my glass of water, set the cup on the end table, and nod. "We won," I say, hanging my head, not wanting to look Kara in the eye.

"We're *safe*." I know Kara well enough that that's her way of saying yes and no, and the real answer can wait.

Just like waking with a hangover, I want to know what happened, rip off the band-aid fast so I can have time to process everything and come up with a reasonable response for my actions when talking to the next person I run into. "How many?"

"Don't concern yourself with that right now."

"No," says Lexa from a chair in the corner. "She needs to know, and so do we."

They've obviously been discussing me and my other self, the Raven, while I slept. "I can handle it," I say, putting on a brave face, forcing myself to look Kara in the eye.

She glances down at my hand she's rubbing, and takes a breath. "Nikki was right—we lost a little over half."

"Lukas?"

"He's fine, so is Ben."

"And the caravan of Broadsword?"

"Two are alive, chained up in the dungeon."

I glance at Lexa. "And the wolves?"

"Eight survived out of over a hundred, along with Eric and me," says Lexa plainly. "They're human again till nightfall, then we'll have to contain them in cells so they don't try to kill everyone…at least until Eric recovers."

"How bad is he?"

"He's been through worse, and he heals faster than other wolves. As long as he's got wine to lick his wounds with, he'll be fine." Lexa waves off my question as if what happened is a normal occurrence. "What *I* want to know is if you remember your name." Lexa leans forward, studying me.

"Of course I do."

"Good, what is it?"

"Lexa," Kara interjects.

"No, I want to hear her say it."

I get it, she wants to know if I'm me, or the Raven. It's almost comforting to know that my other self has a name. But it's concerning as well: two names, two separate identities, two extremely different personalities in one body…and possibly moving toward a fight as to who owns that body. That was what I feared about losing control. Now, I'm not so sure. I gave in to…not my other self, but myself. I took control of the power. I am the Raven. It scares me, but the unknown has a habit of doing that. I have an idea as to what I can do, but truly controlling the Raven with rational thought and not just unchecked emotion is going to take some serious practice and meditation. "My name is Scarlett," I say, answering Lexa. "And the Raven. It just popped out, felt natural. Like I got it from deep within me."

Lexa sighs, rests her forehead in her fingers and rubs her temples. "I didn't want to hear that, not again. I can handle her, but not the Raven," she says more to herself than either me or Kara. She sits there rubbing her forehead until her silence becomes awkward, then she slaps her knee and stands up. "Never too early for a drink."

"What do you mean *her*?" I have to know what's got her so disturbed. "What other name could there be?"

"I would have been happier had you said your grandmother's name, Sorsha." Lexa pauses at the top of the stairs. "Not her alter-ego. The Raven was hard enough to deal with the first time around. I gotta talk to Eric." She turns to head down the steps, still speaking, but to herself. "Least we had a way to pull it out of *her*."

The way she said *her* makes me think that even someone with Lexa's age and knowledge has a right to fear the Raven. To my knowledge, magic mixed with vamp blood has never existed before. The name came up from deep within me, like a blood memory from my ancestors. If the Raven was my grandmother's alter-ego, her other self, my blood remembered it. Was the Raven the first sorceress Dad spoke of back on Lukas's porch and not my grandmother, not Sorsha?

Lexa saying at least they had a way to pull it out of *her* concerns me. It's not like my blood can be pulled out of me. Am I channeling her? The thought of the Raven being more than just my pent-up emotions is more than disturbing, it's downright terrifying. What if the Raven, the world's first sorceress, is channeling through me like Xanatos is through Dad?

Chapter Sixty-Three

Kara lets me get ready for the day alone, as per my request.

I pull on some clean clothes, mulling over Lexa's cryptic wording about the Raven and Sorsha, and what that means for me. I decide I need to know what she does. Maybe Eric knows, too. He's as old as she is. Older maybe, and he might not be as cryptic.

The birdsong outside the window calls to me, and I force myself to follow it to the balcony even though I know I'm going to see what shape the castle's in.

It's a wreck.

The once perfectly toothed catwalk on the wall is missing parts of its teeth and the catwalk itself, along with a section of wall that's collapsed into a pile of rubble beside the main gate. Surprisingly enough, there's still the remnant of an arch on the right. Only one catapult and two giant crossbows survived; the rest are in shambles or burned down to embers like the stables are. The cows and horses that were in the stables are now out in the field with the rest of the herd, chomping on grass in their paddocks well beyond the circular scorched earth and charred vehicles. The normal mulling about of people has been replaced with covered corpses and loved ones kneeling by their sides.

I drop my head. The morning started out so much better when I was still in a dream-like state. Makes sense, though—my life has become a nightmare, and there's no need to make one up as I sleep.

A little boy points at me from the courtyard and is quickly ushered away by his mother. My short-lived appreciation and acceptance by the people vanished overnight. I don't blame them. Sure, they knew, thanks to Nikki's prediction, that half the castle's population would perish. But I'd bet none of them thought I would be the one to do part of the killing. When I strafed the land and incinerated the convoy, I also turned the majority of wolves to ash. Some of those wolves were people from Lincoln, and they would have been people again during the day, people related to those staring up at me from the courtyard. I essentially killed off everyone they knew in one fell swoop.

I pull back from the balcony and head downstairs, directly for the medical wing. I still have hope that Lukas will accept me for who I am despite what I became last night, Kara seems…fine with it. I can track down Lexa and Eric once I check in on him and give myself a sense of normality.

The room Lukas was in yesterday is still standing, but it's empty.

I make for the main hall and stop just before it, press my back against the wall, and listen in to try and get a feeling about the mood and what I'm about to walk into. There's not much talk, not even small talk. Mainly the conversations are about pain, loss, funeral preparations, and open-ended questions with no answers expected like. *What are we gonna do now?*

Ike steps out of the hall and freezes in his tracks at the sight of me.

I give him a downtrodden grin that I know must look pathetic. He clenches his fists and stares at me as he's done in the past, but this time he's close enough I can smell the moonshine on his breath. The apple, Zeke, didn't fall far from the tree. The bulge in the pocket of Ike's coveralls tells me he's got a handgun of some sort with him, and now I really want to know if he suspects foul play on my part in regard to his sons.

Ike pulls the pistol out of his pocket, a snub nose revolver, and points it at my face. He's shaking, with rage, fear, or anticipation—I can't tell. He may be holding a gun in my face, but his finger isn't on the trigger, it's on the guard. He hasn't even pulled back the hammer.

I could take him no problem, but instead I'm fixated on the barrel. Maybe my reaction, or lack thereof, stays his hand. He studies my face and after what seems like an eternity, he says, "How can you live with what you've done?"

If he's speaking about the state of the castle or the entire world, I'm not sure. But I can smell anxiety on him. Its bitter taste pours out of him, overwhelming any trace of moonshine. Then it shifts, and so does the position of his finger on the guard. I'll be damned if I'm going to let this asshole end me before I can get the answers I want from Lexa, stop Xanatos, free Dad, free the Broadsword, free me from the burden of being…me.

Before Ike's finger can reach the trigger, I have his mangled hand in mine, crushing his bones around the revolver. He makes to scream, but I drive palm into his throat. His eyes bulge, and before he can grasp my wrist, I drive my forehead into his face. Warm droplets of blood from his nose spackle my cheek, and Ike falls to the floor.

His breathing is laboured, thanks to his whistling, bent out of shape bloodied nose, but he's alive. I scoop up his gun. Then I haul him to the nearest room and toss him inside. Ike's temporary holding cell is being used to house linens, blankets, and pillows. Satisfied he can use nothing to escape I break off the interior handle, shut the door, and head away from the main hall scanning corridors as I pass them by until I find who I'm looking for. "The drunkard Markus put down is locked in the linen closet by the main hall," I say to a Broadsword as I hand him the gun. "See that he finds a more permanent home."

Before the man can speak, I turn away from him trusting he'll fulfill my request. My mood shifted, either from the exertion or the instinct of self preservation, I decide my next course of action and make my way to the dungeon and the two Broadswords who survived the battle.

Of course they're being watched, and to my relief it's by Toni and Huntly. They're an odd paring but I guess it makes sense—she's Broadsword, he's highly trained military; they can handle the two chained to the floors of their individual cells.

"Get anything out of them?" I ask, concentrating my gaze on the prisoners. They're the engine driving my guilt and anger, at the moment. They're the cause of me losing what semblance of a life would look like. One without children being ushered away from me. One I had a taste of, no matter how briefly, and I intend to take it out on them, one way or another.

Huntly whips his head around. "Nothing pertinent," he says, looking startled. I hope it's because I crept up on him and not because of last night. I chalk up Huntly's shock to my speed and stealth.

"Scarlett, I'm sorry about Kara. You told me to protect her, but to do that I had to follow her. No matter where she went."

"I know, it's not your fault." Toni doesn't seem to be bothered by what I did. 'Course she kinda shares my predicament of not being in control of herself. But I was in control. I may have been guided by lesser evolved instincts and emotions, but I still had a say, a choice, in what I did. How I did it is another story though. The Raven side of me acted on my behalf, on my urges. I chose to fight, but the power took control of the how. "It wasn't my place to treat you the way I did," I say, trying to put her at ease and retain what friendship we have developed.

"Isn't this all warm and fuzzy," says one of the prisoners.

I approach his cell, wrap my fingers around the bars. The word *scraggy* comes to mind. His long black hair is tangled in his unkept foot-long beard. The holes in his shirt don't do him any favors either. He's the polar opposite of his short-cropped blond-haired companion in camo. "What's your deal?" I ask Scraggy. "You get your kicks from kidnapping women?"

"I got a job to do, and I aim to see it done."

"He's been like this since we brought him in," says Huntly.

"All full of vinegar," Toni adds.

"What about him?" I nod at the military Broadsword.

"He's…pleading the fifth," says Toni.

Everyone thinks I'm a monster because of these two, and they probably do as well. So, why not use that to my advantage? "Okay chatty, fess up." I rip the barred door free of its hinges, sending its bolts clanging off the floor. Scraggy scurries back from me as far as his chains will permit. The door rings off the steel frame as I set it aside. He's afraid; I can smell it. He may have the strength and speed of the Broadsword, but he hasn't been trained like Toni was. "I want to know what you know. And you better talk fast, 'cause I'm getting hungry." Slowly, I run my tongue across my fang, letting it sink into Scraggy's mind that monsters *do* exist, and one is literally at his door.

"No, don't, stay back." Scraggy raises his hands defensively.

"Hold your tongue," says the military Broadsword, no longer pleading the fifth.

"I'll get to you in a second," I say to him sharply. "When I've finished my breakfast." I turn back to Scraggy, grab his chains, and haul him closer. He pulls back, but he's no match for me, and I drag him forward with a grin. I could use my mind trick on him, sure, but that would be too easy. I want to enjoy this, enjoy the diminishing buzz Ike gave me while it lasts.

"I'll tell you everything I know."

I release Scraggy's chains, and he falls to the floor, landing hard on his ass. "Talk," I say, folding my arms.

I hear Toni whisper to Huntly, "Now that's how you interrogate someone." Scraggy doesn't catch it.

"We were told to capture you alive and—"

"That's enough," says the military Broadsword.

"You shut up, she's not about to eat you."

"That's right," I say, squatting down to Scraggy's eye level. "I'm here with you, and it seems your door no longer works. So, I either feast on you for security purposes"—I glance at the torn-down door—"or soldier boy over there, depending on how well you cooperate. Then you can have his cell all to yourself."

"Now wait a minute," says the military Broadsword.

I hold up a finger to silence him, and he stops his protest. He reeks of fear as well, but not as much as Scraggy. I stand above him. "I'm growing impatient."

"Like I said, we're supposed to bring you to L.A., alive. He made us do it. We didn't have a choice. He did something to me, so I have to do what he says." I look at my wrist, pretending there's a watch wrapped around it and I'm pressed for time. Scraggy catches his words for a second, then continues rambling. "He said to take care of any who tried to stop us. I swear, that's all I know. Xanatos just wants us to bring you to L.A."

"Xanatos?" The mention of Dad's other self sends shivers up my spine. Dad—*Drago*—wanted no harm to come to me. Xanatos threatened me at every turn. I can almost hear *his* gravelly voice in my head like in my dreams, like when he threatened me outside of Lukas's cabin. "Why, what does he want with me?"

Scraggy drops his head. "I don't know, I swear."

"Not good enough," I say, stepping forward.

"He never told us, never told me; I swear on my mother."

"You do any better?" I say sharply, glaring at the other Broadsword as I grab Scraggy by the hair, craning his head back, exposing his neck.

He looks at Scraggy, then at me, and says, "I might have overheard more than him, but not much."

"Spill it."

"He wants your body. Something about the power of a half-breed. Other than that, I know the same. Take you to Los Angeles."

I shove Scraggy's head aside, and he scurries away as fast as he can.

Power of a half-breed. The words hit me like a punch to the gut. Xanatos wants me and my powers to be his. I'm half vamp, immortal, and can uniquely walk in the sun. But I'm also half witch. Combine those traits with the full force of the amulet and he'd be unstoppable, as if he wasn't already. But if that's the case, then aren't I the unstoppable one, even though I can't yet control myself? I may not have the amulet around my neck, but I have power like Dad…Xanatos…does. Not to mention I'm tapping into blood memories, channeling the untold power of the Raven. My grandmother may have called herself the Raven in the past, but I'm the Raven now. I'm the one with the power.

"Throw him in a new cell," I say, turning my back on Scraggy, walking through the bent steel door frame. I need to think. I need air. I need to go for a ride and clear my head.

"Toni," Huntly says, nodding, indicating she's to relocate Scraggy. Then he's by my side, following me out of the dungeon. "He's lying."

"Yeah," I say, more like a question than an agreement. Ever since he stood up for me against the convoy's ultimatum, I've gained even more respect for Huntly; he's earned it. So, I wait as patiently as possible for him to spit out what he means. He's always been straightforward, and I'm certain this time will be no different.

"Los Angeles is gone."

Chapter Sixty-Four

"Whoa, whoa, whoa, what?" I ask Huntly, stopping dead in my tracks.

"Los Angeles is gone."

"Yeah, I caught that. What do you mean, *gone*? How…I mean…how do you know?" How can an entire city be gone? Aside from the San Andreas dumping it into the ocean like movies have predicted, I can't believe it.

"The information I have is spotty at best. But from what we can discern through the gathered intel over the ham radio is that L.A. is gone, along with anything outside a nine-hundred-mile radius of Lincoln. No communication of any kind has come from outside that radius so far, and from the chatter I don't suspect any ever will."

A pit forms in my stomach. I don't want to hear what Huntly has to say. I've dreaded it since my birthday. I failed to stop the sun in its entirety.

"I didn't know how to tell you, or when, or if I even should until I received confirmation. And we did have a pressing matter at hand that needed our attention." He nods to the captives at our backs. "When I said the government wasn't interest in you anymore when we first met, I wasn't lying. As it stands, I am currently the highest-ranking survivor we've been able to get in contact with. It appears that anything outside nine-hundred-miles is burned. Cities, farmland, vegetation, everything is charred with not a single survivor coming out of what has been deemed the Wasteland. San Francisco, half of Vegas, Kansas City, Minneapolis—they're all gone. We have had word from Seattle, Portland, Salt Lake, Denver, and southern Canada that they are in the same situation. No power, limited operable equipment, nothing with a chip works, and zero communication or signs of life have been reported outside the zone. At first I thought it could just be a lack of ability to communicate. However, the number of ham radios, and other various radio equipment not bearing chips that have popped up is astounding. I see no reason why there would not be any in the Wasteland, only a lack of people to operate them."

Huntly lets this sink in, studying my face and posture. I don't know what he's seeing, but I'm certain he can read me as easily as I can read Lukas. One thing he said stands out more than the rest: *half of Vegas.*

A memory of me holding the line against the sun, and Dad, at that fountain in Vegas surges up in me, grows a pang in my gut, and I want to vomit. "Where in Vegas?" I ask Huntly, though I already know the answer before he says it. It's where I failed to expand my shield past Dad's onslaught of crimson energy.

"The Bellagio, I think, is the southernmost intact hotel."

The Bellagio—that's the name of the hotel with the fountain out front and where I drew the line against Dad with my shield before the sun's flare hit.

I thought I needed to go for a ride to clear my mind before. Now I just want to crawl into a hole and die. This is crushing. No one in the history of the planet has failed so hard. I could puke.

Why I would torture myself by asking Huntly, I don't know. Until now, I hoped the entire world was just like us, back in the Dark Ages with limited technology. But I had a gut feeling, an instinct that not all was right from what I saw my other self, the Raven, protecting.

Now there *is* no rest of the world.

I hammer the meaty part of my fist into the stone wall and lean my forehead against its cold surface, fighting to contain the tears that threaten to fall. How much more is a person supposed to endure? How much can one woman take? I can't do this anymore, live like this. Every turn I take there's another catastrophe waiting for me around the corner, and I've failed to stop every one.

"There you are," says Abby, turning her walk into a jog down the hallway as she spots me, her arms crammed with sealed gauze bottles of liquid. "I need you."

Here we go again—another catastrophe, another-world ending decision I have to make. "What now?" I bark. Abby slows her jog to stop a few paces from me. I was louder than I intended to be, but I can't help it, something needs to give.

"I've had people looking for you."

"Now you've found me."

"Scarlett, Mel is dying."

Oh come on. Gimme a break. Heat flushes my chest, overtaking my urge to vomit. I catch myself. Sweet little knobby-kneed Mel is on her deathbed and here I am pissed off that *I'm* getting bad news. "Where?"

"The main hall."

I take a breath, and Huntly puts a hand on my shoulder. "Nothing that I have told you will change anytime soon. Go to the girl. I can answer any questions you have once you are ready," says Huntly, giving me a nod, then heading to go back to the dungeon with Toni and the two Broadsword without another word.

I make for the main hall in silence. Abby takes the hint. I don't want to know what happened, because I'm already sure that whatever it is, it's my fault. Sure, Abby said Mel was going to die from her diabetes, but that would have been a month or three from now depending on the insulin and how Kara could refrigerate it. Part of me wants to think that in that time, I could use my gift, use the Raven side of me to…I don't know…pull the diabetes out of her.

I shake my head. The notion is asinine. *She's born with a sugar imbalance due to her liver or kidneys or something. A transplant maybe? No. Stop it Scarlett, don't do this to yourself. You can't play God. No matter how powerful you've become, no matter how much you learn to control the Raven side of yourself. Accept it. Breathe, and live in the moment. As shitty as it may be, live in it. Grow from it.*

I step into the hall. Abby points to where Mel is. Right in the center of all the injured who are either eyeing me or turning their gaze from me with a scowl. Dried blood, spent gun powder, sweat, fear, it all mixes for a pungent aroma. I want to sprint out the doors in a blur, but I'm here for Mel. I just hope she doesn't have the same look in her eyes as everyone else.

Lukas's broad shoulders obscure my view of Mel with his back to me. I catch myself lurching forward a step and restrain myself from running through the crowd to hold him, to see her. Thank God he's all right. That's the first positive thing I've had since I woke.

I guess the cease of the room's hum makes him turn. I want to drop my gaze, from the onlookers, but I hold my composure and step forward trying not to show any emotion on my face. His lips are nearly healed, and the swelling in his eyes has come down. He has the book in his hand that Mel was reading to him—such a gentleman he is, reading to her. He stands from his chair and sighs, shaking his head. The book in his hand is shut tight under his white-knuckled grip.

All that remains of the buzz from Ike's blood coursing through my veins vanishes.

I sidestep Lukas as fast as I can, but I know I'm too late even before Mel fully comes into sight.

She's covered in a white sheet up to her chest with her tiny arms folded over it and hands wrapped around her cracked glasses. The bandaging barely covers the top of her forehead, but it's stained with a large red blotch and wadded with gauze. Her sweet face is void of all emotion yet is calm and peaceful like she's going to wake the second I make too much noise. I swallow what little I can, and sit on the side of her bed, wrap my hand over hers. "When?"

"Twenty minutes, half hour ago," says Lukas resting his hand on my shoulder.

Insult to injury, has there ever been a better phrase? Had I not run away from the hall to take my anger out on the captured Broadsword I would have been at Mel's side too, comforting her, and reading to her in her final moments. Instead, I tried to escape the judgmental eyes of the castle and go in search of those who wouldn't blame me for the death of their loved ones. Here I am, too late again to help someone I care about.

"She didn't suffer," says Abby. "She's been unconscious since she got the injury. There wasn't any more I could do than bandage her up and hope."

"Thank you," I tell Abby. I know there isn't much she can do with such limited supplies, especially for a head trauma. It is somewhat comforting knowing Mel didn't suffer. I guess, in the end, going to sleep is a better way to die than the long painful way without her diabetic medicine. Still, a tear rolls down my cheek, lands on Mel's arm. "Thanks for the ride," I tell Mel, leaning closer to her face. "Be sure to give Spirit some good exercise for me."

I kiss her on the forehead just below her bandage, run the back of my fingers against her cheek, and pull away. Silently, I thank her for naming my pegasus and for showing me that not everything that's happened is horrible.

The canvas of faces around me has daggers for eyes. Yes, sweet little Mel is dead now because of me…just like those they loved who turned to wolves and I obliterated…just like those who fought by my side…just like the rest of the world. I drag Lukas's hand from my shoulder, not wanting to be touched or comforted, but wanting to feel Mel's death to mourn, to move on, more so to own the fact that she's dead due to me.

She didn't die from my hand, but she might as well have. Anger grows in me, wants me to hurt those directly responsible. I want to kill the two in the dungeon, but there'd be no point. That won't bring her back.

I hold my composure all the way to the doors, then a flood of everything that's happened since I first rolled into Lincoln hits me as one. As if on rewind, everything comes back, replayed like a living nightmare: Broadsword attacks, Mom, being hunted, Dad's history lesson, *Dad*, Ovando, Lukas nearly dying, Nikki's death. It's ironic that the only person she couldn't predict dying was herself. Matt, Markus, Spirit—they're all dead along with God knows how many others. Fearing my other self will decimate those I care about by accident. Owning my other self, naming it the Raven…Lexa's ramblings of not knowing how she can free me from the Raven's hold. Or if it's possible. I'm not certain I even want to now. I did, but so far, my inner demon is not as terrifying as I imagined it to be. But where'd that get me? A castle full of death. A world deemed the Wasteland? *Good job, Scar.* Finding out Xanatos wants to inhabit my body and push my soul to the side. Huntly says the world is a crispy piece of toast.

It all hits so hard that innocent little Mel is the tipping point, and something snaps inside me.

I sprint through the courtyard, forgoing Kara's pegasus, Swiftwind, and my dirt bike Ducati altogether. I'm through the tattered gate and down the cobblestone road as fast as I can move, trailing violet as I pass through the gates of the outer wall.

Pushing my body to its limits until my veins pump acid and the trees speed past me in a blurry haze, I finally collapse on a guardrail. Shaking, trying to draw in air and pull the heat from my face, I peek over the rail. My breath catches. My other self, the Raven, or my subconscious has carried me to a place I never wanted to return to—the lookout above the cabin where Mom was murdered.

Charred, half fallen down, and surrounded by yellow police tape, the remnants of the cabin stand like a cruel tombstone marking the spot of my worst failure, and the beginning of so many more that came to pass.

I collapse to my knees, sobbing, hating myself for existing, wishing for it all to end. Wishing, for just an instant, that I'd let Ike pull the trigger.

The Raven flares up in me, driving such a foolish thought away. It's a survival instinct, and I get it, welcome it.

Death doesn't end the chances of life getting worse: it eliminates the possibility of it ever getting better.

I have to suck it up.

I pluck a stone from the road, crush it in my palm. I have to do more than survive. I have to win.

Chapter Sixty-Five

A car driving by slowly, with my name being shouted out the passenger window by a member of the Broadsword, pulls me back to reality, jars me into rational thought. The car passes the turn up the gravel road leading to the lookout and continues rolling away from the charred cabin. Amid the burned timber, police tape, and tiny yellow triangle markers is a white outline of where Mom died. How disappointed she would be in me if she knew what I had thought, had wanted to do for even the briefest of moments. Give up? She raised me to be stronger than that.

What are mistakes for, Scarlett? Mom's lesson calls out to me from the beyond, a distant memory from my youth.

Mistakes are lessons. Some lessons are learned the hard way through repetitive failure due to stubbornness of not changing an approach to a problem. Others are picked up immediately. So what are you going to do, sweetie? You have to choose for yourself. No one else can do that for you.

That day I learned immediately, thanks to a broken leg, that riding my bicycle off a garage roof was a poor choice. Sure, once the bone was set, I healed quickly, but the pain etched Mom's words into my mind even through my sobs.

"I'm sorry," I whisper. *Sorry for failing you. Sorry for...everything. I'll make it up to you. I swear.*

A branch snaps so loud behind me it gives me a start.

A wolf stands a few yards away.

I make to back away and stumble over the guardrail. I'm done for sure, lying on my back, defenseless, but for some reason I have time; it's not on top of me yet. I roll back, fists up, flashing violet. The wolf hasn't moved. It's just squatting there with a branch as thick as my arm in its clawed hands. It gave away its position deliberately and isn't making to attack. A crimson mane glimmers in the sunlight, and it hits me—the wolf is Eric. He's tracked me down, even evaded my senses so I didn't pick up his scent or the sound of his approach until he was right on top of me.

He tosses the broken branch aside and lays a pair of jeans out in the gravel. A rumble grows in his throat. He shuts his eyes, and his fur begins to shed. Muscles shrink beneath thick hide that softens to become pink, irritated skin. Bones loudly reshape themselves as Eric grunts at the painful transformation. Aside from his cotton belt, he's naked as the day he was born, curled up in a ball and drenched in sweat.

I step over the guardrail letting the Raven fade away, relieved I'm no longer in peril, and thankful for what he did whether he did it knowingly or not. His surprise presence forced me into action, to react without thought, and all I wanted was to live, to survive. Fight or flight, they call it. I partially did both, but more importantly I didn't just lie there with my belly exposed waiting to be gutted. Proving to myself just how selfish my single thought of letting Ike pull the trigger was. There are those who need me, the world needs me, and now that I'm in control of the Raven—to a degree—I have a chance at rectifying my shortcomings even more so than I ever imagined before.

I make to help him up, but he throws a hand out, urging me to stop without words. Eric takes a few breaths, wipes the sweat from his brow, and pulls on the pants he brought with him. "Thanks for not going too far," he says, standing up, stretching. "I'm as game for a stroll through the forest as the next guy but having to change in order to track you down is…irritating."

Irritating? His transformation looked downright painful, at least it sounded that way. "Sorry," I say, dropping my head.

"It's all good." He steps over the guardrail, sits down, then stares out over the cabin. "You got a plan, kid? Or are you just out for a mornin' stroll?"

His entire back is one big scar, along with his arms and half his face. "Are you—"

"Oh, I'm fine." He waves me off. "You don't pack as big a punch as your grandmother, thankfully."

Oh God, I did that to him, gave him those scars when I snapped and let the Raven out.

It must be written on my face—the remorse—because after a glance at me, Eric says, "I've been through worse, and I'll heal." He rolls his shoulder, letting out a bone-on-bone scraping coming from the socket. "See now, your little friend Kara there, thinks you took off to clear your head. Lexa says you're running away. She's pretty intuitive, trust me. Over time I've come to understand that if a person isn't running *away* from something, they're running *toward* something. So, I figure they're both wrong, and you're running to something. Whether you know what that is or not, I'm not sure. But make no mistake, you are running. I'll give you a moment to decide which. Take your time—after all, we're immortal, you and me, and I'm patient…to a degree."

They say with age comes wisdom and *they* do say a lot. But that particular nugget rings true. Eric gets me thinking. I've spent my whole life running—on my bike mostly, constantly on the move, evading the Broadsword. Now, it's not entirely clear who is on whose side, and who exactly I should be running from—or as Eric put it, who I'm running to.

We sit there on the guardrail for a while. Eric is silent, unflinching, and lost in his own thoughts. Giving me a chance to ponder his question. It must be around lunch time from the looks of the sun before I finally come to a conclusion.

"I thought I was doing the right thing, waiting for Dad…rather Xanatos to sweep across the land in his dumb-assed idea to take over the world. Waiting to take him on and strip him of that amulet of his. Hopefully freeing Dad along with the Broadsword's souls if I'm lucky. But after what happened, I know what I must do. I've known for a while now, secretly. I'm no longer going to be the lamb waiting to be slaughtered behind walls of stone. That, for all I know, was Xanatos's doing and not Dad's."

"That's possible," Eric says, tilting his head and raising an eyebrow. "He was strategic."

"I'm going after him. I'm going to stop Xanatos myself."

Chapter Sixty-Six

"Go after the Last Atlantean, eh?" asks Eric, stretching his arms to his sides as he shifts his weight on the guardrail.

"Yeah, but if I stay at the castle he knows where I am, and I don't think it's wise to wait for another wave of his troops to come at us. Castle's in shambles, we've lost half the people in it, not to mention your pack. In truth, I don't think I have it in me to fend off another caravan of the Broadsword."

"But you think you're strong enough to go on the hunt and take on Xanatos by yourself?"

"I have to be, and if I can catch him off guard maybe I can defeat him. An army marching over a hill would alert him, but me on my own, I'd at least have a chance of sneaking up on him." I picture myself, a stealthy assassin, hooded, and slipping through a crowd of the Broadsword to come up behind Dad.

"Then what?"

"I rip that amulet away from him and smash it on the spot."

Eric chuckles.

"What?"

"I could swear I'm sitting here with Sorsha. I forgot just how impetuous she was. Bold. Willing to charge into battle, but not so headstrong as to do it blindly. You got a bit of your grandfather in you too. *World's greatest tactician*," Eric says, wiggling his fingers like quotes. "Good friend." He pauses for a moment, as if reminiscing about my bloodline. "Good plan, though. That's how we beat him the first time. Well, how Sorsha did."

He's opening up, and I see my chance to pull from him what Lexa withheld when she stormed out of the queen's chambers. "Dad, I mean Xanatos"—I correct myself—"said something about my ancestor putting a blade through his heart. That was Sorsha? My grandmother?"

"Yep. He was damn hard to kill. But she did it. 'Course that's how she turned into the Raven." He leans closer to me. "Got a shard of the amulet imbedded in her chest when she drove her sword through it and his heart. Watch out for that, if you ever get your chance to smash his amulet."

I nod, mulling over his tale, hoping history won't repeat itself entirely and I'm able to win without driving a blade through my father's heart. "That's what Lexa meant? About pulling it out of her. She meant the shard. You guys pulled the shard out of the Raven, making her Sorsha again. Right?"

"Pretty much. The Raven might have been her chosen battle name, but when that thing got in her it changed her, gave her power not unlike yours or Xanatos's. She was never the same once she was free of the amulet shard. She wasn't crazy and possessed anymore, and she still had most of her magic. Not all, but enough."

"Possessed?" I can't help it; it just blurts out. "I've had dreams of Xanatos. When he threatened me. When I did my thing at the castle, I called myself the Raven. I even sounded different."

"Yeah you did," Eric says like a laugh.

What the hell? There's nothing comical about being possessed. Dad has no control of himself, not all the time. But what I did to the caravan felt like it was still me. Not some other entity taking over me but a freeing of my primal desires. "Now I'm possessed? Like my grandmother was? By Xanatos through my blood? And I'm calling his possession the Raven? How am I—"

"Nooo," says Eric, cutting me off as if I'm being ridiculous. "You were confident. There's a difference. I've seen what the amulet can do to a person and not just Sorsha. You don't have that problem."

Him confirming what I had hoped to believe lifts a weight from me. To be scared of oneself, then to come to terms with my newfound gift, to name it, and become one with it gave me self-assurance. Eric didn't say it, but I took it as if he suggested I was possessed. I got a taste of how Dad must feel, and I don't like it.

"But I hate to break it to ya, kid. You have a completely different problem. One just as difficult as separating a sorcerer from a person."

"What's that?"

"Lexa and I have been trying to track Xanatos down for a real long time. Now without any kind of tech it won't be as easy as it was finding you. 'Course we thought you were with him due to the castle. He almost got it right, too, your dad. How do you explain Lexa and I knowing about the secret entrance behind the mirror leading to the stables or the concealed arch on the outer wall that let my pack in? Your dad must have had me tell him those stories a couple dozen times. Forgot to build the taverns though and got the grand hall wrong. That was a hundred percent Xanatos. Damn near a perfect replica of his mountaintop lair."

"That's why the main hall felt creepy. It was Xanatos'." I crane my neck, trying not to let the feeling of being in the hall set in. "But you're wrong about one thing. I do know where he is. He's in Los Angeles. At least he's supposed to be. So, I'll start there." I have to start there. Not only to go in search of Dad but I have to see it for myself. See if Huntly's right. See if my shield stopped in Vegas. "And I won't stop until I find him."

Eric grins. "Quoth the Raven." I know he's quoting a famous poem, but part of me thinks he's referring to my grandmother and not the poem or myself. He slaps his knee, and stands up. "Well, it's settled then. Now that you are clear as to who you're running to, let the adventure begin. But before it does, you'll need provisions."

Eric doesn't say another word as he strips off his pants and transforms into his massive furry form, bending the guardrail under his growing hands. It looks painful, but as soon as he's turned, he howls repeatedly as if he's speaking at length in his own language. I expect him to revert back to his human form, continue speaking with me, but he doesn't. Instead, he curls up in a ball at my feet. It's an odd thing, to have the creator of all wolves beside me like a faithful lapdog. One that's larger than me and shaped more like a man than a dog. I run my fingers through his fur, watching as his scars shrink and heal. I must have really done a number on him for him to still be healing. I think about trying to get more out of him, about what he did, what he knows, what his origins are, but with him in his wolf form he can't answer me so there's no point, and I think that's why he remains in it.

A few hours pass, letting me ponder Eric's words while I study the vast Montana skyline, and look deeper into myself. More so now than ever I'm convinced I'm on the right path going on the offensive. I'm annoyed that I didn't follow my gut and do it earlier, before the caravan arrived. I can't change history, but I damned well better learn from it. My plan to smash the amulet worked in the past, aside from Sorsha turning into the Raven. Separating her from it saved her from Xanatos's influence, so it stands to reason the same can work for Dad. It's nice to know where I got the name from, and how I got the power running through my veins other than it just being handed down to me by Dad. It's like knowing about my family tree. The fact that I get the heebie-jeebies only in the grand hall of the castle makes sense now. Dad did try to give me protection. He did try to help me, but Xanatos was in him altering his creation. I decide I'll have to put blinders on when I find Dad and focus on nothing else other than the amulet. The source of all that is wrong in my world.

Eric moves from my feet. Lifting his head with his ears standing on end, he rises to his hind legs, stretching, then picks up his pants and prods me down the gravel road toward the highway. I listen hard to see if I can pick up what he did, but my hearing is obviously not as developed as his. It's not until we round the last of the winding corners of the gravel road that I know what he heard, engines.

One car and three pickup trucks pull over on the road. One's towing a long cattle trailer, another has my Ducati strapped down in its box, and the other is loaded with suitcases, coolers, and gas cans. Wings thrash about in the cattle trailer—they brought Swiftwind with them, and from the length of the trailer I'm guessing another five horses. Eric's long-winded howl must have been a one-sided conversation with Lexa.

As Kara climbs out of the car, Eric changes into his human form and says, "If we're going on a journey, it's nice not to do it alone."

"We?" I ask him, doing my best to abstain from staring at his nakedness which doesn't seem to bother him as he slowly tugs on his pants.

"Yeah, we're going with you."

"Just like that?"

"Just like that." Eric's chatty, but to the point, and he jests like no other I've met. A little more time with him would be nice if he's willing to divulge more about Dad. It sounds as if Eric was somewhat of a mentor to him; telling him stories about the castle repeatedly makes me think Dad was a boy prodding Eric for answers just the same as Mel did to me. I'll have to probe him more, but not at the moment as he leaves my side and heads for Lexa's truck.

Ben tips his hat at me, followed by Lukas hanging out the passenger window of the truck loaded with my bike. Lexa is behind them, alone in the extended cab. Huntly's at the wheel of the pickup with the trailer and gives me a nod, as does Toni in the passenger seat.

Kara leans against her door, folding her arms. I drop my eyes, not so much ashamed of running away like I used to do, but ashamed I was willing to go off on my own without so much as a goodbye to her. The bond we have has been an emotional rollercoaster, filled with highs and lows which I have trouble dealing with.

Eric climbs in the passenger seat of Lexa's truck and is hit with a bundled-up shirt in the face.

"Going somewhere without me?" Kara says. "I've got half a mind to kick your ass."

"Kara I—"

"No, I don't wanna hear it." She points at me. "No excuses. No debate. We go somewhere, we do it together. You can't abandon us like that. Because like it or not, you're part of a family." Kara looks down the line of trucks. "A really messed up one, but still a family. Packed with those who are willing to die for each other if need be. Sure, she's here because of a command,"—she means Toni—"but the rest of us…we give a shit what happens to you. So don't you go pulling another stunt like that again or so help me I'll—"

I wrap my arms around her, cutting her off. "Thank you," I tell her softly.

She hugs me back. It's the best thing that has happened all day. She pulls away, stares me in the eye. "Now that that's settled, we better hit the road if we're going to make it to a decent hotel before dark."

I let her go, holding back a tear, and can't help but think how lucky I am to have her in my life. Even if it's just emotional support as I go after Dad, she fuels me from within and makes me think I can do anything. "I wouldn't want you to slum it," I say.

"Damn rights," she says rounding her car, strutting and flipping her hair.

I look over the line of trucks. "Gimme a second."

Kara rolls her eyes. "Make it quick." She sighs.

Part of me wants to blow Lukas a kiss—childish, I know—and jump in with Kara. But he's still injured, and the last thing I want to do is put another person in unnecessary danger. I approach his truck and before he can say a word, I kiss him, gently. Pulling back, I can see it on his face, he knows it's a goodbye kiss. We stare into each other's eyes until Ben clears his throat.

"You come back to us now," Lukas says.

I catch myself pursing my lips and harden up. "We will." I walk away, letting his fingers trace away from mine as Ben questions Lukas.

"We'll keep the home fires burnin' for when they return," Lukas tells Ben.

Ben grumbles, starts his truck, shouts out the window, "I'll fancy up the place for…you guys." He meant to say for Kara but caught himself. He pulls out of the procession, slows as he passes Kara and says something about them not being even, and she's going to get it good when she makes it back home.

The guys spin around and head back toward Lukas's ranch. I wave bye as they pass and continue on to Kara's Caddy. Home. The ranch, the homestead, the castle—they're Lukas's home for certain. He came for me; they all have. Kara's right. We have each other, and I realize how ungrateful I've been to these people who have done nothing less than have my back. They've forgiven me for my transgressions, and, like a family, they are still here, ready to follow me to the ends of the earth. A kind of peace falls over me, like when I was with Mom. Perhaps I could call the castle home, if I succeed and redeem myself for the past couple weeks. If that's even possible I have no idea. Scenarios run through my head of various outcomes that could have happened had I made different choices. Along with what could come to pass, and all the infinite possibilities that could be.

"Would you get your head out of the clouds and into the car already," says Kara, opening her car door. I reach for the rusty old handle of her Cadillac, and it shimmers into a polished black paint. A phoenix appears on the hood. "The fire chicken's waiting to soar."

She knows me so well, opening a window into my soul in such a short time. Part of me wonders if it's the bond between our two bloodlines, or something more. I smile and get in. New-car smell fills the cab.

"I get it, you wanna keep the eye candy locked up, but a little entertainment on the road could have been nice."

I try to tell her the reasoning behind my decision, sending the guys back, which she isn't protesting against, but she won't let me get a word out in her unique way of jabbering on.

"Guess I'll have to settle for some girl time. A night on the town. Ready, set…" Kara inks and peels out down the road, speeding toward a future that for once feels as if we are writing for ourselves.

"I don't think you'll find your room service," I say, moving past the fact that I sent the guys packing.

"Oh, I will," Kara says, sitting forward in her seat, ecstatic to locate her much sought after pampering. "You can bet on that."

I glance in the side mirror at the two trucks following us and Ben's heading in the opposite direction. I can't help but think I've finally gotten what I needed, not necessarily what I thought I wanted, but what I needed. My bestie by my side, even if she's just recently earned the title. A wealth of knowledge and power trailing us; though I'm not entirely clear on Eric and Lexa's intentions, I don't get the feeling they mean to cause me any ill will, and I so want to know what they do, about…well…everything. After all, they were turning people immortal, not killing them. Sure, they were turning them into wolves, but I'm starting to see what Toni meant about them.

Toni and Huntly I'd like to think of as friends, Toni for sure. We have a kind of bond through our own personal demons and metaphorical chains weighing us down, and it's brought us closer. She is after all the only Broadsword who chose to come rather than stay back and protect the castle. *Protect her and her castle with your lives.* Dads orders I had Markus repeat back to me. She, like the others, had the option from what I recall. Huntly has accepted me, protected me, and he strikes me as the straightforward no bullshit kind of man who can keep my head clear, something I may be in desperate need of when we finally catch up with Dad.

Ben's taillights leading toward the castle give me a feeling I had not expected, certainty. No matter what, they'll have the castle ready for us and, more importantly, they'll be waiting for us. Lukas will be waiting for me like it's my home too. After a lifetime on the road, moving from place to place, Mom and I never had a single place to call home, not really. But I had her, and now that I think about it, she was what made it all okay: I wasn't alone. After she died, I didn't think anything could fill the hole she left in my heart, but it seems to hurt a little less every day, though not by much. The motley band of supernatural beings surrounding me, along with the few humans I've let in, have opened my eyes.

I'm not alone.

Chapter Sixty-Seven

Kara figured it'd take a solid fifteen hours to reach Vegas, the outermost edge of the Wasteland, and so far, we've been making good time. We decide to keep clear of Great Falls, and any other major cities, and meet up with I-90 at Garrison. Aside from the odd vehicle, dead on the road, it's smooth sailing.

Slowly, the highway becomes cluttered with more and more abandoned cars, though. I have to put my strength to work, with aid from either Toni or the wolves, in order to clear a path for us. If we didn't have the horse trailer, we could use the ditches, but Huntly doesn't want to risk tipping it. These little stops have proven useful, not only to stretch our legs, but to plan our route. Huntly, being as organized as he is, takes the lead of our little caravan with Toni in charge of the map.

Kara and I drop to the back, despite grumblings from Toni. It's as if I'm the president and she wants me in the middle of our group, surrounded by steel, bullets, and an enhanced Secret Service. I get it; she's sworn to protect me and the castle. At least she chose me over the latter, unlike the rest of the Broadsword who remained on the ranch. Kara slows until the group follows suit, waiting for us, then pins it. The Caddy is no Trans Am, but it does have really comfortable seats.

Kara seems to have forgiven my transgression of taking off and tells me how Lexa, via wolf communication, told her of my plans to track down Dad. Lexa spread the word; the others loaded up. Kara, bless her heart, she's always thinking of me and my thoughts before I have them. She had the foresight to not leave the castle in shambles. After all, we worked hard to defend it and the people within. She mumbled the wall back up along with the water tower. Brian insisted he could rig something to the well she sprang up in order to keep water flowing year-round. I'm sure whatever he thought up is complete now that Lukas and Ben are back there with him. It's good to know the people will stand a chance at survival, even though I up and abandoned them. Huntly told them it was my plan to draw away any more aggressors, and Lexa ensured they were safe from those within who are now wolves. She tested the dungeon's cells and left explicit instructions as to how to keep the *pups*, as she put it, locked up prior to sunset.

We stick to the interstate and skirt a town named Deer Lodge. From the size of it there can't be more than a couple thousand people living there. In the distance children are playing football and people are working in a massive garden. It looks as if the community has come together to feed themselves, and they'll have to. If they got word about the world, they'll know that there is no assistance coming. Crops surrounding us are growing, but with no running equipment to harvest them, it all has to be done by hand unless some older tractors are still running. Though I'm sure there are more than a few handy farmers living in this state that can rig anything to work for them, like Brian.

We pass a few turn-offs, and when the sign for Fairmount Hot Springs comes up, I wish I had a radio to signal the caravan to take the exit, but I don't. So, I point at the sign and tell Kara I found her resort. She doesn't hesitate; her telepathy sounds out loud and clear telling the others to take the exit. I smile. I could really use a shower, or at least settle for a dip in the springs. Kara fragranced the car and herself and said I should have no problem doing myself after the things I've done. She doesn't even mention the tornado I manifested the first time I tried it.

It's not a far drive. There's a bunch of motorhomes in a campground, either abandoned or their owners are keeping their heads down, just before the resort.

The resort itself looks to be intact. I get hopes to give the waterslide a rip, but I doubt it'll work without power. There are a lot of vehicles in the parking lot. It makes sense—the world shut down on the Fourth of July, so this place would have probably been packed with those willing to pay the jacked-up holiday pricing. It's odd there isn't a soul in sight, though.

We circle the resort, getting a good look at it. There's no one here. The patches of grass are overgrown and full of weeds. Kara follows the caravan past the golf course that's in no better shape and into a housing development, all the while complaining that we should be pulling over and finding the penthouse. She gets her wish, partially. We slowly roll around the block and come to a stop just before an all-brick bungalow.

"What are they doing?" Kara asks, glancing back over her shoulder at the resort. "It's right there."

I don't get it myself; the entire place must have been evacuated as there is no sign of life, not even a stray pet. Then I look closer at the brick house, more so its yard. "That lawn is mowed."

Upon closer inspection, this brick house sticks out like a sore thumb. Mowed lawn, flowerpots void of weeds, polished golf cart in the driveway, and steps swept clean of debris. "If this is the only place with someone in it, why not head back to the resort?" asks Kara.

"Don't you think we should find out what happened here?"

"Does it matter? The place is ours, we're safe, this guy obviously is, and we'll be off tomorrow. I say leave him be."

She really wants that five-star experience—I don't blame her—a sense of normality even without electricity would be nice. I'm sure it'll bring some much-needed sanity to an uneasy mind, particularly mine.

Eric gets out of his truck and heads for the house, followed by Huntly with his hand on his pistol and Toni with her rifle in hand. Probably not the best way to knock on someone's door, looking like you're going to ransack the place, but we live in a different time now.

A voice calls out from the house, and Huntly responds. I can't make out what's being said through the closed window, so I open the door, get out.

"—only looking for information." I catch Huntly's conversation midsentence. "We are just passing through and are in search of a place to stay."

"Hotel's not locked. Go there," calls a man's voice from inside the house.

"We mean you no harm."

"Prove it. Leave."

Huntly shifts his weight, says something to Toni, and the door to the house flies open with a barrel pointing out of it. It's in Eric's hand so fast it's hard to believe he crossed the street, the yard, and climbed the steps faster than the man could get off a shot, but Eric did. "I don't want any of them getting hurt; they're growing on me," Eric says to the man.

They're far enough away and speaking softly enough that even I'm hard-pressed to hear them, but I do catch the man's response. "One of *them*, are ya?" Eric cocks his head to the side and the man continues. "Don't suppose I have a choice."

"You do. We can leave, but you're not getting this back," Eric says holding the shotgun, "until they're out of range."

"What about you? Not afraid of buckshot?"

"Nope."

"What do you want?"

"Information, like soldier boy says." Eric nods at Huntly behind him.

"In exchange for…?"

"What we know."

The man takes a second, weighing his options. "Deal."

"Deal," Eric says, shaking the man's hand, then rests the shotgun against the wall. "Eric."

"Dwayne."

Eric turns around, heads for his truck and Lexa. "Dwayne's offered to impart you with some knowledge," Eric says, patting Huntly on the shoulder as he passes him by.

Tension still exists, but it's minimal compared to when we first pulled up. Huntly holsters his pistol and Toni slings her rifle over her shoulder. Dwayne looks down to his shotgun but doesn't make a play for it. He scans the caravan and when his eyes rest on me, they stop scanning. *Yes, Dwayne, the one who caused all this is staring at you from across the street. So, what are you going to do now?* He ducks inside the house and comes out after a second, lobs a can at me. I hesitate, thinking it's one of those weird grenades the Broadsword had. A glimpse of two blue triangles on the spinning can tells me what it is, and I catch it before it hits the ground. His beer is chilled to perfection.

I hold it up for Kara to see, and she calls out the window, "Got one for me?"

Dwayne takes one look at her, then looks back at me, putting it together. *Yes, she is the other woman on the news, the one whose face they didn't quite capture.* Dwayne waves us over, inviting us in as he disappears inside.

I walk over to Huntly, cracking my beer.

"Think we can trust him?" Huntly asks.

I take a swig, cold Coors Light never tasted better. Kara could mumble it cold, but there is no comparison to a can that's been chilling for hours. The garage door opens, and the faint hum of a generator escapes. Dwayne rummages around, pulls out a chair at a table and sits down with a cooler in what has to be the most highly decorated man cave I've ever seen, including on the internet.

"We can trust him," I tell Huntly as I head for the man cave littered in metal signs painted with tidbits of knowledge, posters of beer girls, tools, a rather large TV for the size of the wall, a full standing fridge, a dart board, a pool table, golf clubs, and a two-seater leather couch. "Thank you," I say to Dwayne hoisting up my beer and plopping down on the couch. I highly doubt he'll pull a stunt, there are many of us and only one of him. Besides, he looks like he's the type of man who spends his retirement soaking in the hot springs, going golfing, and entertaining neighbors.

Kara walks into the garage and Dwayne hands her a beer from a cooler. "There you are, good-looking," he says to her in the way only an old man—probably in his late sixties or early seventies—can get away with. He's managed to keep most of his hair, neatly combed to one side, and avoided growing too large of a beer belly. "Help yourselves, gentlemen," he says to the others, pointing at the fridge as they file in. Toni sits at the table, and he produces another beer for her. "I'm a lucky guy to have such a vision at my table today." Toni blushes and takes the beer. Dwayne hands Lexa a beer and winks at her. She accepts, smiling back. Dwayne is a gentleman, like Lukas and Ben, serving us ladies and letting the men fend for themselves. Must be a Montana thing.

"We appreciate the hospitality," says Huntly, taking a beer from the fridge and passing it to Eric.

"Likewise," says Eric, leaning against the pool table.

"Two rules," Dwayne says to Eric, but loud enough he's making a statement to the rest of us. "No drinks on the table and no jump balls."

Eric stands up, away from the pool table, and nods.

"You look like a man of action," Dwayne says to Eric, then turns his attention to me and Kara. "But it's your tale I want to hear before I tell you mine. Consider it the price of admission." He holds his hands up, indicating his man cave.

"What do you want to know?" I ask.

"Are you...the One...that the guy on the flying horse is looking for?"

Chapter Sixty-Eight

I'm taken aback. Dwayne just referenced me as the One, and he knows about Dad on his pegasus. We came here, by happenstance, for information. If Dwayne knows something that can help us get to Dad, then I guess I have no choice but to let him know what I know, to a degree. "I am…the One," I say, though it feels wrong.

"You've got a powerful enemy hunting you down, and I don't mean our nations finest." Dwayne glances at Huntly, salutes him, and looks back at me. "But something tells me you already know that, and if that's true, then you also know what he did to my neighbours, the people from the hotel, and the National Guard who were here." He glances at Toni.

"I have an idea," I say at the mention of the National Guard. If I had to guess from the size of the hotel and few houses, this was Dad's first stop, and where he made his army of Broadsword that he sent to fetch me from the castle. "He took control of them."

"That's an understatement," Dwayne says, taking a long pull on his beer. "Never seen anything like it. Our boys didn't even get off a shot."

"What *did* he do, exactly?" asks Toni, leaning forward.

Dwayne studies her. "Same as he did to you. Turned them gray, took away their will."

"But how?" Toni's voice is getting laced with urgency, like she herself doesn't know what Dad did to her. She knows, of course she does, but the *how* is a different story. Come to think of it, Markus was evasive as to how it happened to him as well.

"With a shiny rock. Must have been two hundred beams, one for every man, woman, and child. He shot the crowd with it while they were listening to the boys."

"And you weren't affected?" Huntly interjects.

"I had a few too many on the course and was sleeping them off. Joe, my neighbor, woke me, said the boys had an update for us. I doubted it was anything more than I knew." Dwayne nods toward a mess of equipment on a table against the wall. Some of it's new, some old, and the older stuff looks like it was made around the time Huntly's ham radio was. "Not that I don't have respect for the boys," Dwayne says to Huntly as he rolls up his sleeve revealing a tattoo of an anchor. "Indiana. I was the radio man, and some habits die hard. So, I made a sandwich and figured I'd catch up with Joe before the boys started. Never thought a couple slices of bologna would make the difference between free will and unchallenged obedience." Dwayne slides another beer from his cooler to Toni even though she's barely sipped at her first one. "Sorry, kid."

"Wasn't your doing," says Toni. "But thank you."

"What happened to them?" asks Huntly.

"They packed up and went north looking for the One. No matter what I said, I couldn't stop Joe or the others."

"And the man on the pegasus?" I ask.

"Flew off to L.A."

"You sure about that?" Kara asks.

"Yes, dear. I am. I didn't catch all his speech, but I caught that. 'Bring the One to L.A.' Now it's your turn," Dwayne says, leaning back in his chair.

I don't have the heart to tell him that his neighbors, and Joe, are dead. He'll find out one day. Right now, we need Dwayne to keep his emotions in check if he has anything else to divulge. Huntly has been eyeing up Dwayne's equipment and I'm sure he has a lot of questions for him, as do I, especially when it comes to the Wasteland. "We haven't run into them," I tell Dwayne. "For the most part we've been keeping to backroads."

"Where you headed?"

"L.A. To stop the man on the pegasus."

"Good luck with that," says Dwayne. "You six against an army? You better have more tricks up your sleeve than you did at the rodeo."

"What do you mean…army?" asks Lexa as she polishes off her beer, makes for the pool table, and racks the balls.

Dwayne checks her out from head to toe, then does the same to Eric picking up a pool cue. "I've seen plenty of fighters in my day, they all have a certain gait to them. A walk, a way of moving that sets them apart from the untrained man, or woman. So let me assure you, my dear, it doesn't matter how well-trained you are. You are not prepared in the slightest to take this man on."

"I can handle myself," says Lexa, breaking the racked balls, sinking one.

"Even if you're as fast as he is," Dwayne says indicating Eric, "being overly cocky can end you. You showed up at my door unarmed. This old sailor could have taken you out before you set foot on the street, if I wanted to."

"Perhaps," says Lexa, sinking another ball. "Or perhaps I know things you do not." Lexa bends over, lines up her next shot, and winks at Eric. "Just a taste now, hon."

Eric grins and turns toward Dwayne. Their eyes lock, Eric's flash crimson, and he lets out a short loud growl.

Dwayne jerks so hard he nearly falls out of his chair.

It takes a minute, and a few swigs of beer for Dwayne to calm himself as he assesses us. Pondering what abilities we might actually have. "So, handsome," says Kara, pulling another cold one out of the fridge and handing it to Dwayne. "What are we up against?"

Dwayne stares at her with what I take as pity in his eyes. "A hundred thousand if you're lucky."

We freeze. No one moves, not even the centuries-old battle-tested wolves.

A hundred thousand Broadsword under Dad's command puts a pang in my stomach, and I have the urge to vomit. We can't take on numbers like that. The vision I had of me slipping through a few Broadsword as a stealthy assassin slips so far away it might as well have never existed.

"How do you know?" asks Eric, his brow furrowed.

"If you look at who has stopped communicating," Dwayne says, pulling a map of the US from a drawer and spreading it out on the table, "there are only two possibilities. Either everyone is dead, or they are like Joe. Sorry," he apologizes to Toni once again.

His map has a perfectly drawn circle on it in thick red ink with Lincoln at its center. Immediately I focus on Vegas, and sure enough, the line slices right through the center of it. The circle extends to the middle states—Colorado, Nebraska, the Dakotas—then drops off where the map ends at the Canadian border. *Wasteland* is spelled out in the southeastern half of the country. Dwayne's been picking up on the same chatter Huntly has.

"Had a contact in Salt Lake, a trusted one," says Dwayne, spinning a knob on one of his older-looking pieces of radio equipment. Static crackles, filling the mancave. "He stopped transmitting three days ago."

Huntly makes for Dwayne's gear, leans in close, inspecting it. "There could be any number of reasons for that to happen. There's no need to jump to conclusions."

"If these were working," says Dwayne, patting a monitor next to a keyboard, "we'd know more, but I suspect they'll never work again. But Old Betsie here"—he caresses the top of the old gear—"she's stubborn as hell. It's not just Salt Lake. Updates and regular chatter have all but ceased heading pretty much in a straight line for Vegas. Nothing's coming out of what's left. Reno and Grand Junction are still transmitting. So, it stands to reason that this fella has cut a swath to Vegas, making others into Joes." Dwayne glances at Toni yet holds his apology this time.

"Vegas it is then," says Lexa, resuming her game of pool as if the shock of the sheer overwhelming numbers of the Broadsword barely fazed her.

"Are you mad?" says Kara. "We can't go up against numbers like that."

"We'll drop in on 'em." Lexa waves off Kara and chalks her pool cue. "We need more winged horses," she says after missing her shot and glancing at me.

"You know how I feel about those things," says Eric.

"Really? After all this time I'd have thought you would have gotten over that."

"Oh you know I can handle it. If I have to. I'm just saying that if there's an alternate means of transportation we can find, we should take it."

Lexa makes a *bakaw* sound, imitating a chicken and Eric gives her the stink eye, missing his shot.

"You can't be serious," says Kara. "Why not let him come for us? We set up, get ready for him. Not go marching right into the heart of the wolves' den." She doesn't hesitate on her phrasing. She means it as an insult, and the wolves do not miss it, but instead of speaking up they both continue on with their game. I don't know how they're keeping a cool head—maybe it's experience, maybe it's the blood running through their veins, or maybe, because they are from Dad's time, they're bat-shit crazy. "Scar, this is suicide."

"Not for her," says Eric, not looking away from his game. He's right. I'm the one Xanatos and the Broadsword want alive. He ordered the caravan from here to capture me and slaughter anyone who got in their way.

Kara's pursing her lips. She steps forward, and I'm sure she's about to give Eric a tongue lashing until Huntly cuts her off before she can begin. "He's right. Scarlett might as well be bulletproof. Maybe we can use that to get close to him, or in the least, a diversion."

"We can't do this." Kara throws her hands in the air.

"We have to," says Toni. "Or else he'll turn what's left of the world into the Broadsword just as he did here."

"Not you too."

"They're right, Kara," I say. "Our goal hasn't changed, just the playing field has. Thanks to Dwayne"—I tip my beer at him—"we have an idea what we're up against. No matter how crappy it is." I admit it, but I don't really want to accept it. Xanatos has to be stopped, no matter the cost.

I'm finding the courage of the wolves rubbing off on me, nurturing the seed Kara planted by being at my side all this time. "I can make more pegasuses." *At least I think I can. Hope I can. The last time might have been a fluke.*

Kara rolls her eyes at the notion of flying. I know she despises it, but the strategy is sound. Even Huntly is nodding his approval.

"And I can show you how to control them without mumbling a carrot in front of them," I add.

"This isn't going to go well," Kara says, dropping back onto the couch, twirling her hair around her fingers with her deep in thought expression on her face.

"Vegas might have that fancy hotel you're after," I say, trying to lift her spirits. She shoots me a look I haven't seen since I was sixteen. Thankfully, it softens as she goes back to twirling her hair. She's not happy, but she's accepted fate has once again ripped choice from our grasp. We have no option but to go forward. Just like my lack of knowledge for stopping the sun, I have absolutely no idea how we're going to stop Xanatos other than tearing the amulet away from him. He can stop bullets in midair after all. Now he potentially has an army of a hundred thousand Broadsword.

What we need is a plan, a viable one. I need to think, and I need some air. One thing I know I can do to feel not so overwhelmed is get our rides ready.

"I'll see to the pegasuses," I tell them, downing my beer for a little liquid courage, and buying time to come up with a diplomatic approach of obtaining the knowledge I seek, just like Mom would.

"This I have to see," says Dwayne, leaving Huntly to look over his gear. "We'll check in with the others after the show." Dwayne grabs another beer and follows me out of the garage, eager to watch a magic show like a little kid instead of the retired Navy man who welcomed us into his home.

I raise my hands, calling upon the Raven, and we open the back of the trailer, letting my violet energy illuminate the horses within.

Chapter Sixty-Nine

As luck would have it, I don't disappoint Dwayne or the others in converting our horses into pegasuses. After all I've accomplished, as the Raven, I should be more confident in my magical abilities, but I still find it difficult to accept that I can create a wonderous creature of legend. They're mythical after all, or so I used to think. Dwayne's enthusiasm helps, though. I drink up the feeling of success as there has been so little of it lately, and I'm going to want to manifest that feeling again in the days to come when I catch up with Xanatos.

We decide we're going to head out in the morning and go as far as we can on back roads until we have no choice but to use the pegasuses. Kara insists on delaying the use of them and Eric agrees with her, but that's as far as we've gotten when it comes to an actual plan. Lexa says we need to relax if we're going to come up with anything, and I agree. A level head is what we need now. Since we're a long way from Vegas, Dwayne gives us a verbal tour to make ourselves at home in the hotel. He invites us to join him for dinner in a few hours. We accept, and all of us head for the hotel except for Huntly who chooses to learn what he can from Dwayne about the old radio gear.

In no time we've scavenged some chips from the eatery, avoiding the stench of rotting fruit left out in bowls and sandwiches turned green in the double-door coolers. We pick out our rooms on the top floor, allowing both a sense of security and a view of not only the land but the only road leading up to the resort in the chance we are discovered. Nothing moves on the highway in the distance, nor in the surrounding hills. Nothing to be concerned of at least. Toni sets herself up near the stairs and picks out a room for Huntly across from the other staircase.

Toni heads back to see what Dwayne and Huntly are up to after checking out our accommodations, and Kara disappears to find the bar.

Eric and Lexa don't even poke their heads in a room and instead opt for a dip in the hot spring-fed pool, deciding my next course of action for me.

I make my way down to ground level with one of those soft fluffy resort towels under my arm. I skirt the enclosed indoor pool and push open the door. I pull back, holding my breath. The sulfuric rotten-egg smell of the hot springs hits me like a punch to the face. A second whiff and I realize it's the bacteria growing in the pool. With no power to circulate the water with a fresh supply from the source, the pool has become stagnant, and the sulfur is doing its best not to let it turn green. I let the door close and head for the outdoor pool where I can hear Eric and Lexa.

I step outside, and the difference between the two pools is like night and day. This one still has that unique hot spring scent, but it's not laced with bacteria. The overflowing water in one corner leading to the bushes makes me think there's a valve that has to shut to divert the water from filling the pool; that's why it's not stagnant and reeking. Since no one has packed a swimsuit, underwear is the attire at the pool. Thankfully Eric has kept his on. He cannon-balls into the pool from a diving board. I've seen him naked more than I'd like to. Sure, he's easy on the eyes, but there's something about staring at another woman's naked husband that rubs me the wrong way.

I strip down to my bra and panties and slip in to let the heat engulf me. It's no shower, but it's still awesome, way warmer than the July summer air.

"Heads up," calls Eric from the pool's edge. I just have enough time to catch the bottle of wine trailing its deep-red contents through the air. Somewhere from Dwayne's to the pool, Eric and Lexa have procured a half dozen bottles, and it doesn't look like they intend on slowing down. Maybe it's a wolf thing, or an immortal thing, but I get the sense these two have lived a life of partying. It's not like they're going to get cirrhosis of the liver or anything, of course neither will I, but I do have my limits. I take a tiny sip, raise the bottle in thanks, place it on the pool's edge, and submerge myself. Kicking off the wall I glide through the warm water.

I rise above the surface closer to the deep end where Lexa is lounging half submerged against the pool's edge. So far, she seems harder to pull information out of than Eric, but she strikes me as the more serious one of the two. As if emphasizing my take on him, Eric jumps into a cartwheel and lands on his ribs in the pool. "He's a big kid, isn't he?" she says.

"Aren't all men?"

"Touché," Lexa says, raising her own bottle and taking a sip. "The world would fall apart if it weren't for us women to keep them in check. Can you imagine it? They probably wouldn't have even invented the wheel if they discovered wine first."

I laugh but can't help but kibitz back with her. "He's not the only one who enjoys a fine wine." I tap the bottom of her bottle. Maybe she's easier to talk to than I thought.

"When in Rome?"

"Right you are," I say, seeing my opportunity to get her to open up about her past. "Have you ever been?" Who doesn't like telling stories about where they've traveled to?

"It's okay."

I guess if you're as old as the hills, conversation about exotic destinations is a bit dull.

"I'm more of a tropical girl."

Maybe not.

"You've been around for thousands of years. Tell me, where's your favorite spot? I always thought Bora Bora would be the pinnacle of vacation destinations."

Lexa pauses before taking another gulp of wine and grins. "You nailed it. Pretty much anywhere in French Polynesia is the cherry on top. Good guess for someone so young, and I'm only just over one thousand years old, thank you. Don't look a day over thirty, though, do I?" Lexa raises her chin, smirking.

I'm confused. She said she was there in the beginning, when Atlantis fell, when Dad first took hold of the amulet. How can she only be a thousand years old?

"Careful now, you're so deep in thought I can almost see smoke coming out of your ears. That'll give you wrinkles."

"No chance in that," I tell her.

"Yeah, immortality has its advantages. Keeps everything tight," she says, looking back over her shoulder at Eric climbing up the side of the tubular waterslide.

He jumps a good fifteen feet, spinning in a tight circle as good as any Olympic diver I've ever seen, and leaves only the smallest of splashes on the surface of the water. "Impressive," I say.

"What about that cowboy you sent away? Is he…impressive?" I don't say anything, but I must be blushing as Lexa adds, "Then why did you send him back? A journey is far less pleasurable if you're alone."

Heat rushes to my cheeks, confirming the color I suspected in them. I look to Eric and then to her. They've been together forever, and what's more impressive is they're *still* together. Old age or disease won't separate them, so it's choice that keeps them bound to each other, like an unending family. Lukas is mortal, and he'll someday leave this world. 'Course I might not survive the week going up against a hundred thousand Broadsword.

I haven't known Lukas that long, but I know one thing's for sure—I want to be with him again. There's an unexplainable natural comfort with him. I want to hold him, kiss him, dance with him, make love to him. He provides a comfort I didn't know I needed. He's the shoulder to rest my head on as we dance, the heater that warms my bed. Most of all, he's the kind of man who I want to spend the rest of my life with. Intellectually I know our relationship is in its infancy, but my heart tells me to risk potential hurt and pain down the road to let it leap when I'm in his arms.

Sometimes intellect has to take the back seat in decision making, and at the moment I'm certain I've made the right decision. I will give myself to Lukas. Give him my time, my future, my heart, just as soon as I get back to his farm.

I do what I can to push down any further physical response. "Just keeping him safe for when we get back," I tell Lexa, waving my hand as if to brush off her question. Then I change the subject. "How can you only be a thousand—nice by the way—and have been around with Dad and Atlantis? Didn't the city sink like a million years ago or something?"

Lexa laughs so hard wine sprays from her nose. "Damn, I do look good." She takes a breath. "I don't know how long it's has been since Atlantis sunk. Or the continent."

"Continent?"

"Yeah, historians haven't gotten a thing right. Once it went under, we managed to settle the new world for a time. It was nice, peaceful, even between us." Lexa points between myself and her. "But then *he* returned. We tried to stop Xanatos. Somehow, we got trapped thanks to that damned amulet. Got free about a thousand years ago." Lexa shrugs. "So yeah, I'm a thousand years old." She smirks.

"Trapped in what? How'd you get free? How—"

Lexa holds up a finger, silencing me, then shrugs. "Someone cracks you on the head and drags you somewhere, do you know how you got to that somewhere? Well, you go into battle against a sorcerer and get a magical crack on the head; there you go." She tilts her bottle toward me. "Trapped, imprisoned, time jumped, whatever. No point in speculating about the how's, why's, and where's of what happened. It doesn't matter, some of us got lucky, and we're here now." She glances at Eric, raises her bottle, and then pours a generous helping of wine onto the concrete. "Most of us weren't so lucky."

This may be ancient history to her, but it's incredible to me and she's telling me it so nonchalantly like she's describing cooking. Maybe getting her to talk will be easier than I thought, unless she gets bored. She strikes me as the type that needs entertaining; that would explain one of the reasons why she's with Eric, who's anything but dull.

"That's why no one knows where we came from," I say more to myself than her.

"Smoke and mirrors, kiddo. Goblins, pegasuses, trolls, everything in fairy tales have been passed down through generations of campfire stories from the survivors of continental Atlantis. Trust me, they were far more gruesome than any silver screen can produce."

"So, we came from Atlantis too. Vamps I mean."

Lexa sighs. "Same as wolves and witches. Born and bred on the same continent, wiped off the face of the earth only to make a resurgence when we were freed *a thousand years ago.*"

Lexa's tiring of my questioning, emphasizing the timeframe like that. I have to ramp it up. Keep her engaged. "What's with Eric's white karate belt? I've never seen him without it."

"He may be a lot of things, but secretly, he's a true romantic. You get hitched, you get a ring, but when you're a wolf, rings tend to snap off your fingers when you change." Lexa points, beaming at Eric's shadow under the water. "That my dear, is where he keeps the token I gave him on the first night we met."

"Really?"

Eric pops up from the water's surface a few yards away. He could be of use to help me get a little more out of Lexa if I play my cards right. After all, he opened up to me quite a lot when we were overlooking the remnants of the cabin. "You ladies been talking about me?" he asks, wiping his face.

"You and no other, babe," says Lexa.

"We were just discussing a little history," I tell Eric.

"Dull. I told you all you need to know about the past." Eric swims to the side of the pool. "Now's more fun." He can switch from a monotone voice to an upbeat one so fast he could be the poster child for bipolar disorder. "We weren't like that, were we, darlin'?"

"Like what?" I ask before Lexa can answer Eric.

"Impetuous. Eager to know everything about everything. Where did we come from? Why did Atlantis fall? Why is the sky blue? Where'd the first two cows come from? Bah." Eric waves his words away, skipping his palm across the water's surface. "All you need to know is we're here now, and now is good. Appreciate it, enjoy it, it's all we really have."

"I seem to recall a man with ambitions to raid the king's coffers and nothing else."

"That's when we were mortal, living with an expiration date, and that was a long time ago. We have all we need right here." Eric pats his chest. "Air in our lungs, good wine…and great company." He winks at Lexa as he swims toward her. "Over time the gold lost its luster, but you"—Eric plants a brief kiss on Lexa's lips—"are as fetching as the first night I set eyes on you."

Lexa rolls her eyes.

"Mom always said we have to learn from the past if we're going to survive in the future. Don't you think we should come up with some sort of plan of attack? Something a little more than drop in on him from a pegasus?"

"I do. We attack." Eric reaches for Lexa's wine. She pulls it back enough for him to get close and returns his kiss before relinquishing the bottle. "Worked before, it'll work again. Hit him from enough sides so he can't concentrate on his manifestations. Just improvise, kid. It'll all work out."

Lexa squirms away from Eric like he pinched her below the water's surface. "Listen, Scarlett. We'll know more once we get closer to him and check out his lair. With Xanatos's memories he's probably built another castle like he did in Lincoln."

"Hopefully he'll get the main hall right this time," Eric chimes in.

"For the moment, learn to live here, in this one. Have some fun." Lexa quoting Eric—and Mom—is something I don't expect. *Live in the moment. Just breathe.* It's as if the older an immortal gets, the more they enjoy the simpler things in life.

"You two have had enough fun for the rest of us already." Kara sits down on the foot of the lounge chair closest to us, picking up one of the wine bottles Eric and Lexa had found. I'm guessing since she's empty-handed they cleaned out the bar.

"Not yet," says Eric, making Lexa squirm again.

"It's time we got back to Dwayne's for dinner," Kara says. "The food could do all of us some good." It's funny to see Kara being the responsible one and not wanting to throw back some wine like she's done nightly. Let alone take a shot at the werewolves for acting like they just turned twenty-one and the bars are open. She must feel the way I do, aside from the decision to use the pegasus. She, for all her flamboyance and spontaneity, needs more to go on than simply *attack*. "Then you two can grace us with the wisdom of how you think we can stop her dad."

"Sorsha's sword through the amulet and the heart shut Xanatos down…for a bit anyway. But that's a last resort," says Eric.

"We owe Sorsha that much." Lexa climbs out of the pool. "The short of it is, we separate him from the amulet and see what happens. Hopefully we won't have to kill him, and he becomes himself again."

That bit was directed at Eric, following her lead with a look of disappointment on his face. I assume it's from his playtime ending, but something tells me they've had this conversation many times before I came into their lives. "I know, I know," he says.

"Something might still linger inside him, but we can deal with that as long as it's just power and not Xanatos's influence," Lexa says as if she's speaking to herself, wrapping a towel around her waist and picking up another bottle of wine. Then she stares me in the eye. "We did before with your grandmother. If anything, take a word of her advice. Before she was possessed and all full of magic, she was the most feared *and revered* mercenary leader of all time. She said in the past—and I'm sure she would now if she were here—that we should wait for the opportune moment."

Waiting hasn't worked out so much in the past. I did that at the castle and it's in shambles. What worries me is not acting in time and letting Xanatos get the better of me. But that's the least of it. Dad's possessor, Xanatos, might be part of him forever. We're on the same page about stripping Dad of the amulet and hopefully setting him free. But the power is in my veins, and it stands to reason it's in his as well after such a long time of it saturating his cells. So, would Xanatos's influence remain as well? If he does, he'd most likely still want to take over the world, take over my body. I shudder at the thought. Then there's the Broadsword. Sorsha split the amulet in the past, according to Eric. Will smashing it to bits return the souls to all the Broadswords?

A person could go nuts trying to figure this all out, lost in an endless loop of what ifs. *Keep your sanity by living in the present, the immediate present.* I decide that's exactly what I'm going to do. Right here and now. I'm going to let the warmth of the hot springs be the only thing that penetrates my mind.

Lexa and Eric go inside the resort to get ready for dinner. I can have a minute soaking in the warm water with no one but Kara by my side. She shakes her head at the wolves' backs as they leave and spreads out on the lounge chair reassuring me with a "We'll figure it out, Scar, together." I tell her I know, but don't believe it one bit.

I take a deep breath and let myself sink to the bottom of the pool, hoping the minerals in the water will wash away everything and give me peace. It doesn't work as well as I want it to. I can't help rolling over the *what if's* in my head. I come up, brush my hair back and look to Kara. She's sound asleep with her mouth hanging slack and her arm dangling in the air off the lounger.

There's a silver dart with a red fluffy end stuck in her shoulder.

A sharp pain hits my neck, and my fingers find a cylinder sticking from it. Then all goes dark.

Chapter Seventy

I drift back to consciousness to a full-body ache. I had to have been drugged with something hard for my system to leave me like this. I roll to my side and want to crawl out of my skin as a cotton sheet glides over me; a weighty one. It clings to my tank, creating static electricity as I move. I fling the sheet, and the heavy quilt above it, to the side and sit up. My head swirls—vertigo—and I fall back to the bed, straining to focus through blurred vision to see where I am. I rub the crust from my eyes. I'm in a hotel room, a rather large one with its white curtains drawn shut. The glow of sunlight filling the room hurts my eyes, makes me squint.

I slip out of bed and crawl along the floor to the window, use the sill to pull myself up, and open the curtain enough to look out. I have to blink a few times to adjust to the light before I can stick my face in the opening. A stone-slab deck with a hot tub in its center presents itself with columns supporting the roofs of the two buildings to either side of it. Beyond the deck's glass rail is an almost blinding white building with hundreds of windows leading to a red sign: CAESARS PALACE.

I drop to the floor, letting the curtain fall shut, and lean against the wall. I'm in Vegas. Dad, or at least the Broadsword, drugged me, kidnapped me, brought me here. The hotel is fitting if Dad, rather Xanatos, thinks he's going to rule what's left of the world. Then it hits me. A glimmer of hope despite my current situation. Hope that Huntly and Dwayne were wrong. Hope that the Wasteland is only propaganda.

I look through the window again. Beyond the towering building of Caesars is the Eiffel Tower, and past that…nothing but black-charred buildings. Vegas is as shimmering as I've seen it in the movies, less the hordes of people. But beyond that, there's nothing resembling the once iconic landscape. A vast expanse of rubble, charred…everything. Ruined civilization stretches as far as I can see.

I drop back down. The Wasteland is real. I claw at my scalp with my nails as if self inflicted pain will somehow make the world better; erase my failure.

Part of me wants to think it's an illusion put on by Xanatos, but that's just a childish thought. Seeing it waters my already hazy vision. Sorrow turns to anger. I hate him. Hate him for everything he's done. Everything he's going to do. The Raven rises up from deep within my chest, warming me, strengthening me, giving me my sight back. I rise to my feet and any remnants of vertigo are gone.

I push through the room's door, certain I'm going to find Xanatos on the other side, or a large number of the Broadsword.

Instead, I'm met with an empty room with an inoperable fountain in the middle, its water green. I cross past it, swing open a door to an empty bedroom. The sheets are untouched and neatly folded in place. The main guestroom of the penthouse is also void of any remnant of someone's presence. Frustration builds, further charging up the Raven in me as I search the rest of the rooms and make it to the deck. I'm alone. Kara is nowhere to be found. She was drugged too but must have been left behind at the hot springs, I hope. I don't know why I thought they might have brought her with me. It's more wishful thinking that I won't have to face Xanatos alone. But he's not here either. No one is.

Aside from the odd pigeon cooing, Vegas is as silent as the dead.

I race back through the penthouse, down the stairs, and across the massive casino with statues of Greek guys as the only witnesses to my actions. I make the street, sprint past the Eiffel Tower.

The adjacent Bellagio's fountain where I held my ground against Dad isn't running—no surprise there. Just beyond it is what I need to touch. The scent of burned…everything…fills my lungs, and I drop to my knees on a palm tree-littered boulevard in the middle of the Strip, just before a perfect unwavering line of distinction between life and death.

I'm on the exact spot where my shield held its own against Dad and the flare. The exact spot where I failed to push myself further.

Dry brown grass beneath me is replaced by black soot sifting through my fingers. Fire raged through here in a torrent of destruction, melting the tires from cars, cracking stone, crumbling buildings, and stopped dead in its tracks where I held the line against Dad and the solar flare's ferocious approach. A few hundred yards away, the broken sign of Planet Hollywood hangs precariously from what's left of the hotel, and it draws a scoff of desperation out of me. Hollywood…has fallen. The sign, combined with the phrase in my mind, cements my reality. I'll never get to see another movie again. I knew that... know that…but for some reason the fallen hotel sign makes it worse.

I wish now, more than ever, I wasn't alone. That Kara, my rock, was here by my side. I'd even settle for Eric and Lexa to give me some words of encouragement as I stare out into the lifeless abyss. With all that's happened, and all that's been taken from me, I want to break down. But there's nothing left; either that or the Raven in me won't let me show weakness even to the void.

I wish with all I am that she and the others are still alive. But the Broadsword isn't known for taking prisoners. Me, yeah, they wanted me for Xanatos, and the ones who attacked the castle didn't hesitate to mow every person down to get to me. I squeeze my eyes shut, try to will Kara's life force to me from the distance between us, whether that be from miles or from the beyond. Nothing…I can't feel her, not even with aid from the Raven. It's not like I ever could before, but I have to do something to push down the thought that I may never see her again.

A scraping of feet on the ground turns my attention to what's not burned to a crisp, and I realize how much I underappreciated my solitude.

Men, women, and children are filing onto the Strip's sidewalk, all with grayed skin. A bridal party dressed in 1980s clothing surround a woman in a veil. Children stand beside parents in flip flops and brightly colored shirts. Showgirls stare at me with large poufy feathers on their heads, along with more than one Elvis look-alike and people dressed as superheroes. Vegas isn't deserted—it has been enslaved. Scattered among the growing crowd is the odd Broadsword—not that Vegas's population isn't all Broadsword, but these ones stand with a gait of well-trained assassins bearing bulges beneath their clothes where weapons are kept.

My other self ramps up the heat of the desert already baking me, then I feel her…. A surge of confidence, along with fist clenching, teeth gritting, rage rises up. The Raven wants out.

I want to let her out. Let myself be free once again. But the Raven retreats within me, acting on my instincts as one of the people on the Strip approaches me: a young girl with gray skin, long dark hair, a yellow summer dress, glasses hanging on the tip of her nose, and a bottle of water in her hand. Her age, and the glasses, remind me of sweet little knobby-kneed Mel.

The girl kneels then sets the water bottle in the dry grass beside me. "We're supposed to keep you safe," she says.

Xanatos's orders. Keep *my body* safe she means.

"Mom says we have to listen to him, that you're here to help him. But you know what I think?" She leans closer, whispers, "I think you're here to save us from him." The girl flashes me a grin, stands, and heads back toward the crowd staying put on the sidewalk. As her hand brushes through her flowing dress, I catch a glimpse of a tiny figurine clutched within her fingers. I don't know whose likeness it's supposed to mimic, but it has long dark hair and a cape. She needs a hero and thinks I'm it.

Little does she know the last girl her age who believed in me paid the ultimate price. I'm no hero. I'm not the cool Russian assassin. I'm a failure.

A horse's neigh breaks the silence of the crowd. A pegasus touches down in the middle of the Strip. Dad is sitting tall on its back, shirtless, with the amulet hanging from his neck, dangling down on his chest by a gold chain. Exposed to the sun, it shimmers brilliantly against his skin. If one touch of the amulet gave me visions, I can't imagine what Dad is seeing, or what it's doing to him.

"Come, child," he says in a gravelly voice. Xanatos is in command of Dad's mind, and with the amulet pressed against him as it is, I doubt I'll ever hear my father's real voice again. "No harm will befall you by my hand or theirs. You're far to precious to let that happen." Xanatos turns his pegasus, starts off down the Strip.

The nerve of him! The overwhelming confidence he imbues is infuriating. Rip the amulet from his neck, smash it on the pavement into bits—that's what I want to do. But for some reason I don't rise from my knees. I stay put, wallowing in my failures.

"It's nearly time, child. Let us take refuge in a grand palace."

I look at the water bottle the little girl gave me. *Think of Mel, of Kara, of Lukas, and all the people counting on me. Toni, Huntly, Lexa, Eric, and all those who reside in the castle.* They're all counting on me, and here I am on my knees.

Screw that.

Sorsha, revered and respected by the wolves, freed the world from the grip of Xanatos's plague once. I rise to my feet with her words, passed down to me by Lexa, repeating in my head. *Wait for the opportune moment.*

"Yes, Father," I tell Xanatos in the most dispirited voice I can muster as I scan the thousands of Broadswords lining the Vegas Strip.

Now isn't the moment to strike, surrounded by an army of thousands under Xanatos's command. I'll have to be patient, bide my time. He doesn't acknowledge me and keeps to his intended destination. I pick up the water bottle, shoot a wink at the little girl, and follow Xanatos.

I may be alone physically, without Kara, but I have the next best thing, the magic of the world's first and most powerful sorceress coursing through my veins.

Chapter Seventy-One

I follow Xanatos in silence to the Venetian. The water filled canals surrounding the hotel have not turned to that putrid skunky smell of stagnant bacteria. I'm certain it is due to Xanatos's magic.

Making our way through the grand oval-shaped lobby of the Venetian, Xanatos on his pegasus, me on foot, and a horde of the Broadsword following, I understand more than ever the phrase *wait for the opportune moment.*

If I lunge at Xanatos, I'll be overrun by sheer numbers before I can bring up the Raven.

"This city shall become grander than Atlantis ever was," he says more to himself than to me or the others as he holds his hand out, his palm facing the wall. Concrete, wood, drywall, mortar, and paint crack and crumble as the lobby forms into a wide ramp leading up to the roof. "No pyramid of gold though, man's currency is obsolete. Homes of crystal can still come in handy for their vibrational properties." He chuckles. "And they'll be a good way to house the slaves." His simple gesture, without even mumbling, makes me thank Sorsha silently for telling me, from the beyond, to wait. I need to build up some nerve if I'm going to do what needs to be done. "But which slaves?" He looks over his shoulder at the Broadsword, and me. "Won't need enhanced immortals to conquer a world overpopulated with man anymore." I follow Xanatos to the roof. He has only given us access to the top of the main building, not the entire hotel towering above us. He dismounts, walks to the roof's edge, and looks out over the horizon. "Or witches for rejuvenating the scorch, I can do that better than any of them could dare dream to. Could keep the comeliest ones for pleasure though." I want to give him a shove, let him plummet to the street below. But I know better than that. He could probably save himself from a fall before he drops six feet. "Take every soul this time."

I hesitate at his last rant to himself but force myself to make my way to his side and look between the white triangles mounted on the ledge to the Strip below, hoping he'll stop his insane planning.

It works, and Xanatos keeps his thoughts to himself as he drums his fingers on his amulet. It makes sense why we're here. The triangles remind me of the teeth of the castle. The main entrance over the canal with its tiny Italian stick-propelled boats looks like a moat from the movies with the main drawbridge lowered over it. He's a man out of time. Why else would he have chosen this location? Why else would he have made the castle in Lincoln?

"So, you got me here. Now what?" I ask.

"Patience, it is almost time," Xanatos says gazing to the east and then straight up. "It will only be another five or six turns of the glass."

"What?" I don't know what he means, but five or six of anything other than days is not long enough. I need more time, need to get him alone, need a chance to draw on everything I have in me to fully let the Raven side out. I can't just flip a switch and let my emotions go nuts.

He looks at me, makes me feel as if I'm a small child who doesn't know a thing about the world. "Hours until the moon is fully risen, child. Then I shall shed this mortal husk and take on a far more robust one." He eyes me from head to toe. "Shame, but perhaps with time a male one will present itself."

"What, I'm not good enough to have my body snatched?"

"Watch your tone, child."

"Stop calling me that." He's getting under my skin, and I'm letting him. I can't help it. He wants to do God knows what with me…the real me…my soul. "My name is Scarlett."

"Not for long." He smirks.

I slap it from his face as fast as it appears, and immediately I know I screwed up from the rage in his eyes. "I'm your daughter," I say, trying to coax Dad to the forefront.

"You," he says wrapping his hand around my throat, "are the descendant of the wench who thwarted my plans, took my kingdom from me."

I cling to his wrist, stretch my legs out to find the roof's surface, but he's holding me too high. I try to speak, to chastise him, but his one-handed grip is crushing.

"If you didn't have the closest ties to Atlantis and my creature mixed in your veins, I'd have made you into one of my soulless by now." Xanatos tosses me a dozen paces across the roof. I land, skinning my palms, burring tiny bits of stinging gravel into my flesh. "Stop acting like an ungrateful whelp. I'm granting you more power than you could ever imagine. You won't be able to have any say in how it's used, but I'll let you watch for eternity."

The roof crunching beneath his boots tells me he's getting closer. If ever there was a time for some help, now is it.

Mentally, I call on the Raven, try to use my frustration, my anger, and the pain in my palms to aid me in using my power. Heat flushes me. I'm doing it. Faster than I have in the past. I'm letting myself go.

"The first thing we shall do together is set up the castle your father left you in the hills. The vermin living within will have to be eradicated first."

I stare back at him, pushing up from the roof. My face must be an open book telling him what I think about that idea, because he smiles, maliciously. I let that smile fuel me.

"Give it a good cleansing." He holds his finger up in the air like he's just had an epiphany. "I know. We can have them turn on each other. Tear each other apart with their bare hands until only one stands. Then he, or she, can be placed at the head of my army skewered on a pike. Unable to die, unable to live with thought. Yes, I do believe it's time I reanimated a corpse."

"No!" I charge toward him. Violet energy bursts from within me. The crisp white roof is bathed in my power's aura as I reach out for Xanatos's throat.

His hands circle each other, one on top of the other; one shoots skyward, the other points at me.

Lightning channels through him from a cloudless sky.

I'm only halfway to him, and I skid to a halt as the lightning surrounds me in a writhing crimson electric cage. The power swirling around me makes my hair try to defy gravity and curls the tips up. "Predictable," Xanatos says. "Funny how some of the oldest tricks are the best."

"How's this for a trick?" I throw out a tendril at the bars. It sizzles, disintegrating on contact.

Xanatos laughs.

I can't let him do this. I dig deep, pull all kinds of emotion up from Mom's death to making love with Lukas. I form a violet suit of armor around me. Thicken it, strengthen it.

Xanatos stops laughing, cocks his head. "You have some skill, little one. But you're out of your league."

It'll only take a second, I tell myself. *A second of pain and I'll be free of this cage to do what I've set out to do.* If I can't survive grabbing hold of a bolt of lightning, as powered up as I am, then I'll die trying. Now, I have to be the hero, no matter the cost.

I take in a deep breath, muster up as much courage as I can. It'll only take a second. "I told you, my name is Scarlett."

I grab hold of the crackling bars shifting around the orb.

~ * ~

I open my eyes. The cage is gone—and so is the daylight, replaced by a star-filled sky with a rising moon that illuminates the city that never sleeps. I knocked myself out cold. Must've cooked my retinas too because the moon looks to be taking on a red hue.

I make a fist and my knuckles crack, split open, letting warm lines of blood trace along the back of my hand to drip free. Wincing at my palms touching stone, the cool helps to soften the pain, but only a little. I'm still on the roof of the hotel, and it looks as it should. I look up at the moon. It's not my vision that's shot, the moon is slightly red.

A blood moon. One needed for Xanatos's body swap no doubt.

"Woke before the ceremony. Didn't want to miss it, did you?" the gravelly voice of Xanatos says from my side. I swear, through his words, I can hear him grinning maliciously. "I hope those wounds heal fast. I'd hate for my first experience in my new form to be that of anguish."

His cockiness is exasperating, assuming he's going to win and that I'm not going to put up a fight. I make to stand and shackles tug at my burns, making me shudder. I guess he thinks I might have a little fight left in me.

"Relax, child, we have some time for your vampire blood to work its ability on those wounds, and if not, I can work up something that'll speed the process."

But he won't speed up the process for me now. He strikes me as the type who gets his kicks from the suffering of others, sitting there, lounging on a throne of gold with a handful of the Broadsword by his side just waiting for a command.

"Go to hell," I tell him. I'm still charged up. The Raven is writhing just below the surface. The burns coupled with Xanatos's presence see to that.

He just grins and motions to one of the Broadsword beside him, a slim woman in her twenties, who pours some wine into a gold cup resting on the arm of Xanatos's throne. *Keep it up. Get wasted drunk, and I'll have my chance to tear that amulet from your neck.*

I screwed up, attacking him like I did without any plan at all. Stupid. I have to play the part and be patient—not one of my strongest qualities. Going toe to toe with him isn't an option, especially chained up. I need to get free. That shouldn't be a problem. But I have to keep my powers hidden until he is close enough yet make him think I'm incapable of being even the tiniest threat. Though it's not like he thinks of me as one anyway. Now I'm pissed I told him to go to hell; it's hard to look weak after lashing out at him—or is it?

I raise my hands toward him like I'm trying to hit him with a tendril, pique his interest, but only enough to get him to raise one eyebrow. "Come on," I say trying to look frustrated as I vibrate my hand. I grunt in frustration, drop my arms to my sides, and jerk as the shackles bite into my charred flesh.

"What did you do to my powers?" I ask him in the most defeated voice I can come up with as I slump to the stone roof.

Xanatos frowns. "Hmm, must be the proximity to…no, that can't be it." He's talking to himself again, gazing up to the moon. "Perhaps the injuries…no…that's not it either. Ah, I got it, she's lying."

Crap, there goes that idea.

"I wasn't born yesterday, child." He toasts himself.

Time to come up with a plan B. Feigning a lack of power didn't work, so now what? Even if I was free, it's not like I can take him by myself. I need help, big powerful help loaded with magic, and I see it just beyond the dimly lit hotels of Vegas—a phoenix rising above the desert.

Kara's alive.

Chapter Seventy-Two

Kara's alive.

The Broadsword left her alone by the pool or the others came to her rescue—either way, she's coming to mine now. But why expose herself from such a distance? The phoenix stands out like a winged sun surging toward us against the night sky, and it's gotta be at least a mile away.

Distraction—she wants Xanatos's attention. That's gotta be it.

Hoping I'm right, I play along and take a deep breath of relief as I stare at Kara's fire chicken. Xanatos catches me, as I hoped he would, and turns his gaze.

"Ah, the other child has come. Chalk up one more to kneel before me," he says, standing from his throne and heading to the roof's edge.

Frantically, while his back is to me, I search with my eyes only, scanning the surrounding rooftops only to find them void of all life. Then I hear it—the faint beating of wings coming from high above.

I glance up just as Eric, in wolf form, plummets from the sky head first and slams into Xanatos, driving him into the roof with claws embedded in his back.

My opportune moment has arrived.

"Son of a bitch!" Xanatos screams. Crimson tendrils hurl Eric aside.

Xanatos may have been able to stop bullets, but the blood pouring from his back and shoulder prove he had to know they were coming.

Eric skids across the roof as my violet other self illuminates it and snaps the shackles from my wrists, freeing me. "Together," I say to Eric. He gives me a kind of wolf-nod and charges forward.

"No you don't!" Xanatos lashes out at Eric with a crimson beam of energy shot from his amulet. The beam is so fast I barely see its advance; it's as if it was always there.

Eric, thankfully, is far faster than me and not only sees the beam but sidesteps it and slashes with his claws. They stop dead in their path, just inches from the amulet, held firm in a crimson fog.

My power rages. Eric was so close to our goal, and now he's frozen stiff.

I leap, launching violet tendrils down in search of my prize, seizing the moment.

Xanatos bats my tendrils aside with his, and I'm immobilized by the crimson fog beside Eric. So much for my moment. It's more than frustrating, it's frightening how Xanatos can stop us with no more than a thought. No wonder Sorsha is spoken of as a legend. She was mortal and she stopped Xanatos. I can't fail—she didn't—not when my goal is a few yards from my face.

I grit my teeth, push against the crimson fog with my strength and my power.

It doesn't budge. What I need is a distraction, like Eric said. Attack from all sides and maybe this blasted fog holding me in place will dissipate enough for me to break free. Dad lost control before. I recall when I broke his nose on Lukas's deck, and I was inadvertently freed of his fog, but I can't even budge a muscle to strike him and get to the amulet. My power surges yet remains as trapped as my body.

Xanatos rolls his shoulder. Crimson flashes over his wounds, sealing them. *Crap.* Like this wasn't hard enough already.

"That was a mistake, Eric," Xanatos says. "I should have known you of all people would have survived into my new world. You've been a thorn in my side for far too long. But I assure you, you will not live long enough to bear witness to its progression."

Eric snaps his fangs forward, growling. Xanatos jerks back. They are too far apart to have made contact, but Eric gets his point across.

It's up to Kara now, wherever she is, to come to my aid once again. I can see it in Xanatos's eyes; he's thinking the same thing. He swats Eric on the nose and looks out to the ever-closing phoenix.

"She'll be easy enough to contend with, but tell me, did your one-armed harlot come here with you? Or did I finally get the best of her?"

Eric growls, low and deep, though I can't tell if he's putting on a show or if he's pissed that Xanatos, or possibly the Broadsword, killed Lexa back at the hot springs. It stands to reason she would have survived if Eric and Kara did, and I can't see her going down easy.

"Get ready." Kara's telepathy rings loud and clear.

All I can do is blink. How am I supposed to get ready? And for what? Her phoenix surges in size, blinding me, forcing my eyes shut.

In a heartbeat the phoenix vanishes.

Blinking the spots from my vision is no help; I'm blinded till they go away on their own, but I'm not deaf, and I catch the thud of something heavy hitting the roof, followed by another, and then a scream, and Xanatos ordering the Broadsword to his aid.

"Do your Raven thing," says Kara in my head.

Damn it, I'm trying Kara. But I can't get…wait. The fog. It's less dense. I can move a little.

I dig deep, calling on all I have.

A surge of energy flashes from me, dispersing the fog holding Eric and me. I can make out Lexa on the roof, in her wolf form, dispatching the remaining Broadswords using her sword and her teeth in a whirlwind of steel and fur.

Toni and Huntly are grappling, trading blows with each other, and after two hits Huntly is knocked out cold.

They all came together, as a unit, with the phoenix and Eric as distractions. They probably didn't figure on having Toni turn on them. I knew it was a possibility, but one I hoped wouldn't come to pass.

Toni charges Lexa, and I catch sight of Kara behind the pair about to square off, she's mumbling.

Xanatos is on his back, and the amulet is lifting from his chest, levitating by some unseen force. Kara's moving it, I bet.

Eric lunges at it and bounces off a translucent rainbow barrier surrounding Xanatos. "Enough!" Xanatos shouts. The barrier expands, churning up the roof's concrete and rebar, flinging every soul on their backs, except for me.

I take the hit, arms crossed before myself, violet energy deflecting Xanatos's blow.

God, if he would just let me get near him, drop his guard if only for a second. But there's no way he'll ever let up. No way he'll ever stop after centuries of unprecedented patience and effort.

Wait. Maybe he can pause—not for long, but for a few seconds.

"Stop attacking us!" I scream, utilizing an ability wholly unique to myself, one Xanatos would not know about, my Jedi mind trick. "Drop your defenses!"

The barrier doesn't drop, but it weakens. Xanatos's face is scrunched, wrought with struggle fighting my command. He's strong, mentally.

I let the Raven out in all her glory, revel in the moment and nothing else, and feel my power slice through Xanatos's barrier.

"Look up," I growl using my power, creating my opportune moment.

Xanatos cranes his head skyward—exposing Dad's strong jaw.

A battle cry, one I can't believe is mine, booms from my chest.

I sprint forward with more speed than I could have ever imagined. My fist flies, catches Xanatos square on the chin, sending him to his back, knocking him unconscious.

I rip the amulet free from Xanatos's chest, snapping the chain holding it around his neck.

I did it. I got it. I won.

But Xanatos won't be out cold for long.

My first encounter with Dad on Lukas's porch comes to mind. Dad lost the amulet, only for a short time, but he still had his power. I have to get rid of the amulet, destroy it, or at the very least put some distance between it and Xanatos.

A hint of pain registers beneath my fingers. The stench of burning meat fills my lungs, turns up my nose. Smoke wafts from my palm—my hand is the source of the burning meat.

Xanatos's warning about casting a spell on the amulet ensuring only he could possess it springs to mind.

The power of the amulet in my hand is terrifying, freezing me stiff. I doubt I'm even drawing a breath as I watch its crimson power overtake the violet energy encasing me, trying to protect me.

I force myself to gasp in air, and rancid burning flesh chokes me, closes my throat. The full force of the amulet surges up my forearm, crisping it, and searing already charred flesh. "What do I do with it?" I call out.

"Destroy it," answers Kara, focusing my mind.

I have no idea how to destroy it. They broke it in pieces in the past, but it's whole again, so smashing it won't work. After all, it contains the power of Atlantis. I need to magic its destruction. But how? My arm's killing me; I can barely think as the burns creep past my elbow. It's like I'm holding the sun.

The sun.

Through the anguish and the tears flowing down my cheeks, a single memory comes back. One from when I first touched the amulet—that of the sun's writhing surface.

Then another memory creeps forward, one that isn't mine. The amulet is showing me it, as if it's responding to me. Is this how it worked for Xanatos? A kind of telepathic link to it?

The amulet shows me Xanatos standing on a mountaintop holding two gems. One is sapping the color and magic from a blood moon, the same as the one hanging in the night sky above my head. The other gem is drinking in the sun's first rays cresting the horizon. He slams the gems together; wisps of violet smoke rise from scrolls, and the amulet I hold in my hand forges into existence.

The amulet was born of the sun, the moon, and a spell from ancient scrolls.

I don't have the scrolls, nor would I be able to read them if I did, of that I'm sure. I know I won't survive holding on to the amulet much longer.

So, I gamble, bet on the sun and its awesome destructive power.

Wrapping both hands around the amulet I look to the stars, scream, and launch skyward. My vision is blurred—not from tears, but from a haze of violet. Higher and higher I climb. Xanatos, awake now, is coming too and his shout of "No!" drives me faster. I'm on the right path.

It's getting harder to breathe; the atmosphere's cooling, thinning. My power fills my lungs, giving me air, warming me against the void I'm on the cusp of entering.

I'm twitching uncontrollably from my power, fighting the elements, and the burns covering me from what feels like my chin to my waist. My throat is hoarse from screaming, little sound reaches my ears.

The curvature of the earth presents itself, and a barrier of violet forms before me, shielding me from the sun's unfiltered force about to hit me just beyond the horizon. Even though the planet is draped in darkness I can still make out the stark contrast between the scorched land and the oasis of life with Lincoln at its epicenter. The sun, and Xanatos, really did devastate the globe.

Trying not to look at the damage done to my hand, I hold the amulet up, ready to hurl it at the sun the moment it's in sight.

An incantation runs through my mind. Words I can't pronounce, nor understand, come forth as if I'm willing them to, as if the amulet knows what I wish of it, as if it can tap into every exact memory of its creation, or at the very least, Xanatos's.

Violet smoke flows from my mouth, carried by the words.

Bathed in the blood moon's light, the cresting sun washes over the amulet, which shimmers.

My violet aura seethes around the amulet, dives in and out of its surface, and splits it in two, releasing a shower of millions of tiny white lights.

The two pieces of the amulet reshape into the gems I somehow recognized. The final word of the spell leaves my lips, and my power starts to draw out of me, dividing itself to sink beneath the surface of each gem.

My strength is fading, but I have to finish this no matter the cost.

With the waning power I have left, I hurl the gems in opposite directions—one toward the sun, and one toward the moon and its blood-red hue. My power leaves me, trailing the gems, and shoves me back, leaving me freezing in the high atmosphere and lacking oxygen.

I can't breathe.

I plummet back toward earth, gasping for air, surrounded by brilliant white lights streaking down with me.

Chapter Seventy-Three

Freefall. I never truly understood the meaning of that word until now, as I watch the curvature of the earth sap away the sun's light. The wind rushing by me is so loud it's deafening and freezing what skin I have left that isn't charred. *Agony, torture, searing, blistered, roasted, cooked*—words my brain tells me of my condition. Worse yet, I'm alone again, and possibly like no other soul on earth has ever been. I have no power, no other self to aid me, no Raven to have my back. Somehow the amulet's destruction pulled the magic from my veins, returning it to wherever it originated from. Not even Kara's telepathy reaches me as I plummet toward the earth.

The millions of tiny white lights the amulet set loose start to scatter, spreading over the globe on their individual destinations, and I realize what they are—souls.

I did it.

I did everything I set out to do. Dad is free. He must be. Xanatos was part of the amulet, and it is restored to its original harmless form, not to mention cast out of anyone's reach. The Broadsword, every one of them is getting their soul back.

Despite the pain, I'm relieved that I can rest now. I fulfilled my chosen destiny. All I can do is fall, and pray I reach the ground fast for a quick death.

The wind picks up against my back, if that's even possible, and I'm grateful my back isn't burned to add to the anguish of my chest as my clothes ripple over scorched flesh. Faster and faster the wind hits me, and I swear I'm actually slowing down despite it. Then I hear it—wing beats, and a voice in my head.

"We got you, Scar."

Huh, Scar, that's one name I think I've earned tonight.

I start to laugh and cry, like I'm an emotional wreck in need of serious therapy. Strong hands cradle me and pull me up against a bare muscular chest. Eric holds me tight, yet gently absorbs the jarring motion of Swiftwind. Lexa's beside us on one of the other pegasus and held tight in her arms is an extremely pale Kara, half her torso soaked in blood.

"Kara?" I croak out, reaching for her.

"You did it, Scar. You saved us all."

"She insisted on coming to find you," says Eric. "Said I could bring you back on my own, but she wouldn't listen."

"What—"

"She's pretty banged up. Caught a piece of rebar in the gut. Surprised she stayed conscious this long. We'll patch her up as soon as we land."

Landing takes far too long for my liking, but we finally set down on the jagged roof of the Venetian. Eric leans me against the roof's edging. As gentle as he is, I still wince from my burns. He turns for Lexa and I realize that while she's wearing a short blue silk robe, he's naked aside from his cotton belt. I stifle a laugh. A half-witch, half-vamp that just destroyed the power of

Atlantis is waiting to lay her eyes on her childhood bully who has become her friend, and bringing us together is the world's oldest werewolf, naked as the day he was born.

Toni's vacant lifeless expression from the far end of the roof pulls any levity from me. Her skin no longer has its gray tone to it, confirming my thoughts about the tiny white lights. Four gashes stretching across her throat tell how Lexa took her down. Huntly, lying near her, with his head crooked to the side, his neck broken, will not rise again either.

Immediately I search for Xanatos, hoping to see Dad, but all I find is an elderly man in what I guess to be his sixties. Shirtless with wrinkled skin, a shock of silver hair, and in impeccable shape for his age, but with a trace of the familiar face of my tormentor-slash-father.

It makes sense, time has caught up with him. He's not a vamp, nor a wolf, and the amulet was the only thing keeping him alive all this time. Without the sorcery he once wielded coursing through his veins, he's wasting away, and fast. He forces a grin as he slowly, cautiously, makes his way toward me over the rubble that once was the roof.

"Thank you, daughter," he says. I'm not sure if my jaw drops, but it should. What the hell does he have to be thankful for, let alone be thanking me for it? I want to save him—well, *wanted* to save him from the grip of Xanatos. It looks as if I have at least done that, but the entire planet has paid the price, along with those I had come to consider my friends. "You freed me from him," Dad says, his voice no longer bearing a trace of gravel in it.

What do I say? Do I even try, or do I let him turn to dust before my eyes? I came to free him and get some answers. Now, it looks as if he's going to take them to the grave—and that pisses me off.

My cheeks warm from the blood rush, right up to my forehead, but no magic rises from within me. Not even at this moment do I have any extraordinary abilities, and it hits me. This is what I wanted when my power first reared its head.

I'm free.

Sure, I had gotten used to having them, sorta. But I'm far more used to being a vamp. The loss of the Raven side of me suits me fine. Though it's not as if I have any say in the matter.

I lock eyes with Dad, stare with more uncertainty than I've ever had, and Eric breaks my gaze just as words are about to pass my lips. What those words were, I'll never know, because Kara's limp body in his arms draws my attention.

Eric lays Kara on the roof beside me. She's unconscious, breathing in shallow breaths thankfully, and most likely blacked out from the blood loss. The rebar looks to have gone in through her lower back and stuck her straight through to come out of her side. I'm no doctor, but it doesn't look good, especially the nearly black-blood soaking her—the liver's blood, that much I do know.

"She's fading fast," says Eric.

Dad kneels beside Kara, looking over her wound. "You know what you have to do," he says to Eric, then nods at me. "She's too weak to do it."

"Scarlett, we have to do something to save her life," says Lexa. "She may not like it, but if she can hang on long enough, she'll live."

I know what she intends to do, what Dad's proposing, before Lexa can say it out loud. I nod in agreement and take Kara's hand in mine. "Do it."

Without another word Eric transforms and gingerly sinks his fangs into Kara's forearm.

"Are we too late?" asks Dad.

Lexa wraps Kara's arm with a strip of her robe the moment Eric releases his bite. "It's close," she says, staring up to the moon. "Hopefully she'll turn tonight, but if we missed it, she'll have to hang on for one more to rise."

I squeeze Kara's hand. "You can do this," I say to her, my voice already returning. I know wolves are made through a bite, and that it takes the rising of the next moon, full or not, to change them after they've been bitten. But Eric is the first, and Lexa is calm, which makes me hope there's a chance the bite might be early enough in the evening to induce a change.

Eric shrinks down, becomes a man again, and runs the back of his hand over Kara's cheek. Lexa and Dad wait, motionless, as if there's something they know that I don't. Like Eric is about to perform a ritual or something. Eric closes his eyes, rests his palm on Kara's chest.

"Anything?" asks Dad, who's shushed by Lexa.

After what seems like an eternity, Eric quietly says, "Ah, there you are." He stands, pulls Lexa close, kisses her, and leans back. "Add another pup to the litter. Now, I need some pants."

Lexa smiles and looks at me. "He can feel her, like he can feel all the others. She'll be fine. It's not like she lost an arm or anything." Lexa shakes her stump at Eric.

"What? I saved you."

"Just to bed me for an eternity no doubt," Lexa says back to Eric, pinching his bare cheeks as he walks away from us, heading for a slain man who once was a member of the Broadsword.

He holds up his foot to the sole of the man's boot, sighs, and starts tugging them off. "Never heard any complaints," he murmurs.

"So…she's going—"

"She'll be fine," says Lexa, cutting me off. "She may not turn tonight, and if she does Eric can control her. But if he can feel her, then she's already healing internally, perhaps not enough to change, but enough to live another day."

Tears run unchecked, stinging my burns, but I don't care. Kara's going to be all right. Neither one of us will go mad from separation if we're both immortal.

"I wish I had more time with you, daughter, but fate it seems has other plans." Dad shuts his eyes, tilts his head to the stars and hauls in a deep breath. "At least I've left a castle for my little princess to rule from." Evidently Dad's habit of talking to himself didn't vanish with Xanatos. "Center of the new world. The cradle of civilization. One filled with followers." He leans over the toothed wall. "It's been so long since I've been alone. Thank you, both of you." He looks at Lexa, then Eric tugging on his borrowed pants.

"You were a good boy," says Lexa. "Just picked up the wrong shiny rock, that's all."

"You always did have a way with words, Auntie."

"What about me?" asks Eric. "I charmed her, you know, so who *really* has the way with words?"

"Only with the ladies. I remember your tales, Uncle."

"Legendary," says Eric, nodding to himself.

A rock to the shoulder from Lexa stops his prideful reminiscence before it begins. "That's all they are…tales," she says. Eric doesn't retort.

Auntie and Uncle? Lexa and Eric? I barely have time to register it and Dad crouches beside me. "I owe it all to you, daughter." Already he's aged since we made it back to the roof. He's hunched, his hands have spots on them, and his muscle mass has all but faded away, leaving sagging skin to cling between the depressions of his bones. Eric and Lexa don't seem to be bothered by it—neither does he—or maybe they know what's happening and have accepted it with such ease that they are able to kibitz with each other. My gut feeling about Lexa and Eric having discussed this moment long before meeting me seems to have been spot on.

Dad puts his boney hand on mine and Kara's, smiles, and says, "Hmm." Shakily he stands and tries to pull himself up onto Swiftwind. Lexa gives him a hand up, and I swear I catch a single tear roll down her face. "Looks like for the first time…in a long time…the world is in the right hands."

Three steps and Swiftwind is in the air, soaring into the night sky, whisking Dad away to his final moments.

Lexa is crying, not sobbing, but tears are rolling down her face freely. Just as mine are. I didn't know Dad, but I wanted to.

"It's okay," says Eric, wrapping an arm around Lexa, drawing her close, and pulling a single blue feather from his white cotton belt. "He's himself again. Sorsha knows it. We fulfilled our oath."

Their oath? An oath to set Dad free, just as they freed Sorsha from the Raven. That was their agenda all along that I wasn't entirely sure of. I get it—they were around when Dad was born, and would have watched him grow, even loved him to a degree I suppose.

"I know, it's still hard though." Lexa wipes her eyes, takes the feather and runs it across her lips. "We've been chasing him for so long, and to have it end so fast…"

"I know, I'll miss the little brat too."

Kara gasps, sits up, and nearly crushes my fingers in her grip.

"Calm down," says Eric in a commanding tone like he's telling a dog to sit.

Kara's hand relaxes, releases mine, and moves to her chest.

"It'll pass. You're on the verge of changing, but the sun's about to come up. You'll be fine," Eric assures her.

Kara looks to her bandaged arm. Her eyes widen as she realizes what Eric is referring to.

"We had to," I tell her. "It was the only thing we could do to save your life."

She opens her mouth but only a rough grumble comes out.

"Guess she was closer to changing than I thought," says Eric. "Musta been strong genes." He flexes his bicep.

"You'd think after all these years a little humility would set in," Lexa says.

"Where's the fun in that, babe? Besides…well, would you look at that." Eric points out over the desert as the sun's first rays wash over him. I push myself up and look out over the toothed wall. Beyond the rubble of Vegas, out in the Wasteland, are two women approaching on foot bearing fireballs floating above their hands and followed by a dozen or so people. "Witches sure are resilient."

"They sure are," I say, looking to Kara clearing her throat. I smile at her. She returns it. Then shoots a phoenix into the sky.

I frown at her. "Why?"

"We brought a surprise for you," says Eric, pointing down the Strip at headlights turning on, and moving this way. It's just bright enough I can make out Lukas's old pickup. "Stubborn one he is. Wouldn't take no for an answer when they found us at the hot springs. Though someone may have enticed them into a journey." Eric tightens his grip around Lexa's waist.

"Got Huntly to get a hold of them after our chat in the hot springs," Lexa says, wiping the tears from her cheeks. "He insisted he come to you, something about a celebratory dance."

I can't contain the smile on my face, and I don't want to. I wish I looked better for when Lukas gets here, but I recall his non-judgmental eyes and have to restrain a tear from forming in mine.

"So, what's the plan?" asks Lexa. Eric opens his mouth to answer but is silenced by an elbow in the gut. "I wasn't asking you."

"We rebuild," I tell her. "Though I have no idea where to begin."

"Together, Scar. We'll do it together," says Kara.

END OF THE CRIMSON SERIES

Made in the USA
Monee, IL
08 June 2024

58301458R00156